EXPLICIT INSTRUCTION

SCARLETT FINN

Also by Scarlett Finn

TO DIE FOR...
TO DIE FOR TRUTH
TO DIE FOR HONOR
TO DIE FOR VIRTUE
TO DIE FOR DUTY
TO DIE FOR LOVE

GO NOVELS
GO WITH IT
GO IT ALONE
GO ALL OUT
GO ALL IN
GO FULL CIRCLE

KINDRED SERIES
RAVEN
SWALLOW
CUCKOO
SWIFT
FALCON
FINCH

LOVE AGAINST THE ODDS STANDALONE COLLECTION
SWEET SEAS
HEIR'S AFFAIR
RESCUED
MAESTRO'S MUSE
GETTING TRICKY
THIRTEEN
REMEMBER WHEN...
RELUCTANT SUSPICION
XY FACTOR

EXILE
HIDE & SEEK
KISS CHASE

THE EXPLICIT SERIES
EXPLICIT INSTRUCTION
EXPLICIT DETAIL
EXPLICIT MEMORY

WRECK & RUIN
RUIN ME
RUIN HIM

MISTAKE DUET
MISTAKE ME NOT
SLEIGHT MISTAKE

NOTHING TO...
NOTHING TO HIDE
NOTHING TO LOSE
NOTHING TO DECLARE
NOTHING TO US
NOTHING TO SAY
NOTHING TO GAIN
NOTHING TO YOU
NOTHING TO THIS

THE BRANDED SERIES
BRANDED
SCARRED
MARKED

RISQUÉ & HARROW INTERTWINED
TAKE A RISK
FIGHTING FATE
RISK IT ALL
FIGHTING BACK
GAME OF RISK

FORBIDDEN PREQUEL DUET
ALL. ONLY.
ONLY YOURS

THE FORBIDDEN NOVELS
FORBIDDEN DESIRE
FORBIDDEN WANT
FORBIDDEN WISH
FORBIDDEN NEED

LOST & FOUND
LOST
FOUND

ONE

"I WOULDN'T DO THAT IF I WERE YOU."

Flick shouldn't have bothered getting out of bed that day. The alarm hadn't gone off and her shower went on the fritz. With no other choice, she'd washed in the trickle of cold water that greeted her.

When she got into work, late, her colleague, Tamara, delighted in pointing out the run in her pantyhose. That meant a quick trip to the washroom to take them off. On her return to the front desk, her boss had been waiting. Though he was pissed off she wasn't at her post, he hadn't hesitated to commandeer her in his office.

Geoffrey loved the sound of his own voice. What should have been a quick chat took up almost an hour. His berating her for not completing a delegated assignment took up more of her day than completing the task actually did.

From there, the day had gone from bad to worse. The cherry on her cake was the cab breaking down on the way to a date she hadn't even wanted to go on in the first place. Her phone battery was dead. Of course. Because she had forgotten, for maybe the first time ever, to charge it overnight.

The cab driver was lost or taking the scenic route. Whatever the reason, when the vehicle sputtered and stopped, all she could do was roll her eyes to the heavens.

The driver shouted in some unknown language and got out to pop the hood, though it was clear he didn't have a clue what he was doing. After five minutes of him babbling in her face like it was her fault, she'd turned on her heels and started to walk.

In the cab, miles had passed since she'd seen anything familiar. So there she was traipsing through a crappy area in the dark, searching for salvation. Her four-inch spikes were nipping at her toes. If it hadn't been raining, she'd have taken them off. Though her feet screamed, the pair she'd elected to wear weren't her most painful. Small mercies. Topping out at five three she needed the height boost. All her shoes were heels, even those she wore to work.

The first sign of life she'd seen for six blocks was the lights in a corner bar. Oddly, there were no windows. A sign hung above the door calling the place "*Dell's*" and the beer bottle beneath revealed it was a bar.

Hoping they would have a phone, and a number for the nearest cab company, she reached for the long brass handle. She didn't get a chance to push before a deep masculine voice came from seemingly nowhere.

"I wouldn't do that if I were you."

She hadn't been aware of anyone but peered into the black of the alleyway to her left where it seemed the voice had come from.

"Excuse me?" she asked, though she still didn't see anyone.

"Keep walking, Red," he grumbled.

His casual impatience grated. "Last time I checked, this was a free country."

"Check again."

"Do you own this establishment?"

"No," he said.

"Then what right do you have to prohibit my entry?"

"Trust me," he said. "You want to keep walking."

"I don't actually. I really don't," Flick said. "Who are you?"

"A good Samaritan."

"Somehow, I doubt that," she said. "Excuse me."

"No—"

His impatience was gone in that exclamation, but she ignored him and swung open the door to stride inside.

Immediately she regretted it. Six men sat around one table in the center of the room. Two more stood at the bar, two more were positioned behind it. A group of eight loitered around the pool table. The space was small, dim, and reeked of cigarette smoke. With bare floorboards, no decoration, and a single lazy ceiling fan, this wasn't her usual locale. The unexpected entrance drew the attention of every man in the room.

Her parched throat wouldn't allow words to pass. While three of the men at the center table wore suits, it was possible the others hadn't bathed for weeks judging by the look of them.

"What the hell is this?" one of the suited men exclaimed. "I thought you had a guy on look out."

"She don't look like a cop to me," one of the men from the pool table said. He discarded his cue to move in her direction with half a dozen others in his wake. "We'll take care of her."

It took time for her feet to register what that glint in his eye meant. As soon as they did, she turned to flee, except the pack of hungry wolves closed in around her.

Three of them grabbed her, ignoring her scream to lift her off her feet.

"No!" she shouted, fighting to free herself as they dragged her past the table of seated men. "No! Please! I'm sorry! I'll leave!"

"Not now you won't," one of her assailants said.

The gang wrestled her past the pool table, following the two that scurried over to open a door in a shadowy corner. Her screams, her pleading, her kicking and fighting, none of it meant anything to these attackers. They hoisted her through the door into a dark room.

No lights, no windows, no sense of anything tangible until she was tossed down onto what felt like a thin mattress. The blackness was disorienting. Where should she go? Where was out? How could she run when she didn't know where the men were? Where was the exit? How many of them were there now?

Someone snatched her arm and jerked it against a metal bar. With a grating snick, a cuff locked around her wrist. She yanked and objected, metal rattled against metal, but her arm couldn't get free.

It had to be a bed. They'd secured her to a bed.

The men grumbled and laughed with delight at their apparent good fortune.

"No, please, I'm sorry. There's been a mistake," Flick said, still tugging at the cuff. "I want to leave. I need to go."

"We've got uses for a chick like you," someone snarled.

"No, you don't want to do this."

When her other arm was grabbed, she fought as best she could. These goddamn men were stronger than her. They forced her onto her back and another cuff clamped around her other wrist. No! Goddamn! They were cuffing her to the bedframe!

"Who's first?" they asked each other.

Tears burned in her eyes, her muscles screamed while adrenaline surged. She had to fight, to shout and kick. What chance was there for rescue? No one passed her on her walk. Even if someone heard her, would they come to her aid? Would they have a hope of saving her given the number of assailants?

"Shut it! You'll piss off the boss. He'll make us kill you before we get our fun!"

Doing nothing wasn't an option. The hope of rescue was slim, but she wouldn't surrender without a fight. Death would be preferable to letting these men assault her. How had her life changed so fast? She didn't want to die, didn't want to lose her life. Yet there she was, trapped and terrified, contemplating the end.

The mattress shifted and a hot, moist hand squeezed her breast. "Big melons for such a little thing, you think she's legal?"

"You care?"

"No," the one who fondled her breast said. "She'll do."

"Or we'll do… her!" one of them exclaimed to the laughter of the others.

The assaulting hand moved, but relief was premature. It landed on her thigh and went up under her skirt to touch the lace of her underwear. Clamping her legs closed, she forced her thighs to bar his entry.

He snorted a laugh. "I think she's gonna fight it," he said, taking hold of her underwear band.

"I love it when they fight," another said.

The fabric was pulled, yanked apart and torn from her skin. Tears slipped from her eyes, their heat trailing down her temples to her ears. Her thighs stayed together; it was all she could do to protect her virtue. What were her options? There had to be a way out. A something. Anything. She needed a miracle, salvation, her desperation grew. This couldn't be it. It couldn't be happening.

The bed shifted again. A heavy body landed on hers, squashing her down so hard, the springs from beneath dug into her back.

A wet tongue lapped at her neck. "You're gonna love what we have in store," the slobberer said.

Keeping his weight on her, he wrestled with the skirt of her dress, forcing it up to her waist. He tried to get his hand between the clamp of her thighs, but she thrashed around, using all her strength, striving to buck him off. It didn't work. Damn, the bastard just stayed right there, the slick moisture of his rancid breath flooding her skin.

"Open up for me, little thing, you'll love it. I'm gonna take good care of you."

"Please," she whimpered. "Please let me go."

"Can't do that," he said, trying to wiggle a finger downward, "you've seen us."

Licking from her chin to her cleavage, he bit her breast.

She screamed again. Screamed until her throat burned in agony.

"It's not your turn!" one of the others said.

By the way the body on top of her rocked, she guessed he'd been shoved by one of his cohorts.

"Yeah! You went first last time!"

Her body vibrated in trembling terror. Her head swam like she could pass out at any second. Still, she cried, trying to keep her wits about her while her body sought to shut down.

The disgusting weight of this lump on top of her was bigger and stronger. Her attempt to free herself was fruitless, but she couldn't give in. She just couldn't.

Three men sniped at each other until a door opened. There wasn't much more light from the outer room. A tall, broad silhouette blocked a lot of it out, it stayed there, looming on the threshold.

The illumination was just enough to see that yes, she was cuffed to the bed, and there wasn't another stick of furniture in the room.

With the men distracted, she tried to battle her bonds. They were secure, she had no hope of escape, yet she fought anyway.

"What the hell you doing in here?" one of the guys shouted. "You're meant to be outside."

"Your turn on watch," the silhouette said.

"Hey no! We got fun here, man!"

"Don't worry," the silhouette grumbled. "I'll take over."

"You?" a second said.

The foul-smelling lump on top of her shifted to roll off and speak to the silhouette too. "You never have a go."

"This one got past me," the silhouette said. "Gotta teach her a lesson."

The man above her mumbled, fumbling each of her breasts again before getting up and stomping out of the room past the silhouette.

"You can go first but you've got five minutes—"

"Out," the silhouette said. "Both of you."

"Wait a fuck—"

"Make me say it twice, and it'll be the last thing you hear."

"Okay, but I'm next, and I—"

"I don't share," the silhouette said to the men who tramped past him.

Though both stopped, evidently ready to say more, the silhouette stepped into the room and closed the door in their faces.

Silence unnerved her. In the darkness, she had no idea where he was, or what he was doing. Was he about to attack? Loosening his jeans so he could… The man was bigger, wider, and far more terrifying than the other three.

The other three had been scared of this man. They'd followed his orders. Would it be worse to have the three of them taking turns or this one man taking until there was nothing left of her?

"Please," she whispered. "I won't tell a soul anything I've seen. I promise if you let me go—"

"I told you to keep walking, Red," he muttered.

"I'm sorry. I didn't understand. If I'd known, I… please let me go."

"Can't do that. It's impossible… Do you want to know what these men do to women?"

"No."

"Whatever the hell they want," he said, carrying on regardless. "Women don't make it out alive. They take turns. They'll beat you. They'll rape you. They'll make you do every painful and demeaning thing they can think of, and then they'll torture you. They won't just kill you. They'll make sure you know about it. A while back a lucky one was asphyxiated by Skeeve's cock. He liked that one. He still tells the story of fucking her windpipe. Skeeve's the small guy with the creepy eyes. The one on top of you we call Shiv. He likes to cut. He tells the story of one, he amputated her breasts and fucked her with a pocketknife. She bled out for an age before she died."

She didn't want to hear it. Any thought of freedom dissolved with his words. Her throat wanted to close. As much as she didn't want these men to touch her, she didn't want them to kill her either. The sobbing became unbearable, and she screamed again. Helpless, chained up there like an animal, she could hardly move.

"What about you?" she wept. "What are you going to do with me?"

"Boss is diversifying into trafficking. We'd get a good price for a little thing like you. I'd get a nod for that, 'specially if you were untouched."

"You don't have to do this," she said. "Please."

"We'll be out of here in minutes, business is nearly done."

"You're going to kill me? Now?"

"I told you it's not quick," he said. "Shooting you now would be a mercy."

"So… what are you going to do?" she asked. A surge of adrenaline boosted her heartrate. "My family will notice I'm gone! My boyfriend will call the police! They know where I am! They'll find you!"

"No, they won't," he said, humor in his voice.

"Do you think this is funny?"

"No," he said. "But maybe next time you'll think twice about doing what you're told."

"If you had… I didn't know what was in here. If you'd told me outside—"

"I tried. If it wasn't so fucking tragic, I'd say it serves you right."

"You think I deserve this?" she asked, pulling against her restraints. "You think any woman—"

"No," he said, suddenly solemn.

"Let me go," she whispered. "Please."

"What's your name?"

"My name?"

Her impulse was to scream, to shout. His benign question took her off guard. Maybe if she could put a human face on the situation, he'd show some mercy. Like naming the stray who comes to your stoop, you choose to keep and care for him after he has a name.

"Felicity," she said. "Felicity Hughes. Everyone calls me Flick."

"Flick," he said.

The mattress moved.

She tensed ready to scream again, but he didn't touch her. "What's your name?"

"They call me Rushe," he said. "What are you doing in this neighborhood?"

"Cab broke down," she said. "I was looking for a phone."

"You don't carry a cellphone?"

"Battery is dead. I thought it was a hellish day before this…"

"I'll say. Chances of you getting out of this alive are slim."

Fresh tears burned her eyes. "You can let me go." Her wobbling chin tried to contain another scream. "Right now. Please, just let me go."

"To what?" he asked. "You'll have to walk back through that room. If they think I'm not… they'll finish what I haven't started yet."

"Yet?"

Three heavy thumps shook on the door startling her again. The bed moved then he was off it.

"I'll uncuff you, but you've got to stay close to me," he said. "Do as you're told."

"You're going to let me go?"

"No. I haven't had my fun with you yet."

"Please!" she screeched in the desperation from her heart.

Any thought this man might be better than the others disappeared with those words. The cuffs were loosened, and she was pulled to her feet. Her weak, wobbling legs didn't hold out, so she snatched for an anchor, only to come up against him.

Solid didn't begin to describe this man. Every part of him was hard muscle. His huge hand curled all the way around her upper arm. He tugged her body away from his, keeping hold of her with a vice grip.

Her torn underwear slid downwards, so she grabbed for it.

Rushe pulled her up, probably thinking she was about to pass out. "Am I gonna have to carry you?"

"No, my… my underwear, your friend tore it and…"

If it got tangled up and she fell over, smashing her face somewhere, these men would have free rein over her unconscious body.

"Get it," Rushe demanded and tossed her back to the bed again.

Hooking it off her bare feet, her shoes had been lost somewhere, sometime. That was the least of her worries.

TWO

AS IF HE COULD SEE in the dark, Rushe snatched the thong and grabbed her again to haul her back to her feet.

It took him two strides to get to the door while she needed twice as many. He didn't slow down. Jerking the door from its frame, he marched out. Anger emanated from him; she could feel it in the way he moved.

She hadn't seen his face, but in the gloom of the bar she got a better look at his frame. Being small she was used to people, men especially, being bigger than her. This Rushe was a clear foot taller, if not more, with wide shoulders, narrow hips, and long strong legs wrapped in faded jeans.

"You got our toy?" the man Rushe had identified as Skeeve asked practically buzzing with excitement.

There were fewer men around, only five left including Rushe. Shiv was holding open the door she'd used to enter. One door. How could opening one door change your whole life?

"Glen's first," Shiv said. "Then I'm up."

Rushe said nothing. He dragged her out onto the wet street, and any distant dream of freedom disappeared when she was thrown headfirst into the back of a truck idling by the curb. Still on her face, Rushe got in behind her and shunted her against the far door. The cold glass of the window came up harshly on her cheek.

"Put your seatbelt on," he grumbled at her.

Rushe didn't look at her when he said it, but his diligence surprised her, and she did as told. Three others piled in the front and the truck got moving. The speed would have concerned her if she wasn't desperately in need of a cop to stop them. Soon they were out of the street, the town, and on the highway.

"If you're not having your go, I'm going now," Skeeve said from Rushe's other side.

"You'll keep it in your pants," Rushe said. "I ain't watching that."

The three up front laughed.

"Yeah!" Shiv exclaimed. "You'll embarrass yourself."

Panic gripped her again. This wasn't a quick trip around the corner. They were traveling somewhere. The further they went, the greater her urge to jump out became. Except on the interstate, traveling at what felt like ninety, she couldn't leap from the car and hope to survive.

The reality of her situation clawed at her. Unlike she'd claimed, her family wouldn't miss her. She hadn't seen her parents or sisters for almost a year. None of them kept in touch. That was as much on her as it was on them.

She didn't have a boyfriend either. The date that put her in the cab and set her on this path was a first date, and he'd likely just think she stood him up. Hayden and she had met in a coffeeshop, so he wouldn't notice she was missing from work.

And work, Tamara couldn't stand her, and Geoffrey had been prickly since she'd refused to go on a date with him. Plus, this was a long weekend, and being Friday night, she wasn't due back into work until Wednesday. They'd let her miss a few days without thinking anything other than she was being unreliable. Then the weekend would come, so it would be more than a week before anyone thought about reporting her missing.

"You're gonna be right at home little girl," Skeeve drawled. "Right at home."

Sitting in the back of this truck, Flick stared blindly at her knees. Rushe took up most of the space, but she was glad that he sat next to Skeeve instead of her.

When she did glance up Shiv was peering over his shoulder at her. Skeeve was creepy and eager, but Shiv was evil. With that leering smile and those narrow eyes she could believe he'd killed a woman for no reason other than his own entertainment. Killing someone in the way Rushe had described was not out of necessity. The man at Shiv's side stole glances too but he seemed younger, jumpier, a bit twitchy, and nervous.

Skeeve shifted his hips forward and began to fumble with his belt. "I say the girl's gotta earn her keep," he said.

"Hey, yeah!" Shiv said from the front. "Give her something to eat! A taste of what's to come."

The men guffawed. Her fingernails bit into her thighs. Her body was so tightly coiled she wanted to scream and self-combust.

"You don't touch my property," Rushe rumbled. "None of you. You not clear on the rules?"

When he spoke, she was never aware of his lips moving, or eyes, or anything. And they weren't words as much as a bassy variety of vibrations from his chest. The third man was nervous. She had no read on the driver. And Rushe…? He was unreadable.

Keeping her attention on her knees, she tried to forget her surroundings, the men, and what lay ahead.

The length of the journey offered a reprieve. Whatever her future held, she didn't want to think about potential details.

All the men muttered, but none of them stood up to Rushe. If he claimed her the others would respect that. Maybe respect wasn't the word, but they wouldn't refute it.

Rushe was broad but lean, and the heat of his rock-hard thigh against her made her physically quiver. This man was athletic but agile, and while he might not say much an awareness shimmered around him that spoke of a quick mind.

But these men feared him. His position had to be superior to theirs, or he'd asserted his authority somehow. The muttering continued, but Rushe was unaffected.

The air was thick, humid, and the tension apparent. In this vehicle, there was no honor among thieves.

Life went on. How many people were going about their oblivious business while people like her were traumatized and assaulted? No one thought about it. Her included. What it would be like to be a victim of a crime… until it happened to them.

Hayden would've left the restaurant assuming she was rude or callous. No one would miss her. He'd be in a cab, on his way home, cursing her name. Flick was alone.

When her family cast her out a year ago, she'd learned the hard way what being alone meant. She'd staggered like Bambi on ice, unable to find her feet. After having her purse snatched on two separate occasions, she'd thought herself independent and bad ass. Boy did this scenario put that into perspective.

The black of night stretched into the souls of the men in this vehicle, and when it left the highway, they drove for more than twenty minutes into more gloom. Streetlights and civilization were a long-forgotten dream; darkness and trees were the only things outside now.

The trees thickened, and their vehicle swung around a narrow bend into a side lane. From the bumping and bouncing Flick knew they were off-road. This wasn't a concrete thoroughfare. They dodged trees and the bumping increased. Cresting a ridge, they fell into a dip and Flick came out of her seat, landing on top of Rushe.

Skeeve whooped and took the chance to grab for her breast. Rushe shoved her aside as an inconvenience but that took her out of Skeeve's reach. Thank God.

Then after a series of mounds the whole vehicle lurched to a stop. All the men piled out. Rushe reached over her to open the door, then shoved her out.

Any thought Flick had about running vanished when mud seeped between her toes and over her feet. Trees barred her view from every angle. All she could see was the truck and a shack.

Calling it a shack was polite. A rickety old porch seemed to hold the walls in place like a belt holding in the beer gut of a darts player.

As she was still stuttering at the view that didn't even allow moonlight through the canopy, Rushe grabbed her arm and regardless of her unstable footing, dragged her toward the shack in the wake of the rowdy men leading the way.

Going up the creaking wooden stairs, it hit her that walking in there was final. Taking the chance, she dug in her heels and tried to liberate her arm. Rushe wasn't deterred. In spite of her struggling and screaming, he hoisted her off her feet and stomped into the shack to cross the width of the room.

Without thought for the others, he shoved open a door, carried her in, and threw her down onto the floor with a thud. Before she could scramble away, he caught her hands to tie them to the pipe that ran along the wall.

The room was small, little more than a cell, ten-foot square with a single bed, and a short set of drawers at its side. Rushe yanked open the top one and pulled out a folded pair of socks, which he held up to her.

"You gonna keep your mouth shut?" he said.

Rushe hadn't put a light on, so she still didn't get a good look at him. But the angles of his face told her he wasn't to be messed with.

"I—"

"There's no one around here for thirty miles," he said. "Scream yourself raw and you'll only piss me off. You want this in your mouth?"

"I got something she can put in there."

Rushe spun on the man she hadn't noticed either. "You get the fuck out of here."

After he hurled the door into its frame, he came back to her.

"Please let me go."

"I'm not letting you go," he said. "If you keep your mouth shut and stay put, we won't have a problem… Are you gonna do what you're told this time?"

Argument died on her lips; reason wouldn't get her anywhere. In fairness, the last time she hadn't heeded his word she'd got herself into this mess, so she nodded.

"Good girl."

With that he left her alone in the darkness. The finality of that closing door sent tears skittering down her cheeks. She'd never leave this house again, or at least she wouldn't leave it alive, of that she was absolutely sure.

THREE

SHE'D GIVEN UP her attempts to hear what was going on beyond the room. Voices came and went. They got louder then dimmed. Voices laughed then growled, jeered and joked. It went on for hours.

At least she assumed it was hours. With her hands restrained against the pipe, she couldn't see her watch. Not that it would matter, because there was no light but for the slither glowing under the door.

Everything had happened so fast. She replayed events over in her mind. How had she gotten into this mess? From being on the street dwelling on her crappy day, to there, alone in this small room, waiting for her jailer to return.

Rushe hadn't harmed her physically, but she couldn't be sure that would last. For all she knew they were out there getting drunk, waiting to attack her when they got up the courage. But men like those in that back room at Dell's didn't need an excuse to assault a woman. They'd been willing to do it since they set eyes on her.

Rushe hadn't. He had tried to warn her against going into that bar.

She'd never been known for toeing any line. Perhaps she entered Dell's in defiance of Rushe's request. That did sound like something she'd do. Once again, her stubbornness had gotten her into trouble.

But the how didn't matter, she was there now. In that isolated shack, with at least five men. The only thing standing between her and further harm was Rushe. His motivation was unclear, and he hadn't clued her in on his intentions. All she could do was wait.

Hope didn't linger. If she had believed that kicking and screaming and raising bloody hell would liberate her, she would do it. But Rushe had warned her against it. Pissing him off could lead to him stepping aside, leaving her at the mercy of the depraved animals who had tethered her to the bed in Dell's.

Her body grew heavy. Her feet were cold, and her legs had fallen asleep from the hardness of the bare boards beneath her rear. Her hands had long since gone numb. The weight of the night settled on her, so her eyes began to drift closed.

Just when the exhaustion was about to overcome her, footfalls came closer, and the door opened. She squinted into the burst of light that died when the door closed again. There was one step, then a squeak of the bed.

Unexpectedly, light flooded the space dazzling her. But she couldn't raise her hand to shield her eyes, so she blinked into it. The light came from a lamp on top of the drawers. Rushe sat there on the bed with his elbows on his knees and his hands clasped, just looking at her.

The harsh line of his brow intimidated, but his mid-length thick dark brown hair was wild, finger-combed and curled over his ears. Though it needed a wash it looked butter soft. The stubble on his jaw was more than a couple of days of growth. But his coloring and rough look was nothing to the ferocity of his black-as-night eyes. The longer he sat there looking at her the more self-conscious she became.

"What are you looking at?" she asked.

"How old are you?" Again, his lips never moved.

"Fifteen if it makes a difference."

"It doesn't."

"I'm twenty-seven. Are you going to let me go now?"

"No," he said, still studying her.

"Where are we?"

"Far away from everything."

Noise from elsewhere in the shack had died down. Had the others left? No. Luck certainly wasn't shining on her.

"What are you going to do with me?" she asked. "You told me what the others were into. Are you going to turn me out to them when you've had your way?"

"Are you going to behave?"

"I've been quiet, just like I said I would be. Please tell me what you're going to do."

When she blinked, hot moisture rolled over her lashes.

"Don't do that," he said, almost wincing.

"Do what?" she asked as another sob shook her throat. "Please, I want to go home!"

With blurred vision and a gasping sob, she dropped her face to her knees. Reality had become unbearable. Each hair on her skin shuddered with fear and exhaustion.

Reflecting on past decisions led to regret. Things she hadn't considered for years, she rethought, wishing things went differently. Now she wouldn't have a chance to fix her mistakes.

She didn't hear him move. The clench around her heart was all-consuming. The weight in her chest came with the knowledge her life was going to be brutally cut short.

Someone touched the back of her head. Raising her face from her knees, she found him seated on the floor right in front of her. As more tears escaped, he tucked her hair away, and shifted closer to gather her into his arms.

Much as she knew this man was to be feared, the strength in his hold and the stability of his chest gave her a security that she needed to lean on in that minute. He held her body against his, offering comfort without taking advantage, or copping a feel.

Her tears dried. Falling apart in the embrace of a stranger wasn't typical behavior. But the shock of his gentle, unfamiliar act wasn't the reason for her upset vanishing. For some reason, he actually made her feel better. These arms, if used for good, would be formidable.

"Are you going to have sex with me?" she asked, resting her weight against him.

"No," he said. The vibration of bass in his chest rumbled through her. "But it will be in your interest to let Skeeve and the others think otherwise."

"Why?"

"Because if they think I'm doing you they'll leave you alone… Do you want them to touch you?"

"Of course not," she said, shaking her head. "Why can't you let me go?"

"I was serious, there's nothing around here for miles. You wouldn't get far. These men are into serious shit you don't want to get mixed up in. I can't guarantee that you're going to get out of this."

"You're not like them, are you?"

In an instant, he let her go and got back onto his feet. "You better not get comfortable, Red," he said. "You walked right into the snake pit. Don't trust anyone. Everyone here has an agenda."

"What's your agenda?"

Producing a pocketknife, he cut through her bonds. "Are you hungry?"

"No," she said.

The socks he'd threatened her with earlier lay on the bed until he grabbed them up and lobbed them at her.

"Put those on, it gets cold in here."

"Where are we?" she asked, rubbing the blood back into her legs.

"Get up and walk," he said. "You'll cramp."

While this sounded like a suggestion, he snatched her, and yanked her up to her feet. "You haven't spent much time around people, have you?"

She shouldn't sass the man who held her captive, but it didn't matter because just as he'd ignored her questions, he ignored her statement. Rushe retrieved a dark red and black flannel shirt, which he threw at her.

"Put that on."

Her extremities were still tingling with the cramp he'd warned her about, but she managed to catch the items. "I…"

"Take off the dress," he said, dropping onto the bed to unlace his boots.

"What? But you… you said—"

"Take it off," he said, kicking his boots off.

When he stood up, he turned his back on her. It took her a second to figure out he was giving her privacy, respecting her modesty.

Not wanting to miss the window she unzipped her dress and let it drop while stuffing her arms into the soft material of his shirt.

It smelled clean, and masculine, something in it gave her refuge. The sleeves hung down well past her hands and the length reached her knees. Despite not wearing underwear, this garment actually gave her more cover than her own clothes had.

At the same time she bent to pick up her dress he turned and snatched it away from her. His reason for doing so was no clearer to her when he ripped the silk and flung it aside.

"Why did you…?"

"Do you want to have sex?"

"No!"

"Then you weren't going to strip down willingly for me."

Tearing the dress as he would have to if he was going to force himself on her. "You want them to think… why would you want them to think that you're a rapist?"

"Street cred," he grumbled and whipped off his tee-shirt.

She froze at the sight of his torso, his broad chest and washboard abs. In all her experience with men, she'd never seen such a perfect specimen. Every sinewy inch of him was toned, his muscular stance was lean but powerful. Her temptation to touch, to see if he was real, had her transfixed.

"Get on the bed."

"What?" she asked, snapping out of her trance.

"Get on the bed," he said, retrieving some twine from a drawer.

"But I don't—"

"There are two other rooms like this one," Rushe said. "The other guys sleep out there. If you run, you'll meet them on your way out."

Grabbing her arm, he began to bind her wrist. "What are you doing?"

"If you fight against this it will cut you, and you don't want an open wound out here. Infection's a certainty," he said, tying the twine. "Come."

Using the twine leash on her wrist, Rushe led her to the bed. When he leaned to the far corner, she fell on the bed, and he tied the other end of the twine to the metal bedpost.

"Why are you binding me?"

"I don't want to look for you in the woods when you do something stupid. If those guys get hold of you, you're on your own."

"What?"

"Don't get any big ideas," he said. "If you're a nuisance, I'll let them have you."

"Why did you stop them?"

Rushe gave her a shove toward the far corner, and she scrambled out of the way when he dropped onto the bed. On his side, he turned off the lamp and kept his back to her. Briefly, he punched at the wafer-thin pillow, before he folded his arms with a grunt.

"Get some sleep."

She slithered down onto her side on the bed at his back. She didn't have much space but keeping herself tucked away against the wall, she managed to prevent them from touching. Tears burned her sinuses again.

The more that was revealed of her savior, the more questions she had. Her tears receded as she pondered the perplexity. He'd comforted her, then he'd bound her. He'd given her privacy, then demanded her submission. Rushe was a contradiction in so many ways.

She wondered if he'd let her understand where they were, and what was happening… and what her fate might be. But he hadn't answered questions. That may not change.

Being bound to the metal bedpost was awkward on her wrist; sleep would be elusive. At least for now she was out of harm's way, and in this situation that was the most she could hope for.

FOUR

WITH THERE BEING NO windows in the room, morning couldn't intrude upon them. But the shack must have awoken because something made her stir. The woodsy smell mingled with a musky something she couldn't identify.

In the mumbling of her dream-soaked mind, she wriggled into the warmth that encircled her. This fog was comfy and cozy. She'd be happy to stay in it for a while.

Except on another sigh, something vibrated against her chest. The hard bed that heated her seemed to be grumbling. Opening her eyes, her bed was breathing. Hot, humid breath clouded her hair and the memory of last night smashed into her.

Trying to shove upward, her arm stalled against the post he'd tied her to. Flattening her palm on his naked pectoral, she pushed up, taking her head out from beneath his chin, snagging her hair on his stubble.

She was on top of him, their bodies chest to chest. Rushe's eyes were closed still in sleep, she guessed. With him on his back, taking up all the bed space, and her tethered, there was nowhere to go. His arms were heavy and strong around her. One of his hands twined through her hair on the back of her skull.

The other hand was under the shirt she was wearing. His shirt. The apparel had been shoved out of the way to allow his large hand to palm her buttock. It rested there with complete entitlement.

If she was offended, she got over it fast with the distraction of what was under her, pressing into her abdomen. Thick and long… and hard. The daunting lump could only be one thing, and it made her eyes water. If he forced that on her, or any woman, she'd be split in two.

Trying desperately to stay still, she became hyperaware of every breath. The deeper she inhaled the farther that intruding, pulsing wood beneath her became. Her experience with men was limited. She wouldn't for a second consider herself worldly. In her first life, the life she'd left when her parents cast her out, men were careful. Or maybe they weren't that worldly themselves.

Having two older sisters meant she was used to being in shadow. Both of her sisters were gregarious and got the attention of the playboys who came to the Country Club. Her parents turned a blind eye to dalliances in their younger days, and both women fell into line when their father deemed it time.

Lucia married Roger Willis three years ago. When Flick last saw them, Vivian had been engaged to Martin Schifford. Both men were now executives in their father's firm.

Despite how they'd left things, she thought about her family every day. The disappointment she'd caused them hung like a lead weight around her neck.

Reliving past pain wouldn't help. Thinking about what had happened was difficult enough without acknowledging she'd likely never see any of them again.

She wouldn't have the chance to air her grievances or make amends.

Thus far a truce had been impossible because her family refused to accept their own fault in the situation. The only concession they'd been interested in was hers. It was only when she refused for a final time that all ties between them had been cut.

Her shack mattress grumbled and sucked in a breath, raising her up, digging that lump further into her. Thinking about family relaxed her, considering the issue, she stroked her hand up and down his muscled flesh.

On another mutter, she was thrown aside, and he sprang out of bed, stretched, and strode out of the room without a word.

The cold he'd warned her about seeped in, and the twine nipped at her wrist. Using her one free hand, she tried to shift it out of the furrow it had created in her skin. But she couldn't move it so went to work on the bedpost. No luck loosening it from there either.

After at least ten minutes of trying, she gave up… until the nightstand caught her eye. In the top drawer, she shoved aside socks and tee-shirts and other useless items like gum and deodorant trying to find something that could cut the twine.

She grazed cold metal and paused. Pushing a tee-shirt aside, she identified it… a gun. Letting her fingers slide over the textured surface of the grip, she picked it up to be surprised by the weight.

The door opened, startling her. Rushe noticed the gun in her grip and lowered the towel he'd been using to dry his hair, shoving the door closed at his back.

"What you gonna do with that?" he asked.

He threw the towel to the corner, on top of her discarded dress.

"Let me go," she said, trying to stop the weapon shaking in her hand.

"'kay," he said, producing a knife from his pocket.

The line of hair that descended from his navel disappeared into his unbuttoned jeans. She hadn't seen any underwear in the drawer, which meant he couldn't be wearing any.

Rushe came toward her with the knife. Her clarity stuck in a mental groove. With a swift knock on her wrist, the gun was gone and somehow in his grip.

The speed of his maneuver left her head spinning. She sat back on her haunches, somehow not surprised by his surprising action.

"What's your boyfriend's name?" Rushe asked, stashing the gun back in the drawer then buttoning his jeans.

"What?" she asked. "I threaten you with a gun, and that's your question?"

"You didn't threaten me, Red," he said. "You didn't do much of anything. What's his name?"

"Why?" she asked. "Why would you ask me that?"

"'Cause when we're through here, I'm gonna pay him a visit."

"A visit? Why would—"

"He's got no sense sending his woman out into the world—"

"His woman?" she asked.

"You could've helped yourself," he said. "That, with the gun, what was that?"

"I—"

"You've been threatened with sexual and physical harm," he said, opening the drawer and pulling out the gun again.

He thrust it into her hands and fell to his knees at the side of the bed.

"What are you—"

Rushe grabbed the barrel and brought it to his forehead. "Shoot," he said. "Shoot me, take the guys out there by surprise, kill them, find the truck keys, and get the hell out of here."

"You want me to kill you?"

"When I came through that door, you should've shot first and asked questions later."

"But… but I…"

Rushe still held the barrel but the shaking in her hands increased. "You can't do it," he said, shoving the gun aside with disgust. "If your life is in danger, you pull the trigger. Don't think about it. Shoot. Do you know how dangerous the knowledge you've just given me is? You can't defend yourself. I can do whatever the hell I want with you."

Snagging a tee-shirt from the drawer, he tossed the gun back to its place. When Rushe put on his shirt, she was hit with a barb of disappointment that his body was no longer on show for her.

"You've been nice to me," she whispered.

He immediately stopped. "What?"

"You haven't threatened me," she said. "If I shot you, I'd lose my only ally here."

"I'm not your ally," he said. "I told you not to be a nuisance."

When he began to move her hand shot out to catch his jeans pocket, stalling him. "I won't hurt you," she said. "You haven't hurt me."

"I tied you up."

"For my own good," she said. "You said it yourself that your colleagues are out there."

"If I had stopped you going into that bar—"

"You blame yourself. That's why you've been looking after me."

"I told you not to trust anyone."

"You've given me no reason not to trust you," she said.

"I woke up molesting you."

"Is that why you stormed out of here?" she asked. "You were asleep. There was no harm done. I was the one on top of you. Do you want me to apologize?"

Rushe lunged down, grabbing her chin to force her face up to within an inch of his. The maneuver stretched her imprisoned arm, sending a stinging pain through it.

"What the fuck do I have to do to you? I'm dangerous. You're in a lot of trouble here, Red. You better watch yourself, or I'll throw you out there."

"But you wouldn't hurt me yourself," she said. "If you were going to let them have me, you'd have done it already… that's why I trust you." He said nothing. "Do you know how dangerous the knowledge you've just given me is?"

"You're coming out of here to get some food," he said, choosing not to respond to her statement.

"Out?" she said, tensing and regretting her sass. "I'm sorry, I didn't—"

"You're not being punished," he said. "You can't stay in here. You need to eat… unless you want to starve?"

"Couldn't you bring something in?"

"I'm no waiter and this is no hotel."

Rushe leaned in to slash her restraints. As soon as she was free, he hauled her to her feet and unwound the twine.

"It hurts," she said.

"I told you not to fight it," he said, tossing the twine to the floor. "Why don't you do what you're told?"

"I was sleeping."

With her in his grip, Rushe yanked her to the door. "Do not talk to anyone," he ordered. "You speak only to me and only when spoken to."

"But—"

"Consider this free advice that will keep you alive. All of them will touch and taunt. As far as they're concerned, we've been in here all night fucking. You are my bitch."

"Touch?" she asked.

"You're going to eat, sit quietly, and do exactly what you're told, understand?"

That might have been a question, but Rushe didn't wait for a response. He dragged her out of the closest thing she'd had to a safe space in this shack and straight into the lion's den.

FIVE

STARVATION WAS PREFERABLE over what was outside that bedroom. The living space stretched the full width of the structure. A couch and a pull out bed were at the far end. Closest to their room, a TV occupied a cardboard box table with a few other chairs next to an empty fireplace.

Another door stood next to their bedroom. Rushe took her to the ramshackle kitchen, jutting away from the middle of the living room forming the lower part of a T shape. Two doors on the other side, she guessed, were bedrooms too.

"Breakfast and a show," Skeeve said when Rushe nudged her down into a chair at the central table. "Come sit over here." Skeeve pushed away from the table and rubbed his lap.

Shiv sat at another side of the table with the twitchy kid and the driver in another two places. In the harsh light of day, all four of them appeared pathetic but no less sinister. Her estimations of them didn't change though the Kid seemed more interested in her today.

"You had your fill yet?" Shiv asked the room while leering at her chest, though it was covered by Rushe's shirt.

"It's hot in here little girl," Skeeve smirked. "Why don't you undo a few of those buttons?"

Shiv snickered, and the Kid's eyes flared in hope. Skeeve leaned forward and took hold of her knee. Pulling it aside his other hand groped up her thigh.

Rushe stood at the kitchen counter with his back to proceedings. Just like he'd said, she was on her own.

Trying to free herself she pulled away, but Shiv lunged forward to grab her shoulders.

"Glen get the shirt!" Shiv exclaimed and the driver pounced to his feet.

Without escape, options were bleak, but she wouldn't surrender without a fight. Everyone froze when a deep, rumbling punch of a single unamused laugh came from the corner. The men all poised to attack her desisted to slink back and find the source of the single flat note.

Slowly Rushe turned and flung a jelly sandwich to the table. "You're some kind of pathetic. All of you. Have you never seen a woman in your lives?"

The men slunk back to their seats at the same time Rushe returned to whatever he'd been doing.

"Eat," Rushe commanded.

Her? She snatched up the sandwich he'd tossed down and began to gobble. Her desire to leave the safe bedroom wouldn't increase, so she might stay put for her next meal… or the next five.

"We need our fun," Skeeve said. "It's our turn with the bitch."

"You don't touch my stuff and you know it," Rushe said. "Don't want your dirty paws on her; God knows what diseases you vermin have."

"You think she's lily white?" Shiv exclaimed. "Bet she's a dirty, little slut."

"You're not gonna find out," Rushe said.

Having practically inhaled the food, she only had a few bites left when Rushe stormed over to yank her up out of the seat he'd not long ago dumped her in.

"Move," Rushe said.

She lost her footing, but his grip kept her upright. By the time he got her back to the bedroom, he was practically carrying her.

He threw the door aside and flung her down on the bed. The shirt bunched at her waist in her fall; she tugged it down while trying to regain her composure. When she turned, a damp towel landed in her face.

"You've got three minutes," Rushe stated.

"Three… for what?"

"Move."

But she didn't. "Rushe—"

"If I've been fucking you all night you need a shower. Move."

"You're annoyed," she said, casting the towel aside.

"Get up," he demanded and reached for her.

She slanted away from him. "You're really irritated, what upset you?"

"I'm not upset. Men like me don't get upset. I'm not one of your pretty boys, Red!"

"You're shouting at me," she said, crawling to the edge of the bed, hooking her hand into his jeans pocket to draw him closer. "Why are you shouting?"

"Damn you," he growled, snatching her arm to jerk her off the bed.

She didn't have her balance so collapsed to the floor. Rushe wrenched her up, and holding the damp towel in one hand, he dragged her out of the bedroom and into the room next to theirs. He hurled her forward into a dirty shower stall with a black mildew covered shower curtain. Seconds later, a slew of icy water cascaded over her. She shrieked, trying to scramble out, but his legs got in her way.

"Do you want me to strip you down and scrub you myself?" he hollered and shoved her back under the water using his knee.

Fumbling her way up the wall, she pushed the wet curtains of her hair from her eyes. Against the wall, she shivered and blinked her webbed lashes at the broad, invincible form of Rushe. A foot higher than her, he blocked her only exit with a hand on either side of the stall.

The ferocity in his manner was anger. As she stared up into those growling bullet eyes, she realized this was the first time they were making direct eye contact. Everything about him screamed danger. Intimidation radiated from him. She should be terrified given the circumstances and his stance, but she wasn't. Everything about him was brutish; from the way he handled her and spoke to her, to everything in his mood. But whatever anger he had inside him, it wasn't aimed at her.

"Thank you," she murmured.

His rigidity faltered.

She reached through the water and drew the curtain across in front of him, blocking him out. She took off the soaked shirt and hung it up over the curtain rail only for it to be whipped away. The water heated slightly while she sorted through various bottles on the narrow shelf of the frosted window ledge seeking the one that smelled like Rushe.

When she found it, she lathered up, washing her body, and her hair. Rinsing quickly, she shut off the water and a towel appeared over the curtain rail.

Despite being naked, she hadn't been in much of a hurry to finish her shower. Rushe was in the room. He wouldn't intrude and stood sentry. No one would get through him, of that, she was sure.

Slipping the towel down from the rail, she wrapped it around herself and pulled the curtain aside. Sure enough, Rushe stood next to the door, arms folded and ankles crossed, the growl hadn't left his expression. If anything, more clouds had gathered above him.

She tiptoed toward him. Rushe yanked open the door and didn't touch her when she passed. Skeeve and Glen were loitering, clearly hoping for a peek, but she went straight into Rushe's room.

The door closed and he barged her aside to yank a tee-shirt from his drawer, which he threw backwards at her, then stormed into the corner keeping his back to her.

Quickly drying off, she trusted him not to look. But this was his space, and it wouldn't be right to take liberties. She put on the tee-shirt, then tossed the towel to the floor at his feet to show she was finished.

Rushe turned and kicked it across to her crumpled dress. "Get on the bed," he grumbled.

She sat down on the edge and watched him retrieve a length of twine from the ball he had in the bottom drawer. Grabbing her, he pulled her the width of the bed like she weighed the same as the pillow.

"Please don't bind me," she said, but he wound it around her wrist. "Please, Rushe."

When she rested her hand on his corded forearm, he stopped to examine the contact like he was a puzzled dog. Remaining static for more than a few seconds, he shook off his confusion and carried on with the twine.

"I'm heading into town."

"You're leaving?" she asked. Her newly found confidence in her guardian faltered. "For how long?"

"Don't know," he responded without moving his lips while he finished attaching her to the bedpost.

"Please, please don't do this, Rushe," she begged. "You can't leave me here. If you leave me with them…"

"No one will touch you."

"But this morning—"

"You belong to me," he said, grabbing her chin to haul her up onto her knees. "As long as you are here, you're my property. You do what you're told, and we won't have any issues."

"They scare me," she said. "The minute you walk out that door, they'll…"

She didn't want to give voice to her concerns. Vivid images of what might be flashed in her mind's eye.

"You're learning."

"I can't trust them. Please don't leave me here with them, Rushe."

The mild pain caused by his fingers curled tightly around her chin was nothing to what was behind his anger. Something in Rushe hurt, the brutality was a mask, but she didn't know what for.

"Will you defend yourself?" he asked her with his jaw set. "If you see that handle move you shoot."

"Rushe," she whispered. "Please don't leave me here with them."

His jaw tick and nasal inhale betrayed his impatience. "Fine," he barked.

With his concession, she expected to be released from the restraint. Instead, he backed away, abandoning her in the middle of the bed.

Very slowly, his gaze slid down her body and paused at her chest. Of their own volition, her nipples hardened. Cool air cascaded over them; the wetness of her hair must've soaked through the material. She didn't check, in fact she didn't move.

The important thing was showing she wouldn't cower under his scrutiny. While interest from the other lodgers repulsed her, being studied by Rushe stimulated her center to swell with a potency she'd never known before.

Her body's response to him was instant instinct. She couldn't explain it because she'd never known a man like him. So strong. So savage. So masculine.

"No one touches what's mine," he growled to himself more than to her.

The ache in her breasts grew. Being bound to the bed felt more restrictive than ever. "Rushe," she whispered.

"We'll all clear out."

She desperately wanted him to come to her, though she didn't know why. His height, his strength, and his machismo made him a force to be reckoned with. From the second their eyes met in the shower, she'd seen something else, a vulnerability he'd never admit to.

Rushe didn't come to her. He went straight past her, out the door, and corralled the others despite their audible complaints. The main door eventually closed and then they were gone.

She settled onto her back, contemplating the events of the last twenty-four hours. The experience was surreal. The previous night, she'd been so terrified. The only thing that saved her from the horror of the letches was Rushe.

He'd stepped in and protected her, clothed her, fed her, bathed her. Gave her tips for survival, lied to his colleagues for her, and compromised for her fear.

Rushe wasn't like the others, but that didn't mean she had any better handle on him. She didn't know what was going to happen, or if she would get out of this. The only thing she could be sure of, as long as Rushe was on her side, she would be okay.

SIX

BEING STUCK IN ONE place meant there was little to do. She had no range of movement. All she could do was lie and stare at the ceiling. She thought more about her family, and their estrangement. About her life in general.

At work, she often got bored with the banality of some tasks. Who didn't? But working with books, with information, was the only thing she'd ever loved. No one was at work that weekend, but she imagined when her colleagues got back to the library they worked at, and she didn't show up, gossip would start. Foot traffic at the library was regular. Some of the same faces popped up often, but she wasn't particularly close to anyone.

Since she and her family parted ways, she hadn't been close to anyone. Something was always missing. She was personable enough and could shoot the breeze with the best of them, but none of that meant anything. She was a reactor, she reacted to situations rather than being proactive about shaping them. She would coast along from task to task at work thankful for the variety of researching different subjects.

One week she could be gathering information about a gruesome crime, or a starlet's biography. The next week she might be researching wars, mysteries, or epic historical romances. Sure, sometimes she was stuck with the history of a gnat, but other times she'd get swept along with the words and see herself there, in the ancient world, or on the distant planet or… Imagining another time and another place was easy, but picturing her own future was more difficult.

She liked to believe that if something felt right, she'd go out and get it, fight for what she wanted. The trouble was that she hadn't found that something. It was difficult to shape your future, your environment, when you didn't know what you wanted it to look like. So she coasted along hoping to stumble upon it.

Except now she found herself there, tied to a bed, in a remote location, with no certainty of any future at all. At some point after that haunting thought, she must have drifted off to sleep.

With no way to measure time, because her watch had been destroyed in the shower, when rowdy noises jarred her awake, she had no idea if she'd been alone ten minutes or ten hours.

Not long after the initial racket disturbed her the bedroom door opened. Rushe's silhouette filled the doorway, just like in Dell's. She'd never been so glad to see a person. Now he was there, it didn't matter how rowdy the others got.

He closed the door and came straight to her. Clicking on the lamp, he took a seat on the bed at her side. She recoiled and mewed in protest at the illumination, but at least she had one free hand to shade her eyes.

A large paper bag was dumped on her stomach, and he leaned over again to free her from the twine.

"What's this?" she asked on a yawn.

Rushe left her to rifle through a paper bag of his own. She sat up and opened the bag he'd given her. Underwear and jeans, clothes that would cover her up and provide a denim barrier for the others.

Beyond the clothes were toiletries like soap and a toothbrush. She found bacitracin, and two bottles, antibiotics and…

"This is the morning after pill," she said of the other bottle.

"Yeah," he said, dropping his bag to the floor and kicking it under the bed. "There's water in that bag down there and food enough to last you a few days. I also got…" Reaching behind himself, he took something from his back pocket and held it up. Handcuffs. "These won't cut you. There's meds in the bag, and bandages, a first aid kit—"

"You're going to leave me," she said. Her earlier panic paled into insignificance to the new feeling. "You're going to leave me here to them. Why? Why Rushe? What did I do? Where are you going?"

"Nowhere," he responded. "These are dangerous people, Red. We don't know what's going to happen."

"You think they'll hurt you? But they fear you."

"These are scumbags who'd shoot a man in the back. If they kill me, you're on your own."

He'd got her a plan B. Apparently Rushe was a planner, he thought ahead. Hopefully, she wouldn't need his contingency plan. Despite whatever reason he'd gone into town, he had taken time out for her, to get her clothes and comforts, and prepared her for what could be the worst-case scenario.

"I need to pee."

"Come," he said with a sideways nod.

She scurried quickly from their bedroom into the bathroom, not taking the time to look at anyone. Rushe closed the door behind her and would stand guard again. She knew it even without him telling her. Quickly finishing up her business, she stayed behind Rushe when going back to the bedroom as the noise level had increased.

Rushe kept her sheltered and followed her into the bedroom.

"It's rowdy out there," she said, sitting on the bed.

"They've been drinking. It's after midnight."

"Have you been drinking?"

"Implying?" he asked, taking off his tee-shirt. "Lie down."

She complied, scooting into her corner. Rushe brought the cuffs to her and fastened her wrist to the bedframe.

"I stayed here," she said, objecting to the restraint. "All day I stayed. You told me to. I did what I was told."

"The cuffs are for your protection," he said, flopping down onto the bed and turning off the lamp.

The men were getting louder. She appreciated Rushe staying with her. Though, it was as likely he was just tired than actually there to comfort her.

His breathing evened out but wasn't asleep yet.

"Rushe," she exhaled.

He rolled to his back, perhaps to talk to her, or not. Last night she'd kept them apart, ensuring not to touch him. But tonight, she set her head on his shoulder.

With considerable hesitation on his part, Rushe eventually curved his arm around her. She snuggled closer to his body heat. Much as Rushe might have claimed not to be her ally, she was safe there, curled in close to his solid body. Despite the situation, she'd never felt safer, and with that awareness, she descended into slumber again.

SEVEN

SHE AWOKE ON TOP of him just like the previous day, except her body was much lower on his. Her legs were between his, her feet under his calves. She hadn't put socks on, undoubtedly her extremities had been seeking out heat.

Shuffling down, she pressed her cheek to his abdomen. The warmth of him gave her comfort. The skin-to-skin human contact made her feel safe. This was a man who wouldn't be beaten no matter the odds.

Letting her eyes close again, she sighed out and felt that lump was there again. The solid line that had been against her abdomen yesterday was now nestled between her breasts.

Rushe slept in his jeans just as before. That day, they were loose. The hot ember of his ore gave her body a heat that didn't stop at temperature. He was thick, as bold in size as the man was virile. There could be no mistaking his length as anything other than monstrous.

In her life, she'd only been penetrated by one man. She'd got somewhat intimate with others, though none as massive as the one beneath her. While his length was formidable, it was the girth that left her with doubts he could ever fit inside an average woman. She didn't fear the man but did fear the organ.

When he sucked in a long breath, she was lifted, and the appendage seemed to expand further.

Her eyes still closed, she braced to be cast aside again. A score of seconds went by, and it hadn't happened. She got the shock of her life when his hand settled on her head and slid down her hair, stroking her. Though her hair carried on almost to her waist, his hand stopped on her shoulder. He spread his fingers, letting her locks slip between them.

Something in his touch was tentative. From such a strong man, that seemed foreign, which reinforced the glimmer of vulnerability she'd spied so briefly yesterday.

If she stayed still, he might reveal more of himself, but letting him know she was safe for him was important. If he learned she was aware of his softer side and welcomed his gentle curiosity, maybe he'd open up more. Being tough was his job, but he'd protected her, didn't that mean she was different, that he felt something for her? It definitely meant he at least had honor somewhere inside.

She lifted her head to prop her chin on his abs. Their eyes met and his hand stayed put. A good sign. He pulsed in her cleavage and swelled further.

A man like him didn't feel fear and wouldn't back down. Nerves of steel were a requirement around the type of scum he had in his life. The others in the shack feared him, but she didn't, even while under the scrutiny of his penetrating eye contact.

Nothing in his expression flinched; his stare was practiced. Still locked in his gaze, her free hand drifted up, seeking his empty one. When she linked her fingers between his, he didn't respond or pull away. They could stay there for hours. Given who lay beyond their room, that idea wasn't so bad.

His hand left her shoulder, moving slowly to the top of her head to stroke her again. Tears pricked her eyes. The conquering act meant something. Was it something in himself he wanted to vanquish?

The throbbing between her breasts intensified, speeding her heart. She considered fulfilling her curiosity about the hard flesh in her cleavage. Would that be biting off more than she could chew…? Figuratively speaking.

Without warning, the door flew open. Instantly, Rushe was on his feet. Somehow, he shifted her back to the top corner of the bed and put himself between her and potential danger.

Skeeve and Shiv in the doorway couldn't have cared less about her right then.

"Boss is on the phone," Skeeve announced, then he and Shiv shuffled out.

Rushe turned on her long enough to unlock her manacles. "Get washed," he grumbled and departed.

He left the bedroom door open. As she unlocked the cuff, she caught sight of him crossing the living room and going straight out of the front door.

These men had to be in this location for a reason. Certainly, Rushe couldn't consider them friends. Being subjected to men like Skeeve and his cohorts was a punishment, not a reward.

But being there, so out of the way, they had to be waiting for something… it couldn't be something good.

Following Rushe's instructions was in her best interests. He hadn't steered her wrong and was the only reason she still had her life. Skeeve and Shiv hadn't shown any interest that morning, Thank God. While they were distracted with the boss and whatever, she snuck out of the bedroom and into the bathroom.

Just because she hadn't seen anyone didn't mean that they weren't there. She went through her routine quickly, getting into the shower in record time. Knowing her guard wasn't there washed away yesterday's ease in the ice-cold water that flowed over her.

In fairness, the water was probably warmer that day, marginally, but her shivering wouldn't stop. She turned off the spray and reached for the towel only to see it slide away to the other side of the curtain. Rushe wouldn't do that. He wouldn't leave her there vulnerable and naked… but the alternative didn't bear thinking about.

"Problem, little girl?" A snicker confirmed her worst fear. "You can't stay in there all day."

Naked, cold, and with no way out, when the curtain was snatched and rattled aside, she could do nothing but stand there while Skeeve, Shiv, Glen, and the Kid examined her. All of them crowded into the small bathroom to ogle her.

Her skin prickled with revulsion that turned her stomach too. She wanted to close her eyes, to scream and run. But the thought of touching any of these men, even in the interest of self-preservation, repulsed her.

"Lookie, lookie," Skeeve said, clucking his tongue. "You must be a good little girl."

"There's not a mark on her," Shiv said.

There were bruises on her arms, but if Rushe truly had been raping her, she would have far more injuries. She didn't care about that. Couldn't focus on anything. Not with Skeeve moving in closer.

"Glen's first," Shiv drawled.

"That's right," Glen said, shuffling past Shiv.

Glen was the heaviest of the four with a big potbelly. From his baldhead to his worn-out boots, every inch of him disgusted her.

"You don't have to do this," she murmured, hoping they would think twice.

Except while they had this gang mentality, showing fear would only spur them on.

Skeeve's hand came up and squeezed around her breast. His hard, dirty fingers made her gag, bile leaped up into her throat. He snickered again and increased his grip only to grab at her nipple with his other hand.

Closing her eyes against the intrusion, it didn't matter that fighting wouldn't help. She couldn't do nothing. Snatching the showerhead from its holder, she swung it at Skeeve's skull, and by catching him off-guard, she sent him to the floor. She jumped over him and barged through Shiv and Glen, which was an easier escape than she'd imagined. The Kid stepped out of her way, and she came up against the immovable object.

Tipping her chin higher, she looked into the man blocking the doorway. Rushe. But he wasn't looking at her, he was looking over her head at the men she'd run from.

"Get to bed," Rushe rumbled without his lips moving.

Those terrifying eyes should remind the slime of their place. If they regretted their actions, maybe she'd be saved from ever reliving it.

She didn't need to be told twice and slunk around Rushe to get back into the bedroom and snagged a tee-shirt from the drawer. A clatter preceded at thud. Shouting ensued, though she couldn't pick out individual voices. None of them were Rushe's, she knew that. After a few more shouts and bangs, an eerie silence descended.

Tears soaked her cheeks, she climbed onto the bed, gathering the pillow in an embrace as she brought her knees up to her chin. In that corner, where Rushe restrained her, she wasn't scared. Silence dragged, provoking concern for her protector, out there with the pack of hyenas.

Just as she was about to move, the door flew open. It ricocheted off the wall and careened back into its frame with a bang. The whole room shuddered with the heat of his fury exploding around them.

"What the fuck was that?" he seethed, clenching and unclenching his fists at his sides.

"I—"

"Never get naked unless I'm in the room! The only man allowed to see you bare is me! You belong to me!"

"You told me to wash—"

"In the sink! Get up!"

"Wha—"

"Get up!"

So often he told her to get on the bed, he'd never told her to get off it before. But she stumbled to her feet nonetheless.

"Do you like it rough? Is that what gets you off?" With one stride, he got hold of her, lifting her off her feet to thrust her against the wall. "You enjoy it? You want me to force you? Is that it?"

Her tears were in free flow. "No," she squeaked.

After another jolt, he backed off, leaving her to fall to the floor. "Get up!"

Walking her hands up the wall, she used the support of it to get her shuddering body upright.

"Take off the tee-shirt," he said, baring his teeth.

"Wha… What?"

"Take. It. Off."

Until then, Rushe always turned his back to give her privacy when she was changing. But the huffing predator looming over her now was in no mood to be reasonable.

"Bu—"

"Now!"

Refusing him wasn't an option, she took her arms from the sleeves and pulled it over her head. Rushe snatched it, tossing it aside while dragging his gaze all over her exposed flesh.

After his perusal, he leaped forward to grab the breast Skeeve had been groping. Rushe's hand was bigger and stronger. The force of his action pressed her into the wall.

He snatched hold of her chin to force her head up, still gnashing his teeth. His eyes were black as night.

"You like that? Hmm? You want to be violated? You want me to take from you what I want? Anything I want? To use you?"

His hands left her body, offering a moment of relief that was quickly reversed by the thrum of his jeans buttons being torn open. She inhaled but his elbows hooked her knees, and she was hoisted up the wall again, this time he spread her wide, opening her for his anticipated intrusion.

Her hands leaped to his torso. "No, you're too big!"

His shoulders dropped. His blind fury receded to become something else. Their position didn't change. Still, he held her open. Her nipples heated against the fabric covering his chest. She wasn't sure what to do… so she rested her palm on his rough jaw.

"I'm sorry," she whispered. "Thank you. For bailing me out… again." He didn't say anything. Amazement relaxed his expression in a way she'd never seen before. "Rushe?"

"Your only problem is…"

He didn't finish the thought but placed her back on her feet and withdrew. She flattened her hands on the wall while he scanned her figure again. His interest wasn't as feral, but it was no less heated.

For the first time, it hit her he might be attracted to her. As quickly as she had the thought, she dismissed it.

A man like Rushe would have no use for her. Her short, skinny stature wasn't complimented by her disproportionate breasts. A very generous C cup that would be normal on any other woman made her top heavy.

The weight of her breasts often niggled her back. Except under Rushe's scrutiny, for the first time, she was proud of them. Maybe the sight could distract him from the trouble in his life and this tense situation.

"What did you do to them?" she whispered.

"They're unconscious," he said, lowering his attention from her chest.

"All of them?"

"No one touches what's mine," he growled, and took an involuntary step toward her. "You can cover up now."

"I know."

Bold wasn't usually her nature. Her confidence had been knocked so many times growing up that remaining in the shade of her sisters had become habit. There in that room with this man she trusted despite everything, she was happy to be on show for him.

His eyes rose to hers; his feral aura was back. "You don't cower."

"Not from you," she said.

"Do you want it? Do you want me to turn you out to them?"

"No."

Rushe had been sure in every exchange they'd ever had; he was the most adamant man she'd met. But a question mark hung over his head now. With one more lingering gaze over her figure, he turned on his heels.

"Stay," he ordered and slammed out of the room.

EIGHT

ACTIVITY DIDN'T START for quite a while. Though movement increased, no one out there spoke. The light from the gap under the door faded, still no one came to her, not until it was almost gone.

Rushe pushed open the bedroom door. "Out," he ordered.

She didn't want to leave the safety of the room, but he gave her no choice. The jeans he'd bought at least fortified her against prying hands. The black and red shirt he'd given her on day one gave her comfort, so she wore that and his thick socks too.

The television was on in the living room. No other lights, just the glare of the TV screen. Loitering by the bedroom, she wasn't sure what to do.

"Here," Rushe barked.

None of the men took their attention from the football on TV.

She went to him as instructed. He snagged the shirt to pull her down onto his lap. Still, they remained fixated on the TV.

Rushe fumbled with the fabric. "Undo the bottom four buttons," he said. The moment she did, his hand slipped inside to stroke her abdomen. "Pizza." He semi-nodded to the open pizza box on the coffee table, two boxes actually. "Eat."

As she leaned over, reaching for the box, his hand drifted up, making contact with the underside of her breast. Not that he seemed to notice. She sat back and ate the pizza slice with the heat of his hand heavy on her stomach.

It shifted higher to her ribcage. "Get us a beer," he said, boosting her to her feet with his knee then smacking her ass.

No man had ever… At a loss, she went to the fridge, hoping the bottles were there. Retrieving one, she went back to him. He twisted it open and tossed the lid to the floor before pulling her into his lap again.

As he settled in the seat, he took her backward to lean on his chest. One of his hands stayed around his beer on the arm of the chair while the other slipped under her shirt again. Only this time, it went straight to her breast. Her nipple immediately pebbled. If he noticed, he didn't react.

She'd never watched a football game. The more she watched, the less she understood how it could transfix so many grown men. Rushe slurped the beer then touched the cold bottle to her bare abdomen. It took a second to realize he was offering her the liquid.

She accepted and drank a long slug, nearly choking when Rushe squeezed her breast. She'd never done this. Never sat in the lap of a man, and certainly never one who'd claimed her as his property.

The other men didn't look at her or Rushe. From stolen glances she caught their way, it was clear they wore fresh bruises. Rushe must've put them there after the altercation this afternoon.

Someone causing physical harm to protect her honor should shock and disgust her... but it didn't. It awoke something in her gut, and despite it being against the vulnerable-victim character being held against her will, she turned her face toward Rushe, tucking her head under his chin. Looking at nothing was preferable to watching sport. As surprising as it was, her little nest was more than safe, it was her haven.

THE NEXT THING she was aware of was being shifted from a seated position to a lying one. Blinking open her eyes, she watched Rushe closing the bedroom door then shirking his tee-shirt.

With the door closed, the room was in darkness, he couldn't have noticed her awareness. He kicked off his boots and tugged open the buttons of his jeans. Before there was a chance to speak, he scooped her up and settled her body on top of his. If they were going to end up in that position anyway, they might as well start that way.

He stroked her hair as he had that morning. That hand eventually settled on her crown as the other snaked under her shirt. No accident this time. When he patted her rump, the denim dampening the contact was frustrating.

Distraction came with the welcome intrusion of the bulge she'd become familiar with. It flattered her. On a sigh, she closed her eyes and enjoyed the intimacy of their position... He hadn't cuffed her, she was free. For a man who told her to trust no one, he put his faith in her. With that thought, she fell asleep with a smile on her face.

NINE

THE NEXT DAY, her protector stood guard while she washed. After, he put her in the kitchen for breakfast and let her sit there for most of the morning. None of the men bothered her. Hopefully that meant they'd learned their lesson.

As soon as the talk between the men turned serious, Rushe ordered her back to the bedroom. Whatever was going on, he didn't want her to hear any of the details, not in front of the others anyway. Rushe gave commands, and she complied. When she got back to the bedroom, she pushed the door but didn't let it close all the way.

"Six days he said." She recognized Skeeve's voice.

"It'll be longer," Glen said.

"He's got a week."

"We gotta go break some legs tomorrow," Skeeve tittered.

"You're not gonna break nothing," Rushe said. "You're scared shitless of your own shadow."

"Fuck off," Skeeve replied.

"Tomorrow's when we get answers," Rushe said.

"One way or another," Shiv said, "tomorrow's gonna include a body count."

"Who gives a fuck?" Rushe said. "We go in cool and get out. No looking for trouble."

"You skinned that last guy," Shiv said. "Who the fuck are you to tell us what to do?"

"He pissed me off," Rushe said. "Don't make the same mistake."

"Who put you in charge?" Skeeve announced.

Chair legs scraped on the floor.

"We let you get away with that shit yesterday," Shiv said.

"You think you're a gang now?" Rushe asked.

"Maybe we get rid of you and take control."

"Victor won't deal with any of you," Rushe said.

"If you're not here, he'll have to."

"You think you can take me with that blade? Don't make me laugh."

One thump followed another. Judging by the clatter someone hit the floor. A crash of furniture came as the scuffling increased with the shouting.

They were fighting, the weight of fists met faces. He was out there alone. Rushe versus the four of them.

"Get the blade," Skeeve shouted. "Hold him!"

Without thinking, she grabbed the gun from the drawer and rushed to the kitchen, weapon raised. Splinters of wood were scattered on the floor, interspersed with shards of broken crockery, but the mess paled in the shade of the gang blocking their victim from her view.

"Let him go!" she shouted, clasping the weapon in both hands.

Skeeve and the Kid were holding Rushe's torso down while Glen lay on his legs. Shiv was half up, half down on his way to an alarmingly vicious blade on the floor a few feet away.

"Hey, little girl," Skeeve laughed. "You're gonna be all ours soon."

"She's not gonna shoot no one," Glen said.

Shiv took a step closer to the blade. On reflex, she shifted aim and pulled the trigger. She'd never shot a gun, and the kick sent her backwards, but the echoing scream of Shiv canceled out her shock.

"What the fuck!" Skeeve hollered.

The Kid fell away and Rushe pounced to his feet. He didn't waste any time pandering to the bleeding Shiv in a heap on the floor.

Rushe came straight to her, seized her arm, and dragged her back to the bedroom. He slammed the door, snatching the gun out of her hands. Simultaneously, he dropped the weapon into the drawer and threw her down on the bed.

"What the fuck were you thinking?"

The blood on his head and the bruise forming on his jaw infused her with terrified shock.

Clambering to her knees, she snagged his jeans pocket. "You're bleeding!" she exclaimed.

Releasing him, she scrambled to the floor to get the bag he'd stashed under the bed. As she rummaged through it for the first aid kit, Rushe got hold of her, dragging her away from the task to dump her back on the bed.

"Answer me!"

"I didn't want you to get hurt," she said.

"You came out there… you could've been hurt! You could've been killed!"

"They wanted to hurt you!" she said, getting onto her feet on the bed.

"You fired," he said. "You actually shot him."

"Yes."

His arm came around, sweeping her legs from under her, planting her back on the bed to come down on top. With bruising force, his mouth came down on hers. The rasp of his stubble and the taste of his tongue were like nothing she'd ever experienced.

Parting her thighs, she resented the fabric barriers between them. In her need, she grabbed his hair in her fists and raised her chin, consuming more of him. The rumble of his chest on hers drew a scratching screech from her throat.

"Why would you do that?" he panted, snagging her lower lip in his teeth. "Why did you come out there and put yourself in danger?"

Between swallowed breaths, she managed to speak. "No one touches my stuff." She couldn't take her eyes from his mouth. "Kiss me again."

He didn't. "You're telling me this is consensual."

"Yes."

"That's… kind."

"Kiss me again, Rushe," she said, her hands descending to each side of his neck. "Please."

Commotion beyond their door continued but faded away beneath the significance of his mouth devouring hers. As he massaged her breast, her legs coiled around him, hooking her feet around his thighs to urge her center up while pulling him down.

Wriggling, she massaged her own swollen tissues against his. "Rushe," she exhaled when he kissed down to her throat.

He tore open her shirt and sucked on her neck conveying his harsh, unforgiving need. The pain only made her yelp again… and not in fear. She locked her ankles around him as he moved lower covering her breasts in hot, wet kisses. Scraping his teeth over her nipple drove another squeal from her, she arched up into his mouth.

"Rushe," she panted, running her hands through his hair.

He lifted up to yank off his tee-shirt. "You gonna let me fuck you?" he grumbled.

Every raw nerve ending tingled.

With a rush of blood to her engorged flesh, she shuddered. "Yes."

Patience was for other men. Rushe didn't have any interest in subtlety. His world was black and white, you wanted sex, or you didn't, and right now she wanted it. On opening her jeans, Rushe rammed them down to her knees and settled over her. His long finger parted her folds and slid through her juices, coating itself with them.

He sampled her neck again. "You're wet," he said, nipping her earlobe. When he brought his finger up to her lips, she opened to lap her taste from him. "Good girl."

Circling her hard nipples with his still damp digit, he trailed it back down to her wet center. Pushing at her clit, he slid his finger down until it dipped into her. That invasion provoked another whimper and she pushed up, pressing herself against him.

"You'll get it, Red," he said, squeezing her nipple hard inside the joint of his thumb. "Don't you worry, you're gonna get it good. I'm gonna fuck your sweet little pussy now, right here. You want that? You want me to fuck you, don't you?" She nodded past her crossing eyes as he plundered her with a second finger. "Say it." When he shoved a third inside her, she cried out and bucked in response to the climax that blasted her body. "Say it!"

"Fuck me, oh God, Rushe! Please fuck me now!"

The vibration of his sinister laugh only made her writhe against his hand still playing inside her while tickling her clit. The heel of his hand pushed down on her pubis, fixing her in place with his solid weight.

"Jeans off," he demanded.

She quickly kicked them from her legs, getting herself naked for him while he unbuttoned his jeans with one tug.

"Open your legs," he said, though she already had them around him.

She lifted and locked her limbs higher. "You're big," she whispered when his fierce eyes met hers.

"You're tight," he said. "But you're wet. I'm gonna slide in real easy, Red. Your greedy little pussy's gonna gobble my cock and beg for more."

He toyed with her clit, rubbing her in long, languorous strokes until her juices seeped from inside her.

"Want me to eat you first?" he said, wrapping her hair around his fist.

"I want you in me," she confessed, lifting her mouth to his.

Rushe dutifully returned her kiss, but his fingers slid away to take hold of her hips. One hand disappeared before she heard the rustle of paper. What was he doing? That question was answered by him opening a condom pack with his teeth.

"You bought condoms?" she asked, learning why she hadn't been allowed to look in that second bag.

"I've wanted to fuck you since I saw you on that street."

She wasn't surprised by his arrogance or his forethought. Those were two things he had in abundance.

"Look at me," he demanded after rolling on the condom. She complied. "I'm gonna fuck you."

She nodded. "Yes, Rushe, I want you to."

"I won't ask again."

Her hand was pale and feeble against his face, but she smiled in consent. His gaze stayed locked on her as he pushed inside.

The consuming fizzle of him forging ahead tensed her to wince and he stopped.

"You don't get a guy like me to here then back out."

Maybe he was trying to threaten her, but she didn't believe it. If she said stop, he'd stop.

"I don't want you to stop," she whispered and rocked her hips.

When she sucked the first two inches of him into her, he growled. He actually bared his teeth and growled down at her. God, he was so… primal.

"More," she said, her breathing growing shallower. "I want more."

He surged forward, she screamed at the stinging pain his intrusion caused. The girth of him wanted to rip her in two, and she was about to beg for mercy when his mouth covered hers in a much more tender, slower sampling of every crevice of her mouth.

Her whole body sagged into the bed until she was dead weight, incapable of much. Slinging her arms up around his neck, Rushe took his time fondling her breasts, growing rougher as his need increased.

The deep kiss with such slow intention narrowed her world to his two lips, his tongue, and his calloused fingers so coarse yet so gentle.

When his mouth receded, hers tried to follow but he pinched her nipple and she opened her eyes.

Her insides ached. Her slick passage burst with the invasion of his probe, but his gentle kiss had relaxed her enough to push himself in deep.

"Fuck me."

No sooner had she said the words than he slid out only to plunge back into her.

"You like that?" He snagged her nipple between his fingers and tugged. His lips moved to the shell of her ear. "I'm gonna fuck you so hard right now, and anytime

I want, you hear me? You're for my pleasure now. You're never gonna say no to me. Your hot little pussy wants more." He pulled out and drove in again. "Yeah, your tight little cunt feels good, sucking my cock in deep. You want it, don't you? You want more?"

"Yes," she breathed, tracing her fingertips over his muscles. "Give it to me, Rushe. Own me. Show me what you want from me."

He hammered out and into her holding her hips to force himself in deeper than she'd known was possible. While she screamed out his name and panted for more, he took her to climax three more times. With a growl, he propelled into her again, digging his strong fingers into her hips, branding ownership into her skin, into her body and soul.

Rushe paused for barely five seconds. Without looking at her he left the bed, and then left the room.

TEN

SHE HADN'T SEEN MUCH of his body. He'd kept his jeans on while she was all but naked. Closing the shirt around herself as she sat up, she wondered what to do next. Shiv could be dead. Maybe the others had taken him to a hospital, or maybe they were mad and wanted revenge. Although if they did, they wouldn't have let her and Rushe finish, would they? The slimeballs didn't strike her as the patient types.

Being intimate with Rushe was unplanned, from her side anyway. He'd known it, somehow, why else would he have bought protection? Of all the people in the world, he didn't seem like her obvious type. That a criminal would be her type at all. A criminal who may have sinister intentions, if not towards her then certainly toward others. Still, she didn't fear him.

The mattress was thin and her back hurt a little, but when she examined her body, the signs of their union all over her made every second worth it. Deep red welts formed over her hips; the stubble burn on her breasts reddened her. The evidence made her quiver.

Rushe had been in her. The man had saved her life, she'd assumed he could never want her or fit inside her, but he'd climaxed in her body. Inside little Felicity Hughes, a woman of no consequence to anyone.

On the other side of the closed bedroom door, frantic voices snagged her attention, but she couldn't decipher what was being said. It might be important for her to defend herself soon. Lounging around naked wouldn't be a good spot to be discovered in. She shirked her disbelief and rolled off the bed only to collapse on the floor.

Her jelly legs wobbled, her knees had given out, and the passage that had welcomed him now ached, her cervix bruised inside. He'd wanted her so badly the need had consumed him, both of them.

The door opened and Rushe came in, back in his jeans with wet hair, he must've been in the shower. He literally stepped over her to snag his tee-shirt then crouched at her side. Still no acknowledgement.

He took the bottom drawer off its runners then reached to the back and pulled out a roll of banknotes. He threw them down to her while thumping the drawer shut.

"What's this?"

"We're going to get Shiv patched up," Rushe said, stuffing his feet into his boots. "Get out of here."

"What?" she asked, picking up the roll of money.

"There's five hundred bucks there. Out the front go left. In a mile you'll find a fence, follow it south. Dress warm; take the water and the first-aid stuff."

"You said I couldn't go," she said. "That you wouldn't let me go."

"The cash will get you a room and transport when you get back to town. Go home to your boyfriend."

He finished tying his boots and was about to stand up.

She snatched his forearm. "What about you?" she asked. "They wanted to kill you."

"I've faced worse with longer odds," he said. "Get out of here."

"I don't want to leave you."

"You've served your purpose. I don't need you around no more."

"You wanted to have sex with me," she said. "You kept me here until I… until it was consensual."

The smirk on his face was enough to confirm her fear. "Wait sixty seconds, then leave," he said, and this time he did get up.

She scrambled to her feet to grab him again. "You're in danger here."

Rushe wrenched his arm from her grip. "You got one use, sweetheart," he said, palming her breast. "Wasn't good enough for a replay."

"So that's it?"

"Wait sixty seconds."

With a leer, he scanned her figure. For the first time, he made her feel ugly and used. Then without meeting her gaze he left the room, and the house.

Long after she'd listened to the truck drive away, she still sat on the bed wearing only his open shirt. He'd told her to clear out, yet something didn't fit. Maybe Rushe wasn't warm and fuzzy, but he'd never been cruel. She'd seen hints of a vulnerability in him and a gentleness it would be difficult for him to admit. He'd used her for sex, for his own pleasure, although he'd ensured hers too.

Sitting there was wasting time. She had to make a move. Her first aim was to shower. The building was empty. No one could threaten her but that didn't mean she hung around. Using Rushe's soap instead of the one he'd bought specifically for her, she washed her body and saved time by not washing her hair. With no way to dry it, she didn't want to be out in the cold with it wet.

In the bedroom, she hit a snag. None of the clothes Rushe bought for her could be considered warm. Granted, he hadn't had a lot of time, and probably didn't want to let the others know he was making purchases on her behalf, he couldn't have come back with a complete wardrobe.

Choosing the jeans and the two thickest tops, she dressed then grabbed up his shirt and tied it around her hips. The next problem was transport. Filling one of the paper bags with the things she might need stretched its ability to hold. Would a paper bag be strong enough? After searching the shack and finding no alternative, she didn't have a choice.

Almost ready to leave, she stalled again. Shoes? Boots? Footwear? She had none. Her own shoes had been missing since Dell's, and the only thing she'd worn on her feet since getting to the shack was Rushe's socks. Pulling on two pairs, she snatched up her paper bag and headed out the door to follow Rushe's instructions.

The goons could be back at any time. She didn't know where they were taking Shiv though she doubted it was a hospital. Maybe they had a local contact who could patch him up. In movies, the bad guys always leaned on some doctor somewhere to do what was needed without reporting the injury to authorities.

But this wasn't a movie. Rushe might not be like the others, but there was no love lost between him and Shiv. It was as likely they were taking the injured Shiv to a deserted place to put him out of his misery. No one could ask questions if they didn't witness the result of her crime.

The sun was hot, or maybe it was her pace that caused perspiration to quickly spring from her pores. Whatever the reason, she couldn't let up. Getting distance between herself and the shack was her most important goal.

Rushe had said civilization was miles away. He'd told her to dress warm and take supplies. That had to mean her escape trek would take a while. The afternoon sun should be past its peak, but her temperature stayed high. Losing water right now could be detrimental later but slowing down wasn't an option.

She paused a couple of hours into her hike, long after finding the fence Rushe referred to, and retrieved some water. The bold blue sky she'd caught glimpses of had become decidedly gray. Heat hung in the humid air, dense and oppressive around her. But she got moving again, she had to keep moving.

Her thoughts kept returning to Rushe, to what had happened that day, to his parting words. She'd spent her life trying not to ruffle feathers. The only time she'd asserted herself in the past led to estrangement from her family. She'd stood up for herself then out of necessity. Rushe had stood up for her at Dell's, and that day she'd stood up for him.

But the fact remained the goons didn't like Rushe. He wouldn't be safe alone. Rushe was the toughest, strongest man she'd ever known. But out there the hyenas could do what they wanted, and they would play dirty. Rushe himself had said these men would shoot a man in the back.

She'd never see Rushe again. He'd never blip on her radar. Why would he? They'd met by accident and walking away meant never knowing what became of him. Rushe was alone, surrounded by men who wished him dead. He had an authority they resented. If he walked away from this criminal plot alive, she'd be surprised.

More likely was the lowlifes shooting him while he slept. They could dispose of his body, and no one would ever know. She would never know. Walking away, abandoning him, meant her own desertion of him. Wouldn't that make her partially responsible for his death? He'd been there to defend her when no one could, but now he was alone.

The heavy plop of rain hitting her wrist shook her from her thoughts. In the moment she registered the moisture, the heavens opened and rain cascaded from the sky. Still following the fence, she pushed on, hoping sanctuary was close. The arduous trip would be worth it if it freed her. Doubts crept in though, three hours must have passed, and she hadn't seen a glimmer of hope or civilization.

Worrying about Rushe was self-indulgent. A man like him was tough. He was more than capable of looking after himself. Believing she could impact his life, or help him, was flattering herself with little evidence to back it up. In the kitchen, shooting Shiv, had been a fluke. Sure, Rushe got himself in a jam but maybe he would've got out of it without her interruption.

She stopped to untie the shirt from her hips and put it on. Her soaked clothes stuck to her, her jeans heavy, and already her socks were caked in mud. She propped the paper bag on a fencepost to button up the shirt. Before she could grab it again, the bag fell from its perch, scattering its contents.

The beat of the heavy drops splatted into the mud seeping between her toes. Thunder crashed far above. The longer she stood there, the deeper she sank. What should she do?

Scrambling to gather the necessities, she lifted the hem of her shirt to make a pouch for them. Not ideal. She'd need the water, and the food that hadn't been ruined by the mud. Most of the first-aid items were lost. As hope dwindled, a flash of lightening in the darkening air startled her upright.

Being in the trees wasn't the safest place in that kind of weather. Though she could see the line of the fence stretched out in front of her, it got lost in the foliage far up ahead. Maybe there could be a clearing nearby, she started into the trees looking for shelter.

The rumble of an engine inspired optimism. She cast her eyes upward, thankful for this serendipity. If the fence was around someone's property, it stood to reason that person could be patrolling the perimeter. If the landowner found her, she could get to shelter, to a phone, and be home by the morning.

Progress was slow going as her sodden feet had to be hauled from the viscous mud one after the other.

A flash of light lifted her chin. Her hands dropped, sending the items in her shirt pouch to the ground. That wasn't the lightening, that flare was headlights. Picking up the pace, she raced as fast as she could toward the noise. When those lights became a solid beam, she lifted her hands to wave, begging not to get lost in the shadows.

The light stayed on, came closer, her cheeks burned with the width of the grin on her face. This was it, the moment she'd be saved. The rumble slowed until the vehicle came to a stop. The glare from the headlights kept her from picking out details beyond. Her hand rose to block it out as she heard a door opening.

"Lookie, lookie."

Her blood froze. Her smile fell. Her body screamed in dismay. "Skeeve," she exhaled.

"In the flesh," he said, moving closer. "You going somewhere or just on the welcoming committee? You're pretty far from home. What were you doing? Running away? You'll pay for that little girl."

She took a step away but slipped in the mud and fell backwards. Another door opened, producing a familiar silhouette. A silent silhouette. Skeeve sidled closer, like a scavenger creeping up on a carcass, ready to pick it clean.

Rushe wasn't so shifty. He strode over to snatch her up, and carried her into the truck, tossing her on the floor rather than giving her a seat. Skeeve's cackle came back into the truck, and then Glen was driving again.

Rushe hadn't said a single word, but she didn't need him to spell out his mood. He was pissed. Seriously pissed.

ELEVEN

SHE'D MISSED HER CHANCE. Now she was back with these men, who were capable of anything. Freedom had been brief. Too brief. The rain, the terrain, the loss of her supplies, despite those negatives, there was hope of a chance... or there would've been if the goons hadn't been out there too.

Rushe and the others were heading back to the hideout. The first night they arrived there, she hadn't been aware of their surroundings, or known their destination. On her expedition, she'd learned most of the environment looked the same as the rest. It didn't matter that she'd walked in the opposite direction to the one they'd driven on her first arrival there. Apparently, danger could come from any angle.

They got back to the shack and the men piled out like she was trapped in a recurring nightmare. Rushe seized her before she even got out of the truck and carried her inside to the bedroom without her ever touching the floor. Not until he dropped her down onto it. It was dark. Cold. She was wet and dirty. But it was

Rushe's seething figure that commanded urgent attention.

"Sixty seconds," he muttered, anger hot in his words. "I said sixty seconds. Can you count?"

"I'm sorry," she said. "When the rain started… and the lightening… the mud. I didn't have anything on my feet."

He grabbed her again, hauling her to the tips of her toes to flatten her against the wall.

She blinked into the darkness and tried to apologize again, but his hand closed over her mouth.

"You like it here?" he snarled. "I told you to take a hike. I was never supposed to see you again."

With his usual finesse, he released her, and she collapsed to the floor. His brusqueness was almost familiar. The light of the lamp that came on was so harsh, she held up a hand to block the bright intrusion and got back to her feet. Rushe paced the width of the room in front of the door, like a caged wildcat. Like before, he clenched and unclenched his fists.

"Can I go get cleaned up?"

Rushe stopped pacing. "Take off your clothes."

"Excuse me?"

"Now," he rumbled.

Exhaustion waned as she observed him, chin down, his eyes black, his short, shallow breaths. He made demands, yet she felt powerful. This man wanted something he'd only get if she complied. He'd proved he wouldn't take it by force.

After the disastrous day, this was the comfort she needed, and it was the only way Rushe knew how to give it. She unzipped her jeans and unbuttoned the shirt, letting it drop. One top came off, then the other, peeling back the layers with excruciating diligence.

His fingers began to flex again. He wanted her to move faster. She didn't. With his eyes on hers, she very slowly pushed her jeans down, and stepped out of them, kicking off the dirty socks in the process. In front of him, completely naked, she let him look his fill.

"Turn around."

When his voice rumbled and his lips didn't move, she got chills, but she did as told. Without seeing him, she knew he was examining this new angle of her as intently as the first.

Rushe made no noise when he moved closer. The first she knew of his proximity was the crushing hold of his hands on her ass. He squeezed and stroked her, then drew his hand down between her cheeks until he reached her clit. His other arm came around to grip her breast.

Two of his fingers slid into her, then a third, in and out. Urging her hard against the wall, his fingers worked in and out of her.

"You want more of this?" he growled into her ear. The humidity of his breath dampened her hair. "You dirty little whore, you're soaking me. You like this?"

From how she squirmed against him, there could be no denying how amazing he made her feel. Too soon, his hand was gone.

"Put your hands on the wall," he said, yanking her hips back until she was bent to ninety degrees.

"Rushe—"

He smacked her ass. "I don't want to hear you. I'm gonna fuck you good. Fuck some sense into that pretty little head of yours. I don't want to hear one sound from you, not one single sound."

Reaching between her legs, he pinched her clit. Her knees tried to buckle but he kicked her feet apart and pulled his buttons open. She heard him access the drawer, and then the rustle of the condom packet being torn. Her vague awareness of his hand landing on the wall above her dissipated the second he plunged into her.

This wasn't slow like the last time; he rammed himself into her right to the hilt with one thrust.

Her insides screamed and he battered her cervix with every advance, but he got faster, harder, propelling himself into her until… he stopped. Deep inside her, he froze. She wanted to ask why, to beg more, but stayed silent, as per his request.

"Do you feel that?" he growled, lowering himself to speak into her hair while his hands groped her breasts. "You feel my dick in you? Does your pussy like that?" He twiddled her nipples between his thumb and forefinger. "Speak."

"Yes," she whispered.

"You like my long, fat cock in you? You better get used to it now. You hungry for my dick? Speak!"

"Yes," she said with the shimmering awareness of orgasm coming from her shoulders to her core.

"That's okay," he said, rubbing his face in her hair. "You want to come all over my cock you do it. You better get used to it. Your only purpose in life now is to accommodate my cock in your cunt. Morning, noon, or night, you're gonna get fucked when I want it. You gonna do as you're told, Kitten?" He began to slide back and forth so slow it was agonizing. "I'm gonna fuck you any time I want, how I want. If I want it fast and dirty, I'm gonna take it. When I tell you to eat, you're gonna suck your breakfast from my balls. You gonna do as you're told? Speak."

"Yes," she croaked, pushing back against his invasion.

"Sir," he said. "Yes, sir."

"Yes, sir," she repeated on a whine.

"You want me to fuck you?" he asked, stopping again.

"Yes, sir."

"What's the magic word?" he sneered.

"Please," she said. "Please, fuck me."

One hand shot from her breast to her clit, squeezing again. "Don't think about coming until I tell you to," he said. "You hear me?"

"Yes, sir."

He surged in deep, angling her hips for deeper penetration. She cried out and he spanked her again, harder, much harder.

She wanted more and struggled not to call out for it. "Please!" she begged. "Oh God, Rushe! Please! Yes!"

With one more slap, he grabbed her hips and shoved into her faster until he growled. "Now."

Just like that, her inner muscles clamped around him, and she shouted for him again. The impact of orgasm was ruthless and all-consuming. She wasn't sure she could handle it, wasn't sure she could feel everywhere all at once and it just kept going and going.

With another thrust into her, Rushe stopped and grabbed a butt cheek in each hand. She shuddered and whimpered when he withdrew without a word. Two beats passed then the door slammed… so much for no replays.

She righted herself, leaning on the wall, not entirely sure what to do next.

The door opened again and Rushe returned, buttoned up as though previous events hadn't happened at all. What should she say? She couldn't even form words.

"Shiv will be back," Rushe said. "It's your blood he'll want."

Revenge? This life was supposed to be in her past and suddenly she got it. Rushe had told her to go because Shiv would come back angry.

"I'll deal with it," she said.

"Will you?"

"Yeah," she said. Her confidence was bravado, that was all she had to draw upon.

"You were supposed to be gone," he said. "You're in it now. You're stuck here."

"You watch my back, I'll watch yours."

Implying he might need help from a feeble woman wouldn't be appreciated by a man like Rushe. Whether or not he wanted a reminder, she had helped him out by shooting Shiv.

"I'm not gonna fall for you, Kitten," he said, almost snickering at her. "You've got a tight, little pussy that's good for strangling my cock, that's it."

"Yet," she said, moving across the room. "Earlier you said it wasn't good enough for a replay… I think that's what we just had."

"I don't see a lot of options around here, do you?"

"I think you like having sex with me," she said, sliding her hands into his front jeans pockets when she reached him.

"I'm a guy, damn right I like sex."

"With me," she said. "I think you like having sex… with me."

"One pussy's as good as the next."

"We'll see," she said, levering up to kiss his jaw. "I like having sex with you."

Rushe tugged the towel from the end of the bed. "You better get washed."

"Are you going to join me in the shower?"

"Why would you want to get mixed up with a guy like me?" he asked.

Something in him was softer, though he did his best to disguise it.

"I'll let you soap my back," Flick said.

"Answer my question."

"About getting mixed up?"

"There's no happy ever after. I'm not a bad guy with a good heart, this is no fantasy. If you knew who I was, the things I've done, you'd cry and run for your mama."

She took the towel, wrapped it around her body, and left the bedroom to head for the shower. The answer to his question wasn't simple. It would mean admitting to him something she struggled with: she cared about him. Movement behind her as she switched on the shower caused her to glance back over her shoulder. Rushe was by the door with his back to her, on sentry duty.

Quickly washing the muck, sweat, and grime from her body, she finished up and wrapped herself in the towel again. As Rushe ushered her out of the bathroom, Skeeve was yelling at the Kid about something in the kitchen.

The toil of the day caught up with her. She cast the towel aside after a quickly swiping away the droplets remaining on her skin and crawled onto the bed to lie out flat on her belly. Something landed on her back, she twisted to figure out what it was: another of Rushe's shirts. With a question in them, her eyes rose to his.

"I don't trust those guys not to walk in here," he said.

She sat up to untangle the shirt and put her arms in the sleeves without buttoning it. Rushe removed his tee-shirt and kicked off his boots.

When he came toward her, she held up a hand. "Take off your jeans," she said. His brow sloped, probably because he was the one who gave orders. "Please."

"I don't wear underwear."

"I know," she said. "You have nothing to be modest about. I promise I'll keep him shielded from prying eyes if there are any."

"Him," Rushe muttered while complying with her request.

Though she couldn't be completely sure, there might have been a whisper of a laugh in his voice.

When he kicked his jeans away, she prepared to be scooped up on top of him as his usual blanket. Instead, he fell down on top of her, bracing his forearms at either side of her head.

"I'm gonna fuck you again," he said.

Her fingertips searched his chest. "Okay."

"And through the night, whenever I want it."

"I heard you when you said that the first time." She planted her feet on his calves and drew them up to his thighs. "Ready when you are."

"Just like that," he said. "You're giving me complete access."

"I know how important it is to you that this be consensual."

"How do you know that?"

"Because I do," she said. "I like having sex with you. I want to have sex with you."

"I really thought I got rid of you today," he said, in a gentler tone than earlier when making the same point.

"Rushe, fuck me," she said, letting a smile curl her lips. "Please, sir."

And without pushing the subject, he pushed into her over and over again all night long.

TWELVE

BY THE TIME HER EYES opened the next morning, every single inch of her screamed.

She'd never had so much sex. Every encounter with Rushe outweighed every remotely sexual episode she'd ever had previously in her whole life. Yet when she awoke, with her naked skin sticking to his, the musky smell of man merged with the scent of their joining, and she purred, stretching out her stiff muscles. His own stiffness nudged her thigh. Was he always aroused this often or was it related to her presence?

Sliding her body up, she kissed his jaw, feathering her fingers down his chest and up the muscles of his arm, learning his incredible physique. Still slumbering, he didn't respond to her exploration. She carried on down his body, taking the time to admire him in a way she wouldn't be able to when he awoke.

Choosing not to linger over his impressive abs, there was another part of him she wanted to learn. She followed the column of dark hair from his navel down to the length of him.

Her eyes watered at the sight of his penis in all its glory. Had it really been inside her? It had. Deep, deep inside her, invading her stretched passage that now cried in agony. Running her finger from its base to his head, it jumped in response. The silk of his skin begged more attention, and she rubbed her cheek over him, closing her eyes to sink into the luxury of his hide.

The mammoth intruder had given her pleasure, pulsed in and out of her, been used as a weapon to fulfill their desires. She pressed her lips to him, placing kisses the length and width of him. Drawing her hands up his thighs, she cupped his testicles, drumming her fingers around them gently testing their weight. With another kiss on his tip, she flicked her tongue across the glistening liquid seeping from him.

She wasn't naive enough to think she could ever pleasure him with her mouth. She'd be awkward and inexperienced. Also, given his size, she'd never be able to take him deep in her throat. But while he remained asleep, she let herself believe it was possible. That she was capable of dispensing pleasure.

A man as virile as Rushe would be difficult to conquer. If a woman could control his pleasure, she'd be formidable. With Rushe in her power she'd be capable of anything.

She sucked his head into her mouth, circling him with her tongue, still fingering his balls she tasted more liquid. Spurred on by her imagination, she closed her eyes and dreamed of delivering Rushe to ecstasy. Sucking more, she took him as deep as she could. Sucking and licking, one hand circled him and began to squeeze, copying the milking action of her vagina he seemed to enjoy so much.

Her lack of experience was nothing in her mind. Her timidity didn't exist. She had Rushe at her beck and call, utterly devoted to the bliss she supplied. The man in her imagination was drawn to her, with her, proud of her.

Fervor burst in her so hard that she sucked him deep, pressing her own legs together. Her action and imagination had taken her to the brink of her own orgasm. Reveling in the fantasy when a thick liquid spurted in her mouth, she automatically swallowed him down, sucking his hot seed into her belly.

When his hand landed on her head, she opened her eyes and blinked up to see his head angled on the pillow, her in his sights, the usual flat expression on his face.

Slowly, her mouth slid away, his head trailed down her chin. Licking her lips, she could still taste him in her throat; every corner of her whole body was tingling.

She kneeled up between his legs. "Sorry," she whispered.

"Yeah," he said without moving his lips.

In her curiosity, the one thing she hadn't considered was consent. So much had been made of her approval that her not offering him the same choice suddenly appalled her. Tipping her head back, she willed tears not to fall.

She tried to climb over his leg to stand, but he sat up and grabbed her wrist. "Explain," he demanded. "The tears… explain."

No actual tears had fallen, he must've just sensed them in her. If she didn't know him better, she'd think concern colored his voice.

"I took advantage of you," she said, watching blood route back into his penis. Her efforts had pleased him for only a few seconds. "That wasn't consensual."

A bark of his bleak laugh startled her, but by the time she looked up his face was blank again.

"Any time you wanna suck my cock, Kitten, you go right ahead."

"Really?"

Though he might consider it crude, she was warmed by his generosity. Not about the act, but about alleviating her upset. Maybe her surprise showed because he gave her a shove.

"Move."

She clambered over him to stay on the bed as he got up and snagged the towel she'd hung at the end of the bed. When he slammed out of the room, she flopped onto her back.

If Rushe was going to shower, she'd have a few minutes alone. He'd no doubt let her shower after him. Rather than just projecting the appearance of fucking all night, they actually had been fucking all night.

With an involuntary blush, she smiled at the memory of the things they'd done. About the things he said that made her come. Those words, his words, could almost bring her to climax on their own. Crude and domineering as it was, being owned by him was enlivening. Freeing. Being united with him made her feel powerful, like his strength transferred to her, wrapping them both in an invincible embrace.

Her thoughts drifting to that morning, about how he tasted in her mouth. Despite not having permission, she'd made him come. Had it been possible? She didn't think so. Practice taught her something different. He'd given her free rein to pleasure him in that way at any time. For one moment, her distant dream of that formidable woman with Rushe under her power could've been her.

Tracing her hand over her breast to her abdomen, her knees rose, and her fingers slid over her clit. Still moist from her own almost climax during her assault on Rushe, she closed her eyes to fall back into her dream.

Rushe was strong and bold, but she imagined falling to her knees in front of him, stopping him in his tracks, unfastening his jeans so gradually it would drive him insane. He liked fast and hard, but she took him down a gear. On a moan, her hips came upward imagining what he would do when she breathed him into her, halting him, controlling him.

"What the fuck do you think you're doing?"

It seemed every single time he walked into this room he asked her a question with the word "fuck" in it.

Under any other circumstances she might have been embarrassed to be caught playing with herself, but they'd lived in close quarters long enough.

"Shh," she sighed, hanging on to the fantasy.

He'd get changed and storm out of the bedroom again. She didn't want to start over. Rushe had seen her orgasm. Plenty. That was the worst, or the best, outcome that could happen here.

The bed shifted, and her hand was snatched away. She blinked at the fury on his face.

As angry as his expression was, she sensed some of that vulnerability he hid. "I left you unsatisfied," he stated.

"No," she said, using his grip to pull herself up. Though it was out of character for their relationship, she placed a short kiss on his mouth. "I don't have a lot of experience with… well let's just say I enjoyed… this morning."

His expression didn't change in the three seconds it took him to speak. "Your pussy is my plaything, not yours."

"Okay," she said. "Next time I'll ask permission first."

His nostrils flared just slightly, in the first direct positive response she'd witnessed from him over something she had said.

"Would you like me to do that?" she asked, leaning in close. "Ask your permission before I fantasize about pleasuring you. That's what I was doing, Rushe. I was thinking about you, about how you felt in my mouth, about the taste of you, the thick, hard length of you—"

Grabbing her arms, he pinned her down on the bed, his heavy weight pressing into her. "You're playing a dangerous game… is that what you think this is? A game?"

She shook her head wondering if she'd made a misstep. "No."

"You think you can play with me? Push my buttons? A thing like you has no place on my level. You think you can rough it for a while then run home and tell your Country Club Bitches about being with a bad boy, is that it?"

She shook her head again. His grip bit into her arms. His weight was beginning to suffocate her, but he didn't move, he just sneered at her.

"You like dirty talk? You think it makes you sexy? Let me tell you a secret, Kitten, every guy that looks at you, do you know what they see? A pair of tits." His hands left her arms and moved to her breasts. "You got a great rack. Huge and pointy, all high and bouncy, you've got great boobs. No guy looks at your face. They sure don't give a fuck about your mouth. I told you that you can suck me off anytime because you need the practice."

He caught her lower lip, biting it until she tasted a whisper of blood. Closing his mouth on her throat over an already tender bruise, he pushed her deeper into their mattress. He must have heard her hiss at the pain his suction caused her bruised neck, because he lifted his head and snickered at her. The low, humorless laugh rattled her bones.

He carried on down to bite her breast. "This isn't a game," he said, licking her nipple before drawing it between his teeth. "You let your guard down. If you think for a second that this is fun, you're gonna get hurt. I told you not to trust anyone. We all have an agenda, and you're not a part of mine. When I'm done with you, do you know what I'm gonna do with you?"

Rushe reached down between them while biting her other nipple. Wedging his knee between her thighs, he opened her to probe his fingers into her, his weight still pinning her down.

"You're gonna stay here and be my plaything," he said, nuzzling at her neck. He bit her earlobe and poked another two fingers into her. "I'm gonna fuck you when I need something to do. You're a pussy to me. Nothing but a walking pair of tits with a sweet, little ass, and I'm gonna own that too, Kitten. Make no mistake, you belong to me. You're my possession, an object I keep in my room to get me off. A breathing porno, that's your only use."

Backing onto his haunches, his fingers came out as his weight receded.

Poised there at the end of the bed, he glared at her. "Finish."

"Wha... what?" she stuttered.

"You want to get yourself off in my bed, you're gonna do it with an audience."

"But—"

"You want me to call in Skeeve? Glen and the Kid?"

"No," she said.

"Stick your finger in your pussy."

Definitely not. If it meant being spared them... She did as told.

"Fuck yourself with it," he said, so she slid it in and out. "Like you mean it, Kitten."

She closed her eyes to try blocking out his attitude, but he slapped her breast.

"This is no fantasy," he said. "You've got the real thing, eyes open." Taking her wrist, he pulled out her fingers and took them to her lips. "Clean yourself up."

Licking her fingers wasn't enough so he pushed them into her mouth, making her taste every drop.

"Do it again," he commanded, sitting back at the foot of the bed. "Play with your clit. Put your other hand on your tit."

The sinister grumble quivered her belly. "I'm coming in here with a camera later. The guys would love seeing this. Put your finger in your pussy again, two of them."

She rubbed from her clit to her opening. As they slipped into her, she squeezed her breast, her nipple immediately pebbled. He might be demeaning her, but she could see the erection he was ignoring.

Watching her put on a private show turned him on, and if she stopped… He'd never hurt her, he'd never force her. This was a game whether he admitted it or not. There in that room, in their safe space, he played with her just as she could play with him.

She arched up into her hand at the same moment he took his own erection in hand. Pulling her knees higher, she whimpered at the glory of her revelation. Rushe came forward on his knees, shoving them under her ass. As she increased her stroke, so did he, she played with one of her breasts and his hand snatched the other.

She sighed out his name and pushed up. Bringing her clit to her hand, she fell through the precipice of orgasm. At the same time she cried out, he roared, and blazing jets of his milky semen streamed from her pubis to her cleavage.

Both panted from their own release, he studied his seed on her skin until he found her eyes. She smiled and was about to quip when he spoke.

"You're mine for as long as I want you," he said, delivering the line so coldly, she frowned. "But when I'm done with you, they get you. You're not getting out of this."

"But yesterday," she said.

He left the bed. "You missed your chance." Flick propped up on her elbows. "Stay. I want you exactly where I left you. Consider my spunk your leash. Leave it exactly where it is."

"Rushe," she said when he went for the door.

"You're not the first, Kitten," he said. "You won't be the last either."

He slammed out as he always did, and she lay back down. She hadn't considered he could've played this sequence with other women.

Rushe got a kick from her giving in to him. That was where his desire for approval came from. The other hooligans wanted the power and control of forcing themselves on a woman. But Rushe wanted a woman to willingly submit.

When he was finished with her, what would he do? Would he let her walk away? Rushe certainly wouldn't follow her. But would he trust her not to speak to law enforcement about him and the others in the gang?

She trusted Rushe not to hurt her, but that didn't mean he wouldn't walk away. If he was finished and ready to move on, all he had to do was tell Skeeve he was done and leave. She would be alone.

Trusting Rushe would make or break her; it was the difference between living and dying. Sometimes he was cold, other times she feared his capability, but rough sex and dirty talk did not a criminal make. Until she knew what was going on here, she would have no way to judge the potential outcomes.

So far, she'd been the only one in the shack to commit a serious criminal offence. Other than the guys kidnapping her in the first place. But who was Victor? Why was there going to be a body count? Who had a week, and for what? Who really was Rushe?

THIRTEEN

WHEN RUSHE CAME BACK into the bedroom a while later, his face was just as grumpy; but she was where he'd left her. That was as much because she had nothing better to do than to lounge around and wait for him to return.

"Is Rushe your first name or your last name?" she asked, dropping her hands onto her breasts.

"What?"

"It's an unusual name and—"

"You writing a book?"

"No, I just wondered if—"

"Don't," he said. "Do yourself a favor, don't try to get into my head. Shower time."

She stretched and yawned as she got to her feet. "Everyone comes from somewhere," she said. "Even if a lot of us would rather forget that place."

Rushe grabbed her arm, halting her progress. Whether he wanted to ask about her past or give out some of his own history was a mystery. There were words on his lips that he didn't share.

"Get washed," he said and pushed her toward the door with a towel.

RUSHE DIDN'T STAY in the bathroom that day. When she emerged, he was sitting in one of the armchairs watching the door, though he turned away when she caught him staring.

In the bedroom, one of the living room's heavy armchairs occupied the confined space, making it feel much smaller. Why? She had no idea.

Pulling on a sundress Rushe had bought at the same time as the jeans, she wouldn't be going outdoors. The storm had raged through the night. All morning she'd heard the rain battering the roof. The ground would be beyond saturated; it would be a swamp out there. How long did these downpours usually last?

The bedroom door opened, and she flipped her head back to ask. "How—" The question died on her lips. "What's wrong?"

Rushe might have looked the same by all outward appearances, but she read him in a second.

"We have to leave today," he said.

"Where are we going?"

"Not us," he said. "Me and the guys."

"Are you coming back?"

"Yes," he said. "But I don't know when. We've got a meeting and then we're pairing off, Glen's with me and Skeeve has the Kid."

"Okay," she said, a dozen questions flying through her mind. "Unless you have a pair of rain boots, some waders, and a backpack in those jeans, I'll have to wait for you to come back."

"It's not as easy as that," Rushe said. "I told you to leave yesterday for a reason."

"To protect me from Shiv, I know." He didn't play with her intelligence by denying it.

"We could be a couple of days, and I don't know which of us will come back first."

"So I could be left alone with Skeeve," she said. "That's okay, I shot a guy."

"Except the gun is coming with me."

"Sure, it would be hard to threaten people without one," she said, then read from his expression he didn't appreciate her eavesdropping. "Sorry."

"Skeeve's not going to touch you."

"Yeah, because he's a coward," she said. "He talks the talk in front of his buddies but on his own he's chicken."

"You're observant. What do you do when you're not a prisoner?"

"I'm a kickboxing instructor."

"Really?" he asked with a disbelieving look.

"No," she said and grinned. "But I had you there for a second."

"Half of one maybe, I've seen how you defend yourself."

"I'm a research assistant at the National Library."

"A book worm," he said, whether that was meant as a compliment or an insult, she wasn't sure.

"Can I come with you?"

"No."

"Why not?"

"You don't want to get yourself mixed up in my world. Skeeve's already told our boss about you, he's too curious. I won't present you on a plate."

Something about the last statement wasn't meant for her ears but Rushe hid his carelessness well.

"Stay here until I come back," he said.

"Okay."

"The Kid's a perv but he won't threaten you. Skeeve talks a good fight but if they get back before I do, don't wait to feel threatened. Get in here and wedge the armchair between the door and the end of the bed. Skeeve has no strength, and the Kid's a weed. The barrier will keep you safe. I've made sure there's enough water under the bed to keep you going until I get back."

"Rushe," she said. "Whatever it is you're going to do… is it dangerous?"

"Yes," he said, again not insulting her intelligence.

"I know you have an agenda, and you're using me," she said because those were his words. Something bubbled beneath his shield. "I don't know about anything you do but…"

"But…?"

"Wouldn't you rather stay here and screw me stupid than go out there and possibly get yourself hurt… or worse."

"I can get pussy anywhere."

And that shut her up in an instant because he was right. "I didn't mean to imply that mine was special to you," she said. "I meant isn't it preferable to getting hurt… in general."

"I'm not the one who'll be getting hurt," he said, showing that sneer again.

"Have you killed people?"

"What's the matter, Kitten? You wondering about the guy you've had in your bed?"

"I don't care what you've done," she said. "I don't care about what you're going to do. I don't know anything about you, how can I judge what I don't know?"

"But you want to know if I'm capable?"

"I know you're capable," she said. "I think you're capable of anything."

"Is this where you convince yourself that I'm a saint? What I am doesn't matter," he said slowly coming toward her. "Neither does what I'm not."

"What does matter?"

Rushe stopped in front of her. "You're not getting out of this alive."

She held eye contact. "I can be wily."

"I told you this morning this wasn't a game, you have to take this situation seriously."

So that's what he'd been trying to do, him and his forethought. Rushe did nothing to suit immediate needs; everything he did was in deference to what may come next. Not what was but what would be.

Touching his tee-shirt covered abs, she startled him, but his reaction spurred her on. Her hands slid around him, continuing until her cheek rested on his torso.

"What are you doing?" he asked.

"I'm holding you."

"Why?"

"If I'm going to die soon, do my motives matter?" she said, deliberately keeping the smile out of her voice.

"You have an agenda. If you think sweetening me up—"

"You saved my life already," she said. "What matters is now, this minute. Someone could walk in and put a bullet in either of us at any second. But right now we have this, doesn't this feel nice?"

"Nice?" he said as though she'd just asked him to eat shit. He forced her shoulders back to push her body away from his. "You think I'm your sissy little boyfriend? I'm not gonna hold you. I don't care how you feel about anything, and you sure don't have anything to offer me."

She wasn't discouraged when he pushed her away. After they'd shared something personal, he always did. Not just after physical intimacy, but when a connection began to form between them. When he sensed that she cared, or thought his own care for her was showing, he'd hurry to put up a wall. Moving closer, Flick kept her eyes on his when she began to pop open the buttons of his jeans.

"What do you think you're doing?"

"What you told me I could do any time I want," she said, sliding her hand into his jeans to coil her fingers around his cock. Like it sensed her desire, it shot to steel in her grip. "You might not like me very much, but he does. You told me that you don't know when you'll be back, and I'm going to miss him."

"Why do you refer to my dick in the third person?"

"You don't like it if I'm nice to you, and you don't like being nice to me. So I'll be nice to your dick, he seems to like me."

Three hard knocks vibrated their door. "Move it!"

"Yeah!" Rushe shifted out of her reach while tucking himself away. "She's sending me out the door with this," he mumbled to himself.

"We could be quick," she said, trying to mosey closer but he clasped her shoulders, holding her at arm's length.

"I've killed men," he said. "I've gutted them and watched them die slow. Why don't you fear me?"

Obviously, he was getting to the end of his wick. She dipped in to slide her hands into his front jeans pockets.

"There's more to you than that," she said.

"How do you know?"

"Because I do."

"Whatever," he said, turning his back on her. "Stay."

"Rushe," she said when he got to the door. "Kiss me goodbye."

"What?"

Their bedroom exploits were passionate, but since their first time together he hadn't kissed her mouth.

"By your reckoning I'm going to die soon," she said. "Consider it my last request."

"Not a chance. I'll get back to fucking you soon enough, and I'll fuck that sweet little mouth of yours too."

This time when he slammed out, she jumped. He'd told her he'd be back but as she listened to the men pile out and the truck trundle away through the slopping mud, something in her prickled. Her sixth sense believed something was about to change. She didn't know what, or if it would be positive, which was unsettling. If only she'd had the power to see twenty-four hours ahead.

FOURTEEN

ACTUALLY, SLIGHTLY MORE THAN twenty-four hours had passed when the squelch of tires in mud and the rumble of an engine signaled someone's return. Closing the mystery novel she'd found with a bunch of others in the box under the television, she craned to hear the vehicle's progress.

Since the gang left, the rain hadn't let up for long. Her one attempt to get out of there was thwarted pretty quickly. Heaving her way through the mud, the rain continued to pour, and after ten minutes outside she was exhausted, soaked, and freezing cold.

Quickly deciding it was insanity, and quite possibly suicide, she'd made her way back to the shack and searched the property for anything that might aid her escape. But there were no phone lines into the structure. Starting a fire would only lead to more problems; she doubted it was even possible given the wet conditions. Eventually she'd resolved to wait for Rushe, and trust he would get her through this, as he had so far.

Surprisingly, during the night, she'd experienced an unsettling fear. Being out there in the middle of nowhere, in the pitch black, all alone, made her uneasy. For some reason, she felt more comfortable when the criminals were there. Sleeping without Rushe had been impossible, she'd been cold and uncomfortable. It wasn't until she curled up in the chair that sleep came at all, even then it hadn't lasted long.

That day she'd spent most of her time reading on the porch, protected from the torrential rain by the overhang. Even with the men gone, she was still a prisoner, to the horrendous weather. Skeeve couldn't have planned it better himself.

On realizing the vehicle was closing in, she left the porch to retreat into the shack. Eager as she was to see Rushe again, and to make sure he was okay, he wouldn't be happy with her sitting outside exposed. And it may not be Rushe at all; it could just as easily be somebody else.

Not taking any chances, she went into the bedroom with her book and followed Rushe's instructions to wedge the chair between the door and the bed. If Rushe was back, she would let him in. Taking risks with the others was unnecessary. At least that was what she initially, in her naivety, thought.

The front door opened, heralding a lot of shouting. Low male voices yammered with excitement. Skeeve's tone she recognized; the second wasn't so familiar. Though with the heightened enthusiasm, she suspected it may be the Kid.

To her horror, a third voice rose. An unhappy, feminine voice. As though she'd fallen through thin ice, her body temperature plummeted.

"Please," the woman pleaded. "Please let me go!"

She must've sounded much the same on first meeting Skeeve herself. She'd lived that terror, and her protector wasn't around to bail this woman out. Still, Rushe hadn't left her defenseless. She'd seen the pocketknife in the drawer, so hurried over to get it.

Leaving that woman out there alone wasn't an option; that didn't mean she relished being the one to break up Skeeve's party.

Holding the folded knife in her palm, she dragged the chair from its role as barricade and tried to project confidence as she opened the bedroom door. "What's going on?" she asked.

True enough, the Kid was grinning like a Cheshire Cat while Skeeve was equally gleeful. At the sound of her voice, Skeeve turned, opening up the view of a terrified woman on her knees in front of the slimy thug. His fist was balled on the top of his victim's head, lodged in red hair much the same shade as hers. From the bruises on the woman's body and the streaks of make-up on her face, the poor soul had already been through an ordeal.

"Hey, little girl," Skeeve drawled. "Your boyfriend back yet?"

"No," she said, looking at the woman again. "What are you doing with her?"

"Your boyfriend says your goods are his," Skeeve said, checking her figure out.

She didn't care about his leering. Sad, but she was getting used to it. "It's going to be okay," she said to the crying woman.

"You might be hands-off, but the rest of us gotta have fun too. Maybe if I screw her enough, she'll fall goo-goo in love with me like you and your boyfriend."

"If he comes back to find this, do you think he'll be happy?" she asked. "It's not exactly lying low."

"We've been out here a goddamn month!" Skeeve barked, jerking his hand out of the woman's tangled hair.

When the victim tried to scramble away the Kid caught hold of her.

"So?"

Skeeve marched over. "Your boyfriend's told you all about it I'll bet. We've lived here with that superior sonofabitch every day, thinks he's better, thinks he's smarter. I've worked for Victor for three years; you know how many times I've been called to the house? None! Your boyfriend strolls in three months ago and he's at the house every other week!"

Skeeve stopped and glared at her breasts, she didn't need him to give his thoughts voice. "Ah, ah, ah," she said, feeling oddly empowered. "You keep thinking like that and he'll gut you."

Using his name was unnecessary.

"You get into your room," he demanded, "leave me to my fun!"

"I can't do that," she said as Skeeve was about to turn away. "You have to let her go."

"I don't take orders from you! Or your boyfriend!"

"It's not right."

"I don't give a fuck what you think! Shiv's gonna get back here and rip your arms off for what you did to him!"

"I don't care," she said. "I did the right thing."

"The right thing?" Skeeve spat. "You saved the life of your boyfriend, the life of a guy whose job it is to torture and kill whoever Victor points at! How do you think they feel about what you did? Pah! The right thing…" He moved in closer. "You know how many women he's fucked? You think you're something special, don't you? Last night he took three strippers back to his hotel room, what do you think they did for him all night?"

Hearing Rushe had been intimate with other women stung deeper than it should. He'd told her she needed practice and took the lead in their intimacy. What had she done? Nothing. Rushe was right, he could get pussy anywhere. Hers offered him nothing different than the millions of others on the planet. In fact, with her inexperience, it offered him less.

"Aww, you thought you were something special, didn't you?" Skeeve laughed. "How many times did he force himself on you before you fell for him? You're a dumb little bitch; I love it when he does a number on you sluts. I'm gonna try it with my own. Bring her!"

Skeeve started toward another of the bedrooms. The Kid dragged the woman that way and she started screaming.

"No!" she said, shaking off her insecurities. "Let her go, Skeeve!"

"What are you gonna do?" he asked. "You gonna shoot me?"

If wishing made it so. "Maybe."

Reaching around, Skeeve pulled a gun from his waistband to point at her. "Let's see who gets to the trigger first."

"You're not going to shoot me," she said.

"Nah, your boyfriend wouldn't like that," Skeeve said. "Maybe he'd like another hole in you to fuck."

"You're scared of him," she said, poking at Skeeve's pride. "You cower when he walks into the room."

In his fuming, Skeeve came back to her. "I'm not scared of nothing!"

"Sure, I've seen how he orders you all around. He's a man in charge… what do you think I see in him?"

With a swift slap, he backhanded her. "You bitches aren't worth nothing!"

"Neither are you it seems," she said, continuing to poke. "You're here for the scut work, to do the jobs below the man in charge. This is beneath him, you're beneath him… you're beneath me."

By the way he seethed, steam should be streaming from his ears. His short, huffing breaths assaulted her nose. Being this close to him made her nauseous, but she held her ground.

"You're nothing."

The next hit was a punch that sent her to the ground, quickly followed by a kick to her ribs. He spat at the floor only an inch from her face. She pulled herself to her knees, wiping blood from her chin that dribbled from the cut inside her cheek.

He stormed off, but she couldn't let him win. Couldn't let him violate that woman. She'd never be able to live with herself if she gave up. With some struggle, she got back to her feet before Skeeve reached the bedroom.

"You're weak," she called, halting him in his tracks. "You'll never be a quarter of the man Rushe is. I don't care if he fucked a hundred women last night, I'd still suck him off and ask for more. He's a real man!"

Maybe some of that dirty talk had rubbed off on her.

"You're a whore."

"Yeah," she said, widening her stance as Skeeve approached. "I'm *his* whore."

"Is that right?"

"Yeah," she said, swallowing down the coppery taste from her tongue.

"Let's see," he barked and grabbed hold of her.

Despite her resistance, he rushed her to the heaviest armchair to bend her over the back.

She kicked out, but he kicked straight back.

"Get over here!" Skeeve shouted at the Kid.

She didn't see the Kid coming until he jumped onto the armchair and braced her shoulders, holding her in place with his weight.

"You're gonna get it from a real man now," Skeeve drawled, pulling up her dress to rip her underwear away.

Thrashing around, she tried to fight but the two of them held her down. Her defiance seemed to spur them on. Flicking open the concealed knife, she'd give him half a second then make sure he'd lose the ability to violate any woman ever again.

Skeeve grabbed at her ass. "Is this what you like? Rushe been up your asshole yet? You like that? Hey!"

She guessed the last word wasn't for her when Skeeve's hands vanished. The Kid ran and Skeeve went too. Out the front door. The woman was gone, she must've made a break for it.

What should she do? How could she help? Hope as she did that the woman would get free, running out after her wouldn't help.

Options were still flickering through her mind when a gunshot cracked outside. Panic burst. Silence followed. Maybe the shooter wasn't a great shot. Just because she'd heard a shot didn't mean… two more shots startled her.

Were those point blank?

Half a beat later, clarity snapped her from her daze, and she ran into the bedroom, barricading the door with the chair again. Skeeve would be mad, madder than before and he'd blame her for ruining his fun.

Crawling into the corner by the pipe she'd been tethered to on her first night, she hugged her knees to her chest as the tears started. That woman was dead, no doubt about it. She'd gone out there to help the stranger and now the stranger was dead. If she'd stayed right there, in the bedroom, the stranger would be alive. Alive and violated, but alive in any form was better than dead.

The woman's demise was her fault. Reality numbed her but the tears didn't stop. It was all her fault.

FIFTEEN

THE NIGHT PASSED SLOWLY but quietly, considering the circumstances. The men hadn't stayed outside for long. They came inside, the TV went on, and then from what she could gather they drank themselves to sleep.

She didn't sit in the chair or use the bed. It seemed wrong she should have any comfort given her role in a woman's death. From the moment she'd got there, Rushe had looked out for her. If she'd needed a demonstration of what would happen without that protection, the previous day was it. Skeeve was slimy, and clearly short more than a few IQ points, but he'd proved he could pull the trigger.

Until then, she hadn't known hate. The coil of it twisted inside her. The foul sense of impotence provoked anger. Looking beyond her shame over how events played out, she couldn't ignore that Skeeve had a choice. He hadn't wanted the woman to escape, sure, but it was more than desperation. Pulling that trigger would've made him feel powerful.

The walls closed in around her. During her hours of crying, she tried to hatch escape plans. Each one came to a dead end. She had no survival skills and wouldn't last a minute in the elements without supplies. For the time being, she was stuck there silently begging Rushe's return so she could sheath herself in the shelter he provided.

The specific time eluded her, though she was sure the next day had come when the thud of the front door bounced back against the wall to be followed by heavy footfalls.

"Flick!"

He'd never used her actual name. It was him. Rushe. He was back. Crawling across the floor, she yanked the chair away and got to her feet while opening the door. Instantly, Rushe was upon her; she didn't even have time to look at him. He wrenched her off her feet, kicked the door shut, and carried her to the bed.

"Look at me," he said, seating her on the pillow, perching himself at the edge of the bed, stroking her hair away from her face to inspect her wounds. "I'll kill him. I'm gonna fucking kill him."

"Rushe," she sobbed, clawing at him, at his arms and his chest like she could crawl inside him. "They killed her… they killed her…"

"I know," he said. "I know." Yanking her against him, his embrace was crushing but exactly what she needed. Crying into his chest, events played in a loop in her mind. "I'm here now. You're safe. I'm here."

She welcomed his comfort even though it was surprising. He let her cry and held her through it all. This was the same man who'd told her he'd turn her out to the others; her doubts about the veracity of that were confirmed.

She pushed away from his chest but stayed in his arms. "It was my fault," she said. "They came in and I heard her… I went out there but… it was my fault. I provoked him. When the two of them had me pinned over the armchair she ran and… it was my fault."

Rushe bared his teeth. "They had you pinned? Did they touch you?"

"Rushe," she said, trying to grab him back when he moved away.

It was too late, he was up and out of the room. All she could do was dart after him. Rushe was already at Skeeve's chair hauling him up by his throat. He dragged the choking man to the wall and threw him against it from three feet away.

"No second chances," Rushe said, producing a gun from his waistband. "You think you can fuck around? Abuse my woman? Was it worth it, big guy?"

"Rushe!" she exclaimed, running to his side when he cocked the gun. "He's not worth it! He won't do it again! He's learned his lesson!"

"Yeah, yeah, boss," Skeeve said, cowering in the corner with no way out. "You got it! Hands off! You got it, boss."

Rushe leaned down. "You touch one hair on her head again, a gunshot will be the least of your problems… and you know what that means."

"Yeah, yeah, boss."

Sticking his gun back in his waistband, Rushe grabbed hold of her arm, and trailed her across the room to hole them in their bedroom again. After tossing her down on the bed, he began to pace only to stop and rake around in the nightstand drawer.

"What are you looking for?" she asked when he slammed one drawer shut and moved onto the next.

"Take off your clothes," he mumbled.

"You want to have sex? A woman is dead and you—"

"I warned you I'd fuck you anytime I wanted," Rushe said, his glare cutting to her. "I want you naked, you get fucking naked."

After the comfort he'd given on his arrival, she didn't want to deny him. Sex with him meant less knowing he'd been enjoying strippers and God knew who else. Skulking out of her clothes, she folded them at her side. He smacked the drawer closed and sat on the bed.

When he reached past her, she tried to see what he was doing. "What are you do—"

Cold metal closed around her wrist. Alarmed, she tried pulling away, but it was too late, he'd cuffed her to the bedframe.

"What?" she asked, tugging on the restraint. "Why?"

Rushe went to the middle of the room, tucking the key in his pocket. "I left you alone and told you to stay in here if they got back before me. You didn't do that."

"You can't lock me up."

"I made a mistake thinking you could follow instructions. Every time I tell you to fucking do something, you fail. This proves you're still not capable of doing what you're told."

"So you're locking me up?"

"Yes," he said. "You'll be locked up for your own safety."

"Why do I have to be naked?"

He scrutinized her figure. "For the art."

"I thought you were concerned about the others coming in."

"I can only figure you like being pawed."

"I didn't ask him to touch me," she said. "I couldn't listen to her screams and do nothing."

"That's exactly what you should've done."

"You didn't," she said, rising to her knees. "You listened to me scream, and you came to my rescue."

"You think that's what I did?"

"I think that's exactly what you did."

"Have you seen her body?" he demanded, striding to her. "Did you go out there? She's been lying face down in the mud, just left there to rot!"

"They left her there?"

"I thought it was you! Driving up here, her body was lying out there and I thought…"

Now his strong reaction made sense. Was this the same guy who'd claimed not to care about her?

She snagged his jeans pocket, Rushe complied to her unspoken request and dipped to smother her mouth with his. He might not kiss her often but when he did, he made it count.

Pushing her hair away, he tipped up her chin, beckoning her tongue with his. She parted her lips, and the soft, moist motion of his lips wasn't like the first bruising kiss they'd shared, or the soothing motion of the second.

Moisture tumbled from her lashes at the feel of his large hands cupping her face without force, urging her to fulfill his will.

"I'm gonna take you home," he said against her, smudging the tears on her face. "Okay? Don't worry, Kitten. I'm gonna get you home."

"What happened to turning me out to them?"

"I thought it was you."

Something in the way he said the words stabbed at her heart. He was more open and vulnerable with those five words than she'd ever thought he could be.

Still cuffed to the bed, she used her free hand to tug at the buttons of his jeans.

"Not now," he said, joining their mouths again.

"Yes, now," she whispered, surprised he'd ever be reluctant.

That reluctance was short lived. He backed off to put the gun back in the drawer and kick out of his boots. His tee-shirt and socks went next, then he came back toward her.

"Jeans too," she said, and he shirked them without argument.

Already fully erect, he swept her body under his to lay over her, bracing his weight on his forearms.

Linking their mouths, he kissed her for what seemed like hours, his fingertips combing through her hair. Her whole body became liquid, a thick soup of hormones and raging want. She locked her ankles at his back to try tempting him into her but his superior strength kept control.

"I could be of a lot more use to you if I had both hands."

"I'm not unlocking you," he said, kissing her jaw then shifting to kiss her throat, right on her voice-box down to her cleavage, and back up again.

"I want to touch you."

He spent some time kissing her breasts and took her free hand down to roll her fingers around his cock.

"There," he said, suckling her nipple.

This wasn't like any time they'd been intimate before, compared to that he was being positively gentle.

"There's more to you than him."

"That's the only part of me that's good for you."

Her smile burst into a laugh, and he froze. Running her free fingers through his hair, her grin made her cheeks ache.

Rushe lifted his head to look down at her. "I've told you not to let your guard down," he said. "Don't think that this is fun."

"Okay."

Rushe cursed and pounced away from her, standing with his back to the bed. "How am I supposed to keep you safe?" he mumbled.

Did he expect an answer? "You've done okay so far."

On spinning to face her, Rushe's attention scanned down every inch of her spread out figure.

"When I'm on a job I don't have women," he said, stooping to grope each of her breasts before he scooped her clothes from the floor to dump them on her. "Get dressed."

"I thought I wasn't the first or the last," she said.

"I lied. Get dressed."

"What about the strippers?"

"What strippers?"

"That you took to bed night before last," she said.

"Skeeve told you that?" She nodded. "How did you feel hearing that?"

"Do you care?"

"No," he said, shaking sense into his head. "No, I don't care. Get dressed."

"You do care," she said, rising to her knees again. "Why can't you be honest with me?"

"I'm honest."

"You lied about that, about me not being the first, about turning me out to your gang. What have you been honest about?"

"I don't argue with women," he said, snatching up his own jeans to pull them on.

"Funny, I'm sure I'm a woman," she said, touching her breasts. "Yeah, I am."

"And I'm not arguing with you, get dressed."

"No," she said. "Not until you admit you care."

"About what?"

"About me."

Rushe sneered. "I don't care about nothing."

"You don't have women on the job. You just admitted that, but you have me. I'm different."

"As different as the strippers the other night."

"You implied that was false," she said.

"I lied."

"But you don't have women on the job."

"Sex and women aren't the same thing," he said.

"So you had sex while you were gone from here? While I was here waiting for you?"

"Yes."

"You're a good liar. I imagine in your line of work that's an asset."

"Here we go," he said. "You don't know anything about me."

"I might not know the physical details of your life, but I know that you keep me at arm's length to protect me. You tell me not to trust anyone, to always be on guard. You don't want me to trust you because you don't want to let me down, and you don't want me to rely on you. If I do that and things go wrong, you don't want to be responsible."

"Put your clothes on," he growled.

"No," she said. "You won't hurt me. Being crude won't work either because I like it when you talk dirty to me. You can tell me you don't care and make fun of me for my lack of sexual expertise all you want, but I've seen the truth."

"And what's that, Kitten?"

"When you thought I was dead, you panicked. The thought hurt you. Just like it hurt me when I thought you were screwing around."

"You think we run off and get married now?" he snickered in his condescending way. "You gonna take me home to your daddy?"

The notion was ridiculous. "My family don't want anything to do with me," she admitted, figuring at least one of them should be honest. "They don't want me around, so I doubt they'd welcome you."

"Why don't they want you around?"

"Because I didn't do as I was told," she said, not missing the irony.

"Good to know it's not just me you ignore … when was the last time you spoke to them?"

"A year ago," she said. "A little longer maybe."

"What did they want you to do?"

"Marry a man I felt nothing for."

"Why?"

"Because it's what's done… it was good for business."

"You high society or something?"

"Not anymore," she said. "Now it's just me in my studio apartment…" She picked at the corner of the pillow. "It's funny how our lives can change so drastically with just one decision."

"Do you regret it?"

"No," she immediately answered. "My life might be different than what I'd envisioned, but it's better… I'm better."

"Until you walked into Dell's."

"I don't regret that either," she said, taking her eyes up to his.

"Don't say that. Think of what you've been through."

"We are the sum total of our experiences," she said. "You don't have to worry. No one will shed any tears for me if this experience turns out to be my last."

She hadn't realized she'd looked away until he sat on the bed by her.

"Are you hungry?" he asked. "You look tired."

"I didn't sleep while you were away. This place is spooky at night, and you weren't here to keep me warm."

"You were spooked when all the hired guns were away? That's backwards, isn't it?"

"I've never thanked you," she said, "for saving me at Dell's and for keeping me safe since."

"My last," he said, scooping her up, giving himself room to lie down and settle her on top of him.

"What?"

"Rushe is my last name," he said, stroking her hair away from his face. "Get some sleep."

"Sex?"

"I'll wake you up in a while," he said. "You're not gonna get out of it."

"Thank you for coming back."

"I told you I would."

"I trust you, Rushe, like it or not, it's the truth; no argument required."

SIXTEEN

BY HER TENTH NIGHT in the shack with Rushe, things had levelled out. She moved freely around Skeeve, Glen, and the Kid, though it was clear they all bristled in her company.

She and Rushe had sex a minimum of five times a day. He'd brought a truckload of condoms back after his trip, and it seemed he was on a mission to use them all.

She sat on the porch to read, and when the rain stopped, she and Rushe ventured into the trees. The ground was still soft, so she'd gone in her bare feet, wearing a sundress. They came across a lake, and she actually managed to convince Rushe to join her in the water. She'd never skinny-dipped before, not that there was much swimming involved. Just like Rushe to be carrying condoms, even out in the wilderness. At least now she could add sex outside and in water to her list of experiences.

They didn't talk much, but his tells were becoming easier to read. She recognized the look in his eye when he was thinking about sex, and that was certainly a place words were welcome.

Alone with him in the kitchen, she took her toast from the toaster to the kitchen table and leaned across it for the butter, except she couldn't reach it. As she was about to right herself to go around the table, Rushe's hand landed between her shoulder blades keeping her bent over.

"What are you…" she asked, trailing off when he lifted up her dress and pulled her underwear down to her knees. "Here? Like this? It's lunchtime."

"I know," he rumbled, sliding two fingers into her while rubbing her clit with his thumb.

"Don't, Rushe," she whispered. "You know I can't be quiet. I always fail at that."

"That your only objection?" he asked, still concerned with her consent.

"Yes."

"Good, then I can ignore it."

His hands slid down her outer thighs, stalling her words. What was he doing? Pressuring her thighs apart, he kissed each of them and closed his lips around her clit, first sucking on her, then flicking her with his tongue.

"Rushe," she gasped. "Do you want to go to bed?"

"No," he hummed around her. "It's lunchtime."

Her smile spread, but when she tried to push away from the table, he held her hips in place. His tongue circled her then probed inside until her knees almost gave out. He licked at her and sucked her clit between his teeth while his fingers dipped into her again.

No man had ever done this for her. She'd had no idea what she'd been missing. His pace increased.

She squeaked and wriggled against him. "Rushe," she groaned.

"I'm gonna take my time," he mumbled against her, his tongue moving faster.

Less than a minute later, she cried out at the explosion in her womb. Sharing this intimacy brought her closer to him. Rushe might not agree, but he'd given her something selflessly, he got nothing in that orgasm except the knowledge he'd spoiled her.

On his feet again, he pulled up her underwear, then lowered her dress, giving her back her modesty.

She reached back to steal his wrist. If she said thank you, he'd rebuke her. What could she say to show her gratitude?

"You should stop wearing underwear," he said.

Her solemnity vanished into a smile. Sandwiched between him and the table, she turned to him More and more he invaded her personal space, and he never apologized for it. Even then she had to lean back a little where her breasts pressed to his torso. There wasn't quite enough room for her, but he didn't apologize and didn't back off.

"You bought underwear for me," she said.

"On day two," he said. "Its job was to keep those bastards out."

"It doesn't still do that?"

"None of them are going to touch you. They know better. Now it's just keeping me out."

"It delays things by like two seconds," she said. "I like wearing your gift."

Rushe leaned down, his face came close to hers. "If I bought you underwear as a gift, it sure wouldn't look like that."

"I'm scared to ask," she said, curling her fingers into his jeans pockets. "If you want me to stop wearing it, I'll stop wearing it."

"Damn right you will," he said, sweeping his hand under her hair to cup the back of her skull and tip her mouth up for his consumption.

He kissed her a lot more these days but reserved it for when they were in private. At night when the men lounged around the TV, he'd keep her in his lap, fondle her, do whatever he wanted, but he still instructed her to get beer, food, and fulfill his commands.

When the others were around, their familiarity was subdued. He pawed her and commanded her but showed no affection. Flick trusted Rushe and followed his direction. If the others saw her as a weakness, they could hurt Rushe, she didn't want that.

"Could we maybe go to bed?" she asked, sinking her hands deeper into his pockets to explore the now solid length of him.

"You're turning into a randy little slut, aren't you?"

"Only for you," she said, pressing her breasts against him. "I have to return the favor… I need the practice, remember?"

Sucking him off had become something of a morning routine.

"You hungry for my cock?"

"Yeah," she breathed. "Right now, please… sir."

Gathering her skirt up, he gripped her rear, forcing her against his erection. "You get it when I want it," he growled. "I fuck you to satisfy my appetite."

"I want you to fuck me," she murmured. "Every minute of the day I want you inside me."

"Ah, my dirty little whore, I've trained you well."

"I love being your whore, Rushe," she said. "The things we do together… the way it makes me feel."

A door banged open, she didn't bother to turn, she didn't need too. Rushe's grip on her butt strengthened.

"Phone," Skeeve snapped.

Rushe smacked her ass. "Get naked," he said to her quietly, then left her alone to take the phone from Skeeve.

The only phone in the place was a cellphone. No outgoing calls were made; it was there purely for Victor to get in touch with these men. Skeeve's job it appeared was to play secretary, look after the device, and answer it when needed.

Rushe took it outside as he always did, leaving her alone with Skeeve. She spread the butter on her cold toast. From experience, these calls could take time, there was no hurry to comply with Rushe's order.

"Tick, tock, little girl," Skeeve said. "Time's running out for you." She ignored him but he carried on. "Boss has got orders, we'll split soon. Pieces are moving on the board."

"I'm sure that's lovely for you," she said.

With her toast in hand, her aim was the bedroom, but Skeeve blocked her way between the fridge and the table.

"Boss gets anything he wants," Skeeve sniped. "You're gonna be on the market, or in the boss's bed... your boy's gonna be in his place then."

The grating sound of the slimeball's laughter followed her to the bedroom. Long after he'd quieted, it still echoed in her head.

SEVENTEEN

RUSHE DIDN'T COME to her after the phone call. He didn't come to her at dinner, or while the men sat around watching television in the evening.

Long after light had disappeared from under the door, she lay awake listening to the sound of nothing from the rest of the house.

Where was he? Would he come to her at all? Worrying about Rushe's welfare did nothing to help, but she doubted he'd appreciate her going out to look for him.

When the bedroom door did eventually open, she didn't disguise being awake, but he didn't look at her. Rushe shirked everything but his jeans and scooped her on top of him when he lay down.

He didn't speak. In their recent nights together, he hadn't kept his jeans on. Every night he touched her too, unlike right then.

"None of this is your fault," she whispered, drawing her index finger up his chest. "What will be, will be, Rushe."

"You don't know what you're talking about," he grumbled in his petulant way.

"Either I'm trafficked, or I have to become your boss's sex slave," she said. "I'd put my money on the former because my lack of experience won't impress him much." Rushe said nothing. "I trust you."

"You shouldn't," he said. "If I had stopped you from walking into Dell's—"

"I walked into Dell's," she said, smacking his chest then sitting up to straddle his abdomen, meeting his eye. "I walked in there. Me. I'm here because of my own actions."

"I'm going to take you into town tomorrow," he said.

"Okay."

"Me and the guys have to pick up a couple of things."

"And you're going to take me?" she asked, excited about the concept of an outing. "Should I buy new underwear?"

"You're not coming back here. None of us are," he said. "But you're gonna take the five hundred and run."

"I know what happened to the last woman who ran from Skeeve."

"We'll be in town," he said. "There will be people everywhere. If you see a cop—"

"What am I supposed to do?" she asked. "Turn you in?"

"Providing there hasn't been a national campaign about your disappearance, the cop won't put the pieces together until we're long gone."

"What will Victor say?"

"He won't give a fuck. We have bigger things to worry about."

"Like what?" she asked. "Are you in danger?"

"Every day of my life. We play with live ammo," he said. "Nothing is more dangerous now than it has been the rest of my life."

"You expect me to just walk away?"

"Yes."

"When you're in trouble?"

"I'm always in trouble," he said, sliding his finger down to her clit. "Lean back."

"No," she said, swatting his hand away. "We have to talk."

"Are you refusing me sex?"

"Yes," she said, swallowing her apprehension.

"You don't get to do that," he growled.

Rushe sat up, sending her down to sit on his erection while he ripped open her dress, exposing her breasts.

Snagging one nipple, he tugged on it hard while biting the other. "You want it," he said, thrusting two fingers into her. "You're a dirty little whore, you've been thinking about my cock all day."

"Rushe—"

Spinning her around, he got her face down at the foot of the bed and fumbled around for something. With his weight on hers, he locked both of her wrists in the cuffs around the metal bar at the end of the bed. Then he let her go. Naked and alone, she had no idea what to do next.

He parted her legs with his own then hooked one forearm under her hips to lift them higher. "Consent," he demanded in a primal growl.

She couldn't ignore the heat building in her belly. "Yes."

Stabbing one finger into her, he said nothing as two others joined it. "Do you like that?" he sneered, his speed increasing. "Your little pussy's dripping back here, you want to say no to me?"

With the arm braced under her, he twisted his hand up to squeeze her nipple, a yelp joined the pain shooting through her.

He drove his fingers deeper. "You're a horny little slut, you like that, you like me playing with your soaking pussy. Yeah, you want me to fuck you bad, don't you? Are you thinking about my dick now? About it fucking that prissy pussy of yours?"

His fingers disappeared. She yelped again, but he took her hips and flipped her onto her back, twisting her wrists in the cuffs on the bar. He stood up just long enough to take off his jeans and snatched a pillow to fold it and stuff it under her head.

Slinging a leg over her, he supported most of his weight when he sat on her chest, nestling his cock in her cleavage. He squeezed her breasts together, rolling them up and down creating a canal to screw her tits. Sliding back and forth, he pushed them harder. The bite of his fingers squeezed the sensitive flesh until she could feel bruises forming.

"Yeah," he said. "Fuck your tits, this is what they're for, whore. Here for my dick, to keep my cock warm, for my pleasure. Your tits are mine, your pussy's mine. I get to fuck you any time I want."

Releasing her breasts, he smudged each of her nipples, then shifted upward holding himself in hand. "Open your mouth," he commanded without moving his lips.

She didn't think twice, this was how he made sense of the world.

Squashing his cock between her lips, his mass rammed further into her than she'd ever imagined possible. With one hand flat on the wall at his side and the other gripping the foot bar, he slid himself back over her tongue. He dragged his bulging head on the inside of her cheek coating her with the pre-come seeping out of him.

Her concentration was occupied by learning how to breathe as he propelled deeper into her throat. His motion picked up pace until he was fucking her mouth with an intensity she could feel to the tips of her toes. On a growl, he grabbed her nose, pulling out of her just enough to drench her tongue in his seed. After the jets stopped, he wiped the tip of his dick around her lips.

"Swallow," he ordered her, holding himself in hand.

While maintaining their eye contact, she did. He jumped up to snatch up his jeans and slammed out of the room… just like the good old days.

EIGHTEEN

A LONG TIME must have passed because she'd fallen asleep. Something she only learned when she felt his fingers inside her.

Not on the bed, he sat on the floor, an elbow on the mattress. "I'm gonna fuck you without a rubber," he grumbled, though he hadn't looked at her. How did he know she was awake? "I'll pull out."

"Okay," she said.

The way he jabbed another finger into her conveyed his frustration. "You're a stupid fucking slut, you know that? I'm a bad guy. Do you know how many women I've fucked?"

"You wouldn't put me in danger," she said, understanding his implication.

"Great," he barked. "You being a hungry little whore lets my fat cock pump into your hot, juicy pussy?"

"Yes," she agreed.

No matter how he lashed out, she wouldn't rise to it. She knew what was going on.

In a blur of movement, he got up and dropped his jeans. Then he was on the bed, on top of her, shoving himself into her. Rushe felt bigger, harder, and so much hotter with the fast rhythm he adopted.

"Do you like that?" he asked. "I'm fucking you bare, my cock in you, you're wet, you're covering me with your dripping pussy. You are a whore, aren't you? Aren't you, Kitten? Say it."

Her hips bucked up into the smash of orgasm that stiffened her body. "Oh, God, I'm a whore!" she screamed out.

Her inner muscles clamped, squeezing him hard, desperately trying to keep him inside, to suck his spunk into her cervix. He yelled and grabbed her hips to push her down, away from where he'd been trying to withdraw. His cock landed on her pubis and a warm wet puddle shot up toward her cleavage.

Both of them panted, neither said a word. Their sexual episodes had never been that short. Rushe always lasted longer, which was probably why he appeared so dumbfounded and fell back to his haunches, transfixed by his seed on her body.

She sighed. "I think that's the best sex I've ever had."

"The quickest," he managed to mumble. With his half joke, she got him back, for the time being at least. "You feel amazing. You grabbed onto me that… skin on skin…"

"You sound surprised."

"I've never fucked a woman without a rubber before," he admitted, and let himself meet her gaze.

"I'm always right," she said, knowing her instinct to trust him had been correct.

"I was tested before the job," he said. "And you're the only woman I've…"

"I don't have enough experience for you to be concerned."

"Just you and your little boyfriend."

She sighed. "My boyfriend."

No one had referenced that lie for a while.

"What's he like?" Rushe asked.

"What?"

"Your boyfriend. He'll be happy when you get back, I guess. But I've ruined you for every man that follows me."

"Yeah, I suppose you have."

"He won't be happy I've stretched your snug little cunt. You'll never feel him again."

"Stop it," she said on a smile, prodding him with her toe.

"Is he gonna hunt me down?" Rushe asked.

"Are you scared?"

"Me? I don't think so, Kitten. Do you want me to kill him for you? I'd do it. No problem."

"Are you joking?" she said not entirely sure because Rushe never smiled, and his humor was so dry.

"If he comes after me—"

"I don't know how anyone would ever find you."

"If you were my woman and another man thought about touching you, I'd let nothing get in my way until I'd watched him die a long, slow death."

"Yes," she said. "As Skeeve would attest to."

"If he comes after me, I'll defend myself. Do you love him?"

"Does that matter?" she sighed.

"If you love him and plan to spend your life with him, it's fair I should leave him with a couple of fingers... Though, I tell you, you won't be having kids."

"Rushe..." she said, ready to tell him the truth.

"If you love him, you shouldn't have consented to sex with me."

"So you do have some redeeming qualities," she said, highlighting he wasn't as evil as he tried to make out.

"You think I feel guilty about screwing around with another man's woman?"

"No," she said. "I meant loyalty and fidelity. Two things you believe in."

"To a man in my line of work they're words without meaning."

"You've been faithful to me," she said. "You just said that I'm the only woman you've been with."

"Yeah, one woman, eleven nights, it's been tough."

"You've been in this place for more than a month," she said. "And you've been on this job for three months. I'm privileged."

"Who's been talking?" he asked.

She slid her feet up his legs when he straightened his out. "I'm glad I met you."

"After tomorrow you'll be free to go back to your life and forget any of this happened."

"I might have asked to come with you if I didn't think I'd be more of a liability than an asset."

"You said it," he said.

Wriggling her toes against his testicles, she lifted his cock with her other foot. "Will I see you again?"

"Are you talking to me or him?"

Though Rushe might not smile himself, that joke stirred hers. "Both of you."

"Don't think your boyfriend would like that."

"You said you were going to have a word with him about sending me out into the world unprepared."

"That was before I knew you were unable to follow basic instructions," he said. "And before I was fucking you."

"You are scared."

He snatched her feet away from his erection. "Do I look like a man in fear?"

"You're very good at hiding your real feelings," she said. "I don't think you could physically fear anyone. But how would you feel about seeing another man with me?"

"He could never be better for you than I was."

She laughed and slipping feet his grip. "Is everything about sex to you?"

"Sex or money," he said. "The only two motivators in the world."

"It's such a shame."

"What?"

He snatched her feet again to wrap them around his dick.

"I have so many questions," she said. "I wish…" She sighed. "I wish we had time. I wish we had…"

"Don't drive yourself crazy with what ifs. I'm a bad guy. You don't want me anywhere near your life."

"My father did tell me that my taste in men would get me into trouble one day. I don't think even he thought that meant falling for a criminal."

"You haven't fallen for me," he stated. "This is Stockholm, believe me, I've seen it before. Why do you think I don't have women while I'm on the job?"

"I don't have Stockholm Syndrome," she said. "I walked into this with my eyes open."

"You walked into this with your pretty little nose poked up in the air."

"I didn't mean the situation," she said. "I meant us. I want to get to know you better, and I want to spend more time with you but…"

"But?"

"But I never thought we'd fall crazy in love, have half a dozen kids, and live happily ever after."

"You got that part right," he said.

"But you've changed who I am, Rushe."

"I'll be your dirty little secret. The crazy fling you tell your grandkids about."

"No." She laughed. "I don't think I would discuss our affair with children of any kind."

"Tomorrow I'll cut you loose, and you'll never say my name again in your life."

"I will," she said.

"Once you tell the cops what—"

"I'm not going to tell the cops anything about you."

"Yeah," he snorted. "You're not a Stockholm case."

"Truth?" she said. "No one will have noticed I'm gone. I guarantee you that the police will have nothing on me."

His brows came together in a show of curiosity. "Maybe I will pay your boyfriend a visit."

"Will you uncuff me now?"

"No," he exhaled. "I want to have sex with you again… a few more times."

"I don't have to be cuffed for that. I'll consent… I'll go on top."

"No," he said with a shake of his head. "It'll drive me nuts."

"Me on top? Are you worried I'll be too slow?"

"I'm worried I'll be too quick," he said. "After that last performance."

"I told you that was the best I ever had," she said. "A man like you doesn't lose control. Knowing in whatever small way I helped you lose it… it's flattering."

"You like playing with fire, don't you, Kitten?"

"What happened to Red?"

The first thing he'd noticed about her was her hair color.

"Collar doesn't match the cuffs, sweetheart, it's not natural."

"No," she said, feeling the burn on her cheeks. "It's not."

"And that was before I got acquainted with your all natural, one hundred percent real pussy."

"You call me Kitten in reference to my vagina?" she asked, incredulous.

He half shrugged. "Walking pussy, right?"

"Rushe!"

Sliding his hands up her shins to her thighs, he lay above her. "Ah, I'll eat you out in the shower, make you feel better."

From somewhere, he produced the key to unlock her.

Her fingers sank into his hair. "Rushe," she asked, keeping him in place. "Will you remember me?"

"The fake red head with a great rack who can't follow instructions? You'll stick in my head for a couple of weeks."

With his teasing, he lifted her off the bed but had to put her down so they could cover up for the journey to the shower, the Kid at least would still be out there.

So this was it, her last night in captivity. If someone had told her eleven nights ago she'd be sorry to see the back of this cabin, she'd have laughed and thrown something at their head. But now, at the end, she was sorry to say goodbye. She'd miss it, miss him. But there wasn't a damn thing she could do to prevent their separation… much like ending up here in the first place.

NINETEEN

AS SOON AS all the shack dwellers were awake, they moved out. Packing everything into the truck, she sensed that although this was a conclusion for her, the men were at the opposite end of their journey. Unable to imagine what lay ahead for them, their trip, it seemed, would be grueling.

With Shiv absent, Rushe made Skeeve sit in the front of the truck. It turned out Skeeve and the Kid had come back in the vehicle belonging to the deceased woman, and now it lay abandoned at the back of the building. Subtly committing the license plate to memory, she vowed to phone in an anonymous tip to law enforcement when she got home.

The only concern was implicating Rushe, she didn't want to do that. But after listening to him go on for half an hour about the need to wipe fingerprints from all objects and surfaces, she was confident he wouldn't be traced or linked to the crime.

It wouldn't be right if Skeeve and the Kid got away with murder, literally.

On the drive, she tried to figure out where they were. Tough job apparently. By the time they rolled into town an hour later, she was mixed up. At that point, all she knew was they were far from the shack. Her sense of direction sucked.

After being in seclusion, it was unsettling to see people going about their lives. They passed fast food restaurants, shops, and banks, everything that anyone would expect of a town. She hadn't considered such basic things in her time away from civilization.

Glen drove them down an alley to a shadowy parking area. The men got out, but Rushe ordered her to stay put. The gang stood in a huddle outside. Should she make a break for it? Wearing only Rushe's thick socks, outrunning the men wouldn't be easy.

Glen peeled off and walked away with Skeeve scuttling after him. Rushe stayed talking to the Kid until Skeeve and Glen were out of sight. Then the Kid ran off in the opposite direction from the other two.

For a few seconds, Rushe stood with his back to the truck, waiting for… what? Eventually, he came and opened the back door, gesturing for her to exit.

"You got the money?" he asked. She nodded. That morning he'd tucked it into her sock and hidden the bulge under her jeans. "Go through that door."

He pointed in a third direction. "Okay."

"Walk through the store, go out the west entrance, it's the cosmetics department. Directly outside there's a cab line. Get in, tell them to take you home, that's it."

"Straight home?"

Rushe closed the truck door at her back. "Change cabs a couple of times if it makes you feel better, but no one will come looking for you."

"No one?" she asked, her fingertips met his abs.

Hope filled her voice. She cringed knowing Rushe would hear it too.

"Do me a favor, Kitten," he said. "Do what you're told. I won't be around to pull you out next time."

She nodded again and swiped tears from her cheeks. "I'll try."

"Good girl… now go away."

She hooked her hands into his jeans pockets, pushing up as he lowered to her. Although he accepted her kiss, he didn't let her prolong it. All too soon he straightened up.

"Thank you, Rushe."

"Get," he mumbled without moving his lips.

Everything in her wanted to stay at his side, but time was running short, and he wouldn't be able to protect her indefinitely. No matter how much he denied caring about her, he did, she could feel it. But in his profession, weakness could leave him open to manipulation.

Touching the stubble on his cheek, she smiled. "You're a good guy, Rushe. I owe you my life… goodbye."

This really was goodbye. The finality of walking away provoked more tears. Following his instructions thus far had kept her out of trouble… or if she'd followed them, they would have. So she walked past the truck, across the alley, and opened the brown door he'd pointed out. She told herself not to look back but couldn't resist.

In the shadows of the surrounding buildings, the truck was just decipherable, his silhouette was harder to define. He was still there. Just like on that very first night. His form eluded her, but she could hear him, though he didn't speak.

This would be the last moment that they would share. So with fresh tears in her eyes, and a weight around her neck, she turned away and followed his instructions.

TWENTY

THE FUNNY THING about returning to her life was finding it was exactly the same. Unlike her.

Throughout her trip home, she expected something to happen. Like being run off the road by a crazy-eyed Skeeve or a vengeful Shiv. At one point, she imagined the driver pulling over and demanding to see her breasts… he didn't.

Her time in that shack had heaved her through so many emotions that her head still spun from the ordeal. She'd never experienced so many extreme emotions in such a short time. From her initial terror to the trust she built with Rushe, through to the panic at being caught naked in the shower. All of it whirled in her mind like a melancholy mirage.

Looking back, the things she'd done with Rushe, the sex, the union of their bodies was surreal. No man had brought her to ecstasy with words and actions in the way Rushe did. Stepping out of her comfort zone, consenting to have sex with him, was the best decision of her life. The misgivings she had about being with him, about her own shortcomings, had been dashed by his confidence. She'd pleasured him, been a part of him, he'd desired her.

Her experience with him had changed her. Something inside was different. The stirrings of her connection with him had awoken it. She felt stronger, more sure of herself. For all the negatives, the fear and anger, she was still alive.

Despite failing to escape or save Skeeve's victim, she'd learned how strong she could be. Standing up to Skeeve showed a new courage in herself. Guilt did chew at her. Some might call it survivor's guilt. She frequently reminded herself Skeeve would've likely pulled the trigger on the woman eventually, it just happened sooner with her intervention.

Most people never got to see what they were capable of. From what she'd seen if her ability, she was proud. Although she did admit to herself Rushe was a big part of her new confidence.

Still, who in their life had been assaulted and kidnapped? How many people were held against their will and found themselves in the clinch of passion with the man who had kept them safe? People didn't know what was in them until they faced it.

In the end, her journey home ended up being uneventful. After a brief conversation with her building superintendent, he let her into her apartment, and gave her a key to copy. Her purse had been missing since Dell's, everything would need to be replaced.

She went through the motions of canceling cards, then dunked herself in her bathtub. When alone in her own home, she didn't know what to do with herself. There were no rules to follow, no men to fear, no one to have sex with. It seemed hollow. How would she sleep without her bad boy to lie on?

Everything was the same, everything but her.

SHE'D BEEN TEMPTED not to go back to work at all. How would she explain her absence? After flirting with the idea for a short spell, the following morning, she got up and went in to face the music. Geoffrey gave her a dressing down. Tamara delighted in the display. The excuse of being unwell and unable to get to a phone was farfetched even to her own ears. Geoffrey eventually accepted it. Then again, short of outright calling her a liar, he had little choice.

She couldn't use the truth even if she wanted to, because there was no proof of it. No police came looking for her. The only messages on her home voicemail were from Geoffrey and Hayden. The latter had called about the date she'd stood him up for, on the night her cab broke down. The night that set all events in motion. She'd almost forgotten about Hayden completely.

Tamara spent the rest of Wednesday filling her in on the latest gossip. Not that there was much to miss at the National Library, it was hardly a buzzing social hub. Students, professors, journalists, and authors made up most of their traffic. Law enforcement were also regular customers, more the state and federal guys than the local ones.

By the following Friday, she hadn't found her groove again. She wondered where Rushe was, what he was doing, and whom he was doing it with. Maybe he got in trouble for releasing her. The danger in his life was very real. Though, like he'd said, no one had come after her.

"You're in one of your dreams again," Tamara said, propping herself against the front desk of the research department.

"What?" she asked the tall blonde.

"You've been all over the place this week, what's up?"

"Nothing," she said, doubting the sincerity of Tamara's interest.

"Do you know what would help?"

"I'm fine."

"Double date tomorrow night." Tamara carried on regardless. "I've been seeing this guy, well, we haven't actually been on a date yet, but he has a roommate. He said if I could come up with a friend for his friend… you know."

Were they friends? Maybe giving her colleague a chance could be worthwhile. Rushe had been the one to point out he wouldn't be around if anything bad happened in the future. It could be wise to incorporate some people into her life who would notice if she went missing.

Although given what she had just been through, the statistical chances of finding herself exposed to that situation in the near future were astronomical. Then again, she'd had her purse snatched twice. Didn't these things tend to come in threes?

"What's he like?" she asked only to be ignored.

Tamara pushed away from the desk with a widening smile and a brightening flirtatious aura. Someone must've caught her colleague's eye. She'd get nothing out of her co-worker until the male was out of her crosshairs.

"Hello," Tamara drawled. "How can we help you today?"

Flick kept typing, giving the pair an illusion of privacy.

"You are one beautiful woman," the man said.

"Why thank you," Tamara said with false modesty. "You're a handsome man yourself. How can I help you? Tell me all your research needs."

"I need some information," he said.

"You came to the right place."

"I work for a man named Victor."

Her fingers froze, hovering above the keys. Without even lifting her head, she knew the stranger's eyes were on her. What should she do? Her mind raced.

"Good to know," Tamara said with no idea what was going on. "But what can—"

"I've got this," Flick said.

"Uh, no, I'm already—"

"Toddle on, beautiful," the man said.

With a clueless air, Tamara walked away.

"What do you want?" she whispered, trying to draw on confidence and detachment to help her through.

"You need to come with me."

Now she looked at him, right into his ice-blue eyes. "Do you think I'm going to get up and walk out with you?"

"I think that's your only option," he said. "Victor wants you…"

"For what?"

Damn, how she craved Rushe.

"I'm not telling you that."

"I really don't want to screw your boss."

"I don't think that's what he wants," the stranger said, snickering. "I walked in here because I thought we could be civilized. If you'd rather be snatched off the street—"

"This has nothing to do with me," she said. "I haven't called the cops. I'm no threat."

"Rushe is in trouble. Come with me and there might be something you can do about that."

"Why should I believe you? If I walk back into that and you're lying—"

"Why would I be lying?" he asked. "I want you to come with me, and I'm gonna take you to Victor. If I was trying to trick you, I'd have come up with a better lie."

"Why didn't Rushe come?"

"Like I said, he's in trouble."

Yes, he could be lying, but how would she wriggle out of complying?

"I think if I show up, I'm going to be in trouble," she said.

"Victor won't hesitate to hurt Rushe."

"Do you think he's afraid?" she asked, wearing a smirk that Rushe would be proud of. "You can come here and threaten me all you like. You can threaten Rushe. You can try to strong arm him, but he's never going to fear you, or your boss."

"He's not invincible," the man said. "And neither are you."

Hadn't she told Rushe she'd be a liability? He'd agreed with her. It wouldn't matter that Rushe's feelings for her didn't run deep; convincing this stranger of that would be tough. This guy had one task to complete. She doubted he concerned himself to look at any reasoning beyond that.

"He won't care if you hold me for ransom."

"But will you care if we hold him?"

And that was the kicker, because she did care if they hurt him, especially if she could in any way prevent his pain.

"What is it you want?" she asked. "Is this about money?"

"I'm here to pick you up," he said. "My sole responsibility is to get you to Victor."

"And if I refuse?"

"You're my sole responsibility," he said again. "If I have to drag you out of here kicking and screaming I will."

"My colleagues will call the cops."

"And by the time they get here we'll be long gone."

Kicking and screaming could lead to others getting hurt. "Are you alone?"

"Do you think you can take me?" he smiled.

"What's your name?"

"Call me John."

"That's imaginative," she said.

"I'll tell my mother you said so. Now get up, we're leaving."

Rushe would kill her for complying, but she wouldn't be responsible for his suffering.

"Okay," she said, rising from her seat. "I have to speak to my boss and—"

"No," John said, losing all good humor. "You're gonna come out from back there and walk out with me. Now."

"But—"

John's hand came up still in his pocket, showing the suspicious slope of a gun. "You don't want anyone to get hurt, do you, Flick? Where did your pretty colleague go? I could call her over, she'd come running. How many people have to die before you do what you're told?"

A group of smiling college kids came through the front entrance.

John followed her line of sight. "They're young," he said. "How many of them do you want me to take out? You're going to do it anyway, one way or another I'll get you to Victor."

It appeared she'd used all her turns. Maybe that wasn't a gun in his pocket. But knowing what she did about Victor's men, she couldn't take the risk.

Without her purse or personal effects, she rounded the front desk, surrendering to the inevitable. John immediately caught hold of her arm to jerk her to his side. With the gun prodding her ribs, they headed for the exit.

"We're gonna walk out of here nice and slow," he mumbled. "If you get any ideas about running just remember it's Rushe's life you're gambling with."

She hadn't forgotten and wouldn't. Rushe had risked his safety for hers. It was only right she return the favor. John pushed her head down to force her into the once white Ford idling at the roadside. One thing was certain, Rushe would be furious with her.

John got in next to the driver. The car started moving before all of the doors were closed. Her attention drifted to the man at her side. Disgust hit her hard: Skeeve.

"Hey little girl," he drooled, grabbing for her thigh.

In an odd reflex, her fist came up and she punched him full force on the nose. Blood spurted in a dozen directions. Commotion in the front joined Skeeve's cursing.

"You fucking bitch!" he roared, swinging at her.

She ducked sideways so the blow only glanced her.

"Calm down!" John shouted.

Skeeve shoved his pelvis forward and grabbed for her hair. "This little bitch has been asking for it since I met her!"

"You think about putting anything anywhere near my mouth and I'll bite it off. I swear to it, Skeeve."

John and the driver laughed, but Skeeve fumed.

"You've got nothing to worry about," John said. "Victor says you've not to be touched… sexually anyway. We all know what Skeeve's like."

"You smug sonofabitch," Skeeve sneered.

"Do your job," John snapped.

Rushe apparently wasn't the only one to have short patience with Skeeve.

"Here for the scut work," she muttered, turning her eyes to the side window.

"We get her to the boss," John said. "You know what you've got to do."

Skeeve's hands swooped around her and fabric was pulled over her eyes. After tightening the blindfold, another length of the thick material came over her mouth. Being blindfolded and gagged evidently wasn't enough, because next he stole her hands and tied her wrists. Fighting the bonds would get her nowhere, but she resented Skeeve's silent victory.

Now unable to ask questions, she doubted her abductors would've answered them anyway. They wouldn't tell her where they were going and didn't want her to see the route. All she could do was wait.

Whatever was going on, they'd used her feelings for Rushe to coerce her. Why? She hadn't figured that out yet. Yes, she believed Rushe cared for her, but not enough to be influenced by her. Whatever he was, or wasn't, doing wouldn't change by her mere presence.

The trip was mostly quiet. The men jeered each other. The radio was switched on and off a few times. After listening without contributing for a number of hours, she rested her head against the window and tried to sleep.

Walking out on her job was the same as handing in her notice given this was the second time she'd be MIA. With no idea what was ahead, employment was the least of her worries.

John had laughed when she refused to sleep with Victor. But his reaction didn't rule out the alternative, the trafficking option. This was a lot of effort to go to just to sell her on.

Did Rushe refuse to do something? Speculation got her nowhere, so while the men argued about sports teams, she counted her breaths, like counting sheep. Whatever lay ahead, she'd need to be at her best.

TWENTY-ONE

WHEN THE VEHICLE STOPPED, the doors opened then shut. The activity got her sitting upright. Without her senses, she couldn't anticipate what was coming. Her own car door opened, and she was hauled out onto gravel. Footsteps surrounded her, increasing her disorientation as she was pulled along.

Smoke scented the air. The crunch of gravel gave way to their ascent of stone stairs. A dozen steps later, the men's voices hushed.

For a few seconds, nothing happened, then a rush of warm air accompanied the sound of a door opening. They were walking. Inside… Somewhere that reeked of expensive perfume.

Her heels stopped clacking when they reached carpet… on stairs, they were ascending again. At the top, they went through another door and walked a few meters until turning sharp to the left and stopping.

"This is you," John said.

Her blindfold was removed. A four-poster bed dressed in peach shades that matched the carpet stood between solid nightstands. One conspicuous characteristic of the room alarmed her.

John removed the gag.

"There are no windows," she said.

"That's right," he said, pushing her toward a wall and up against it to frisk her.

"If I had a weapon, I'd have used it by now," she said.

Once John satisfied himself, he untied her wrists. "You've got some time in here. That's the bathroom."

"So I'm supposed to just sit here? Where's Rushe?"

"Don't know," John said. "Word to the wise, don't be eager to shorten your wait. As long as you're in here, you're safe… You're lucky you were brought upstairs. Women who go down the stairs leave by the back door. Dead or alive."

"Are you trying to scare me?"

"No," he said, smiling again. "I don't need to try. When you realize what goes on around here, you'll need a whole new word for fear… settle in."

He left the room. The snick of the lock seemed to echo. Trapped. Imprisoned… again.

Was Rushe there at all? He had to be. These people had no use for her except to manipulate Rushe. When the timing for maximum impact arrived, no doubt they would parade her out.

If Rushe was here he'd be mad at her, but if he wasn't…

She sighed and took her feet from her shoes. For the moment, she would follow John's instructions and settle in. This could take a while.

TWENTY-TWO

HER TWO EXPERIENCES of being a prisoner were polar opposites. The ten-by-ten-foot cell she and Rushe had shared in the shack doubled in size at this new location. But with so little furniture in the room, most of it was just space.

The disgusting, moldy, and mildew saturated washroom from the shack was now a gleaming fully kitted out bathroom with a double shower and Jacuzzi tub. On investigation, she found ample towels and toiletries stacked in the closet along with clothes and underwear, all new and in her sizes. Whatever her reason for being there, their thorough preparation suggested she was expected to be around for quite a while.

Only seeing Rushe would relax her. Though, when that happened, when they came face to face, she could have a whole new set of problems.

No one had come to her, and she heard no sounds outside her room. Either they'd barricaded her and then abandoned her there, or this room was completely soundproofed. That in itself was worrying. It meant either they didn't want her to hear them on the outside, or that something would happen inside that the bad guys didn't want anyone else to hear.

After kicking around for a few hours, she took a shower to wash Skeeve from her skin. Just being close to the guy made her feel dirty. When finished, she chose to put her own clothes back on. Until she knew what was happening, it wouldn't pay to take chances.

She drank water from the bathroom sink and explored every corner of accessible space for anything that could be used as a weapon. It became clear that these people were well-prepared and didn't want her defending herself. She just hoped it wouldn't be necessary.

No one came so she ended up falling asleep. Sometime later, she woke up. Without windows, or food, her body clock couldn't regulate itself.

When the lock snicked again, she leaped to her feet. John came in with a striking blonde who looked like she'd just walked off the pages of Vogue.

"This is her?" the blonde asked John as though Flick wasn't even present. "She's hideous."

"You think?" John said. "Get saddled up for it."

The woman shook her head. "No."

Her accent was distinctly European. French? Maybe Italian?

"You can't refuse, Simone," John said. "You have time."

"Hmm," Simone pouted. "I'll see what I can do."

"You're a master; you haven't let him down yet."

"This is very inconvenient."

"But necessary," John said to Simone then came to Flick's side. "Come on."

"Where are we going?"

John took hold of her and pulled her out of the room. Two bulky men walked in front of them down a golden-carpeted hallway lined with thick white and gold pinstripe wallpaper. Other doors in the corridor were ignored in deference to the dominating double doors at the end. Opened in ceremony by the men preceding them, she was led inside by John with Simone somewhere in their wake.

This chamber had to be twice the size of her enclosure. A large desk up ahead was the focal point. To one side of the room was an oblong table surrounded by fifteen chairs.

At the other side were leather couches arranged in a square around a fireplace. Behind those was another door, probably a bathroom. This space had windows, or she assumed it did. Flanking the wall behind the desk were heavy drapes that reached the floor. The curtains were closed, she couldn't see light or dark, still no clues as to the time of day.

Without explanation, John led her toward the bathroom. Simone stayed behind to drape herself over one of the couches. When they entered the adjoining room, John didn't close the door, they went forward, through black velvet drapes.

Observing the features of the room, she dug her heels in. Wall to wall bed dominated, fifteen feet of beds with cuffs lining the head wall. Two poles in another corner on separate podiums horrified her. The cove lighting couldn't class up the room's intended use. It was a space designed for one thing, and with one thing in mind.

She dragged in a breath, intending to scream.

John forced her forward. "This isn't for you," he said. "Not yet."

She tried to wrestle free, but John was far stronger and jostled her onto the bed.

"No!"

"Out of interest," John said, "what would you do if you got past me?"

Escape. She had to get out of there. Her gaze darted around the painted walls and wipe-clean floor. Backward wasn't an option with John in her way, but there was a black door, on the same wall as the curtains. That might—

"You don't want to go through that door," he said, cuffing her hands together. "That's spiral stairs right down to the basement… I told you, you don't want a piece of that."

"Are you being nice to me?"

"I'm nice to everyone."

Having an ally might be useful, but John reeked of indifference. Whatever was going on, the outcome wouldn't be in her best interest. A suspicion confirmed when John pulled a length of duct tape from a drawer under the bed and stuck it over her mouth.

"You're going to meet Victor today," he said, pushing her hair away from the adhesive. "You're lucky; most of the girls never see him. You're different, I suppose."

John sat next to her on the bed. What were they waiting for? One minute passed and then another two. They sat there idly together like strangers next to each other at a bus stop.

All became clear when noise from the main room drifted through. The double doors were opened, and a gaggle of voices carried to their ears.

"Yeah, enough," came a strong male voice with a vaguely Spanish accent, then an impatient huff. "Where are we?"

"Ten," someone said.

"Closer to fifteen."

"I've got this to do."

"That's Victor," John said, rising to his feet.

"It's ridiculous!" Simone proclaimed.

"Yeah, you're never happy," Victor said. "You guys get working on the next shipment, and I want that pajero, Jansen over here tonight."

"Yes, boss."

More noise followed then a door closed. "Can we get back to serious business?" Victor asked. "This bullshit pisses me off."

"I have seen her," Simone said. French. The accent was French. "I disagree with your assessment."

"I don't want to hear from you," Victor said.

"I am a valuable part of your team."

"I think the guys would agree with that more than I do."

"You have always found use for me, Victor," she purred.

"I got bored with you months ago," Victor said. "I like variety."

"She's been polishing Rushe's sword," Skeeve said on a snorting laugh.

Her head came up. Rushe?

"I don't give a fuck," Victor said. "We lost a shitload of cash when Jansen screwed us over."

"Yeah."

"The boys have figured out a way for us to get that back," Victor said.

"We've got enforcement."

"Yeah," Victor said. "We've been in the money lending game for a long time, but it's small potatoes. Selling on these bitches is more fun, and lucrative." Various guffaws went around the room. "We have other things to worry about right now."

"What are you worried about?"

Rushe! Recognizing that bored tone, tears pricked her eyes.

"I'm glad you're the one who asked that," Victor said.

"This is gonna be good," Skeeve spoke again.

She wished someone would smack him in the head.

"You let one get by," Victor said. "That's not like you."

"What are you talking about?" Rushe asked.

"Your little bit of fluff," Skeeve grinned.

"If you can't keep your mouth shut, someone will put a bullet in it for you!"

"Yes, boss."

"Boys did a check-up," Victor said. "Wanted to find out if the cops had been on your tail."

She'd made the anonymous call about the dead girl's car, but no one had been in touch with her. She assumed the tip hadn't been traced back to her.

"Glen!" Victor exclaimed. The outer door opened then closed. "Do you know what this is?"

"No," Rushe said.

"This is salvation for us all," Victor said. "Cash enough to get us where we want to be, out of the country and up in the league."

"One card?"

"We need your help on this," Victor said. "You're gonna be point man."

"Fine," Rushe said. "What is it?"

"You gotta be with us. No dicking around."

"You want me to walk, I'll walk. I told you that. I'm sick of the fucking—"

"You're staying," Victor said to Rushe.

Was she there to keep Rushe working for Victor? Rushe would be an asset to any team. Criminal or otherwise.

"Maybe."

Victor definitely wouldn't want Rushe working for the opposition.

"You've got a chance right now," Victor said. "You pull this off and you'll be my new number two."

What had happened to his old number two?

"What's the job?" Rushe asked, she'd bet his lips never moved at all.

"John-boy!" Victor shouted.

John grabbed her, and though she struggled to pull away, he prevailed. Rushe was about to be blindsided.

TWENTY-THREE

WHEN JOHN DRAGGED HER through the fabric, she registered five people in the room. But she fixed on Rushe. The second his eyes touched her, there was a flicker of recognition.

Tears tumbled from her lashes.

"You remember who this is, right?" Victor said.

Her eyes stayed on Rushe's; Victor moseyed in toward him. The pale brown of the boss's skin glowed, but he didn't wear a smile. Something cunning in his tone made her wary.

"Yes," Rushe said.

"You said she ran off, and who cares, right?"

"Right," Rushe said, she'd been right about his stationary lips.

"I agree," Victor said. "She's the bitch who came into Dell's."

"Right."

"Wouldn't have wasted time on it."

Victor was holding a card that looked suspiciously like a driving license. Could that…? Her purse was on the desk. The purse she'd lost at Dell's. Apparently, the bad guys picked it up.

"But…?" Rushe asked, taking the card from Victor.

"The boys checked her out. Made sure her boyfriend wasn't a cop or nothing… but they found out something else about your horny bitch."

"What's that?"

"Her father's worth a couple hundred million bucks."

Damn. Her eyes closed. She hadn't been brought there to coerce Rushe. Maybe that was just a bonus feature of the plot. The Hughes family had money. They were old money. Their wealth hadn't factored into her thoughts. The Hughes hadn't been in her life for so long, and she wasn't that person anymore. She'd learned to live without them, to separate herself. That mental disconnect left her vulnerable.

"So?" Rushe asked.

"How much do you think they'd pay to have their youngest daughter back?"

"The family aren't interested," Rushe said, pocketing her license. "They want nothing to do with her."

"That what she told you?" Victor asked, grinning. "Couldn't hurt to drop her papi a line… you think? She's here now, and you know the end of this."

Rushe said nothing. He was probably cursing his forethought for not anticipating this scenario.

"Okay," Rushe said. "I'll deal with it."

"Put a plan together," Victor said. "I've gotta sort out this crap with Jansen."

"Yeah."

"Breakfast. Take John, and you know Shiv's deal."

"Yeah. Move."

With a sideways nod, Rushe went for the door. John dragged her along behind him. Whatever Shiv's deal, it couldn't be good. Any hope that she might have about Rushe's leadership giving her a fighting chance wasn't supported by the tension he carried in his angry shoulders as they strode down the hallway. She wouldn't put money on him being lenient.

Rushe stopped next to a door that John unlocked. Only then did she notice the two bulky black guys were escorting them again. Having four men covering her seemed excessive; maybe she should consider it flattering.

John gave her a shove back into the bedroom. No one came in immediately after her, but the door remained open an inch. She sat on the bed.

A second later Rushe marched in, closing the door at his back.

He didn't immediately speak. He paced back and forth in front of the door balling and flexing his fists.

"It would serve you right," he said and stopped pacing. "You're a magnet for trouble. I told you that you wouldn't get out of this alive. I should've known getting rid of you wouldn't be that easy."

Her hands were still cuffed, and her mouth taped.

Rushe hadn't been this vocal when they'd first met, but she recognized those bullet black eyes. "Do you know what they do to women in this building?" he asked, stopping in front of her. "Do you?"

Whether the question was an attempt to find out what she'd already been through, or to scare her, both had the same answer, more tears.

"Stop crying," he said. "I can't get you out of this. It doesn't matter if your daddy coughs up. You're going out through the back door."

John had alluded to that too. She still couldn't speak. Rushe snatched her arm and hauled her to her feet to free her hands. As he threw the key and restraints aside, she intended to take the tape from her mouth, but he intercepted her hand before it could get there.

"This is my fault. I wasn't clear. I told you to walk away but didn't tell you not to walk back." Rushe ripped off the gag himself. Her hand leaped to the stinging pain it caused. "Speak," he growled.

"I missed you."

His chest rumbled and he stole her up, right off her feet, flinging her onto the bed to come down on top of her. His tongue delved into her mouth with full entitlement. The need of the kiss tried to sate the want of their separation. Her nails dug into his tee-shirt, her fingers clenching into such tight fists in the fabric that she wished they'd merge and never part.

When the mouth that offered her salvation vanished, she was left cold.

"Where are you going?" she asked, supporting herself on her elbows.

"You want me to fuck you?" he asked. "Right now, you want me to fuck you?"

They didn't have to go that far. A lot came between a brief kiss and sex. Still, he'd abandoned her so suddenly, she wanted to know what was in his mind.

"You don't?" she asked.

A snarl narrowed his eyes. "Your pussy been left hungry, Kitten?" he asked, leaning on the footboard to loom over her. "Your little boyfriend not doing it for you anymore? You come all the way out here to open your legs for me?"

"I was brought here," she said, kicking off her shoes and walking on her knees to the end of the bed to plunge her hands into his jeans pockets. "I was brought here to help you."

"You're a stupid bitch, you know that?"

"Am I?" she asked.

"What did they tell you? That I needed help, or I was in trouble?"

"Yes."

"What kind of trouble?"

"I didn't ask," she said.

"And you thought you could bail me out?"

"He threatened to start shooting in my workplace, what was I supposed to do?" Rushe growled at her. "Do my motives matter?"

"Take off your clothes," he leered.

She shrugged the bolero from her shoulders, which caused him to growl again.

"What?" she asked.

"Are you this easy for other men?"

"What?"

"I snap my fingers and you bend over to be shafted. There are plenty of men in this house who'll tag team you; do you want me to line them up?"

"No."

"When did your boyfriend last fuck you? Last night? This morning? But you're still a hungry little whore."

"I've been here all night, Rushe," she said. "And you've been screwing around with the French chick."

"So?"

"Have you had all the women in the basement? Is it tradition that every man here sample the prisoners?"

"I've fucked my way through plenty of honeys in here," Rushe said. "None of them have been as easy as you."

"I don't believe you."

"All of them put up a fight."

"I meant I don't believe you've been having sex with any of the women in the basement."

"You looking for a fairy tale ending?" he asked.

"No."

"Then—"

"Consent," she said. "You need consent. You would never force—"

"Fuck! Felicity, you're going to die! Worry about that!"

He had never shouted at her, not like that. He'd never just blasted her with the naked truth.

Whatever they'd been was finished. Business was better to focus on than personal. "Are you supposed to be in here asking for my parents' phone number?"

All he could do was inhale and step back. "Getting in touch with your dad is easy. I'll make sure you get to talk to him, you know, to prove that you're alive. During that conversation make sure you tell him not to hand over the money until you're safe."

"My father doesn't know if I'm alive now," she said. "Just how much money are you going to ask for? He'll think twice about paying it, I'll tell you that now. He's a superior individual who really believes he's smarter than everyone, including you and your buddy Victor."

"Victor is not my buddy, and the money isn't an issue."

"The money isn't an issue?" she said. "They cut me off. I had to hock my jewelry to get a deposit for my apartment. I don't have a car, or—"

"Kitten, the money isn't a problem."

"Are you going to tell Victor my family screwed him over?"

"Getting the money to Victor is easy," Rushe said. "But one of two things happens once he has it."

"I go out the back door. Dead or alive."

He exhaled. "Why in the hell did you come back here?"

"I didn't have much of a choice," she said. "John made that clear."

"You'll be a story. A woman who goes missing twice in the same month."

"No one missed me the first time. How long will this take?"

"Victor wants a plan by breakfast," he said. "So you've bought another night."

"Lucky me," she said, falling back to sit on her feet.

"You've been here all night?" She nodded. "Alone?"

"Skeeve tried it on in the car," she said. "Victor doesn't want me touched, sexually."

"Who said that?"

"John." Rushe didn't comment, but she saw his mind working. "What?"

"Victor trusts me right now but… there are… everyone has an agenda."

"You've told me that before."

"This is different," he said. "Everything here is scaled up and tension is high. No one trusts anyone. Things are… volatile."

"You're different here," she said. "More cautious."

"There are more people here, more factors I can't control. It's tough enough to stay alive when I'm only watching my own ass."

Her lips curled. "That must drive your forethought crazy."

"She smiles," he said, throwing up his hands.

"Why are you sleeping with Simone?"

"I'm not," he said but quickly burst her frisson of happiness. "Sex doesn't have anything to do with sleeping. She's a high-maintenance woman, good for nothing but a fuck."

"Yeah," she said. "I know your views on that subject."

The door opened and John came in with a tray of food and a bag. Almost covertly observing them, John put the things down and left without a word.

"Eat," Rushe said. "There are books in the bag. No one will bother you."

"That's it?" she asked when he headed for the door.

"Now I'm gonna do my research on your family and find out what you're worth in currency."

"I thought you didn't want to meet my family."

"I don't have to," he said.

"Do they know?" she asked. "The people here..."

"That I've fucked you? Yeah."

"Should I be scared?"

"You can't follow instructions so I'm not gonna answer that."

"What about Shiv?" she asked.

"I plan to have you out of here before he's back. Victor has him out collecting."

"Are you ever going to explain to me what's going on here?"

"Kitten... just hope you don't find out everything in surround sound and full Technicolor."

"I was right about being a liability for you," she said. "Wasn't I?"

"Yes."

"Tonight, when you're inside Simone think about me down here, alone."

"You better hope you're alone," he said. "But you'll get a visit from Simone before I do. She's supposed to look after you girls. Instead, she's more concerned with having every man in the building."

"No more bareback then," she said.

Empowerment tickled up her spine when his eyes traveled down her body. Why did his desire inspire her pride? She pushed up to her knees again and let the straps of her dress fall from her shoulders.

"Do you remember?" she asked. "What that night was like? What it felt like to slide into me?"

"Don't," he asserted. "Don't play with fire."

"I liked being burned by you the first time."

"Your boyfriend worth any money?" Rushe said. "Will he pay for you? How many times have you had sex with him? If I tally up the going rate—"

"I don't have a boyfriend," she admitted.

The flash of surprise in his expression was a rare show of an honest, immediate reaction. "Are you lying—"

"I lied then," she said. "I thought if I implied people would be looking for me that I might be freed."

"And you didn't think to tell me?"

"Are you upset I lied or that you're the only man I've been intimate with in a long time?"

Rushe immediately left his place near the door to march back to the end of the bed. "How many men have you had sex with?"

"What?" she asked, surprised by his ferocity.

"Tell me!" Rushe grabbed her arm to tug her closer to him.

Though she tried to pull her arm away, he didn't release her. "That's none of your business!"

"I swear to God, Kitten, if you think you can get away without being poked and prodded—"

"Two," she breathed.

Releasing her, Rushe stared with wide eyes, scrubbing a hand over his face. "Including me?"

Flick nodded. "Two total."

Turning his back on her, he walked away then walked back to slam his hands on the footboard of the bed. "I knew you were tight but…"

"Why are you angry? I wanted to have sex with you." Hooking her hands into his jeans, she rested her weight on him. "If you feel guilty—"

"I don't give a fuck," he said. "Damn right I dominated your tight, little cunt. I'd do it again. I'd have fucked you senseless even if you were lily-white."

"Then what's the problem?"

His fingers bit into her shoulders when he shunted her back onto the bed. "The less experience, the higher the price," he said. "Do not answer questions. Do not mention inexperience. Do not let them know about your sexual past. Your inexperience and your family history make you primo goods, and I'm considered a previous owner. I'd rather see you dead than watch them put you through that."

"Simone wasn't impressed."

"She's threatened," he said.

"Because of you?"

"No because you're…"

The thought went unfinished. He didn't leer but he did look her up and down.

"What?"

"Nothing," he said. "Be a good girl. I'll be back eventually."

She could do nothing but watch him leave, and he wasn't as weak as her, he didn't look back.

TWENTY-FOUR

PEOPLE BROUGHT FOOD periodically, but she felt like months must have passed in the room. Despite her sumptuous new surroundings, she actually pined for the shack. For the forest air, and the lake she could swim in.

Victor's place had no natural light. Funny that the mansion should give her cabin fever rather than the cabin. She'd read the books and was rounding for a second pass, but her mind kept wandering. Rushe could be miles away, or he could be right outside the door.

The idea of him with any other woman was sickening. Still, she had to confess to herself that she had no right to think that way and no right to object to any of his actions.

Somehow none of this seemed real. Though women in the basement had been mentioned, she hadn't seen any, which gave her hope it was untrue. Believing that Rushe could be involved in such a thing was almost impossible.

When she'd been vulnerable and in need, he had stepped in to protect her, more than once. Yes, he was crude and domineering, but he wasn't cruel. He was a better man than he gave himself credit for.

If Rushe, or Victor, or anyone, contacted her parents and demanded ransom, it would be fulfilling the Hughes' expectations.

Nothing about her was the same as them; it never had been. The people they associated with, and the sphere they associated in, had always been a mystery to her. She grew up immersed in the fictional worlds she escaped to in books. Being a reader and a loner, she'd always been content with a mind of her own.

Social events, fundraisers, and Country Club functions weren't her style, which would be why she never fitted in. Her parents had been at a loss with her from a young age. She didn't accept the easy way just because it was straightforward. Despite being comfortable alone, away from others, her current situation was extreme on the spectrum.

Until their estrangement, she'd never been far from her parents, or rather from her mother and sisters. Her life had consisted of going from the family home into a limo, into a ballroom, or hotel somewhere. Her sisters, Lucia and Vivian, embraced the spectacle. In contrast, she always felt like just a part of her parents' entourage.

They were allowed to study, though her sisters didn't embrace it as she had. Still, she never got far, she lived in her parents' home, and was escorted to class by her limo driver. After graduating, none of them was expected to work. Of course not, why would they?

The life of a Hughes woman was showing up and looking pretty. Lucia, Vivian, and her mother, Beverley, were always better at that than her. The Hughes clan was all one well-oiled machine. Her sisters and mother went on shopping sprees, while she would stay home to read and study. Occasionally, she got to stay with her paternal grandparents, but it was always on a weekend that coincided with a social occasion, so it was part of the Hughes beast too.

Liberating herself from the family last year had been her first comprehension of freewill. Up until that point, choosing which book to read in the vast Hughes-approved library was the most exciting choice she had to make.

So long as the money Rushe demanded for Victor wasn't off the charts, her parents would pay it… probably. One thing was for sure… If her family had to pay for her life, then they would own it.

She'd have no choice but to go back home with her tail between her legs and fall in line as instructed. Her confession about her financial position was accurate. With no way to pay her father back, she couldn't object to the demands placed on her thereafter.

Maybe Rushe had been right after all. He'd be her dirty little secret. The fling that would keep her warm at night as she lay in bed beside whichever CEO her father chose for her.

EVENTUALLY TURNED OUT to be an accurate assessment. She'd eaten six meals before seeing Rushe again and established they fed her twice a day.

So when the door opened during the fourth day, she sat up expecting another meal. Instead, it was Rushe, with John at his back.

"I assume we're going somewhere," she said.

"We sent your father a message," Rushe said. "He wants proof of life."

"Isn't that nice," she said. "Do you want me to write him a note?"

"No, you're going to get up and come with us now."

"You sound confident," she said.

"I'm bigger than you. Move."

Rushe produced some cuffs. She shook her head. Cuffs were nothing to the other restraints she'd experienced in her time recently; they hurt less. Yet the prevalence of metal handcuffs in this place disturbed her. Handcuffs were quick and easy to put on, they were clean, and could be reused.

"How many women are you holding in the basement?" she asked.

"That's not your business," Rushe said.

"It's not right."

"Worry about yourself."

"I think enough people are doing that already."

"Move."

Rushe's menace reminded her of the night they met. His anger shone out, though she wasn't sure who it was aimed at.

Knowing that options were few, she got up and held out her hands. Rushe came to put the cuffs on, then in his usual manner grabbed hold to drag her out of the room. John fell in line on her other side, and they led her in the direction opposite to Victor's office.

"Don't you feel guilty?" she asked. "Those women are suffering, and you men have the power to do something about it."

"You don't know what you're talking about," John said.

"Don't you have a sister or a mother? Would you like to think of them down there suffering? Haven't either of you ever cared about another human being?"

Rushe halted her with a yank. John opened another door. This room was different to every other one. The floorboards were bare, stained, and blackened in places. Wallpaper curled down from patches of stagnant mold and empty bookcases covered a third wall. The window had been covered with black plastic.

In the center of the room was a rickety wooden chair. Opposite it was an open laptop on a small table.

"Video call," she said.

"They're waiting for your call," Rushe mumbled.

"Wonders of modern technology," she said. "Gone are the days of letters cut from magazines, and pictures of the hostage holding today's newspaper."

"Stop talking, or we'll gag you again," Rushe said.

"Then how will I tell my parents… actually a gag might be a good idea. You'd be doing me a favor."

John pushed her into the hard chair. He produced a balaclava from his back pocket and pulled it over his head, remaining behind her the whole time. The warm metal of a gun barrel touched the side of her neck.

"Now wait…" she beseeched Rushe, who took up position behind the computer. "If you shoot me, you don't get your money."

Her father flashed up on the screen and she stopped, instantly going silent.

"My God," her father, the great Charles Hughes, said. "You look awful."

"Thanks," she said, because she'd actually been taken care of there.

Her father was the picture of refinement, put together with short, neat, gray hair, and his hand-tailored, three-piece charcoal suit.

"Felicity, your mother and I are beside ourselves. How did you get into this mess?"

The answer to that one was quick and simple. "My cab broke down."

Looking past her father's frown, rows of hefty books lined the wall behind the desk in his office. His business office, much, she imagined, what this room she sat in now may have looked like in its heyday.

"Are you safe? What are those barbarians doing to you?"

"I'm alive," she said. "They haven't harmed me. All they want is money."

"Yes, two million dollars is a lot of money."

"Two?" she stuttered and looked over the computer at Rushe. "You want two million dollars? Why not just ask for a billion?"

"Felicity, you must appreciate our position," her father said. "This is all a shock. We haven't heard from you in so long."

"I don't think we have time to catch up now. If you pay the money, I'll… consider me contrite."

"Your mother will be pleased," her father said. "As will your sisters."

"I am very sorry," she said.

"Listening to your parents' guidance would have spared us this."

Argument was inappropriate and would be fruitless. "Yes," she said.

"I will speak with Mathieson and make the arrangements."

"You must be assured of my safety before—"

"Yes, of course," her father said. "Advise your captors we'll be in touch."

Rushe closed the laptop, cutting off conversation. John tucked away the gun and removed the balaclava.

"I feel warm and fuzzy," John said. "Your father's a cold S.O.B."

"Charles Hughes the fourth," she said. "He is the epitome of good breeding."

Even while speaking the words, she knew her captors wouldn't believe them. She didn't believe them either. The trek back to her bedroom was silent. When she was put inside, she expected to be left alone again.

Rushe said something to John, then came in at her back, closing the bedroom door behind them. She held out her hands for him to unlock her cuffs, which he did.

"What—"

"Shh," Rushe said and picked her up.

He carried her to the wall behind the door and held her there with his hips while gathering her skirt into his fists.

"I'm gonna fuck you."

"No, you're not," she said, flattening her hands to the wall at her sides, confident Rushe would steady her.

He frowned. "You're refusing me? You were eager for me to pump your cunt the last day I was in here," he growled.

"You don't like the way my father spoke to me," she said. "You want to have sex with me because you think it will reassure me."

"What the fuck—"

"Rushe, I don't need you to make me feel better. My family have always been this way."

"You're so warm," he said. "You're a bubbling ball of naïvety—"

"This is the way things are. I walked away from my family because I didn't want to be like them."

"He made you apologize."

"No, he didn't," she said. "But I know how things work. I'll go back to that life, and I'll fall in line. This blip they'll put down as a rebellion on my part, and we'll never speak of it again."

"I want to fuck you."

"Because you believe it will make me feel better or because it will make you feel better?"

"I don't give a fuck about better," he asserted.

"Stick with Simone," she said. "I'm sure you can rely on Stockholm from a few of the basement captives."

"You don't get to say no to me," he said. "Consent!"

"No," she said, not in the slightest bit scared of the rumble of his voice, or his erection pressing against her.

"No?"

"I don't know where you've been."

"You're my whore," he said as if unable to comprehend what was happening.

She clasped his face. "Not anymore, Rushe."

"What's different?"

"Everything," she said. "If I end up going home, I'll have to toe the family line. If I don't, I'll end up in the basement with the others as part of the next shipment."

"No," Rushe said. "You're different."

"I'm different because I trusted you, and I can't do that anymore."

"You don't trust me?"

"You told me not to," she said.

"But you did it anyway."

"Yes."

"But you don't trust me now?"

"I told you I couldn't judge what I didn't understand, but I do understand it now. I believe you're a better man than the others here, and I'll concede that you've been an excellent lover. Amazing. But the thought of those women down there, locked up and terrified, it makes me sick."

"What do you want me to do?"

"You helped me."

"That was different; you don't know where we are."

"Those women are to be sold as stock by you and your cohorts. What's your cut of the profit?"

"It's not like that," he said through gritted teeth.

"What is it like?"

"You better be careful."

"Or what?" she asked on an exhaled laugh. "I'll be held prisoner? What's next? Rape? Torture? Death? It seems to me that those things are in the cards anyway. Trusting you hasn't done me any favors. I got some good sex out of it, that's it."

"You think I haven't protected you?"

When he walked away, she slid down the wall and found her feet.

"I don't know," she said. "Yours is the only side I hear. And I never know when you're telling me the truth."

Rushe paused by the bed. "If I tell you what's happening, you'll be at greater risk."

"Greater risk of what? My father will give you the money. But two million is not a debt I can clear by marrying his senior associate."

"Two million isn't a fraction of what you're worth."

"I don't think anyone is worth any amount of money. People shouldn't be bought and sold like cattle."

"There are at least twenty guys on the property, and three times as many guns," Rushe said. "I'm not running this operation alone."

"I didn't say you were. But you are here, and you can walk away anytime you want."

"Do you think so?"

"Yes," she said.

"What good would that do you?"

"What are you going to do when I'm gone? Keep scaring people into repaying debts they'll never be able to cover? Breaking legs and torturing people at Victor's request?"

"You don't understand."

"No, I don't," she said. "But when I see the truth, when I look past the man I romanticized, it scares me.

You're a criminal. And to offer me comfort, you want to have sex with me. I want you to feel something more than that. Something more than the physical. I want to know that you're capable of genuine human compassion or empathy."

"I don't argue with women," he said, marching toward the exit.

"Fine. I don't need you to argue with me. Tell me when my father comes up with the money."

"Whatever," he said and slammed out of the room in a move so typical of him.

TWENTY-FIVE

SHE MIGHT HAVE TOLD RUSHE she didn't need him to argue with her, but she had wanted to yell at him some more. Beyond the stage of denying her feelings, she hated the ache in her gut at the sense she'd been duped.

When Rushe had scared the others off by claiming her as his own, she'd really believed he wanted to protect her out of a fundamental goodness. Her belief had been that his desire for her developed later; that their intimate escapades had been serendipitous, not premeditated. Now she wasn't so sure of that, or of anything.

No one would spend time with men like those in that place, and do the things asked of them by a man like Victor, without having some malevolence in them. Threatening people for money, or selling them for sex was depraved, no two ways about it. Had she made Rushe into something he wasn't? But what would be her motivation?

Struggling with the horrible notion Rushe may have been right about her misplaced trust in the first place, sleep had been difficult to find. She only became aware of her slumber when something startled her awake. The darkness of the room was absolute, but a shuffling sound became a hushed laugh.

"Don't know where to fuck first," Skeeve whispered. "It's like Christmas."

"I get to go first, this bitch is gonna get it good."

It took an extra few seconds to place the second voice. When she did, her blood chilled. Shiv. The bed shifted, but she smelled Skeeve approach before she felt him. His nauseating odor crept up over her.

"Pick a hole," Skeeve said. "We'll do it together."

When Skeeve's tongue made contact with the side of her face, she didn't hesitate to throw back the covers, and smack him in the temple with the wide heel of her shoe. Yes, she slept holding her shoes. The bad guys hadn't offered her a weapon, so she used the ones she'd brought with her.

An agonized wail betrayed she'd hit her target. Shiv let out a string of curses. Pouncing to her feet, she braced to defend herself, but couldn't see from which direction the assault was going to come. Then the game board changed.

The overhead light came on, temporarily dazzling the players. A silenced shot rang out and someone screamed.

Disorientated, it took a second to process Shiv writhing on the floor clasping his blood-soaked leg, the one she hadn't shot. A third figure crossed the room and dispatched the gibbering Skeeve with one punch.

"Move," Rushe said from the foot of the bed.

Rushe. Rushe was the one who'd turned on the light, and shot Shiv, and knocked Skeeve out cold.

"What?" she asked, still on her feet on the bed, braced with a shoe in each hand, ready to fight.

"You sleep in your clothes?" he asked.

"Yes," she answered, looking down at her jeans and heavy sweater provided by Victor. "I don't trust anyone here."

"Good, you're finally getting it. Now move."

"How did you know—"

"I told the guard on your door to let me know who wanted in and when," Rushe said.

Storming around the bed, he grabbed her wrist and hauled her down.

"Where are we going?" she asked when he took her from the bedroom into the darkened corridor.

"I told the guard to beat it, but he'll be back eventually."

"I know what that means," she said, having no choice but to run and keep up with him as he pulled her along.

Rushe took her through a door and down some stairs into the entry lobby. Derelict with falling plaster and cracked tiles, water dripped from the gaps that foliage forged.

"Where are we?"

"Victor got work done on one wing. He says renovating the rest is on the agenda but doesn't have the money. The building doesn't belong to him. It's a squat."

Dragging the heavy front door from its frame seemed redundant given the broken windows on either side. That might explain why all the other windows she'd seen were covered up.

The number of exterior stairs reminded her of entering the building. It was only after Rushe threw her over his shoulder and ran across the wide gravel drive to the overgrown lawn that she realized what was going on.

"We're making a break for it," she said, thankful she'd kept hold of her shoes.

Rushe was grumbling something undecipherable. She had to quell her urge to shriek when he stopped abruptly and opened a car door to toss her inside. Before she righted herself, Rushe was in the driver's seat navigating without lights.

"We are…" she said on a gasp. "You're breaking me out… aren't you?"

Rushe continued to mutter for a few more seconds. "Yes, what did you think? That I was taking you to the highest bidder?"

"Did my father pay you?"

They lumbered through a broken gate onto a deserted road. After three more turns Rushe put on the lights and merged into traffic.

"You think I'm screwing Victor over to take the money for myself?"

"I don't know what you're doing," she said, putting her feet in her shoes.

"You wouldn't have sex with me," he grumbled. "You were that pissed at me."

She replayed his words and their conversation from that afternoon. "You're breaking me out, defying your boss, walking away from the money—"

"It was never about the money."

"Because I refused to have sex with you?" she asked. "You have no idea what it is to be soft, of the degrees of comfort and emotion. Something shitty happened, and your way of processing that emotion was to demand sex from me. When I refused to submit, you realized the strength of my disgust at the situation… you're not a man who does things by halves… Are they going to come after me? Will I be running for the rest of my life?"

"No."

"How do you know?"

"I have a plan," he said.

"Of course you do. Can I be let in on this plan?"

"No."

"Why not?"

"You wouldn't understand it," he said.

"Of course not," she said, folding her arms. "I'm just a walking vagina."

"With a hell of a mouth."

"You are coming with me," she said. "Aren't you?"

"I was never involved with the trafficking," he said. "I don't know why but I need you to know that."

"I'm not letting you go back there. I won't."

"Let me worry about that," he said. "I have something I have to do tomorrow. At daybreak, you get in touch with your father, he won't have to pay anything for your life."

"We could extort the two million and buy ourselves a private island."

Rushe drew his eyes from the road. "Very funny."

"At least now I won't have to marry one of his business buddies. But you could have broken me out before the video call, you know, before I had to admit to the mess I'd gotten myself into."

"You want me to take you back and make him pay the ransom?"

"No," she said. "So what's the next part of the plan?"

"Everything hinges on me getting to this meeting tomorrow, without running into the cops before it. I get there and that sets the wheels in motion. If I can't do that, it's game over."

"Okay," she said. "What's the meeting?"

"I'm not telling you that."

"Why not?"

"I won't put you in that kind of danger."

"Are we meeting with a murderer?"

"We are not meeting with anyone," he said. "I am going to the meeting alone."

"What are you going to do? Tie me to the steering wheel?"

"No, I need the car. I'll tie you to the bed."

"What bed?" she asked. When he drew his eyes around to her again, she didn't miss his intention. "I haven't consented to sex."

"I didn't ask."

"But you will," she said. "I haven't consented."

"But you will," he snarled.

Her hands fell into her lap. "Because you broke me out? I might be thankful, but that doesn't change what was going on back at Victor's place."

"You don't know what was going on there," Rushe said. "Don't judge what you don't know. You said that. Follow your own advice."

"Rushe, don't you feel remorse?"

"I've done a lot of bad things in my life. I've done shitty things that would make you ashamed of me."

"Is that a no?"

"But never like that, at Victor's, with the women, I wouldn't…"

"Tell me," she said, trying to touch his hand, but he swept it around the steering wheel, out of her reach.

"We're not the same," he said. "You can't understand my world any better than I understand yours."

"But—"

"Unless you plan to practice giving head, keep your lips together," he grumbled. "Sleep. You're giving me earache."

She had plenty more to say. But his stern expression focused on the road showed he had things, other than her, on his mind. Leaning over, she kissed his jaw then settled down in her seat. While he didn't look at her, his hands relaxed on the steering wheel. She'd give him time to stew; there would be time to question him later.

TWENTY-SIX

SHE PUT THE ROCKING of her body down to the motion of the car, until an especially intrusive hand jostled her.

On opening her eyes, she was bumped again. "What?" she yawned, settling herself away from his rude gesture against her door.

"Take your clothes off."

"Sure, okay," she said, cuddling her hands into her chest, trying to get comfortable again.

"I mean it. Now."

This time it wasn't a shove, it was a grab, and he pulled her away from the car door.

"We're outside," she said. They were still driving along a darkened road. "It's cold."

Releasing her, Rushe turned up the heat, then shook her again. "I want you naked now."

"Why?" she yawned. "Is this about art?"

"Take off your clothes, Kitten."

"I'll have sex with you when I wake up."

"You're awake."

She took a turn at the muttering, but removed her feet from her shoes, and slid forward to undo her jeans.

"Take off the sweater; I want to see your breasts."

She stopped and let her hands flop into her lap. "Who's doing this me or you? Do you want to do it?"

"I'm driving," he said.

"Exactly, so leave me alone."

In her half fog of sleep, she didn't really think about the implication of wriggling out of her jeans and taking her panties with them. Nor did she really think about pulling her sweater over her head, and unclasping her bra, at least until the cold night air shriveled her nipples instantly.

"It's cold," she said, and made a move to pull her bra back up her arms. Rushe snatched it and threw it over his head into the back seat, at which point she realized he'd done the same with the rest of her clothes. "You didn't think this one through, Driver. You plan to have sex with me, and keep both hands on the wheel?"

She yawned and closed her eyes, resting her head back again.

"Hmm," he hummed. If he was anyone else, she'd say he sounded pleased. "You've got a helluva pair of tits."

With one hand, he stroked and squeezed each of her breasts in turn, back and forth.

"You've told me," she said, swatting his hand. "Drive the car."

Curling away from him in her seat, she gave him a view of her back. Except his hand seemed just as happy palming her ass. The night was cold. To conserve heat, she drew her knees up to her chest. Sleep hung around her, and on another yawn, she folded her arms over her chest.

Somehow, she'd managed to forget her nakedness until his finger twisted into her. His hand on her rear had been happy enough, but when she'd drawn her knees up, she'd given him inadvertent access. Another finger seemed to be trying to prod its way inside.

She sat upright and glared at him. "You did that on purpose. We can't have sex out here."

When she caught a glimpse out the windshield, she saw nothing but abandoned, unlit road, flanked by thick foliage, and dense trees.

"My cock hasn't done anything wrong," he said. "And you like him."

"That wasn't your penis," she said, pinning his offending hand in her sights.

"Stick your own finger in your pussy then," he said. "Got to get you nice and juicy."

"Here, in the car?"

When he looked at her breasts, her reaction was immediate. The tingling in her knew just what he had in mind. Damn her for wanting it so badly. Fighting would only deprive them both, and she wanted him.

Letting her own hand glide up her abdomen, she cupped her breasts and ran her thumbs over her nipples.

"That's it, Kitten," he growled. "Play with them. You think about my hands on you. Squeeze your nipples, roll them in your fingers, those soft little tips that taste so good in my mouth."

She did as he said, playing with the points of her breasts that remembered just how good they felt in his mouth. For now, she was in control of the show. The power she held over him welled to aroused pride in her belly again.

"I'm gonna play with those tits all night. They're mine to touch, to play with any time I want. You're gonna do anything I tell you…"

She increased her grip, letting her fingers nip her while her thumbs grazed over her tips.

"I want to see more of them, all the time, you hear me? You're gonna start giving me a show. I want them on display to every man who craves you. I want them to pant for you, Kitten, but you're mine; mine to touch, mine to see, to play with… only mine."

For as long as he'd been mesmerized by her groping of her breasts those last two words were said into her eyes. Her hands fell, and while one of them rolled back into a recline she drew her heels onto the edge of her seat and let her knees fall apart. He cursed when she fondled her breasts again.

"Do you want me to touch myself?" she whispered.

Her eyelids drooped again, this time it wasn't exhaustion. Her whole body was heavy with slumber, but she wriggled back, unable to stay still.

Her other hand crossed the center console to undo his jeans buttons. As soon as her fingers touched the scorching length of his cock, two of his fingers plunged into her.

With a gasping call she arched up. "Rushe."

"Oh, I'm gonna fuck you so hard," he said, sliding his digits in and out. "Play with your clit. I want you to come now, here, on this road, like this."

With another inhale of his name, she struggled to writhe up against his incursion, and did as told. His focus stayed on the road when his fingers withdrew. She parted her lips in anticipation of them, but he trailed his digits to her breast, circling the pebbles with the juices from his sodden fingers.

"I'm gonna taste those tits."

He took hold of one breast, and with a squeeze, she arched up into her own caress. His hand shifted to impale her with his fingers again. At the sudden motion, she squealed, and orgasm enveloped her fast.

Rushe cursed louder this time, and the car seemed to speed up. Her naked body rocked from one side of her seat to the other. Rushe's intense concentration stayed on the road. With two hands on the wheel, he swerved from one side to the other.

What would happen if they crashed with her like this, naked and undone?

When he hit the brake, the whole car lurched to a screaming stop.

"Stay."

His word was said on the way out of the vehicle. He closed his door with such force the car lurched to the side. If she didn't know him better, she might have been scared; this was a side of him that could intimidate. As it was, she let herself smile because she could see him freeing himself and rolling on the condom as he came around the hood of the car. Then her own door was yanked open, and she was hauled out, naked.

"Consent," he grumbled, while throwing her down against the hood. She'd never seen him so tightly coiled. "Kitten."

"Yes," she said, realizing she hadn't answered. "Yes, of course, I consent."

The last word hadn't left her lips before he was thrusting into her. Because the hood was hot, she pushed her palms down to hold herself away from the metal. His name pulsing over and over on her lips. All of him consumed her. Not so long ago, she'd thought they'd never be united again, that she'd never see him again, and now...

"Fuck!" he said, squeezing her butt cheek in one hand as he drove into her.

His punishing force in and out drew his name to her lips every time he smacked her center.

"Yes," she sighed. "Yes, Rushe, oh yes."

"Fucking dumb bitch," he said, even though she couldn't see them, she knew he was gritting his teeth through his own huffing breaths. "She came back, why the fuck…"

Without thought one of her hands left the hood and reached back. "Rushe," she said again.

Still with a hand squeezing her flesh to move her as he wanted, his other hand came from nowhere to link his fingers between hers.

"I'm gonna fuck you, damn right I fuck you. You're mine to fuck. My whore, my decision, my tight little pussy hungry for my cock… You want to be fed, you want me to feed your little cunt here and now, don't you, Kitten? Don't you!"

"Yes! Oh yes!"

Out there in the dark, on an abandoned roadside, she had no idea where they were, or how far they were from civilization… or discovery. She didn't care that she was naked, or that they were outside, or that the air was cold and the metal under her hot. All that mattered in her world right now was that thick shaft propelling into her.

After orgasm three or four, Rushe roared and smashed into her in sync with the vice of her pelvic muscles squeezing him in place, silently begging him to stay.

In the still of night, she could only hear the rhythm of their shallow breathing. Fog from her mouth misted the night. She was naked. They were outside. But all she wanted to do was stay there, with her cheek on the warm hood, and him embedded within her.

Their hands were still coupled. His other hand slapped her ass then soothed her skin, covering her with the large span.

He didn't speak and didn't move. What should she do? Maybe Rushe was waiting for her to talk or do something. The glory of having sex like this was that he couldn't slam out of the door. There wasn't one.

"You're one fuckable bitch," Rushe said, letting his palm glide up her spine, he'd never… touched her like this.

Tears sprang to her eyes. "Good enough for a replay?" she asked, making herself smile.

"Maybe," he said, and continued to let his rough calloused hand stroke her body, her back, her neck, her shoulders.

He pushed her hair aside and stroked her from brainstem to coccyx.

"Rushe?"

"You said no to me," he said. "You came back… and you said no to me."

"Yeah."

"When I ask a question… no one says no to me."

"I'm not scared of you, Rushe," she said, turning her face the other way. "I know you couldn't hurt me… that you wouldn't."

When he slid out of her body, that was her cue to stand up. She turned and propped herself on the side of the car, as he disposed of the condom and tucked himself away. She stood there with her arms folded under her chest, completely bare, with no compulsion to cover up even when he brought his attention to her.

Her nakedness didn't seem to register to him though, because he marched over and got himself into her personal space. "Explain."

"What?" Rushe pressed his finger into the dampness on her cheek to show her she was leaking. "It's nothing."

"I hurt you?" he asked, stepping away to look at her crotch as though he'd find bloody carnage.

"You've never held my hand before," she said.

The spark of recognition startled him when he looked to her hands to see that yes, he'd linked his fingers between hers again. He snatched his hand away and rubbed it on his shirt like she'd passed him a disease. She smiled at his disgust. They'd shared fluids and had plenty of skin-on-skin contact, but he was suddenly allergic to her hand. This was out of his comfort zone.

"Do you want to snuggle?" she said, not containing her teasing smile.

He silently growled at her. "Get in the car."

While Rushe stomped off in a grump, she took her time getting back into the vehicle. He wouldn't tell her where they were going, or why. But as far as she was concerned, they couldn't get too far away from where they'd been. And the further away they got from Victor, the closer she and Rushe would become. Now they had nothing but alone time.

TWENTY-SEVEN

BEING ALLOWED TO PUT her clothes back on was a battle in itself. Rushe turned up the heat and tried to snatch them away. But he did have to concede because, as she pointed out, the sun was rising, and they were still driving. That alone didn't do it. She also reminded him that the cops were not part of his plan. She queried how long it would take to garner unwanted attention when people saw her naked breasts through the windshield. Only then did he let her get dressed. But hours and hours later, they were still driving.

"Who's the other one?"

"What?" she asked, chewing on the last of the power bar he'd given to her for lunch.

"The guy that popped your cherry."

"I don't know what you…"

"You said there were two of us," he said. "Who's the other guy?"

"Does it matter?"

"You've been yammering on all night. About movies, and books, and music, and some chick called Tamara, and your job, and your boss."

"All very generic topics," she said. "How I lost my virginity is personal."

"Kitten, you were just naked and fucked at the side of the road by the guy who sprung you from a gang of loan sharks and sex traffickers."

"Are you saying I owe you?"

"I'm saying we're past personal."

"Okay," she said, stuffing her trash into the door pocket then turning her attention on him. "How did you lose yours?"

"My what?" he asked.

"Your virginity."

"I don't remember."

"Yeah, right, you're such a stud," she said. "Everyone remembers their first time."

Rushe shrugged and checked both ways at an intersection. "I remember having sex with my foster mother, she could've been... no there was a chick who brought clothes, and food and shit to one of the shelters. I remember her 'cause when she took her top off and had like no tits, I was disappointed. She was before the foster woman. I thought I was actually gonna get my hands on a... are you crying again?"

"No," she asserted because she wasn't, but she must have carried the notion in the air. "You grew up in foster care?"

"What did you expect?" he asked. "You think I had a mom who baked cookies and took me to little league?"

"No," she said. As she folded her arms and sat back, she thought about what he must've been through to make him so tough. "Where are your parents?"

"No idea," he said. "Never met them and never asked. I was abandoned as a baby, cops never found out who dumped me."

She felt petulant, like a spoiled brat who'd stormed out on her family because they'd refused to buy her a pony. "Want me to blow you?"

"Might make me feel better about my life." She went for his fly, but he caught her hand. "I was kidding."

"I didn't know you could do that," she said, which earned her a glare, but he released her hand, and went back to driving. "I could drive for a while."

Rushe shook his head. "You can't follow instructions, wouldn't know what you'd do at a red light."

"I always talk my way out of tickets," she said. His face relaxed, which was the closest he came to a smile. "What?"

"Nothing."

"What are you smirking at?" She dug her nails into his thigh. "Tell me."

"A cop stops you," he said, as though explaining the most obvious thing in the world. "He gets out his vehicle and comes to your window."

"Yeah."

"At that point, Kitten, before you've opened your mouth, that guy knows he's not giving you a ticket."

"How do you know that?"

Drawing his eyes around, he drank in an eyeful of her cleavage. "You've got great jugs."

She looked down at her breasts then back at him; he was driving again. "Are you saying...?"

"You could curse about his mama, his wife, and his sister, he's not listening. You're not getting a ticket. He's imagining what he wants to do to those babies."

She wasn't ignorant of her breasts existence, she just didn't think about them very often. From a young age, she'd been taught how to dress properly and that meant not flaunting your assets. In comparison to her mother, sisters, and most of the women in their sphere, her breasts were an anomaly.

Instead of folding her arms under her chest as she usually did, she tried to fold her arms over them, feeling incredibly self-conscious about these lumps bestowed on her without her permission. She didn't want to be a freak and certainly didn't want to be nothing more than a pair of breasts on legs.

"That shut you up," Rushe said. "If I'd known talking about your cans would do that, I'd have done it last night."

She was not in the mood for his needling. Tiredness was a long distant memory. She'd had enough sleep this week to see her through the rest of the month. But if she could've fallen asleep and blocked him out, she'd have done it.

"Are you sulking?"

"No," she said, aware it sounded as though that was exactly what she was doing.

"Good. I plan to fuck those girls again as soon as I find a motel."

"We're stopping?" she asked, perking up a little.

"Yeah," he said. "It's daylight. Can't fuck you on the roadside in this town."

They were in a built-up area; she couldn't be more specific and hadn't bothered paying attention to location markers. Rushe had been driving all night, but he didn't look tired, he looked… She observed his profile, his features were strong, a square stubbled jaw, his nose had been broken at one time, maybe more, but that only added to the danger shimmering around him. His face was arranged in a permanent scowl, like someone just dared him to a fight. Rushe was ready, alert… angry.

She was curious about his past, if he'd ever been in love, if he'd been hurt, if he'd had anyone to trust. Something about Rushe meant business. Had he ever smiled? Did he find anything funny? Was he capable of stepping down from DEFCON one?

Trusting that Rushe knew what he was doing, she said nothing when he stopped in a dark corner of a motel parking lot, then arranged a room for them. She remained quiet while he retrieved a duffel bag from the trunk and ushered her into room twenty-nine.

He'd been ornery since they escaped Victor. More ornery than usual. With everything that had happened, Rushe must have a lot going on in his head. Her mind kept drifting back to that roadside, and his hand in hers. He'd walked away from everything at Victor's because she was unhappy.

Rushe threw the bag to the floor, locked the motel room door, and headed for the bathroom. Still neither of them addressed the other.

She hadn't been in many motels. The only time she'd slept in one was the night after leaving her parents' house more than a year ago. This one was just the same. Threadbare carpet and curtains, the room smelled musty. The bed looked anything but comfortable or inviting. A mirror hung on the wall above the drawers that served as a stand for the TV at the end of the bed. That was it. She drew the curtains over the window, blocking out the glare of the sun, and then took off her clothes. Rushe would only ask her to do it when he came back into the room anyway.

If she'd known where the condoms were she'd have found one, but she didn't want to snoop in his bag. Rushe was a secretive guy, and she wouldn't for a second want him to question her integrity. If he thought for half a beat that he couldn't trust her, he'd close down tight. So she would do as told and respect his boundaries.

Running her hands into her hair, she could use a shower, but the water hadn't turned on in the bathroom yet. Whatever he was doing in there, she wouldn't want to disturb him. Lying on the bed, she wondered if she should try to arrange herself seductively, or if he would just tease her for trying.

Rushe needed no encouragement; he didn't need her to spell anything out for him. If he wanted sex, he'd ask for it straight out. If he didn't, he'd ignore her no matter how she chose to arrange herself.

Still in the middle of the bed when the bathroom door opened, it was immediately apparent he'd had the same thought. If not the same one, he was prepared to accept her idea. For Rushe stood there as naked as she was, holding himself in hand, condom already on.

Without a word, he came to the bedside and curled his fingers in her hair, guiding her toward his penis to push it into her mouth. The sensation of the taste of latex on his solid offering was novel… exciting.

This was a new skill for her. As nice as it was to have his dick pumping in and out of her again, she preferred him rubber-less. But while his hips moved back and forth and his hand guided her action, she'd keep him happy. Letting her eyes move upward, she watched him watch her. Rushe surged far into her mouth and paused letting her feel the stretch in her throat, the burn of her held breath, the power he had over her, life or death, pleasure or pain.

In one motion he slid out, and she gasped in a breath. His eyes remained on her. Something was different. She couldn't quite figure it out, but he was… looking for something in her, searching for something. What was it? If she knew, she'd give it to him without hesitation.

"Sit on the edge of the bed," he said.

She did as told and he came to stand between her knees, urging her legs apart with his until her thighs burned. He snatched a handful of her hair and pulled her head back forcing her to sit up straight and look right at him.

"You're gonna use your tits to pleasure me, understand?" She didn't speak, just nodded, he increased his hold on her hair. "Now."

Another new trick. She'd never done this before. As Rushe leaned closer, putting himself in her cleavage, sliding in close, his hand stayed in her hair. Because of the angle, she couldn't look down. So with both hands, she pushed her breasts together around him. Mimicking much of the moves he used in the shack, she rolled her breasts up and down around his member.

"Tighter." His fingers had bitten into her when he'd done this himself. "Yeah," he sneered, squeezing one of her nipples, giving it a tug. "Keep going."

With the hand in her hair, he pulled her up sharply. At her responding gasp, his gaze darkened. He'd forced her closer to him, thus her breasts consumed every part of him, balls and all.

"This is what every guy wants," Rushe said without moving his lips, looking her straight in the eye. "That cop, guys in the street, at the store, every man who looks at you wants his cock right where mine is, fucking your jugs." The pinch on her breasts increased. "Your tits make you a slut, every man wants to fuck your titties, Kitten."

Releasing her hair, he tossed her backward to bounce on the bed, then he was over her, inside her, right up to the hilt.

"You missed this," he said, licking the side of her neck. "You missed my fat cock in you." Though he stayed in her, he didn't move. After a long pause, he pushed away and took her legs higher forcing her knees into her shoulders. Only after leaning back did he begin to slide in and out of her. Something in the way he watched the motion of himself move in and out of her was almost... wondrous. Then as quickly as it started, it was over. He was out of her, off the bed, standing there with his back to her.

She at a loss. He hadn't climaxed and neither had she. "Rushe, what's—"

"Quiet!"

Driving his fingers through his hair, he spun to face her. The blackness in his eyes, the clouds that gathered around him, that intensity... All of him was feral, black, devoid of any humanity. His snarl made her mouth dry and her body tense. For the first time, she wasn't sure what he was capable of.

"Give me your ass."

"Rushe."

"Now!"

She turned and closed her eyes, hoping her tension didn't carry to him. Remaining on the bed, she did as told, presenting herself on all fours. Initially, nothing happened. She tried to relax her breathing in anticipation of whatever might come next because she knew Rushe moved silently, and she was right.

His finger speared her pussy and was followed by another. They stilled for a few seconds then he wiggled them inside her, curling them into the cushion of her g-spot. On a groan, she pushed back against his caress. It was like nothing she'd experienced, the automatic desire to writhe against his gift overwhelmed her. Rushe smacked her ass harder than he ever had, and her eyes popped open. Then his fingers were gone. He touched her anus, which caused another automatic desire to seize her. A desire for retreat.

"Any man been up here," he asked. "Don't have any lube, could be painful for you, Kitten. Maybe we just use this?"

Sticking his fingers into her again, he wormed them around as if gathering her juices. "Rushe—"

He spanked her again. "I didn't tell you to talk. I need your permission for anything I'll let you know."

Again, his fingers came out of her and drew their way around to her rear opening. Tense, waiting for what might happen, she didn't know what to feel about what he might do.

His solid urgency spiked into her pussy, and she cried out.

Bracing in fear of the presumed invasion, her hands leaped from the bed, and she came half up, grasping for his hand that lingered on her hip. Maybe she'd expected him to be brutal with her other opening, so the surprise of his intrusion on her vagina took a moment of adjustment

"Consent," he murmured. She sobbed out a laugh. "I like it in here, Flick… I like it too much. I thought if I could treat you… if I could disrespect you, this… it would all be another day at the office… but I like it too much."

She'd never heard him sound so innocent. He spoke like a little boy confessing a terrible crime. Without thinking, she did something for the very first time. She bowed away. He slid out of her body, but she kept his hand and led him around from the end to the head of the bed.

"Sit," she said.

He did as she requested. Keeping their eyes locked, she skimmed her leg over his thighs and took him into her body, all of him, every delicious inch of him, until her clit pressed to his groin. Wriggling herself forward, she skimmed her hands from his shoulders to the back of his head into his hair. With their eyes open, she brought their mouths together.

The kiss was slow, and she thought of the parallel with the kiss Rushe bestowed on her during their first time, when he'd first entered her. Back then his goal had been to relax her enough to penetrate her with greater ease. This was the slide of warm, familiar tongues that had long since craved each other. With a hunger she didn't want their mouths to conquer, she rose onto her knees and descended, going up and down, letting their mouths mate as their bodies mimicked the action.

The solid, quaking length of him inside her was always consuming. His hands gently touched her hips, then moved away and came back again; he wasn't sure what to do with himself. Rushe's mouth was usually for dirty talk, but now she kept it occupied with hers. Usually, his hands were used for pleasure and domination, but she was in control this time around, and pleasure was being taken care of.

Deliberately pushing her clit against him, she drew down steadily, letting the scratch of his hair stimulate her, while simultaneously coating her juices over him, more liquid on him, all over him. She wanted him to know how this made her feel, how their intensity didn't fade without the words, or without the actions. This was what she needed, their simple joining, him inside her; Rushe did it for her even when he didn't know what to do.

Taking her hands from around his head, they trailed down his chest to find his hands. When she linked their fingers, he didn't flinch. In fact, he reciprocated. She tried to guide his hands to her breasts to let him know it was okay to touch her. Rushe took the offering but kept their fingers interlocked, so they caressed her breasts together.

When she smiled on his lips, his actions stopped. Would he berate her for not taking things seriously? On freeing his hands, Rushe took her into his arms and kissed her again, deeper, but just as gently. Pressing her body into his, he lifted her slightly to lay her down on her back, keeping himself in her. When he pushed all the way in, he broke their kiss to look down at her, into her.

Brushing her hands onto his face, she didn't hide her smile. Rushe's expression relaxed, the anger wasn't there now it was… determination that took its place. Sliding out of her, he slithered back in, the rhythm positively sluggish compared to how they'd joined in the past.

Tilting her hips, she took him deeper. When the claws of climax came upon her, she tipped her chin back. But Rushe framed her face and kept their eyes connected through every shudder of her peak, and every aftershock.

When her body had taken from his, he took right back, but this wasn't his typical roar and thump. With this motion, he filled her so completely that she tipped over the edge again. Like their very first union when she wasn't sure if she could accommodate him, she was conquered, owned, this time in more than just the physical.

Rushe didn't pull out, he didn't turn his back on her, and he didn't slam out of the room. He pressed his mouth to hers, then lifted them off the bed together, still intimately merged, and carried her through to the shower where they did it all over again.

TWENTY-EIGHT

"KITTEN, I'M LEAVING… okay?"

She yawned and rolled onto her back to see Rushe sitting on the edge of the bed, his arm over her body supporting his weight.

"What time is it?"

"It doesn't matter," he said, stroking the hair from her face. "I need you to listen. Are you listening? This is important."

"I'm listening," she said, draping her arms over his thighs and curling herself closer.

"It doesn't seem like you're listening."

"That's because I'm near your penis and you're not listening."

"Fair enough," he said, putting up no argument.

She snaked one palm to the thickening member emerging in his jeans. "He's listening."

"He doesn't need to listen. You need to listen." He took her hand away from his groin. "There's a gun in the duffel, and a knife in the second drawer, you hear me? The second drawer, not the top one."

"Mm hmm."

"Kitten," he said. "I'll haul you out of bed if I have to."

"No," she said, sliding down until her cheek met his knee. "See how close my mouth is to him? Why don't you just stay here with me… and my mouth?"

Snatching hold of her arms, he did as he'd threatened and heaved her out of bed to pin her to the wall. "Do you see how quickly things can change?" he growled. "You better take this seriously, or I swear to God…"

She yawned and used the back of her forearm to scoop her hair back over her forehead. "Okay, I'm listening. Gun in duffel, knife in second drawer. I heard you."

"Good."

Sure he was about to turn away, she grasped for his shoulders. "Who's coming in here that I have to shoot?"

"Hopefully no one," he said. "But I won't leave you unprepared. I'm gonna use the cuffs, so you won't—"

"You're going to cuff me?" she said and sagged. "Where am I going to go? You've said it yourself that you can't get rid of me. I want more dynamite sex. I'm not going to run out on you. You're not that lucky."

"I'm not taking any risks."

"Then take me with you," she said. "I don't like being… in this… without you."

"You're not in this without me," he said. "If you get scared…"

"If I get scared what?" she asked. "I can't trust anyone. If I don't know where I am, how do I know I'm not running into danger instead of away from it?"

"There's money in the duffel," he said. "If I'm not back by daybreak I want you to get to your father's, okay? Surround yourself with people, never go anywhere alone."

"Ever again in my whole life? I don't like this, Rushe. Take me with you."

"I should've left you sleeping," he grumbled.

"I'll be good, I promise, I'll follow instructions. I'll do everything you tell me, stay in the car, everything, anything you say."

"You're not dressed. I don't have time to—"

"I'll be fast."

When she nudged him to release her weight, he lowered her back onto her feet. Rounding him, she darted toward the end of the bed, screeching to a halt as her insides objected. She sucked in a breath and dropped to the corner of the mattress.

"What?" he asked, poised beside her.

Pushing a hand to her lower abdomen, she smiled through a wince. "That was a sex marathon."

He growled and straightened. "If you're in pain, why are you smiling?"

She stood and ran her hand down his tee-shirt. "This is good pain, Lover. Pain that reminds me just how much you want me."

Rushe grabbed her ass and hauled her body to his. She let herself fall against him, her arms getting trapped against his chest.

"You forget you're naked," he muttered.

This was something else now; something between them had changed. If she didn't know any better, she'd swear he was more interested in kissing her than fucking her right now. Man, was she glad she'd taught him the virtue of sharing a kiss. Rushe had always been good at the act but stingy in giving them, until now.

With no interested spectators around, they didn't have to worry about rules or chain of command. Alone together, they didn't have to worry about who saw them.

They didn't have to worry about who knew they might care for each other. No one knew who they were, or that they could each be used as collateral against the other. So they were free to relax, to be themselves, to enjoy each other openly.

No matter how he might object to it now, or in future, she'd seen something in him since they left that house. After their conversation in the car, she'd got in, just a little crack had formed, and it was enough to squeeze through. Coupling that with what had happened in their motel room that night, she'd wedged the fissure open and seen what he was, or what he could be. The goodness in him, that she'd always known was there, had been hidden behind a barrier. A shield Rushe built to protect himself, and to protect her, against the evil that circulated around them.

But none of that existed there. He was a man, and she was a woman, and they had trust. He'd ignored his own advice.

If they found themselves back in that arena, he'd be harder again. The protection he put in place to keep them at arm's length from each other would return. The bad guys had to think he didn't care for her or they'd use her as a weapon. Now she realized how deep that ran, what a depth of responsibility he felt. While he'd never had anyone in his life to rely on, he took the job of her welfare very seriously. He wanted to be strong enough, good enough, for her to rely on. Even if he didn't believe himself capable.

Rushe might trust her as she trusted him, but he didn't trust himself.

The kiss was important and so consuming that rational thought got jumbled. His fingers circled around her opening then up to push her clit. Her sandwiched arms rotated to take his tee-shirt in her fists. With a twist and a pull, she got him off-balance enough to land them on the bed. When his weight landed on hers, the sheer solid mass of him made her ache to cower in the safe cocoon of him for the rest of time.

"Kitten," he said, turning his head to break their kiss, but she kept hold of his tee-shirt and wrapped her legs around each of his thighs.

The track of his erection got her at just the right angle, and she tipped her hips to wriggle closer. He clamored with her hands and managed to get them out of his tee-shirt, but when he planted them on the bed, she linked her fingers between his, keeping them connected.

"Kitten, I don't have time," he said, as she tried to kiss him again.

"Please," she murmured. Nipping at his jaw, she closed her knees on his ass, keeping her feet hooked between his thighs, increasing her rubbing on the ridge behind his fly. "I'll beg, Rushe. Do you want me to beg?"

"You're gonna come all over my jeans," he said. "I'm meeting a serious guy."

"You like it when I come all over you," she said, licking the stubble on his chin.

"If I fuck you—no, no, I don't have time. Stop."

"Are you refusing me?" she asked, kissing him again.

This time his lips responded, but she wasn't sure what they were trying to do. She relaxed her head to check him out. Following his lead always worked better for her. Except the sight above her was so startling, she stiffened.

Concern gripped him. "What?"

Her hands rose toward his face but paused. "You smiled at me," she whispered, sure that feeling of his lips, the fleeting look she'd seen on his face before she froze and worried him was…

"What? No, I didn't."

Her expression relaxed, and a smile seeped onto her own lips. "Rushe," she exhaled, more gratified by that brief glimmer than she would have been if he'd presented her with a diamond ring.

"No, I didn't, stop screwing around."

His cantankerous reaction was all the confirmation she needed. But she wouldn't tease him, it might discourage him. If she chased his smile away too far, it might never come back. But it was so satisfying to know she'd caused… or at least been a part of a moment of happiness in his life no matter how fleeting.

"Okay, let's go."

Patting his chest, she let him clamber off her to straighten himself out, and get that frown glued back into place.

He swiped at his jeans, checking what mess she'd made. "Kitten," he scolded, but he slapped his thigh and let it go.

"Let's get moving," she said.

"You're naked."

"I was naked in the car last night."

"I'm not letting you go out there naked," he said. "Not a chance in hell."

"Do you think there are men out there who haven't seen breasts before?" she asked, stepping into her jeans and pulling them up, never having had the notion to go outside without dressing first anyway.

"Probably," he said, retrieving the knife then hauling the duffel off the floor while she put on her sweater and swiped up her underwear, sure to leave nothing behind. "But I don't give a shit about that."

"What do you give a shit about?"

"They're my breasts," he said, opening the motel room door. She paused to look at him. "What?"

"Your breasts?"

"Yes," he said, without shame. "Your tits mean more to me than they do to you, so why haggle over ownership?"

If she hadn't scared his smile away, it might have poked its head over the horizon again. "You're taking ownership of the breasts attached to my body."

"Yeah. Problem?"

"No," she said, with few other options.

While he dumped the bag in the trunk, she settled herself into the passenger side.

Rushe climbed in and got them started. "Seatbelt," he said.

"Can I have your penis?" she asked, while obeying.

"Now?" he asked, a hand on her headrest while he reversed from the parking spot.

"If you own my breasts…"

"We'll work out a timeshare," he said, swinging them out of the lot and through the dark city streets.

"That hardly seems fair. You've already laid claim to my vagina, and now you're claiming my breasts."

"He takes a lot of looking after," he said, as intent on the road and as stoic as ever, even despite the teasing.

"You're amazing," she said and sighed.

"What?"

"Who is this guy you're meeting?" she asked, knowing he'd never understand or accept her point of view on this subject.

She might not know everything about who Rushe was, but he proved the adage that still waters ran deep. He'd yielded to her fear again. When he told her that he wasn't involved with the trafficking, she believed him. Though that didn't explain his reasons for being mixed up with Victor, Skeeve, and the others. There was more going on than met the eye. If Flick ever needed proof of that, all she had to do was remember that look on his face. She'd made him smile.

TWENTY-NINE

NO AMOUNT OF BEGGING would induce Rushe to take her out of the vehicle. While he reminded her she'd promised to behave, she still asked to join him at the meeting. Trying was always the first step toward success. Without it, no chance of succeeding existed. But Rushe wasn't interested in her reasoning.

The car was parked on a well-lit street. He'd told her to stay put, and although part of her wanted to chase after him, she knew better.

Being locked up in a car might not be fun, but if she'd listened to Rushe in the first place, she wouldn't be in this mess, and likely neither would he. Why had she ignored his instruction on the night they met? What reason would he have for cautioning her? It couldn't have been anything nefarious. Clearly, the only trouble on the street was the owner of the warning voice, and he was telling her to keep moving.

Back in the shack, she'd believed Rushe indifferent and thought pleasuring a man like him was beyond her.

Their time in the motel wasn't any typical fuck session. Since they'd rolled in there, what went on between them wasn't animal mating for copulation, it was animal bonding. Women were always jeered for coupling sex and emotion. Rushe would never admit to having feelings for her, it would just never happen. He'd never whisper words of affection and romance to her in the still of night. Maybe she was making more of it than she should.

Much as she didn't want to admit it, they had no future. If they both got through this, and Rushe wasn't sent to jail for a million years, he'd never be happy with a meek librarian. The bond between them was forged because of the danger they could both face at any second.

Maybe she would get a screw out of it, but Rushe wouldn't hang around. She had nothing to offer him beyond her body. A guy like him wouldn't offer much stability. Being with Rushe would mean giving up any dreams she might have of love and security, home and children. But he'd be worth it. Rushe would say different. And that was why there would never be a future. He'd tell her to "get" and disappear into the sunset. She'd never see him again because he'd believe that was in her best interest.

Swiping some errant tears from her face, she slunk down in her seat to look around outside. Then she saw him. Rushe, in a lit diner on the corner of the block diagonally opposite where he'd parked the car. Whether he did it to give her sight of where he was, or so he could keep her in his view, she didn't care.

The view gave her the chance to be a part of this meet. It could give her the chance to understand. If she hadn't caught a glimpse of Rushe before he sat down, she'd have missed him. Just one man sat at the same table, and though she could only see his profile, she was sure she'd seen him somewhere before.

But he wasn't Shiv or Skeeve, Glen or the Kid. No one else had been at the shack. He definitely wasn't in Victor's office. This wasn't John, or the driver in the car that brought her to Victor's place.

Mentally ticking off places, taking careful note of where she'd been, and what she'd seen, she tried to figure it out. She'd make a terrible detective. Recognizing someone wasn't important, placing them was important. His name didn't matter, his job, or his family. If she could put him in a location, details could be established.

He wasn't the cab driver who took her home, her super, or any of the people she'd encountered in family, or life. This person wasn't famous, there wouldn't be a gang of… a gang.

She sat poker straight. In a gang. That's where she'd seen him. He was in the gang, the first gang, at Dell's. That man had been in Dell's the night she walked in on the meeting. He'd been at the table, in the seat next to Victor, whom she placed there too.

Whoever Rushe was talking to was a man who worked with Victor. But they were running from Victor… weren't they? She couldn't believe Rushe would boost her just to hand her back over, that made no sense.

This stranger had definitely sat at Victor's side, so he had to be important. Could he be a competitor of Victor? And their proximity at the meeting table in Dell's merely a coincidence? But why would Rushe talk to an employee of Victor, or to his competitor? Weren't they running for their lives right now?

Every time she'd asked Rushe what was going on, he'd refused to tell her. While she had caught tidbits over the last few weeks. She understood the hierarchy and how the men made a living. The other men anyway, she still didn't know where Rushe fitted in.

While she understood his desire to protect her, she didn't understand why he wouldn't give her information that might help her. At any point, they could be separated. She wouldn't get out of this without him, just as she had no desire to walk away from Rushe while this was going on.

Examining the scene, she couldn't tell who was talking, they were too far away. Rushe made no gestures; he just drank from a mug of coffee. The other man gestured little too. Their lack of hand movement must be thug one-oh-one.

She could push the issue of information but had faith in her lover. If she questioned him too much, he might doubt that conviction. As John had said to her, she shouldn't be in any hurry to end the wait.

Watching the men in that booth at the window of the diner, she started to salivate. Hot coffee would be great right then, in that cold car, on that cold night. Her ally and his cohort sat in the warm diner with the other patrons while she sat out there freezing to death. She could be in bed. If she had just accepted Rushe's terms, she would still be in the motel, except she wouldn't have slept.

Being in the car, observing the scene was better than any alternative. In the motel, she'd have paced, and worried, and jumped at shadows; thinking about Rushe out in the world somewhere that she would never find him.

The minute all this was over, she was getting herself in shape. Well, not in shape because she trained at the gym all the time, but she needed some kind of combat skill. If anything happened in that diner, she wouldn't be able to do a thing about it. She'd probably scream, scramble out of the car and run over there, just to get herself shot, or be a distraction for Rushe.

Getting self-defense training seemed so obvious, though she'd never imagined needing it like this. No one anticipated assault and abduction. Then again, she'd been targeted by two bag snatchers. Maybe learning how to defend herself would be a good thing.

Men like Skeeve were the ones a woman had to really watch out for, and he didn't play fair. Something would be better than nothing, but if someone pulled a gun there wasn't much anyone could do against that.

Considering how crazy Rushe would go if she got out of the car and crossed to grab a coffee from the diner, she saw he was on his feet. He and the Dell's guy still stood together. Were they were leaving or addressing a confrontation between themselves? Maybe they'd seen a danger she'd missed.

He'd been out of the car for a good half hour but had only come into her line of sight in the diner ten minutes ago. Twenty minutes remained unaccounted for. He'd commented on not being back before daybreak. Did that mean he had other meetings or plans?

Rushe was the king of forethought. No doubt he factored in there being a problem. Any trouble around there hadn't jumped up and down waving its hands, so she hadn't seen it. It seemed, from experience, that was what it needed to do in order for her to notice.

Still the men stood in the diner; neither seemed particularly tense. She continued to watch and wait. Then Rushe was walking out, away from the man who quickly went toward the back of the diner and disappeared from sight. When Rushe came outside, he kept moving but was looking around, carefully, not too obvious in his observation but aware of anything and everything, hyper alert as always.

Casual. Right, yeah, she should be casual. Except, uh, there was nothing to distract herself with. Not that she needed to worry. Rushe got back into the car and cranked the engine to pull away at speed without looking at her once. Thank God she hadn't gone into the diner, he may not have noticed her absence.

"Did it go well?" she asked, receiving no response. "Now what?"

"Sex."

One syllable, and her father had called him a barbarian, how apt. "With anyone in particular?"

His knuckles whitened on the steering wheel. "I was gonna fuck you slow," he said. "Now I'm gonna wash that smart mouth of yours out with my spunk, how you feel about that?"

"Say ah," she said and countered his glare with a big grin. "We're alive, Rushe. Give it to me anyway you can, while you can."

The car sped up so suddenly that she was pressured into the backrest of her seat. Wherever they were going, he wanted to get there fast.

Less than ten minutes later, Rushe was dragging her into a different motel room. It looked the same as the first, except the mirror had been replaced with a cheap print, and the bed was on the opposite wall. Rushe dumped the bag on the floor and pushed her to the side.

"Strip."

As was becoming her custom, she did as told. "Rushe, I don't—"

"Get on the bed."

Rushe remained near the door, fully clothed, his arms folded across his chest, and that anger was back on his face. Maybe the meeting hadn't gone well after all.

She crawled onto the bed and lay down on her back.

Scrutinizing her, he sauntered to the end of the bed to look down on her. "Spread your legs," he said, and she did. "Wider… Look at that little pussy of yours. You've got a hot muff. I'm gonna fuck my way through you; fuck you 'til you can't walk." His head tilted though his focus remained at the apex of her thighs. "I'm gonna fuck your tight cunt 'til you beg me to stop, then I'm gonna do it again. I say when. I say how. You do what your told, whore. Speak."

"Yes."

"Yes, what?"

"Yes, sir," she said.

This was the Rushe who'd been with her at the shack. She'd been entirely right about him building those walls if they were exposed to the bad guys again. He would never tell her what happened at the meeting. That was no doubt the reason he hadn't spoken to her in the car. If he'd spoken to her, they would have to acknowledge she'd observed him, and he wanted that to be unspoken.

When Rushe was in this mood, she couldn't play her games, she couldn't tease him. He just wouldn't put up with it.

"I wanna split you in half," he growled, pulling his tee-shirt over his head. "Brand that little pussy as mine, for my use only. You're never gonna have another man, Kitten. No one touches what's mine."

The words were more for effect than rooted in truth. Still, a tremor in her chest wanted him to mean it. If she could have him, if they could have each other, she'd do it. No other man could match up to him, could match up to this, to what they did, what they'd shared.

Kicking off his jeans, he got on the bed and drove his knees beneath hers, compelling her upward for a better viewing angle because he didn't touch her, not with his hands. He prodded her opening with the head of his dick, let it run up between her folds to her clit, and then beyond until the underside of him was against her, his balls against her. He lifted enough to smear his palm and fingers across her juices.

"You're wet, Kitten," he said, licking his fingertips. He did it again, and she ached to push closer.

But he used her juices to coat his cock without entering her. "You're making a mess of me."

Pressing his length between her folds, she gritted her own teeth wishing he would just enter her. "Please, Rushe."

"Not a chance, Kitten," he snickered. "You keep that mouth of your shut now. If you're a good girl, I'll let you lick me clean."

His concentration went back to her pussy, and he began to tug on himself, letting his head bounce against her clit as he jerked himself with her lubricating fluids. He reached for her breast and pinched a nipple, but his eyes remained on the task in hand.

"Rushe," she sighed, as her head drifted back.

Three fingers drove into her, and he hooked them round to yank her from inside. "I told you to be quiet, slut, you're gonna do what you're told."

Curling her lips into her mouth, she nodded but being silent didn't mean she couldn't move. Her sap coated both of them as his cock hammered her clit, and swallowing her scream came on the back of him launching up to grab the back of her neck. He pulled her to sit while rising to his knees. In reflex, she opened her mouth, and he squeezed his own intoxicating liquor into her. When the jets stopped, she lapped out, catching the persisting beads from him. Swallowing him down, she licked her lips, and blinked up at him. Neither had their breath, or their senses, back. Only one word came to mind.

"More."

His face relaxed, she watched the anger and his burden recede some.

Any concern for her was wiped away when he stroked from the top of her head to her jaw. "You're a good girl."

"I want to be naughty," she said, letting her lips curl.

"We've got all night for that, Kitten."

THIRTY

APART FROM THE BRIEF INTERLUDE when Rushe put jeans on to retrieve pizza from the delivery boy, they'd both been naked all night. The pizza was cold in its box, scattered somewhere on the floor.

Rushe sat slouched in the middle at the head of the bed, while she lay on her front between his legs, looking for something to watch on the television. They hadn't bothered with a lamp, so the glare from the TV was their only light. As she flicked through channels, he took her hips to pull her back into his lap, opening her legs over him.

His erection rested on her rear while he rolled his balls around her intimate entrance. But the audacious action wasn't urgent. He explored her, running a finger around her vulva then slipping it inside her. This was play rather than a request for something more.

"What are you in the mood for?" she asked, still flipping through channels.

"Any porn?"

"My God," she exhaled. "That's like giving crack to an addict and asking him not to use it all at once. I already can't walk. Rushe, you did it. I'm crippled."

The words didn't discourage him; he tickled her clit and pushed another finger into her.

Her head fell to the bed. "You're so good at that," she whispered.

"I'm not doing anything," he said like he meant it.

"Okay, keep doing nothing, and if you feel like doing nothing to my clit while you're there…" When he lifted her hips again, she expected to be tossed aside. Instead, the searing heat of him impaled her. She gasped and clenched at the shock.

"Fuck, Kitten," he grumbled. "Give a guy a second to adjust, I'm shirtless back here."

While she liked the intimacy of no barrier, and she definitely preferred his skin to any rubber, her urge was to withdraw.

"If Simone really has had every man, I don't trust the likes of Skeeve to be clean of—"

Her lover spanked her, then took her small hips in his large hands to slide her rear up and down the length of him still embedded within her.

"I didn't fuck Simone," he said, still working her rhythm.

"You didn't?" she asked, peeking at him over her shoulder but he was too interested in watching himself move in and out of her. "Why not?"

Muttering, he released her hips, so she slithered down his shaft. "Do you want me to fuck her?"

"No."

"Then shut up."

Squeezing her internal muscles, his mutter became a curse, and his body went rigid. "I wish you could come in me," she confessed.

"Not a chance."

"I know," she said, undulating on him. "You're too careful for that. A man with your forethought would go crazy with the possibilities."

"I come inside you, there's only one possible outcome. That's not an outcome I'll ever be part of."

"I like it when you come in my mouth. I like how you taste. I like taking a part of you into me."

"There's a part of me in you right now, Kitten."

"But I don't get to keep him."

"You want to keep my spunk?"

Even she had to smile at his skepticism. "Not indefinitely."

"You wanna spread my jizz on toast you go right ahead, Kitten, but you're getting none of it in your happy little pussy. You got enough juice in there already."

With so many things she wanted to say, it broke her heart that she couldn't voice any of them.

"Rushe…" she sighed.

"Tell me about the other guy."

"Who?"

"The pioneer."

"You want to talk about how I lost my virginity when we're having sex?" she asked.

"You like it when I talk during sex."

"Yeah," she conceded. "When you're calling me a whore, and telling me how much you want me, this is more of a conv—"

He shifted and smacked her down onto him bruising her already tender muscles.

"I say when and how… Tell me about the pretty boy your father trotted you out for."

"I never had sex with Robert," she said, pushing back to squirm against him. He'd been playing with her for so long that her body buzzed in anticipation of the promise of his actions. "Oh, Rushe." Humming out her pleasure, she buried her face in the blanket beneath her. Rushe lifted his knees, bringing her up onto her hands. "Please fuck me now."

"No," he said. Staying engaged, he took her with him when he kneeled up and pulled back, leaving only his engorged head to stretch her opening. "Why not?"

"I don't know," she said. "I'm a bad girl… or I'm a good girl?"

He hissed out an exhale. "No, I'm not fucking you because you haven't satisfied me. I want you to tell me why you didn't let your fiancé fuck you."

"Why? Why does it mat—"

He stabbed her deep. On her groan, he withdrew again, letting her pussy kiss the tip of him. The wait for the pleasure she needed tormented every inch of her prickling skin.

"Satisfy me," he growled.

His curiosity? "I wasn't attracted to him… he was boring and self-absorbed."

"Ah," he said, surging in another inch. When she tried to push back to take more of him, he grabbed her hips locking them immobile in his grip. "When I say, Kitten. Did he kiss you?"

"Yes," she squealed, struggling to be patient when she was so ready to be fulfilled.

Foreplay was another of his specialties. His previous tentative exploring had primed her ready for action, yet still he only teased her with the notion.

"Did he buy you flowers and jewelry?"

"Yes."

"You let him get his hands on your cans?"

"My breasts? Yes," she gasped. "Yes."

"Bet he was drooling on you, gagging to seal the deal, when he saw those airbags in the flesh."

She shook her head and brought it up fraught with her desperation. "No," she said, swallowing to moisten her throat.

"No?" He bobbed in deeper then came out of her again, swaying her hips away then back. "You think he didn't want to fuck—"

"On top of the clothes," she panted the words. "Please, Rushe! I was never naked with him! Please! Oh, God! Rushe!"

He thrust into her, fast and kept up the pace of a jackhammer. Fumbling for his hand, she screamed when he took her to climax. Liquid heat burst inside her and her head came up. He wasn't wearing protection.

Without a second to spare, he yanked her hand against his shaft and released his seed into her palm.

He shoved her face first down to the bed. She sat up to look at his semen in her hand. He grabbed her head to force a punishing, brief kiss to her mouth.

With a distant glint in his eye, he nodded at her hand. "Midnight snack."

THIRTY-ONE

SHE TIPPED THE MnM's packet up to pour more into her hand, then raised her curled palm to Rushe's lips. He opened to slurp them into his mouth while keeping his eyes on the road.

"We've been driving for half a day, and you still won't tell me where we're going?"

"No," he said, crunching chocolate. "You've asked me like twenty times."

"Maybe one of these times you'll slip up," she said, knowing it was unlikely. She steeled her courage to ask the question that had been bugging her all day. "Why were you asking me those questions last night?"

"What questions?" he asked, digging some chocolate shell from his teeth.

"About Robert."

"I do what I want," he said. "You don't get that already?"

"It's odd though," she said, putting the candy away. "Asking me about another man when we're having sex… Does that turn you on? The idea of me with another man? I have to be honest, I'm not comfortable with the idea of a threesome—"

"What?"

"Would you prefer it if I had more experience? Do you want to watch me—"

"Kitten!" he snapped, then appeared to think twice about whatever he'd intended to say.

"What?" she asked.

"Nothing."

"Say what you were going to say."

"Why don't you get some sleep?"

"Rushe!" she demanded.

"I've watched men die," Rushe said, confusing her. "Some die fast, some die slower and deserve it but…"

"But?"

He bared his teeth and hesitated again. "When I think about any man…"

"What?"

"You want to know why I asked about him?" he asked, flashing his attention to her then back to the road. "Do you?"

"Yes."

"I want to rip his face off. I want to pull his eyes from their sockets and shove them so far up his ass for looking at you… for thinking… I want to ram my fist through his teeth and down his throat 'cause he had the taste of your mouth. I'd break every finger he touched you with. Do you know the noise a finger makes when it breaks? How quickly I can make a guy cry and beg for his mama?

"I'd cut off his balls and watch him bleed out slow while I make him grovel for mercy for thinking he could ever… for imagining your body, for dreaming about fucking you… I asked those questions because since you told me there had only been two of us, I've wanted to murder any man that got there before me, and any man who thinks he can follow me. Get it? I want him dead, Kitten, and I'm the kinda guy that can make that happen."

He spoke with such venom, such hatred and anger, that she was… astounded. Given she'd thought he would never whisper words of devotion to her, he'd just managed to say the most romantic, and disgusting, thing she'd ever heard.

She sat straight, her eyes stayed on the windshield as she tried to process his statement, and its sentiment. "Okay," she said, unsure exactly how to react to… wow.

"Okay?" he snapped, seemingly happy to shut her up.

"Yeah."

"Good."

No one had ever reacted with such depth of feeling toward her about anything. In her life, she'd attracted indifference and had come to expect it. That was her reason for believing she couldn't pleasure Rushe. No one felt much of anything toward her, or because of her.

But he'd proved her wrong. They'd had replay after replay. If she wanted to, she could persuade him into sex, one way or another. Her experience with him, with this one man, gave her the inside track on how to tempt him.

Her brothers-in-law, and the men in her father's circle, wouldn't know anything about dirty talk. If any of those men thought about demanding anything sexual, she'd probably laugh in their faces. Asking any of them to come in her would be the furthest thing from her mind, and she'd certainly never beg them to fuck her.

Reality came back into focus. When Rushe was gone, she'd have to be celibate for the rest of her life or settle for less than him. She couldn't go back to her independent life expecting happiness. Being with her family, or out on her own, there would be no great love. This was it for her; no man would match up to Rushe. She'd seen her lover go through his own sort of sexual awakening, as he'd schooled her through hers.

Rushe didn't care about her inexperience, and he didn't treat her with kid gloves. He wouldn't fear her father or any of his associates. Last night in the first motel, when he'd been unable to objectify her, she'd taken control. He'd been like a lost puppy and happy to let her sit him down, to kiss him, to take him through their union slowly and gently.

She would never say it to his face, but she doubted he'd ever made love to any woman, until last night when he made love to her. With a taste for the new tempo, he'd mixed things up since, allowing her to relish the variety.

Being intimate with Rushe was electrifying from the first second. But now they'd crossed another barrier, and he could be softer with her, it was more than that. He'd fuck her senseless, then kiss her and stroke her, and she'd felt treasured. She had to keep reminding herself it could never last.

When Rushe walked away she'd be a different person. Would that person ever be whole again?

THIRTY-TWO

AT SOME POINT, she'd fallen asleep, though it couldn't have been for long. He'd stopped at a service station and screwed her in the restroom, at her request. It confused the hell out of him, but he complied.

Now that she sensed the car slowing again, she blinked open her eyes and stretched her muscles, ready to see another motel or a deserted strip of road. When she realized what was actually in front of them, she jerked bolt upright, instantly wide awake.

"Rushe?" she panted. "Rushe, what are we doing here? Rushe?"

He didn't answer her, just drove on right through the still opening iron gates.

"Please, Rushe," she whispered.

His stony expression remained ahead. They broke through the line of trees. Her hands pushed at her gut until she grabbed for his arm, but he yanked it away.

"I'm sorry. Turn around," she begged. "Come on. Let's get out of here. Rushe?"

"This is where you belong, Kitten."

The car stopped. She didn't want to open her eyes to face the mass of white concrete that loomed beyond the windshield. Swallowing away the bile that threatened her throat, she took her shaking chin up to see her hell.

The Hughes family home.

"Get out."

"What?" she asked, cracking her neck with the speed of her head turn.

He didn't look at her. "You heard me."

"Rushe, look at me, baby," she pleaded, and tried to reach for him.

He pulled away again. "Get out."

"No," she said, shaking her head. "No, I won't go. You think you can make this easier? Look at me! Coward!"

"Listen, sweetheart," he snapped, letting those bullet eyes scorch her with disgust. "You were a good fuck, okay? But you're home now; home with your prissy suitors who'll drown you in jewels, just to get your hands on theirs. Go show your pretty boys all the lessons I taught you!"

"I don't believe a word," she said. "I know you."

"What?" he snarled. "You think because I fucked your throat that you can see into my soul? You're good at being easy, go open your legs for one of your wimp-ass rich boys. I'm bored with you."

"You're going back, aren't you?" she whispered. "You're going back to them. This was your plan all along, wasn't it? This was why you wouldn't tell me."

"Yeah," he spat. "If I told you, you might've refused my cock for half a second. Plenty of women back there who'll take care of it now. Don't worry your little head."

"What happened to bareback? What happened to my body belonging to you?"

"Women love that shit," he said, raking his eyes over her.

While he groped each of her breasts, her focus stayed on him. She wouldn't pull away. He shoved her breasts together and kissed her cleavage, then bit her nipple through the fabric. When his eyes dragged back to hers, they crowed, presumably believing he'd have broken her, or convinced her of his cruel indifference.

But she didn't cry, she smiled. "Do you want me to take my clothes off?" she asked, and his swagger faltered. "You could do me right here." She leaned in close. "Right in daddy's driveway. Would you like that? Bend me over the hood like you did night before last? Watch me strip off, slowly, or you want me just to hike up my skirt? Let all the staff watch as you slide your cock into me really slow, into my slick, tight pussy?" Fixated on his mouth, she salved her bottom lip, eager for the taste of him. While she had him off-guard, she kept going. "Or you want me to suck you off, get your dick deep into my throat, fuck my skull with your hand in my hair until you feed me your sweet spunk."

He got hold of her arms and held her body away from him to scrutinize her face. The look in his eyes was… horror. She'd never seen that in him before.

"You want to fuck me, Rushe," she whispered. "I see it in the way you look at me. I've always seen it."

"What the fuck did I do to you?" he murmured.

"Only what I deserved… sir."

Rushe turned his head to one side, and paused, then shook it. "No, Kitten, you're getting out of this car now. You're going up those stairs into your father's house. You'll be taken care of in there. I'll deal with Victor. You have nothing to fear anymore."

"Will you come back?" she asked.

"No."

At least he was honest, but somehow that wasn't a consolation. "You could. You could come and get me."

"For what?" he asked. "I'm not gonna marry you, and I'm not gonna impress your family. Do yourself a favor… and don't embarrass yourself."

A tear skittered down her cheek, but she remained steadfast. "I know you feel something for me, Rushe. I know you do."

"You don't know squat, sweetheart. Guys like me… we don't… feel."

"Yes, you do," she said. "You just can't admit it to yourself because you think it makes you weak. That I make you weak."

"You've already fucked this whole job," he said. "If you'd been any other complication, I'd have put a bullet between your eyes weeks ago. Get out of the car."

"No."

"Get out of the car and walk away, Flick. Don't look back. Forget this whole horrible experience."

A sniffle brought more tears from her lashes. "You're the best thing I've ever had in my life."

A look of alarm and sorrow flitted across his features. "Get out of the car, Kitten."

She shook her head. When his hand rose, she believed he was going to caress her, but he withdrew. On a curse, he slammed out of the car.

She didn't know his plan until he ripped open her door and grabbed her arm. "No!"

Although she tried to resist him, it was useless. With little effort, he carried her tiny frame from the car and took her kicking and screaming onto the front steps. Dropping her down, he tried to walk away.

She grabbed hold of his wrist. "They'll kill you!" she screamed. "I can't let you go back there alone!"

Rushe lunged down and grabbed her chin to haul her face up to within an inch of his. "I don't need a whore like you to give me permission for anything." Through his gritted teeth, his lips didn't move, but he huffed every breath. This was a mask he knew how to don and maintain well after his years of practice. "Another thing, don't believe everything a guy says to get into your cunt… and get yourself tested, God only knows what I gave you."

When he threw her face away, she could only cower, until cursing herself she lifted her head with hope… If he looked back…

Rushe got in the car and with a spray of stone chips, he sped away without a second of hesitation.

"Felicity?"

Her mother's voice was the last thing she needed to hear.

"Oh my goodness!" her sister Lucia called out.

The thunder of footsteps coming down the stairs revealed they had a troupe with them. But she watched the dust settle on the drive and craned in hope of hearing the engine return.

It didn't.

People got in her eye line and crowded around her. Hands touched, explored her, and her injuries. All she could see was him. He'd lied to her. Bringing her there was a swindle. He'd blindsided her, knowing if he'd given her the truth, she'd have run out on him, and done everything in her power to delay and avoid this.

"Felicity," her father demanded.

She swayed, drugged by emotion, by disappointment, by grief. "He didn't look back," she whispered and was swallowed into the belly of the Hughes beast.

THIRTY-THREE

HER FAMILY INSISTED on talking constantly. They questioned her yet continued without waiting for answers. The noise rattled through her, grating on every nerve.

She'd been taken into the house. Her father wanted to call the police, but she wasn't interested in law enforcement, and nothing had happened. Other than them keeping her in captivity, she had not been party to, or witnessed, any other criminal acts. No one had hit her, beat her, or subjected her to anything. Yes, they said there were criminal acts taking place, but she had no evidence of them. She didn't even know the location of Victor's place. Not what city or town it was close to.

So after a frustrating conversation, she'd been forced to allow her mother and sisters to take her up to her old bedroom. They all twittered on while she bathed. Washing the remnants of her last union with Rushe off her body was painful. Under the spray of the luxury power shower, her tears fell, craving to be back in the shitty motel with its terrible water-pressure and fluctuating temperature.

When her energy waned, she leaned against the shower wall and sobbed. On the other side of the fogged glass, her mother and sisters were fussing with clothes and conversation, but she was consumed by the loss.

Even against the wet shower tile she was reminded of him, of what he would do to her if he'd been there, or on the other side of that glass. The hard wall reminded her of his hard body, and the strength of him that would haul her from the floor and plunge himself into her.

Sex wasn't a thing she'd understood before Rushe, and she'd never understand it again. He'd been her guidebook, her mentor.

But the sobbing wasn't for the sex. It wasn't for the harsh way he'd spoken to her, or even for the things he had said. She sobbed because her heart was broken. The only man she'd ever loved was driving into danger. Alone. Rushe drove back there to face the music. To confess his involvement in her escape; she could only imagine what horror would follow. He drove back into the fire because he didn't want those evil men to sell those innocent women, because somehow his purpose hadn't yet been fulfilled. And for her. Rushe was going back into that building to put his body between her and danger.

He'd said it himself. *"I'll deal with Victor. You have nothing to fear anymore."*

She'd asked him if she'd be running for the rest of her life, and he'd told her she wouldn't. Because he had a plan, and this was it. Rushe told her he wasn't involved in the trafficking, and it wasn't about the money. She could think of no reason he'd go back to that place voluntarily, unless it was to protect her and the other women.

Steeling herself from her anguish, she gathered herself together enough to leave the shower.

"Good God."

Her mother gaped. An equally shocked Lucia stood to her side.

"What?" she asked, trying to see what they were…

She didn't have to look far. Vivian stumbled into the room to gawp too, but her lips curled up slowly as she examined her body in the full-length mirror.

He was everywhere, all over her. The rash of his stubble burn covered her body, her face, her neck, her breasts. It went down her abdomen and her thighs. But that wasn't all. Seeing the imprint of his hands on her thighs, and on her butt, she caught her lip in her teeth. He'd wanted her so badly, and so often. Rushe was a man starved for her and she hadn't realized it. Not until she saw the bruises marring her flesh. His urgency, his desire, swathed her in his embrace again, he'd left his mark.

"What did those men do to you?" her mother squawked.

"Men?" she asked, lifting her eyes to the three gaping women in the doorway. "He did this all by himself."

"He?" Vivian asked.

Her sisters were like twins, only a year apart. Both wore the same style of twinset that matched their mother's, all in varying pastel shades. These were sophisticated women who toed the family line and did exactly what was expected of them. She'd bet these women would claim to always follow their partners' instructions. But she doubted any of them had been told to strip naked in a moving car and masturbate.

"Was it just awful?" Lucia asked, pressing a hand to her chest.

The three women inspected her naked body from their place in the doorway.

In her recent experience, she'd learned to shirk any modesty she may have had. Though before Rushe, her experience of being naked in front of anyone was limited. Then again, before Rushe she hadn't had much experience of anything.

"The sex?" she asked, strangely enjoying the blush in her sister's cheeks.

"Oh my…" her mother said and pressed her fingers to her mouth. "We can phone the police. They may be able to get samples of…"

"This was consensual," she said, gesturing to her body.

What would non-consensual sex look like? She had bruises to the tips of her toes, and hickeys on all of her soft spots.

"You had consensual sex with…" Vivian trailed off.

She didn't know if any of them had seen Rushe, or if they were just imagining what a big bad ogre who could do this looked like.

"I've heard of captives who come to care for their captors," Lucia said. "It has a name."

"This isn't that," she said, drying herself off with a thick white towel from the heated rail next to her.

A lot had happened since she and Rushe shared that rough towel in the shack.

"How can you be sure?" Vivian asked. "I can't see why any woman would want—"

"It's been a couple of days since I've been a captive," she said to the renewed alarm of her audience. She hadn't thought of it that way, but it was true. She could actually have walked away from Rushe any of dozens of times. It had never occurred to her, not even as he was throwing her out of their vehicular sanctuary.

"We have to tell daddy," Vivian said to their mother as though Flick wasn't there at all.

"If you tell your father, he'll have a heart attack," her mother muttered to her other daughters.

"What if whoever he is comes back and—"

"He's not coming back," she said.

Her enjoyment of the previous moment was gone. Now wrapped in the towel, only her face was on show in the heated mirror.

"How can you be so sure that—"

"Because it was just sex," she declared, not believing her own statement.

"My goodness, Felicity," her mother scolded. "What a way to speak."

And she found her smile again. She knew something they didn't… she'd been his whore, and if he showed up right then and snapped his fingers, she'd fall to her knees and thank him for the gift of his presence.

THIRTY-FOUR

SHE'D STAYED AT HER PARENTS' house because there was no urgency to be anywhere else. Most of her time was spent sitting at the front window staring into the empty driveway hoping to hear that engine. The sun rose and set. As the world turned on its axis, her pain didn't subside. Could he be out there? Was he thinking about her? She hoped so because the alternative was... He could've walked back into that building and been killed immediately. Even he wouldn't stand up to a hail of bullets... or a knife in the back.

He couldn't have gone back there just to be felled. Wasn't he smarter than that? Stronger than that? He wouldn't have left her there and walked away without knowing she'd be protected. So she watched the sun rise and then she watched it set.

On the third evening, her father joined them from his study, which was unusual. While she remained intent on the driveway, her mother, sisters, and their husbands paused.

"What's the matter?" her mother, Beverley, asked. "Charles?"

"I received a warning," he said.

"A warning? Who would have the gall to warn you about anything?" Lucia's husband, Roger, asked. "Did you remind them of whom they were dealing with?"

"From Felicity's captors," he said, as though Roger hadn't spoken.

She whipped around like a meerkat on high alert. "From whom?" she asked, getting to her feet. "Was it a message? A letter? An email?"

"No," her father said. "It was a telephone call from a blocked number."

This house was her mother's pride and joy. In a building that size, with its twelve bedrooms, someone would be lucky to hear a phone ring from an adjoining room let alone farther. If only, through some kind of serendipity, she could've been the one to answer it.

"What did he say?" she asked, rushing to her father. "Did he tell you his name? What was the message?"

"There was no message," her father said, still put out by the whole affair. "They stated the money had been paid, and that your safety was assured. They warned me if I thought about going to the cops, they could target others in my acquaintance."

Only her father could consider his own daughter an acquaintance. Her disappointment at the lack of communication from Rushe was quelled when she mentally recited her father's words.

"The money's been paid," she said, frowning up at him. Her sisters were five foot seven, just like her mother. Once again, she was the freak of the family. "Even though I was here and safe you paid the two million?" She would be astounded if her father had done that in deference to her safety.

"I did no such thing," he stated.

"But you said the money had been paid."

"Perhaps so, but not by me."

Charles Hughes had always been proud of his acumen. Doing something like paying a ransom after the captive had been set loose had no reason. She was safe, so there would be no need to pay money to the people who may come after her just because they'd been cheated out of their cash by her escape. It took some stretch of forethought to…

"Oh my God," she said aloud to the thought in her head. "Forethought…" Her family probably thought she'd gone crazy. With one step backwards, her hands went to her forehead. "He considered the possibility… He considered what they would do if they… if they thought I'd one-upped them, tricked them somehow."

"What on earth are you talking about?" Beverley asked.

"Don't you get it," she said. Though there would be no way anyone in the room could, she had to give her thoughts voice. There just wasn't enough room in her brain for them. "He… the money isn't a problem, that's what he said. He said I should… that I had to make sure I was free before… getting the money to Victor is easy. He paid it… the idiot."

On an exhale, her legs gave out, and she dropped onto the floor in the middle of her mother's favorite rug, letting her tears start all over again.

"What are you talking about?" Vivian asked.

She and Lucia were glued to the unfolding drama, their mother was just as intent. The men hadn't been following events and were basically bystanders.

"He paid the ransom," she whispered.

"He?" Lucia took her turn to ask.

"Someone paid two million dollars to ensure your safety, when you were already safe?"

"Yes," she said. In spite of the tears, she laughed a half blub that burst up from the swelling of her heart. "He's in… I knew he felt… Why didn't I see this coming? He… he doesn't know how to deal with feelings…" The chill of dread struck her. "They're gonna kill him."

"P's and Q's, Felicity," her mother scolded.

Only her mother could worry about enunciation at a time like that; her parents really were made for each other. She tried to smile, but her love was out there alone, and there wasn't a thing she could do about it. If Victor didn't hang Rushe for screwing up her kidnapping, by actually returning her without further extortion, then Skeeve would get him for ruining the attempt he and Shiv made to get at her. Shiv… if none of the others did it, Shiv would find a way to avenge his injuries caused by her and Rushe.

He could take care of himself. Rushe believed he didn't need anyone. If he got through it, he'd deal with being apart from her better than she would being away from him. All his life, he'd been ignoring his anger. The way he felt about himself was no surprise now that she knew about his parents, and more about how he was raised. Any abandonment issues he had were dealt with when he was young. Fighting and screwing were his outlets, from what she could establish. He hadn't had a healthy channel for it and wouldn't show weakness to anyone. Not even her.

But two million dollars… how could a boy abandoned at birth and brought up in abusive homes get his hands on that amount of money? Could it be blood money? Was he really a hired gun?

What she didn't understand was, if he could get his hands on money like that from whatever he was capable of, then why was he around the likes of Victor and Skeeve? Two million would be enough to knock down their dilapidated lair and build a new one. Could he have handed his life savings to Victor just to ensure her safety?

She didn't have to think for long. Rushe had to know that the likelihood of him getting out of this plot alive was slim. If he expected to be thrown off this mortal coil, he wanted to be sure no one would come looking for her. He'd said it himself; he wouldn't be around to pull her out the next time… Except… hadn't he told her that the last time they were apart?

THIRTY-FIVE

WITH ANOTHER THREE DAYS gone and no sign of Rushe, she consoled herself to the fact he wasn't coming back. She couldn't stand another day of her mother and her sisters, so she went home to her apartment.

Once again, she walked into her one roomed apartment and sighed out her anguish. Rushe was in her mind constantly. After reading the bill for the new duplicate key, it was obvious she had to find some source of income. Much as she wanted to crawl under her duvet for the next month or two, her bank account couldn't be very healthy. She doubted she'd have been paid and the bills in her mailbox were all red.

Despite knowing there was little chance she still had her job, she tried calling Geoffrey and got a frosty reception. Yeah, she'd been replaced, so she was out of work.

Shame, she'd always enjoyed her work and loved to learn new things, to investigate topics she would never otherwise come across. But the bureaucracy always weighed her down, and she struggled to play nicely with her colleagues. It wasn't that she was rude or got into arguments, she just found it difficult to show interest in the melodramatic details of their lives.

She supposed losing her connection to her family put things in perspective. Now, after her time with Rushe, she realized there were real tragedies, profound incidents going on in the world causing harm. With that new discovery, it would be harder to show interest in banality.

Eventually, she would find her way back into research. She wanted to be immersed in books, searching the internet and obscure directories to find clues that led to salient details. Her love was knowledge and discovery, not who her co-worker had slept with last week.

But her priority was money. She had to find work to pay her bills. Anything would have to do; the jobs market was tough for everyone. Luckily, or not, she was employed the next day, at the local coffeeshop.

"A latte… excuse me?"

"Hmm?" She took her chin from her hand to see the woman on the other side of the counter wearing a scowl. The champ of that expression flared in her thoughts. "Sorry?"

Rushe dominated her mind. She couldn't seem to concentrate, no matter how hard she tried.

"Would you like me to write it down for you?" the woman asked. "It's not difficult. I would imagine it's one of the easier orders you've had. People order in these places like they have their own language."

"They do," she said. "Well, not their own language as such, just words used to describe items that are dispensed here."

On a snort, the woman spun and marched away without her drink. That took care of that problem, though she hadn't intended to be rude, just… state a fact.

"If it isn't the disappearing woman herself."

Her head turned toward the next customer before her eyes followed. Seeing Hayden was a surprise.

"Hayden," she said on a sigh. What a rollercoaster she'd been on. Now it seemed she was back at the beginning, paying her fare to ride again.

"You didn't return my call."

"No," she said, after a brief thought for making excuses. "I suppose I didn't."

"I was concerned. You didn't meet me, and you didn't return my call. I tried you at work. They said you'd been ill and had returned briefly only to vanish again. And here you were all the time."

"Not exactly," she said.

From his point of view, her behavior was odd and abhorrent. She'd been having the hottest and most terrifying experience of her life, and there he was, exactly the same.

"Have you been working here long?" he asked. "I'm in several times a week, I've never seen you."

Hayden was tall. Anyone was next to her. With ash blond hair and a narrow nose, he was… the plain to her plainer. No one would ever measure up to Rushe. She'd known that since before he'd thrown her down on her parents' doorstep.

"About six hours," she said. "I'm not banking on my long-term career prospects."

"Not if your last customer was anything to go by," he said. "I promise to give you a glowing reference, if required."

When Hayden smiled, she copied. It was somehow automatic to return the gesture, though it felt like politeness rather than divine will.

"Do you have plans for dinner?"

He was asking her out. "No."

"Could I tempt you into trying the new Italian place down the block? I can pick you up from work, so you won't get lost again… if you want to say no, I understand."

"No," she said, and he nodded. "No, I mean…"

In reflex, she reached for his hand and the touch of him was… nothing. Hayden's fingers curled around hers. He was holding her hand, just like that. This was normality. This was what people did.

People didn't cry while standing naked at the side of a road because a thug slid his fingers between theirs. Rushe holding her hand was almost equivalent to summiting Everest. When she'd pointed it out, he'd pulled it away and tried to scrub her skin from his.

Hayden smiling at her was simple. That's how easy it was to express an emotion. Hayden was happy, so he smiled, end of story.

Hayden was a good person, a nice person, who would never be mean to anyone. In her processing, his gaze slipped to her chest only to quickly leap back to her eyes. She wanted to ask what he was thinking about. Was Rushe right? Of course she couldn't do it, Hayden would blush and babble and do what any normal man would.

If she'd dared ask Rushe what he was thinking about anything, breasts or not, he'd bend her over and show her exactly what he was thinking. There was nothing normal about that.

"Are you okay?" he asked.

She'd been standing here with his hand in hers for about a minute and hadn't said a word.

Convincing herself her time with Rushe was over, that there would never be a future for them, there was only one responsible course of action. She had to move on as though none of it ever happened.

So although there was nothing electric between her and Hayden, this was sane. This was normal; this was the route her life was supposed to take.

Without Rushe this was the best she could get.

Before she could talk herself out of it, she hurried to speak. "Yes," she said. "And, yes, I'll go to dinner with you."

Hayden ordered his drink to go. They made plans to meet at the end of her shift outside the shop. She couldn't blame him for being wary. It wouldn't be much fun sitting alone in a restaurant wondering if your date was going to show up or not.

Now knowing she couldn't have the man she wanted, it didn't matter who she ended up with. That was her reasoning. Maybe she could show Hayden some of the things she'd learned. Maybe she could learn to be a better lover with him too.

The sex wasn't what she missed. It was how he watched her when he thought she wasn't looking. How he stood guard when she took a shower and anticipated her needs before she had them.

Rushe was responsible, and he was good. Just because his life hadn't started well didn't mean that was the sum total of him. If he let himself, or if he'd let her show him, he could have seen what goodness lay in him.

Possibly too much time had passed, he'd learned his behaviors of protectionism from a young age. Yet in that motel room, she'd seen those barriers fall. He would never believe he could be good for her, but she believed it. By letting him walk away, she'd let him down.

But there was nothing she could do about it. She couldn't go after him because she didn't know where he was. He could be anywhere… or nowhere.

She couldn't think like that anymore. Her affair with Rushe had been a blip in regularly scheduled programming. That night she was going out with Hayden. If things worked out, her life wouldn't have missed a step… just gained an extra one that no one could ever know about.

THIRTY-SIX

"YOUR MIND IS ELSEWHERE."

She'd laughed at Hayden's jokes and listened closely when he spoke about his family. Though she couldn't remember any of their names, relationships, or occupations. Maybe it wasn't so closely.

The restaurant was lovely. He'd picked her up on time. He'd given her a corsage to wear on her wrist that matched the pink of her uniform.

Hayden was considerate, sweet, and had reserved a table and pre-ordered wine. But he couldn't plan away his date's distraction.

"No," she said with a wide smile. "I'm having a good time. I just have some things on my mind."

"Like your job," he said. "Forgive me, but how did you end up in the coffee place? You have a degree."

"Yes," she said and sighed. "I've just had a lack of luck I think."

He nodded to the flower on her wrist. "You have luck now. I've heard they warn off evil spirits."

She smiled. "Good. I could use the back up."

"You're a very beautiful woman, Felicity," he said, reaching over the table to take her hand. "I was disappointed we missed each other the last time."

Hayden was too polite to point out they hadn't missed anything, she hadn't shown up at all.

"Yes."

"I hope we can do this again, continue to see each other. I know you have things on your mind but I'll… I want to be patient. I think we could have something worth waiting for."

And if it wasn't so cheesy, she might have been touched. She was touched. But… she wanted him to come around the table and yank her to her feet. She wanted to be thrown down and shouted at for not keeping her head. Rushe would never let her be distracted, he'd tell her to always be on guard. That was the kicker; she wanted Rushe, only Rushe. No amount of telling herself she had to accept he was out of her life could console her to the fact.

Hayden wasn't Rushe, and no man in her future ever would be.

"Thank you," she said. "I have had fun, and I'm sorry if I've been… elsewhere. I'll get things back on track, soon."

"We could have dinner this weekend," he said with an edge of hope. "Is that too soon?"

She shook her head. "That sounds lovely."

Hayden paid the bill and walked her out. He offered to take her home, but she assured him she was within walking distance and waited with him while he hailed a taxi. He'd leaned in to kiss her, and she'd closed her eyes to let him but… fireworks weren't in her future either. A nice man, and a nice kisser, this was her future.

Looping her gypsy purse around her wrist, she wrapped her wide scarf around her shoulders, and held herself in her own embrace. It had been seven days since she'd seen Rushe. The marks of their exploits were fading from her skin. Every morning she checked in the shower to see another bruise had vanished; his fingerprints no longer marred her skin.

She was shedding him from her body, just as she had to shed him from her mind and heart. The memories were so vivid, but most of their adventures still seemed like dreams. Had she really let him eat her for lunch on the kitchen table in the shack? Had she really asked for more after he ejaculated into her mouth?

The Flick her family saw, Hayden, and her colleagues at the library, and now at the coffeeshop saw, wasn't the Flick Rushe had seen. Had he known what was within her, as she'd known what was in him?

She saw goodness and light inside a man who claimed to be nothing but darkness. He'd seen a bold, uninhibited lover in the body of a woman who had never been anything but plain. If there had been a point of no return, she'd missed it. From that very first question, when he'd asked her if she was going to let him fuck her, the spiral had grown sharper and steeper. Even now, walking back from a date with another man, she thought about Rushe. Would he care she'd been on a date with someone else? It didn't matter. He would never know; she would never see him again.

A gray van squealed as it turned into the street. By the way it lurched, it had been lucky not to tip. The street was quiet and dark, so the noise was conspicuous. Under normal circumstances, she wouldn't have thought anything of it. Her recent adventures changed her perspective Were the people in the van running from something? In the midst of a car chase or fleeing a robbery scene?

Tightening her shawl, she smiled, and locked at her shoes again. A long hot bath would soothe her feet, which had blessedly been saved from heels for most of the last few weeks.

Tomorrow, she had to work at the coffeeshop. If she didn't buck up—

The screeching of wheels sounded again. She looked up just in time to see two ski-masked men leap out of the gray van careening to a halt beside her. The men picked her up, and giving her no time to scream, a hand clamped over her mouth. They bundled her into the van, and it started moving again at speed before the door was closed.

"What? No. No!" she objected and reached for the door.

One of the masked men caught her wrists and bound them together with a length of rope. As she tried to resist, the other held her down on the floor. Stuck on her back with no room for movement, when one of the men planted his foot on her shoulder, she was pinned.

The one not standing on her took off his mask. When she recognized John, her head fell to the floor with a thump. Being free hadn't lasted, and this time she had no assurance that Rushe was at the other end, like the last time John picked her up.

"Thought you'd appreciate us mixing it up," John said. "And we knew you'd never fall for the 'Rushe is in trouble' thing again."

"He's going to kill you," she said without doubt of its veracity.

"Might be difficult," John mused.

The other goon sat on a fold down chair opposite and didn't take off his mask, but he didn't seem to be listening either.

"Why?" she asked John.

"He's in trouble," John said with a grin, and she wanted to kill him herself. "For real this time, but you know what they say about the boy who cried wolf, so I figured this was easier."

"People saw me," she said. "They saw what you did on the street."

"A quiet street with its lights busted out, I doubt it. You don't live in the best neighborhood… which I guess you know, given what just happened. People keep themselves to themselves… besides the plates are phony."

"I was on a date with my boyfriend who will call me later. When I don't answer, he'll know something is wrong."

"Long term boyfriend?" John asked.

"Yes," she said, feeling triumphant.

"That didn't walk you home and screw you to the wall?"

"He has an early day tomorrow," she said, looking for an excuse.

"Yeah," John said. The top of her head was against the front seats that John looked over, she supposed, to watch out the windshield. "Guys usually let women with jugs like yours go to bed alone, just so they don't miss their alarm clock."

"You won't get your money again," she said. While she didn't expect them to pull over and let her out on the basis of that declaration, she couldn't just lie there doing nothing. "Does Rushe know? Does he know you're bringing me in?"

"Nope," John said, still looking forward.

"He'll be angry."

"I think that's the point."

"What kind of trouble," she asked. "You said he was in trouble."

Maybe asking this time was a sign of growth.

"The bad kind," John said.

She didn't have to ask about the good kind because she'd met him and mated with him a few million times. "Is he hurt?"

"Do you always talk so much?"

She thought about some of the things she'd said, and heard, of late. "Until Rushe tells me to be quiet."

"Now I'm telling you," John said.

"You don't know the secret password."

When his attention came down to her, she deliberately averted her eyes. Let him think what he wanted; she was done playing mouse. Her strategy didn't have the desired effect. Whatever she'd expected that to be. The rasp of adhesive snapped her head back. With a smug grin, John ripped the duct tape from the roll.

"No, I didn't—"

The tape came over her mouth.

"Much better," he said. "Get comfortable, you'll be down there a while."

The rollercoaster ride apparently wasn't finished. This time she was on her own. Rushe would be beyond livid… if he was still alive.

THIRTY-SEVEN

THE JOURNEY TOOK HOURS. She felt every single pothole as she bounced on the hard metal of the van floor. Every bump drove the boot heel of the man standing on her deeper. It didn't matter how she wriggled, he only pressed harder.

Rushe had paid her ransom, if she'd needed any more proof of him caring for her, that was it. But there she was going back to the place he'd saved her from, and she had no idea why, or what they wanted with her.

She'd prayed for the journey to be over because half of her body cramped and ached. That was until they slowed and she recognized the sound of gravel crunching under the wheels. Now she wanted to stay on the floor and on the road. She'd put up with the pain rather than go into that building again.

No amount of shifting and squealing through the tape moved the men, and why should it? These men were safe. They were workers completing an assignment. This experience was probably what all the women in that basement went through. The terror. Strange men grabbing you, hauling you around, throwing you down, and dragging you up, being bound and gagged, and probably blindfolded too. She'd been spared that last indecency this time around.

The van lurched to a halt, and her heart hammered in her chest so hard she got dizzy and lightheaded. She couldn't suck enough oxygen through her nose to combat her faintness. The rush of heat to her head made her close her eyes against the stars fluttering in her vision. When the drag of the van door opening assaulted her ears, her head rolled, but she was already being heaved out, and that was when she saw it. They weren't at the front of the building, they were at the side, and the stairs... descended. She was being taken downstairs.

SHE DIDN'T KNOW she'd lost consciousness until a slap jolted her head. Blinking up, another slap came, then another. Trying to get away, she found herself on a chair, a metal chair, her hands tied together at her lower back. When she tried to kick her legs, she learned they were tied too. She retched around gag across her mouth. The taste of blood mixed with the acid of vomit that roiled in her throat.

"I told you nothing can be done."

The voice laced with its European lilt was definitely Simone, but she couldn't see much in the darkened room. A light hanging low in front of her filled her view with shadow beyond. Still, she struggled to recover from her fainting spell.

"You awake, little girl?"

If she hadn't felt ill before, the sound of Skeeve's voice would've done it. She could tell by the cold draught over her chest that her uniform was ripped. Letting her head loll forward, she saw that everything but her nipples were on show. Even they peeked over the torn fabric when she breathed deeply.

"You're down here now," Skeeve cackled. "You're goin' out the back little girl, sold to the highest bidder."

"I can do nothing with her," Simone said.

"Keep her alive." That indifferent voice she recognized as Victor's. "For a day or two."

"Then?" Simone asked.

"She'll have served her purpose, won't she?"

With another slap, and a tug on her nipple, Skeeve dissolved into the shadow. With the scrape of metal on wood, a heavy door slammed. She could see nothing but the light and had no idea how big the room was. Was she alone? When would they come back? Rushe wasn't there. If he came back and saw her… he'd do anything they asked of him.

SHE TRIED TO ESCAPE her bounds to no avail. No one had come back. Something she should be thankful for if the feminine wail of desperation from beyond these walls was any indication.

Their screaming was nothing but a pathetic attempt at begging for mercy from the merciless. Useless, she was so pitiful that she appalled herself. She couldn't do anything but sit there and wait for whoever to do whatever they wanted with her.

Hours passed. Her body bawled in the agony it hadn't recovered from since her journey in the van. In the forced position on the chair, her discomfort only grew. Her upper arms were bound to the top corners of the chair back, her knees tied to the sides of the chair, leaving her legs wide open at a horrific angle. But her pain faded as she listened to the vicious cackle of torment punctuating the shrieks of women begging for their lives.

She'd had no food or water. Her blood wasn't circulating to her limbs, and she lost consciousness at least once more. The thump of a lock came before the scrape of the door opening. She tried to fortify herself against what would come, whatever that may be.

Except she heard the pant of breath, someone spat out, then the door was closed again. She wasn't alone. Who had been left there with her?

With the damp, short breaths wheezing from her lungs, panic was beginning to assert itself. She tried to slow her breathing. Except the more she fought it, the worse her hyperventilation became. Being scared wouldn't help anyone. Just like those tortured women who cried out despite being ignored, she couldn't do anything.

Tears stained her gag until she could taste the salt from her own body. Losing the moisture could be crucial if she wasn't hydrated soon, but she couldn't stop the fat rolls of liquid from skidding down her cheeks.

As she fought the urge to scream, another voice came from the ether.

"You're new."

A sobbing started, and seemed to be crowded by a second, then a third. Yet the voice that spoke was calm and quiet.

She couldn't see anyone but sensed someone coming closer. The knot of her gag was pulled from the top of her head, snagging her tooth on her lip in the process.

She gasped for the welcome air. "Who are you?" she coughed out, struggling to control her lungs need to heave in oxygen.

"There are six of us," the female voice said.

The woman who moved around her came into view through the harsh light of the lamp.

Thin as skin on bones, a vaguely blue dress hung on her shoulders. On the fabric, stains of blood, and vomit, and goodness only knew what, matched the bruises over her porcelain skin. She was tall but meek, somehow broken.

"They took me from the street more than a week ago," she said, sitting on the floor next to her.

"Can you untie me?" Flick asked.

"No," the woman said.

"What's your name?"

"Brianna."

"If you can untie me—"

"I can't," Brianna said.

"If we can get the door open—"

"We've tried." Brianna shook her head. "We've tried breaking out. The door is metal. It's three inches thick… Were you taken from the street?"

"Yes, but—"

"I've never seen them… The way they brought you in here… the small one, the Sniveller we call him—"

"Skeeve," she said. "They call him Skeeve. The woman is called Simone, and you're all in a derelict mansion of some kind."

"How do you know those things?"

"What are they going to do with us?" a voice from the blackness asked.

They were all in the same room, and no doubt restrained too.

She didn't want to answer the question. But it seemed only fair to be honest. Her words would be nothing to what these women would face when they were taken out of there.

"They're going to sell you, us…"

"Sell?" Brianna asked.

"Victor, he's a loan shark who wants to get into the big leagues," she said, so that at least if she didn't get out of this, these women would have the means to expose him if need be. "I don't know how, or why, but he's moving into this, human trafficking. Women like us… I think they pick women for their marketability."

Brianna had been pale before, now she was positively transparent. "How do you know this?"

"I've been here before," Flick said. "Not here but… upstairs. They held me for ransom."

"I don't have any money," the woman in the darkness said.

"It doesn't matter," Flick said. "They got paid for me, and a week later they snatched me from the street, just like I said."

"It's almost morning," Brianna said. "I heard them talking about going out today… I don't know why but…"

"Morning…" Flick said.

Dusk had been threatening when she'd been taken out of the van and brought down there. At least that was her guess from the encroaching night of the sky. So she'd been there all night.

"There are no windows down here," Brianna said. "I haven't seen the sun in…"

"Be careful what you wish for," Flick said, trying to order her thoughts.

What she wouldn't give for forethought. She didn't have the first clue how to get out of there, especially when she was still restrained.

"What do you mean?"

Not quite believing she was about to quote the man who'd captured her, twice, Flick answered Brianna. "I wouldn't be so eager to shorten your wait. As long as you're in here, you're safe."

"Safe," Brianna said. "Do you know how they treat us?"

"Alive in any form is better than dead," she said, reminding herself of the redhead she'd tried to save from Skeeve in the shack.

Rushe was right, Flick was different, but it wasn't him who changed her. Not only him. The things she'd seen in these last few weeks showed her the underbelly of humanity. The bottom feeders she'd been surrounded with made her bare her own teeth and she got it, she understood. Her fear wasn't what consumed her. It was anger.

These men had no right to touch her, let alone capture her. She was a human being with her own free will. It wasn't the right of anyone to sell her into slavery. They might be stronger, and they may be able to force her into things she would revolt against, but she wouldn't go quietly. Somehow, she'd see Rushe again, even if just to tell him that he was right: weakness had no place in this world.

THIRTY-EIGHT

SOME OF THE WOMEN CRIED, and then there was silence. She didn't know if they were sleeping, or if they'd been injured, because she still couldn't see them. Sleep was impossible for her with the light so close to her face, and she continued to fight her bonds. It didn't matter that they weren't getting looser. The bite of rope on her skin bloodied her, but she kept trying because she couldn't do nothing. She couldn't sit there and do nothing.

Not all the women were bound, but they stayed where they were, out of her sight. Maybe they'd been exposed to punishment for escape attempts. The goons made their money by breaking the will of others. Brianna seemed to be the strongest of the group, but the dullness in her eyes betrayed that she too had been toppled.

No one fed them and the hours dragged. Conversation was a ridiculous notion in their situation. None of them attempted it. She did try to get information from the other women. But from the pieces she cobbled together they were mostly bound or blindfolded when transported from one place to the next. One man was as faceless as any other when they were subjecting the women to their trauma.

Not all of them had been raped. One of the girls was young. From what the others said on behalf of the mute teenager, she was either underage or untouched. Both would get top dollar, and once again her stomach heaved. The other women, mostly Brianna, spoke on behalf of the youngster. Every word broke her heart.

Where was Rushe? He couldn't know she was down there.

Her eyes had been closed against the harshness of the light that blinded her. She must've lost consciousness again, The snap of ice-cold water gushed over her. With a gasp, she sputtered up as far as she could against her ties.

Skeeve and Glen stood in front of her holding a large metal basin, it must've been filled with the water they'd thrown over her.

"Boss wants to see you," Skeeve sneered.

Glen was behind her. When he loosened the bonds, she tried to stand, to fight, but collapsed to the floor. Her arms and legs had been in stress positions for so long that their strength was gone.

"Up!" Skeeve demanded. She tried to get to her hands and knees. Just as she managed it, he kicked her ribs knocking her over again. "Yeah, you're good and tired aren't you, little girl? No fight left in that stacked body. Up!"

Again, when she got up, he kicked her over, she snarled at him. Her limbs might not work, and her eyes might burn, but she was still better than him.

"Pathetic," she managed to croak. "Scut work again. Fetch, doggy."

"What are you doing?"

Women, six of them, were huddled together at the door. Each had their hands bound and were in various states of undress.

"He's the lackey," she said, not recognizing her own hoarse voice. "He just waits for his boss to throw the ball, like a pathetic puppy."

"He'll kill you," Brianna whispered.

"No, he won't," she said, struggling onto her hands and knees again. "He only does as he's told. He's a slave with perks, like being allowed to rape defenseless women, because there isn't a woman alive who would touch him voluntarily."

"You whore!" Skeeve said.

His boot made contact with her cheekbone, sending her sideways again. Pain burst in her eye, and blood flavored her tongue, but it was nothing compared to what she imagined would come. As she lay there on her back between the cowering women and the vengeful Skeeve, she made herself smile through the pain.

More than that, she laughed and rolled her attention to him. "He's gonna kill you," she said, and suddenly laughter seemed appropriate.

"You fucking slut!"

She didn't know where the burst of energy came from, but when Skeeve's boot swung toward her again, she blocked it and thrust it away, pouncing onto her knees in the process.

"You wanna watch him fuck me before he gouges out your eyes?" Being a victim was a state of mind, and it wasn't one she'd subscribe to, not anymore. "You want to listen to me beg him for more? God, it feels good when he fucks me, real hard, I beg him to fuck me. I want him to fuck me every minute of the day, Skeeve. He's a man, a real man, and you're scum."

Skeeve started toward her with his hands on his fly. "I'm gonna fuck you six ways—"

"Later!" Glen said, shoving him. "Don't keep the boss waiting."

Skeeve snarled and spat down on her.

She strutted with her eyes. "Yeah, do your job, slave."

Glen grabbed her hair and yanked her backward. "You get up on your feet and walk, bitch, or I'll drag you by the hair."

When he propelled her forward, she fell to her face but managed to scramble towards the other women being herded like sheep. New rope was tied on her bloodied wrists behind her back as they shuffled along a black corridor. A door was opened, and they went into another black room. Her fellow prisoners went to line up against the wall, so she followed, tucking herself in the farthest corner.

"On your knees," Glen said.

The other women complied, and she didn't know what else to do. She wanted to fight and object, but her comrades were broken, she'd be on her own.

Glen and Skeeve she knew, but the other three men in the room she didn't. Those three were big, bulky, and much more formidable than a weasel like Skeeve.

Skeeve and Glen went along the line, the former gagged the prisoners one at a time, while the latter put a black hood over each female head. Whatever was about to happen, they didn't want to be looked in the eye. They wanted the women faceless, or they wanted to be faceless to the women. Neither had positive connotations.

Skeeve came to gag her and took great pleasure in pulling the fabric tight. She looked him square in the eye; he would never have the satisfaction of her fear.

A door in the opposite corner opened, allowing light into the dimly lit room. The flash of it was the last thing she saw before the thick hood was tugged over her eyes.

Slimy hands fondled her breasts; she had to suppress the urge to headbutt forward. Luckily for him Skeeve sloped off; she was grateful to have the stench of him retreat.

Footsteps sounded. Were people coming into the room or leaving? Still drowsy from her time without sleep, food, or water, focusing was difficult. Keeping herself on her stinging knees took all her concentration. Then a door closed and the walking stopped.

"Everything under control?"

Victor. She recognized his voice and doubted he'd have traveled alone.

"Yeah," Glen responded.

If no one had departed, there were more men in the room. The three thugs, Glen, Skeeve, Victor, and whoever else. A sniffing sound came from the line. One of the women was crying. The youngster didn't cry. It was amazing that despite her terror, the littlest of them didn't give these men the satisfaction either. Or maybe she was numb to it, she could identify with that too.

"I'm gonna kill her. I swear to it. I'm gonna kill her."

Skeeve's sniveling never stopped. She wanted to crow over him; he could only be referencing her. She'd riled him up, and this time he had no one to shoot. If she hadn't had the gag in her mouth, she'd have started the next round. She would not curl up and play dead just because these men wanted her to.

If Rushe's bedroom games taught her anything, it was that respect was earned, and it wasn't earned when you rolled over in fear. She didn't cower from Rushe. Didn't fear him. If she could stand up to the face of his unflinching angry façade, she could stand up to anything.

The worst she could get was beaten, or raped, or killed. Given her current predicament, all of that would likely be in her future. If it was going to come anyway, why worry about delaying it.

"You shut it," Glen said.

Someone got smacked.

"Who?"

That word halted her thoughts. It stopped her heart and brought her chin up. Rushe. He was there in the room. He was alive. Her tears started again, not out of fear or pain, it was joy, complete relief that her love was there, he was alive.

"New girl," Glen said.

"She is disgusting." Simone was in the room as well.

"What we doing down here?" Rushe asked.

The fact that he didn't know scared her. No doubt they would use her to scare him. Skeeve and Glen had been certain in their words and actions. Victor ran the show. The hooligans were muscle, and Simone was… whatever she was.

"Been some concern," Victor said.

A silence followed, which made her think Rushe was waiting for someone else to speak. Did they know he could be sparse with his words? If no one else spoke, that meant Victor was waiting for Rushe to respond.

"I'm not interested in being fucked around," Rushe said.

"Seems to us you're not interested in being fucked of any kind," Victor said. "You a joto?"

"Yeah, I'm a fag," Rushe said. "Give me the key."

So they were locked in there. He was as much of a prisoner right now as her.

"I don't think that's it," Victor said.

"Think what you want," Rushe said. "Didn't know you spent so much time thinking about my dick."

She'd been right.

If Rushe hadn't been screwing other women, Victor had to suspect he released her. But the money had been paid. Had Rushe told them he handed her over after the cash or did Victor know the money was from Rushe? What reason could Rushe have for paying her ransom unless he admitted his feelings for her? Except if he had admitted his feelings to Victor, then Victor would have no cause to believe he couldn't demand more money.

Rushe was there, with these men, and had to have been for the previous week. The week between him dumping her at her parents, and her being snatched from the street. Rushe had come back. He had to have told Victor that her father paid the ransom, and that was when he handed her over.

Why would Rushe have come back? He didn't like any of the men there, let alone care if they got hurt. He was here alone. Why? And why did they need her?

"Boys have been noticing," Victor said, after the lengthy silence no doubt meant to put Rushe on edge. Victor didn't know his target at all.

"You got shit to say, spit it out," Rushe said, sounding more bored than nervous.

"You've never had any of the girls," Victor said.

"So? I'm not a rapist. Didn't know that was a qualifier for being part of your crew."

"It's not," Victor said, as cool as a cucumber. "You don't have to fuck them though, plenty of pretty girls here, Rushe, you don't even look."

"I'm not screwing around with the merchandise."

"Yeah, but you've not screwed anyone, not since that frisky bitch with the tits… you screw her before you took her back to daddy?"

"What's it to you?"

"You're a tough guy to read. You do what you're told and get the job done. But this isn't your gig, is it? You think every guy in this room here is a piece of shit."

"I don't hire 'em, and if you're gonna ask me to screw one of your fucking—"

"Not one of them," Victor said, switching his intonation like he wanted to be Rushe's buddy. "But look at it like this…You won't look at the merchandise. You haven't pulled a trigger since you've been here, and you think you're better than the rest of us. Why are you here?"

"I get my cut," Rushe said. "If you're gonna fuck me out of my money—"

"You want cash? I'll give you a cut of the ransom and you can walk."

"You want me to walk? Fine."

"Cool, what do you want? Fifty grand? A hundred? How much was the bitch worth? Two? I'll give you two, think of it as payment for servicing her hot bod. Man, she was a peach, how did her titties taste? Was she a squealer or a screamer…? What's up, Rushe? You don't look happy."

"He never looks happy," Simone drawled.

"Yeah," Victor said. "You're a superior sonofabitch… got some of the guys thinking… you a badge?"

No one said anything. What did that mean? What were they asking—it hit her at the same time Rushe spoke.

"You think I'm a cop?" Rushe asked, and damn if he didn't sound like he was smiling. "Right… fuck."

There was movement, then the crack of flesh on bone. Someone called out in pain. She was almost positive it was Skeeve. She would have smiled if she had space behind her gag.

"That doesn't mean shit," Victor said. "We all wanna hit him in the face."

"I'm a cop?" Rushe asked. "Come on…"

Consent, he always needed consent when they had sex. But she didn't have a clue of the rules cops followed, what they were and weren't allowed to do. Surely, they weren't allowed to… some of the places they'd had sex would be considered illegal, but for all she knew cops were above that.

She would be the first to admit Rushe was a better man than every other man there, better than any man she'd met in her life. He'd come back by choice, and that took cojones. But if he was a cop, it made sense, he could be undercover for some reason. It put so many things in perspective, about why he didn't want her hurt, about why he protected her. Cops could talk dirty and have rough sex too… she was almost sure anyway.

"Pride aside, you're small time… why would I waste the time?" Rushe asked. "I've been working with you for months."

"Yeah, but you came from nowhere."

"You know the history of every man you hire?" Rushe asked. "Fuck it. Give me the dough and I'm gone."

"You wanna walk out that door when we're about to make the big sell?" Victor said. "You gonna walk away?"

"It's not worth this shit. You expect me to have some ID number tattooed on my ass? You think that's why I don't get naked with your whores? Who knows what shit they got?"

"You fucked the Dell's bitch."

"Yeah," Rushe said. "You think she was a plant?"

"Could be," Victor pondered.

"Fuck!" Rushe said. "What is it? You want me to fuck one of your bitches? That help you sleep at night? That take your mind off my cock?"

"Yeah," Victor said. "It will."

"Fine," Rushe said. "Give me a rubber and you got it."

"Pick one," Victor said.

Their voices came from the far corner, but they were talking about the line of women on their knees, which included her. Skeeve snickered but abruptly stopped, which must have been on a silent warning from someone else in the room.

"Pick?" Rushe asked.

"Yeah. You can have any one of them you want," Victor said. "Except the one on the end, you can't have her."

"She special?"

"Not to me," Victor said. "But the point is to prove you're capable of mixing it up so you don't want that one."

"Why not?"

"Because..." Victor said. "You've had her."

A rush of air warned her of someone approaching. When the hood was whipped off, she blinked through tears that prevented her from focusing her eyes. There were a dozen forms she could make out the shapes of bodies. While she was drawn to his, she couldn't see his eyes, not through the scratch of her own.

THIRTY-NINE

"FUCK."

On the quiet exhale of breath, Rushe cursed. She wanted to apologize. Wanted to tell him this wasn't his fault and that he could never have foreseen this. They came to her; they came to get her, because they wanted to show him they had something of his.

While she was there, they could try to control him. Being in the basement and with what she'd been told, she was to be sold, just like the other girls. Maybe the point wasn't to keep Rushe in line, or even to have him screw anyone.

If the next shipment went out with her in it, then Victor would know Rushe was capable of anything. Of turning his back on the only thing that anyone had noticed meant anything to him, or at least that was what they suspected.

"We picked her up. Stroke of luck, huh?" Victor said, waiting for Rushe's reaction.

"You want me to fuck her, fine, where's the rubber?"

"Oh no, no," Victor said. "You can't have her. She's got rounds to do."

Through the smear of tears over her lenses, she saw his fists ball and flex. He couldn't lash out and couldn't control this either. The door was locked, and they were outnumbered. He had to hold onto his indifference. She couldn't. Try as she might to muster confidence or detachment from the situation, it only caused more tears to gather.

"I think she's upset. And the boys have been treating her so well too… you'll find a way to cheer her up, won't you, boys?" A collective muttering went around the room then settled again. "Shame you're not into the merchandise," Victor said, moving in at Rushe's side. "You could've showed us just how she likes to be fucked."

"What do you want?" Rushe growled.

Though his lips didn't move, the set of his jaw betrayed he clenched his teeth. When her tears cleared, his eyes were trained on her. The venom in them, the anger, made her own attention drop to the floor. She was exactly what she didn't want to be for him: a liability.

"This is fun," Victor said.

The bastard was just like Skeeve, and Glen, and all the others. Victor was enjoying this perversion. Tormenting Rushe like this was sport. This was all just one big chessboard to Victor. Check.

"What do you want?" Rushe asked again.

She still couldn't bring herself to lift her face.

When the hot copper built in her mouth, she couldn't swallow down the liquid quickly enough. Inhaling made her choke, and with the gag in place, she couldn't cough out. Retching again, she lurched forward, but had no hands to catch herself on.

"Take it off before she chokes on her own blood," Victor demanded, annoyed by her outburst as though it was somehow voluntary or contrived.

Skeeve dug his knee into her back and sliced the gag from her face. She deliberately turned to cough blood on his lap, spraying it up to his tee-shirt.

"Fuck!" he said and grabbed at her throat to shove her away.

"You want to fight again," she snarled, still on her side on the floor. "I think I won the last time. You're so weak, it's pathetic."

"Why you fucking—"

His fist came up, and she closed her eyes, braced for the punch, except someone appeared at his back and snatched Skeeve's raised fist.

In an instant, Rushe had Skeeve off his feet and hurled him to the other side of the room. Rushe didn't follow, he stayed in front of her, his boot heels less than a foot from her face on the black floor. Although it couldn't last, in that half second, she found peace. He gave her the cover to relax, though if he knew it, he'd tell her to get her guard up.

"Everybody relax," Victor said. "Skeeve, you little shit, don't fuck with the woman while he's in the room, you do that once he's gone. Which you're gonna do right now, Rushe. You're going upstairs… with Simone."

She knew what that meant. Rushe wasn't capable of forcing himself on a woman. It seemed Victor was happy to accept that fact. Simone would consent. Perhaps for the men in this gang Simone was a rite of passage.

"What?" Rushe barked at Victor.

Rushe hadn't looked at her. He hadn't turned. But his body remained between her and them, while she cowered like a wounded animal. No, she needed to gather her strength and again dragged herself up to her knees. With one shaking calf, and a screaming thigh, she got her weight onto one foot. Steadying herself on the wall, she'd never be able to hold all her weight but got the other foot under herself and stood.

"You just don't know when to quit," Victor said, admiration glowing in his tone. "You're gonna be a tough one."

Her eyes remained locked on Victor even when Rushe stepped aside to see what the boss had. Victor wouldn't break the stare, so she wouldn't either.

"What's the worst you can do to me?" she asked, once again finding her smile. "Don't send those sacks of shit to do a real man's job." She tipped her chin in the direction of Skeeve and Glen, keeping her focus on the boss.

"The bitch has got game," Victor said, sauntering closer. "I get what you saw in that, Rushe. You've got taste."

When Victor approached, Rushe stepped into his path, getting his shoulder in Victor's way to block her body from the boss's proximity.

Victor drew his eyes around to Rushe while his tongue pressed the inside of his cheek. "You wanna scent the bitch?" Victor asked. "You sure you wanna do that?"

While there was a battle of testosterone, she tried not to make a sound. Rushe's position was impossible, just like hers. Taking his sight from Victor in an instant, Rushe stepped out of his way.

"That's what I thought," Victor said. "You do your business with Simone. The boys here will take care of the girl for you."

Victor leered at her all but exposed chest, and she wanted to spit blood again. But this was the man in charge. If he ordered a bullet, it would happen. She couldn't die until Rushe knew she didn't blame him. He would take the responsibility for her death onto his shoulders and would never forgive himself. Victor's finger touched the swell of one breast and traced down toward her nipple. His hands on her flesh made her nauseous, but she set her jaw. The tears came of their own volition. She couldn't stop him, but wouldn't cower, she was getting used to bullies.

"Go!" Victor hollered

The three hulky men came toward Rushe, but he held up a hand. She sensed his reluctance, the room probably did, and he would hate for anyone to see his weakness. Intentional or not that's what she was. Simone held out a hand showing a key, and when Rushe started toward her, the European put the brass into the lock. On the action, Simone looked back at her, more than pleased to be gaining an advantage. Rushe would screw Simone… but he'd never smile at her.

She didn't expect Rushe to look back and he didn't. Simone opened the door. Rushe had the three hulks at his back. The streak of light behind the door revealed there were three men of equal girth waiting to walk in front. Six guys… She didn't rate their odds.

As soon as the door was closed behind Rushe, Skeeve and Glen were on their way over. She expected another confrontation, but they each started to haul the other women to their feet.

"I'm sending him down," Victor said to Glen. "I've got no patience on this. It's one or the other you hear me?"

She doubted he meant Rushe when he spoke about sending someone down. The door they'd entered by opened, and Glen started to shove the other women back down the corridor.

"Where are we going?" she asked. "What's going on?"

"Rushe is gonna move on now," Victor gloated. "Which means you're going out with the shipment tomorrow."

She'd known that was the next chapter and was under no illusions about that. "What about Rushe? What happens to him?"

"Pastures new," Victor said. "Unless…"

"Unless what?"

"You're luckier than the other girls here," Victor said, moseying in close and propping his arm on the wall beside her head, letting himself lean on her while Glen closed the door behind him, Skeeve, and the other captive girls.

That left her alone with Victor.

"And you're going to tell me why," she said.

"Yeah." Victor touched her navel through what was left of her uniform as his mouth came closer to hers. "I'm the man with all the cards."

"Let me guess," she said. "If I consent to join you in the room next to Rushe and Simone, I get out of jail."

Victor's lips curled up into what was supposed to be a smile, seeing it made her ill. "I get what Rushe saw in you," he said. "But I've got a dozen girls in this place who'll lick my lollipop any time I want it. Not sure I could trust a woman with your…"

"Fangs," she said, ensuring to show her teeth when she smiled.

She'd once warned Skeeve if he put anything unpleasant in her mouth, she'd bite it off. Victor would get exactly the same deal. Only she might not be polite enough to warn him ahead of time.

"I can let you go back to your daddy, forget you ever saw this place."

"Why would you do that?" she asked. "You went to all the trouble of abducting me… twice."

"I did," he said. "And fun as it was to watch Rushe on the hook; I brought you here for something else."

"Something else?"

"If he's a cop that might… stall my expansion."

"If he's a cop you're going to jail. You and your perverted friends."

"I've got friends in high places, sweetheart," Victor said. "So don't bet on that."

She rolled her eyes left to right, before pinning them on him again. "Except word on the street is you've got a bit of a God complex, and… not the goods to back it up."

"That what Rushe told you?"

"Ah," she said in comprehension. "Pillow talk, you wonder if Rushe has a loose tongue. You want to know what I know."

"Could say that," he said, admiring her body again.

She was unmoved. "Problem is… when a woman's had a man like Rushe… well, let's just say, sloppy seconds aren't so appealing."

"He works for me," Victor ground out.

"You're not very sure about that, are you? What is it with you lowlife scum suckers? Why are you so threatened by Rushe? Is it because you take one look at him, and know you'll never be the best, because the best is what you're looking at?"

Victor backed off. Any genial emotion vanished from his face, and his stance. "I thought we could be pleasant about this. You give me what I want, and I let you go… I see you're not a professional."

"I've not been in the game long," she said. "But I was instructed by the best."

"You think a lot of the man who just turned his back on you. How do you feel knowing he's up there fucking another woman? You guys partners? Colleagues? Tell me."

"If I was a cop, I think I'd have called for backup by now."

"Would you?" he asked. "So why hasn't your buddy upstairs called it in?"

"How do you know he hasn't?" she asked. "One thing I've learned about your game is that you've gotta have the stomach for it. You gotta be a man who can hold his load… a man with balls."

With a swift backhand, her head snapped to the side, but her eyes returned to his a second later.

"You're one smart mouthed puta, aren't you? You talk to Rushe like that?"

"Only when I want him to wash my mouth out."

"I can do that too," he sneered.

"Oh, I hope you try it," she said. "Please."

A heavy clunk echoed in the space, and the door Rushe had exited by opened. She held her breath, hoping it could be him coming back for her. It wasn't. It was John… and Shiv.

"Do what you want," Victor said to them. "But she's out the door tomorrow either way."

Victor glared at her, then marched through his men to exit.

"What do you two want?" she asked, uneasy by how Shiv limped.

The vengeance he'd wanted could be his now. The only thing between him and the victory of punishing her was the width of this empty room.

"We want it all bitch…" Shiv said, "and we're gonna get it from you."

FORTY

SHE DIDN'T HAVE MUCH TIME for panic, and there was nowhere to run. John rushed at her, ducking to dig his shoulder into her belly to fling her over it.

Shiv led the way through the door Skeeve and Glen had used. Her attempts to kick loose were fruitless, John's arm just clamped her legs tighter against him. The corridor was narrow, but with her hands still bound behind her back she had no way to reach out.

Shiv waited to get behind them and sneer at her. Whatever lay in her future, he was looking forward to it. The sick bastard. She had no way to help herself, not a fighting chance. How could these men relish triumphing over defenseless women?

Although it wouldn't help, she screamed. Frustration, anger, hate, all the negative emotion burst out of her in a long howl. Only the women still locked in their cell would hear her. They may envy her liberation. But she wasn't free. She was helpless, and Victor was doing all he could to remind Rushe he was powerless too.

Obviously, Victor was worried enough about Rushe's potential identity to kidnap her. To do it in the way that they had, with the van on the street, John and the others must've been watching her. They'd known where she was.

Other than her date with Hayden, she had no reason to be on that street at that time. They'd known where to pick her up. If they knew that, they had to know she wasn't a cop. That didn't mean they were as confident about Rushe.

If he was a cop, there would be some kind of protocol, some way to check in with superiors. Maybe his colleagues would get worried and come looking for him.

Her captors stopped to unlock a door once, twice… three locks. She couldn't see the door from her angle but noted this end of the black painted passage wasn't lit at all. Fingernail scratches in the wall were the only sign anyone had been there before her. The curled paint showed a desperation, a need to live, a fight for life. If her hands were free, she may have left her own mark.

"That's right," Shiv said, leaning in to whisper in her ear. "You ain't never getting out of here."

Shattered, fraught, and completely powerless, she screamed again as John carried her into a dark room. Disorientated again, she tried to fathom something, anything, in the darkness, but was thrown off-kilter again when John tossed her from his shoulder. The awakening of hitting ice-cold water, freezing water that shocked her lungs into taking a desperate gasp was abrupt. She tried to clamber away but was thrust back into it.

A sudden blinding white light spiked her anxiety. What was going on? Where was she? Soaked to the skin, she fought the shivering to get to her feet, and look around through webbed lashes. Another black room. A light on the ceiling. A circular tub, six feet diameter and maybe two or three feet deep, the water lapped at her thighs.

Scanning the room, she turned and paused at a surprising sight. A person, there in the corner, on the floor, blank, motionless. If the stranger hadn't blink through her blind stare, she might have assumed the woman was dead.

"Wanna know how long she's been here?" Shiv said on a depraved laugh. "Shame you're not gonna get the boss's mercy like she did. You wanna know why he kept her alive? Almost offed her a couple of weeks ago, but he wants to make it slow, real painful. He's gonna make it count; make sure he got an audience. You're not gonna get that, you're out the back door."

"Shut up," John said, retrieving a canvas roll from his back pocket. "Got any phobias?"

"Yes," she said, and he glanced up in surprise. "The great outdoors and three course meals."

John smiled. "You're funny," he said. "We don't get a lot of that."

"Worth asking," she said. "That's why you asked about the phobias, right? You don't try, you don't succeed. I'm just adopting your philosophy."

Her teeth chattered, but she glanced back at the woman again. Her body was covered with nothing more than an old shirt, torn and stained, but the woman didn't notice. Still, the blonde hair and the long legs made her a beauty… if someone could look beyond the trauma. They'd broken her, just like they planned to try on her.

"What's her name?" she asked.

"Serendipity," Shiv said. John shoved him, then crouched to unroll the canvas. "What? Bitch isn't gonna make it out of here alive, is she?"

"Ironic, isn't it?" John said, standing up again. "She could use some serendipity… so could you."

"Why am I here?" she asked, then regretted it when Shiv lunged forward and grabbed her to wrestle her to her knees in the water. "You're gonna give us information."

John shoved Shiv aside and crouched in front of her. Just when it appeared John might be kinder, he took a handful of her hair and thrust her face into the water. The blood from her mouth and wrists stained the water. Crimson clouds billowed in front of her burning eyes and soundless scream.

With a tug, he brought her head out of the water. She sputtered and gasped, fighting for oxygen. John kept hold of her hair with one hand, while the other dragged wet hair from her mouth.

"That's a sneak preview," John said.

"What is it?" she asked, still gasping. "What is it that you want?"

"Rushe," Shiv said.

Beyond John, Shiv leaned against the wall, presumably struggling with his limp to stand without aid. That man wanted blood, her blood. His standing there, looking on, with such a malevolent determination, terrorized her. Her guts roiled. This could be it. This could be her end.

"You have Rushe," she said to Shiv. "What are you doing here?"

"We work in shifts," John said. "You don't give me what I want… he gets his turn."

John let her go. Without her hands, she fell face first under the water. Her attempt to push up was thwarted when his hand hit the back of her head on its way back up. She shook, writhing for oxygen, for a glimpse of air. If she let the reality of what was happening, the inevitably of her fate, overtake her, she would die there, in that cold water, without ever telling Rushe none of this was his fault.

In the last prison chamber, she'd been desperate for water, and now she was deprived of air. Hadn't she told Brianna to be careful what she wished for. She should've taken her own advice.

John hauled her head out of the ice-pool by her hair. She tried to shake the water from her body, but the shivering impeded her breathing too.

"It's cold," John said. "What do you think it will be, the hypothermia or the drowning…? Drowning's supposed to be a good way to go, that's what I heard."

"I thought you were nice to everyone?" she spat out, her throat scratchy.

"Don't wish me away," John said. "The water's the kindest option around here. I'd tell you to ask Serendipity, but it's been what…? Four months since she said a word?"

"Four months?" She exhaled. Suddenly her predicament wasn't so bad. "You've had her here for four months?"

"Closer to six," John said. "Are you gonna tell me what I want to know?"

"You haven't asked me anything," she said.

"What do you know about Rushe? What do you know about why he's here?"

"Nothing," she said.

"Who are you really? What is he, your boyfriend?"

"Yes, he's my boyfriend," she chattered, the cold seeping into her bones. "Can I go now?"

"What do you know? What happened on the trip back to your daddy?"

What was she supposed to say?

"He took me to my father."

John dunked her into the water. "Wrong answer," he said, pulling her back up. She barely heard him through her own choking. "He was gone for days, where did you go?"

"To my father."

Another face full of freezing water. She couldn't gasp. Couldn't breathe. If she opened her mouth… Every atom in her body thrashed and bucked, fighting for the chance of air. But he was stronger. Much stronger. On the next ascent, she spat water from her mouth and fought to breathe. Coughing through her burning lungs, her resolve didn't waver. Yes, she wanted to live, but she'd let them hurt her, she would endure this.

Even if she gave in, and told them everything she knew about Rushe, it wouldn't matter. One way or the other, they'd made it clear she wasn't getting out of this. Shiv was sure she wouldn't get out of this room alive and judging by the stories Rushe told her on that first night in Dell's, these men were more than capable of murder.

What she had done to Shiv in the shack was in defense of Rushe. What Rushe had done to him upstairs in this very building was in defense of her. After everything she'd been through, evil was becoming familiar. Talking wouldn't keep her alive, only a miracle would do that.

Rushe was somewhere, on one of the floors above them in the embrace of another woman. His torture was nothing to what she endured there with these men. But, in his own way, he was a prisoner too. Without Victor's trust, Rushe's own card would be marked too.

"Who did he talk to?" John asked. "Does he have a contact? Who is he working with?"

The man in the diner. The one she recognized from Dell's. Rushe could be working both sides. Maybe he was a double agent for one of Victor's competitors. That could pay well. It was a hell of a risk, so she assumed he'd want danger money.

"No one," she said. John lugged her back to slap both of her cheeks. "You're gonna die here, Felicity. Is he worth that? Worth dying for? You're gonna die for a man who's fucking another woman as we speak? Is he worth it?"

"Yes."

"He's up there with Simone. She knows how to do things to a man that will make his eyes roll from their sockets."

"Says the voice of experience," she said. "Did Victor put a gun to your head and make you have sex with her too? What's wrong with the woman that you men don't want to get naked with her? You should get her and Skeeve together."

"Tell me," John shouted, ignoring her taunting. "Tell me who he spoke to, who was with him? Was he alone? Did he have a partner?"

"I don't know anything," she said. "We went to my father's, that's it."

John threw her backwards into the tub. She fell under and immediately scrambled to get out again. At the same instant she broke the surface, the door opened.

Spluttering, she fought to get her bearings. John was at the door talking to someone. Shiv hobbled over to join them. Two men stood behind the one talking to John, rushing them would do no good.

John glanced over his shoulder at her.

Shiv started to swear. "Fuck, no! No way! I get my turn!"

John continued to talk for a few seconds, then shrugged and came back to her. "You've got a reprieve," he said. "For the time being."

Without thought of being gentle, he dragged her out of the tub and across the floor to the other men. Unfortunately, she caught sight of the canvas from John's pocket laid out on the floor. Inside were a bunch of vicious metal tools. She didn't want to imagine what they were for.

One of the men stopped to lock the door behind them again. Why were they so thorough? The Serendipity woman was out of it. They'd broken her. They'd won. Why would they hold onto this one woman, or rather why would she be separated from the others and so well guarded?

They went back down the corridor. Instead of going into the cell with the other women, she was taken past that door, to another on the opposite side.

John fumbled with locks as the men closed in around her. She hadn't had this much attention when they went to the water room. Why would they give her it now? Escape sounded like a great idea, but she wasn't sure how much fight remained in her.

When John got the door open, someone cut the binds from her wrists. He swung the door back, and she was shoved inside. No one followed this time. The door was shut and locked behind her.

FORTY-ONE

NO ONE CAME INTO THE ROOM because there was someone there already. Its tenant looked like thunder itself.

The added protection wouldn't have been adequate if he'd chosen to fight his way through the others. But it was unlikely they would get far in any escape attempt when there were so many variables, and most likely other men in the building. Men who'd shoot to kill.

"Hello, Lover," she said to the man sitting on the single bed in a room not much larger than their accommodation in the shack a lifetime ago.

Seeing him was unexpected. It bolstered her strength, reminded her the fight was worth it. His anger seeped from his every pore; she was familiar with the feeling.

He was sitting forward, elbows on his knees, and his hands clasped. "You're like a fucking boomerang, you know that?"

"Why are you here?"

"Me?" he asked, flying off the bed. "What the fuck are you doing here?"

Her teeth began to clack again. "They snatched me off the street."

"Don't tell me you went back to your old place. You should've stayed with your family."

"You told me there was no more danger. You said no one would come looking for me."

The latter statement had been made when he liberated her the first time. Granted, a lot had transpired since then, but still he had said it.

"You have no idea what you've walked—"

"Look at me!" she screamed, matching his anger with her own. "Do you see the bruises? Do you see the blood? Don't tell me what I know! I know damn well what they're going to do with me! And I know they'll take pleasure in it. Don't you dare fucking stand there and tell me that I don't know, Rushe, don't you do it! Don't you dare!"

"Take off your clothes," he said, grabbing the neck of his tee-shirt to pull it off over his head.

"What?" she asked, somewhat deflated by his indifference to her outburst.

"Your… is that a uniform?"

"Yes," she said. "You want to have sex with me? With everything that's going on you think…? You want to have sex with me?"

She didn't know whether to laugh or beat him about the head.

He thrust his tee-shirt toward her. "You're cold."

With those clipped words, he turned his back. Right. Cold. Her clothes were soaked through. She had to get out of them, get warm.

"Tell me what they did to you," Rushe said, still with his back to her.

He hadn't done that since her early days in the shack, when he knew she felt violated. The tension in his shoulders kept him rigid, his huffed words revealed frustration.

"No," she said, putting on his tee-shirt.

At the clean, masculine smell of him brushing her nose, tears sprang up again.

"No?"

"No," she said again, kicking her sodden uniform to the corner.

Another torn dress, another cell, another single bed, and all because her cab broke down.

The bed was less than two feet away, but when her throat closed, and her legs gave out, she collapsed to the floor. Lying in the fetal position, she covered her face with both hands and let herself sob. Her body ached, her soul screamed for mercy, but no one could deliver.

These horrible, despicable, evil men would taunt and torture her, and then her body would be sold on as property. The possibilities of where she could end up were too petrifying to imagine.

But they couldn't see her there. Soon every tear she shed would be to the depraved pleasure of whoever purchased her. Anyone willing to buy a person had to be sick.

Whatever use they found for her would be humiliating and excruciating. She had to void her thoughts, void any feelings she had for anything. The child in the shared cell seemed to have managed it. Brianna and the others did. Serendipity certainly had. She got it. It wasn't about them breaking her, yes, that gave them pleasure, but she had to break. Fighting would get her nowhere. If she let herself feel, if she let herself hope, then her torture would endure.

Serendipity managed to block it out, after months in that room, and with these men. Numbing yourself to reality, teaching yourself to detach, it was a defense mechanism. She had to make it a way of life. Whatever life she had left would be too unbearable otherwise.

When a heavy hand landed on top of her head, she hissed out, throwing her anger and hatred at whoever dared to touch her. But then she saw him. Saw his concern, his pain, and a torture all of his own.

Rushe sat there in front of her screaming an apology with his eyes. None of this was his fault, and none of it was hers, but that really only made the futility worse.

"Kitten."

One murmured word and everything was said that needed to be. When she crawled toward him, he opened his arms, and she let herself fall into him. His embrace could shield her from everything. Maybe he couldn't make the physical fall away, neither of them could help themselves or each other. But they had this, perhaps the last pleasant experience she would ever have.

He let her sob and stroked her waterlogged hair while holding her so tight, so close, that she wanted to believe their bodies could forever merge to one. When the tears stopped, she was terrified to look at him. He'd never be cruel, not now, but he'd want to comfort her, to tell her that he would take care of things and save her. Except there was nothing he could do.

"Why aren't you with Simone?" she whispered, closing her eyes, and pressing her damp cheek against his hot, bare chest.

"I didn't want Simone," he said.

She tried to figure out what that meant, and how he'd ended up there. When she couldn't come up with anything, she lifted her head, relaxing on his upper arm to look at him.

"You didn't want Simone?" she repeated.

"No."

"I don't know what that means."

"It means she's a whore. I don't want a whore."

"I'm a whore."

With his large hand, he clumsily shoved her hair from her face. "No, you're not."

"I'm not?"

"No," he said.

He wouldn't meet her eye. Reality blurred with fiction. In her dizzy mind, it wasn't easy to recall what was truth and what was lies.

"So much has happened."

"How long have you been here?" he asked.

"I don't know."

"Where have they been keeping you?"

"Down here," she said. "I was in a room with a group of women. They have a teenager in there, Rushe, did you know that?"

His hand stopped. "No."

Urging her back to his chest, he tucked her head under his chin. He wouldn't, or couldn't, look at her face.

"I was in there and then they brought us all into that room where you were."

"Who hit you?"

"Skeeve," she said. "Mostly. But I deserved it… at least I gave it back to him. I might not be strong, but I have a smart mouth… or so I'm frequently told."

"Did anyone touch you…? Did they…?"

"No one raped me," she said. "If that's what you're asking."

"That won't last."

Rushe didn't know how to sugar coat anything.

"Why are you here?" she asked. "Why are you locked up?"

"You heard them out there, they don't trust me."

"Why not?" she asked. "I thought once you were… you didn't have sex with Simone?"

"No."

"When you refused," she said, trying to figure it out, "they put you in here."

"Yes."

"They think you're a cop. They can't just kill you if you're law enforcement, that would bring their house down."

"I guess."

"Victor's a piece of work," she said. "He asked for information."

Rushe tensed. While his body went rigid, his embrace loosened. "What did you tell them?"

"Nothing," she said. "I don't know anything."

"Victor asked you questions?"

"Yes," she said. "But he got angry when I wouldn't answer them. That's when he sent me out with John and Shiv, who brought me back here."

"John? What did he ask?"

"They wanted to know about you. About anything you've told me, about anything I saw."

That last statement made him draw back. She was left alone on the floor when he separated himself from her to sit a few feet away.

"What did you tell them?"

God, he was good. That anger was back, he ground his teeth together.

"I told them that you had a monster stuffed animal collection," she said, but he only glared.

Now that he was angry with her, he could look her in the eye. Distance was so much easier to accept than familiarity.

She used the bed to pull herself up and slithered onto it, letting every muscle in her body loosen.

"What are you doing?" he demanded. "Tell me what you said!"

She didn't even bother to open her eyes. Judging by the angle of his voice, he was on his feet at the side of the bed. But letting her swollen cheek sink into the mattress, she took advantage of this last chance to rest.

"I didn't tell them anything," she said. "Why do you think I'm cold, wet, and covered in bruises? Do I look like someone who blabbed to save themselves?"

"They tortured you," he whispered.

"They didn't get onto the fierce looking metal instruments, so don't trouble yourself. I told them that yes, you were worth dying for. Even though you were fucking another woman at that moment in time. Or we thought you were." She couldn't open her eyes. "Now if you don't mind, I haven't slept or eaten since I got here, and the adrenaline's wearing off. So unless you're willing to share your body heat, leave me alone… please."

Rushe didn't say anything else. She took that as a sign he'd conceded his argument. If she'd told them what they wanted to know, she'd probably be dead already. Shiv would've taken great pleasure in cutting her, according to Rushe, that was his thing. Skeeve might be allowed to take a turn with her, but she doubted Shiv had that kind of restraint. Good. That was actually a comfort. Better dead than let Skeeve come anywhere near her. If not and they beat her again, or she was restrained, or unconscious, she'd never be able to fight him off.

Skeeve would be the tip of a large iceberg if she went out with the other women the next day. Were the women trafficked in this country or overseas? The logistics didn't matter. Bottom line, it was barbarity. Like most of the population, human trafficking were words without meaning. Of course not, how could society face such ugly exploitation?

Soon, she'd be gone and Rushe would be alone. Not that her being present did anything for him. She'd wonder about him… in her final weeks or months… if she got that long.

Someone touched her. In reflex, she recoiled, but Rushe just scooped her up and lay down to drape her over him, just as he'd done in the shack.

Except this time, it was different.

She peeked up at him. With his hand behind his head, his focus stayed on the ceiling. To reassure him, and herself, she pressed her lips to his torso, and gently rubbed her cheek on the same spot. Eventually, they would come to get her or take Rushe away. They lay there together on that narrow bed with the knowledge a bomb hid under them. Only this bomb didn't have a timer that they could watch the seconds descend on. Without warning, they would be torn apart, and after they were, they'd never see each other again.

FORTY-TWO

A PIERCING SCREAM jolted her awake. On springing up, her knee landed in his abdomen. But she ignored Rushe's displeasure to take quick stock of her surroundings. A room, painted black, the bed in the corner, and Rushe.

"Rushe," she sighed out, and flopped back down onto him.

"Harsh wake up call," he grumbled.

"I'm sorry," she said, squeezing her hand between them to pat the part of him she'd kneed.

"No problem. Just don't aim further south next time."

Everywhere was sore with bruises and tense muscles but lying out on Rushe was an experience she'd missed. "What time is it?"

"Eleven thirty," he said.

She peeked at him. "How do you know that?" He took his hand from the back of his head to show his wristwatch. "Ah," she said, settling down again. "At night or in the morning?"

"P.m.," he said. "We've got some time."

"Until what?" she asked, stretching her body over his, yawning. His lack of a response was unsettling. "Until what?"

She sat up. Her knees parted over him, straddling his stomach. At the reminder of her apparel, she looked down. Flesh touched flesh. While she still wore her thong, it didn't offer much of a barrier between them.

"I'm not having sex with you," he said.

She smiled at him. "Isn't that what I'm supposed to say?"

"I know what happens when you get that look," he said. "And I'm not having sex with you."

"Not that I'm saying I want to, but why not?"

"I don't know if they're listening."

As though a bug would suddenly become neon when he said the magic words, she looked around. "Listening?"

"It's the only reason I can come up with that they would put us together."

"Sure," she said. "Except they seem to enjoy watching us squirm."

"I've done everything I can to protect you. I've played all my cards. I pushed you away time and time again, for your own good."

"I know. I just want you to be honest with me. Please do that for me now. No more games, no more lies and misdirection. After tonight… we'll never see each other again."

"I'm sorry you got involved, Kitten," he said, dropping a hand to her hip.

"It's not your fault," she said, tentatively touching her face to explore her bumps and bruises.

"It is my fault," he said. "You're here right now because of me."

"I'm not," she said. "I walked into Dell's of my own free will. How many times do we have to go over this?"

"This isn't about Dell's, not anymore."

"So what's it about?"

"You're here because… because they know I care about you," he hissed through gritted teeth.

"That wasn't so painful, was it?" she said, placing a hand over his heart. "The walls didn't come tumbling down, did they?"

"I've never…" His expression remained as static as ever, but she saw him swallow away the foul taste of his words. "I've never cared about anyone before. I cared about the job, but I… I didn't know it felt like this."

"I make you weak," she said.

"Yeah, and I resent the hell out of you for it but… any resolve I've had before, in the past… I'd do anything to keep you safe, Kitten. I might not be much use to you right now, but—"

"This is not your fault," she soothed with her words.

"You're here because of me."

"I missed you," she said. "If nothing else comes of this, then I'm happy I got to see you again." Sliding her hand up his chest, she cupped his cheek and leaned in. "You're a good man, Rushe. If you saw yourself as I see you…"

"I'm not a cop."

"I know," she said.

"So whatever fantasy you have about a shining hero… you know?"

"I know why you're here."

"How can you possibly…?"

She didn't need to know the specifics. He'd come there with a purpose greater than himself. But law enforcement was a stretch too far. Cops could smile, they didn't hate the world like he did. They weren't strangers to caring for others in the way Rushe was.

"I trust you," she whispered. "That's how I know."

"When I walked out of that room with Simone—"

"What could you have done?" she asked. "I thought about fighting too. I thought about escaping, but where could I go? This is an impossible situation for both of us."

Rushe took his hands under her hair to hold the back of her neck, his thumbs resting over her ears. "I want to have sex with you," he said.

"That was a quick turn around."

"But I think it's because…"

"It's the only way you think you're capable of comforting me or showing me how you feel."

"Look at what they did to your beautiful face," he said, and stroked her bruises with such delicate hesitancy her eyes misted again. "Am I hurting you?"

"No," she said, snatching his hand back to her cheek.

"You've got a black eye, and the blood, the—"

"Bruises heal," she said. "Hearing you admit that you care about me… it's worth every single one of them."

With almost apprehension, Rushe lifted his head and traced his lips on hers. Her cuts didn't make for much thorough kissing, and she couldn't let him taste her tongue for fear he'd taste her blood too. Yet their simple, gentle kiss was so potent. They'd done hungry for each other, desperate, devouring, and much as that lingered, this joining was so much more powerful.

She rested her lips on his and slid her hands between them to unbutton his jeans. Rushe took his head back, showing his uncertainty, but he didn't stop her. He let her ease his erection from its confines as she wriggled down, nudging her underwear aside. Oh, so very slowly, she let his member kiss her opening, then as her eyes closed in the ecstasy they anticipated, she sat up on him. Committing every second of the delicious slither of her impaling herself with him, she didn't want to forget a detail.

Still in her dream, she took his tee-shirt up over her head to present her full naked body for him. But he didn't touch her. As she moved up and down on him, she took her own breasts into her hands and brushed her nipples with her fingertips in a reminder of him.

Though he was there, he wasn't with her. Still bouncing on him, she opened her eyes to let their gazes join. The very second she saw the love in his eyes, orgasm devoured her. The arrangement of his features was foreign, the love on his face was more than a smile. The torture of that love, and his powerlessness to prevent her pain, wrought fresh moisture from her eyes.

Him in her like this, the depth of him inside her most sensitive space, gave her a power that she always drew from him. She'd found her sass in defiance of this adversity, because Rushe would expect nothing less of his woman.

She didn't care if they were listening, she didn't even care if they were watching. As long as she had Rushe there with her, in her, she would savor every second. She wouldn't cower in the face of their aggressors triumph. They could watch and jeer as much as they wanted, she had something they could never take away.

At the thought of it, he sat up as though reading her mind. He closed his arms around her and held her body there pressed to his. He kissed her hair, her forehead, her temple, all on a descent to her ear. She tipped her head to the side, giving him all the access he wanted to her neck. But when he kissed her jaw, then the groove behind her ear lobe, she realized he was whispering something to her.

The words didn't fully register until he said them again. If she'd thought she appreciated him talking in bed before, this was the jackpot, and more than she could ever have dreamed of.

"I love you, Kitten," he exhaled into her ear, while still kissing everywhere he could reach. "I've never in my life… I love you."

He triggered a joyful sob from her throat, and she snatched his head to force his mouth back to hers. Brushing her lips back and forth on his, she tightened her arms around his neck. They couldn't be close enough; she wanted to exist in time with his body.

"I love you too," she breathed onto his lips.

That was it. After this, there was nothing but terror. Wherever she ended up, and no matter what happened to him, she needed him to know, to understand, what she felt for him. To know the bond that blazed them together no matter their physical distance.

With such care, he cradled her body against his, and lifted her against him to switch their positions and lay her down, showing such tender devotion.

"I can't let them have you," he said, his gaze locked on hers. "I can't do it, Flick."

"You have to," she said, enjoying the mass of him occupying its home inside her. "If you try anything they'll kill you." She caressed his stubbled jaw. "If they kill you… they get me anyway."

"You can't ask me to… I can't let them hurt you anymore. I don't care what happens to me. When I saw what they'd done to you, what they've done. I wanna kill them. I wanna kill them all."

The ferocity of his expression was familiar. "They'll get what's coming to them," she said. "You have to worry about getting yourself out of here. You have to gain your freedom from them. Let me go. Let them send me wherever they want to… I'll always be your whore."

And this time when she whispered that word, she meant it as an endearment.

Confusion melted into his anger. "I love you, Flick," he breathed, though she wasn't sure he said it to her. "I didn't know I could… fuck…"

When had he realized his love for her? If his melancholy was any measure, it was very recently, like since they started making love.

"Make love to me," she said, pushing his hair from his forehead. "Show me how you feel."

When their eyes met again, his confusion cleared, his anger evaporated. With stiff muscles, his cheek twitched then he relaxed and… smiled at her.

His whole face changed. His eyes lit up when he shone that beautiful joy down on her. Their odds couldn't get any longer, but while they were there in that room, on that bed, joined together, the world was a beautiful place.

FORTY-THREE

THEY'D MADE LOVE AGAIN, and again. Every time, he pulled out before coming. Certainly, the last thing she wanted, while out there with the lowest form of life on the planet, was to find herself pregnant. If she was carrying his baby and forced to abort, or have it taken from her, she wouldn't be able to live with herself.

Except she wouldn't have much of a life to look forward to, which brought her back to the thought that kept recurring. Soon all choice would be taken from her, and she would be subjected to whatever her "owner" chose to demand.

Lying there in the cocoon of Rushe's body, if she wanted her dignity, to exercise any free will, there was only one thing for it.

"Do you remember…?" she said, warm in his tee-shirt, spooned in front of him, facing into the corner.

His body represented a barrier between her and the evil in this place. Although the protection was an illusion, the gesture was cherished.

"Remember what?" he asked, stroking her neck, her shoulder, her hair, her back.

When they'd met, he wasn't as tactile. Gradually, it had built up, now he couldn't stop touching her.

She anticipated and cherished every caress. "When I was here the first time, upstairs in that room."

"Yeah," he said.

"You… when you found out that I'd only been with two men?"

"What about it?" Rushe asked. "You better have a damn good point to make if you're bringing that up."

In spite of herself, she smiled at the memory of what he'd said in the car after she'd hand-fed him MnM's.

The gravity of her decision wiped contentment away. "You said something to me…"

"What did I say?" he asked, kissing her hair. "Did I hurt your feelings, Kitten?"

Still he could make her smile with his teasing, but they were running out of time. There was no more putting this off.

"You said… you said that you'd… rather than watch them put me through this… that you would…"

His hand stopped. "Yeah?"

"You said you'd rather see me dead, than watch them put me through this."

He didn't say anything. What was he thinking? What was he doing? He remained stiff as a board behind her.

"Would you do it?" she whispered and waited through the silence. She counted to sixty twice, and he still hadn't said anything. "Rushe?"

In an instant his body left hers, making her lurch back into his now vacant space on the bed. When she rolled, she found him pacing, clenching his fists.

"You want me to…"

She let him pace, in hope he'd come around to her logic. "There's no way that I can do it myself in here."

"No," he said, stopping to stomp over and bear down upon her. "You are not talking that way. You are not going to let them—"

"What?" she asked, getting onto her knees and hooking her hands into his jeans pockets. "Rushe, you know what will happen to me when they take me from here!"

"No. I'll stop them. I'll find a way."

"You can't," she said, knowing just how torn apart he was because she felt it too. "You can't stop them, and when I'm out there in the world, I'll never be free. How long do I have? A week? A month? What if I get a guy who likes to beat, and torture, and…? Rushe, I don't even want to imagine what could happen."

"No," he asserted, and swiped the tears from her cheeks. "Stop crying. I can't think when you cry like that. Since that first damn night… stop it!"

"You wanted me to keep my guard up, here it is," she said. "Think this forward, use that forethought of yours, what else is there?"

"What do you expect me to do?" he asked. "We don't have weapons."

They didn't need them. She guided his hands to her throat to show him he was the weapon. A flash of revulsion pulsed through his body. He tried to withdraw from her grasp, but she kept hold and brought his fingers as close as she could.

"I love you," she whispered. "I know you can do this for me… please."

She could feel the vibration in his fingers and see the adrenaline pumping behind his mask. Time crackled, he set his jaw, and his dark bullet eyes detached in determination.

His fingers tightened, immediately constricting her throat. No air, no oxygen, and nothing she could do about it. If the drowning had been bad, this was worse. The panic was primal, it consumed her with the automatic urge to kick, to get away, to beg his release. Her grip on his wrists increased, her fingernails dug deep into his flesh. But her instinct to tug his hands away was useless in the face of his superior strength. The energy in her was waning and when her palms leaped to his chest they didn't push, they slid away.

In hopeless desperation, her head got heavy, and seemed to swell. Terror at being deprived her basic human need sent adrenaline coursing through her, speeding her starved organs. Dread was cold, and it glided through her from skin to bone, until a spasm of frost spiked. Without the ability to move, to breathe, her body gave up, and the fight left her.

Then with an unexpected gasp, oxygen flooded through her again. She was on the bed, on her face, free from his grip. Her throat scratched, she coughed, trying to breathe again. He'd released her, dropped her. Pushing onto her hands, she kept coughing, but her voice wasn't available.

"Fuck!" Rushe shouted and punched a dent in the brick of the wall.

"Rushe," she wheezed, and flipped to her back because it wasn't in her to sit up yet.

"Don't ask me again," he said over his shoulder, giving her only his back to address.

"What's wrong?" she rasped.

Her distressed systems prickled to every nerve ending. Disorientation waylaid her senses. Actions were clumsy, so she gave up trying to move.

"What's wrong?" he shouted and spun to loom over her again. "You just asked me to kill you, Kitten! I almost did! What the fuck…? How the hell did…? What the fuck am I gonna do?"

"I asked you to, Rushe," she said, lifting her hand to hook it into his pocket, though there was no strength in it. "I asked you to do it because I don't want any man to touch me… I only want you, Rushe, and no one touches your stuff."

"If I could do anything about it," he said, dropping to a crouch.

He ran his hands through his hair. For the first time, she saw him lost and disheveled.

"Did you really want me from the first time you saw me on the street?"

"Yes," he answered, still distracted.

"I didn't think that I would ever be able to…"

Rocking to her side, she took her hand to his face. Her other hand remained in his pocket curled against his thigh in his crouched position.

"Able to what?"

Rushe took her hand from his face, maybe as a defense. If he was turning away from her affection, it was because he blamed himself, just like she'd thought he would.

"Pleasure you," she said, trying to make as many happy memories in this dire situation as possible.

With the revelation of their shared love, there was so much she wanted to disclose, so much she wanted to say. But time would be stolen away from them soon, and they would never be together again. That finality was the only reason he'd made his declaration to her. This was the end, and they'd lost the game.

She tried to convey her own depth of emotion, hoping it might ease his burden. "Until you, I didn't… you've given me so much, shown me so much joy. I'm grateful, Rushe, you're a good instructor."

"Yeah, class dismissed," he muttered, wrapping his hand around hers. "We're running out of time."

Again, he glanced at his watch, as he had done so many times since they'd been in there. "When are they coming for me?"

He'd been on the inside of the gang and likely had more information than he'd volunteered.

He scrubbed a hand over his stubble while confirming her suspicions. "They'll leave here at four a.m.," he said. "Journey's about an hour."

"What will happen?" she asked. "Where is it? Who will be there?"

"I don't know," he said. "This is only the second shipment. The first never got through."

"What happened to the first one?"

"Victor's wingman screwed him over and took charge of the merchandise. Hasn't seen him since."

"Jansen," she said, attracting his interest. "I heard the conversation, in Victor's office. I was in the next room with John."

"They'll put you in a van," he said in that deep, flat, detached tone of his, except it wasn't dangerous anger she read on his face.

Witnessing his quiet resignation shattered her heart. By breaking her, they'd broken him—the strongest man she'd ever known.

FORTY-FOUR

"I WON'T GO QUIETLY," she whispered. "I mean the van, the journey, I can handle that but… I won't just bend over for them, Rushe."

"You listen to me," he said, tightening his hold on her hand. "I don't want you to give up. Don't provoke them into hurting you. You've got a mouth on you, Kitten, but it's mine, and I'm telling you to keep it shut."

"You want me to… I can't, Rushe. I can't just let it happen and do nothing."

"You are gonna do nothing," he said. "You're gonna go where you're told, and you're gonna do what you're told."

She snatched her hands from his, recoiling against the wall behind her. "You want me to… Rushe, they're gonna—"

"I know," he said, reaching over the bed for her.

She pulled away. "I won't. I won't do it. I won't let them."

"You will," he said, getting to his feet. "Because I'm gonna come get you. I want you healthy when I get there, do you understand me? For once in your life, follow my instructions."

"You can't… How do you know they'll let you out of here alive? You might never see daylight again. They could take me out of the country, out of the hemisphere for all I know. No, no, I won't do it."

With her head swinging back and forth, she tried to block out the possibilities. But what was going to happen to her wasn't as important as what was going to happen to him. Once Victor found out he wasn't law enforcement, there would be no need to keep him alive. If Rushe had nothing Victor wanted, he was dispensable. She, at least, knew they'd keep her alive long enough to sell her. If she saw an opening, a chance to escape, she would take it.

"We'll get through it," he said, landing on the bed. "I will come for you, Flick… I don't know when, but I promise you I'll come."

"No." She shook her head again. "No, I won't let them touch me." Rushe reached for her, but she batted his hand away and pounced up to perch on her tiptoes in a crouch. "Nobody touches me!"

"Kitten…" he said, shifting up the bed.

She backed up against the bare black wall that served as a headboard. "No! No, I don't want their hands on me!"

"You think I do?" he shouted back. "Do you have any fucking idea—" He punched the wall with the side of his fist, leaving another crater in the brick, but it was the blood on him that speared her with terror.

On reflex, she sprang forward to grab him. "Don't hurt yourself."

She traced her lips back and forth on his wound.

"I'm going to find you," he said, stroking her hair as she kissed his hand. "Trust me."

"I trust you. I've trusted you from the start. Even when you told me not to. But they're going to do things to me… things that might… if I ever got back to you, I might never…"

"We'll deal with it," he said. "All you have to concentrate on is breathing, okay?"

"You won't want me."

"This isn't your fault," he growled with a ferocity that made her shiver. "You are my woman. I don't care how many fuckers I have to kill to get to you, I'll do it. Do you believe me?"

"Yes," she whispered. "How did we not see this coming?"

"There is precedent, but I had no idea Victor—"

"Not Victor," she said. "This."

Alarm flashed on his face when she directed his hand to her heart. "You're the best thing I've ever had in my life," he said, awe in his eyes. "That's what you said to me."

"Yes."

"Why would you want anything to do with a guy like me?"

"You're the strongest, most honorable man I've ever met. I love you, Rushe. It's not a choice. It's not something I can switch on and off. You protected me, fed me, pleasured me, took care of me. You did whatever was needed to accomplish what was in my best interest. You told me to leave that shack to protect me from Shiv, and from this. You sent me home when I didn't want to leave your side.

"You broke me out of here," she said. A salty tear broke onto the crack in her lips. "You took me to my parents, made me believe you didn't care, because it was best for me… In that room earlier, you put your body between mine and danger, even when we were astronomically outnumbered. I love you, Rushe. You treat me like a woman, you see me. You knew what was in me before I did. I had no idea that strength like this existed, not until I met you.

"Skeeve groped me, but I taunted him, I wouldn't let him see me tremble, because I'm better than him. We're better than him. Someone has to stand up for what's right, even against the odds of good sense… just like you did for me in Dell's."

"There are things I should tell you," he said. "Things you should know."

"I don't trust these walls any more than you do… We'll have to hope that… You can tell me everything when we're together again."

"Damn, she's fuckable," he said. "That's the first thing I thought when I saw you. I thought you were going to keep going. But when you stopped… I froze up."

"Out of the frying pan and into the fire," she said. "That's roughly what I thought when I first saw you in that room in Dell's."

"You thought I was going to hurt you."

"I didn't know who you were."

"You keep that guard up, Kitten, but keep your mouth shut. I'll be pissed if I show up and you've stood me up."

"Stood you up," she said, and grabbed for his watch to check the date. "Oops."

"Oops what?" he asked.

"I stood Hayden up again," she said, and pursed her lips to hide the smile that threatened.

"Hayden," he said and frowned. "You're dating?"

"Lover, I'm about to be bundled into a van and sold to the highest bidder. I think you have more pressing concerns about other men."

"Did he fuck you?" he demanded with his angry brow crowding his eyes.

"You found your anger," she said. "And does it matter?"

"Yes. Tell me!"

"Are you jealous?"

"Yes," he said. "Answer me."

Rushe was honest to a fault… when it suited him. "I never sleep with a guy on a first date," she said.

He relaxed some. "I've never taken you on a date."

A statement that she couldn't argue with. "True… and I won't sleep with you the first time you do."

When his exhale was almost a laugh, his face softened when he looked at her. "Suits me. Sex doesn't have anything to do with sleeping."

"You've used that line already, and you were lying to me when you did."

"I don't argue with women."

"No," she said, crawling into his lap. "We can find some other way to settle our differences."

She pushed her mouth up to his. When his tongue touched her lip, she opened to him. Blood or pain was nothing. This could be the last space, and the last time they spent with each other. She'd never realized love like this existed, and Rushe had even less experience of the phenomenon than her.

"Say it again, Rushe," she murmured on his kiss.

His hands snaked up under her tee-shirt to take a breast in each palm. "What?"

She sighed into the caress. "Tell me you love me."

"You gonna stay alive 'til I find you?" he asked. She nodded but he pinched her nipples, which apparently connected to her eyelids because they popped open. "Speak."

"Yes," she said. "I promise."

"Good then."

On an inhale, his mouth came towards hers, but there was a clatter beyond the door. Both of them sat up to fixate in that direction.

"What was that?"

"They're coming," he said, stealing another glance at his watch. He cupped her face to train her eyes on him. "I love you, and I'm going to find you."

More tears escaped as she clawed his chest. "I'll be good, I promise."

"I know."

"Don't let them hurt you," she said. "I'm not worth it."

His mouth tilted to an almost straight diagonal, forming a smile she wanted to picture every second from now until she could see it again.

"Kitten, you're the only damn thing in the world that is."

FORTY-FIVE

SOMEONE WAS AT THE DOOR unfastening locks. She grabbed him to her body and kissed him again with every ounce of sorrow and anger surging through her.

"None of this is your fault," she said. "Don't blame yourself if anything… I love you."

The door swung back. Three hulks of varying ethnicity entered with John and Skeeve behind.

"Time to go, little girl," Skeeve said, practically salivating.

"You gonna give us trouble?" John asked Rushe.

She climbed out of his lap intending to rise from the bed, but Rushe linked his fingers between hers, stalling her. He was holding her hand. When their eyes met, she relived every second of their time together. Rushe didn't have to say the words, they were written all over his face, which surprised her given their audience. Then as she had the thought, all affection left his countenance, and he pinned those bullet eyes on John.

"If I beat the crap out of you, it might make me feel better."

"Doubt it," John said. "We've got another three guys in the hall."

Maybe they hoped Rushe would fight. Had they hidden the other men so that they could sneak up on Rushe when he didn't expect it? Perhaps when he thought he had won, they would unleash the second wave, but it didn't matter.

"There won't be trouble," she said to John who held out rope to tie to her wrists.

The men started out of the door. She stayed put. "I've never been able to walk away from you without looking back."

Deliberately, she turned to see him there on the bed, exactly where she had left him. The pain around him broke her heart. He'd always blame himself and would try to come for her, though he'd probably die in the process. Nothing would make him give up. He took his responsibility for her seriously.

"I'll do as I'm told," she said.

"You could use the practice." He shut down. In one instant, Rushe was the man she'd met in the alleyway. "Get."

John got hold of one arm, Skeeve snatched the other, both tugged her out of the room. The pair dragged her down the corridor with three bulky men in front, leading the way. The sound from behind of locks being put in place reminded her he was in there alone and ripping himself apart for doing nothing to help her.

Nothing could be done.

The three hulks who had come in with John and Skeeve closed ranks behind her. After one door and a corridor, a turn here, and a turn there, she noticed a dull light emanating from the end of the passage. The exit? A rush of cold night air tensed her. The van would be out there. Her instinct was to dig her heels in, to refuse to leave with them, to make a fuss, to fight.

Rushe wanted her to be safe, all his actions were meant to assure her safety, and she hadn't even thanked him for the two million dollars she'd never be able to pay back. So many questions buzzed in her mind, but it was unlikely they would ever be answered. His words kept her warm. His unexpected declaration made her heart swell even then, as she replayed the moment.

Love was a strong word, but she'd meant it, just as she knew he did. The trust she had in him was greater than the trust she had in herself. She didn't want to be the reason for his demise.

The air was thick but cold, and it stuck to her skin. Before they went outside, a hood was shoved over her head. They pulled her up the outer stone stairs to approach an idling engine and the crying women she'd met previously. At least, she assumed they were the same women.

Someone lifted her up, and she was dumped into a cold, hard, plastic, pull down seat. Her feet were bound, and she was contorted into the brace position so they could tie her ankle restraints to the rope on her wrists.

"The gang's all here," John said.

She couldn't see him; she couldn't see anyone. But the women were definitely there. Judging by the elbow that brushed hers, they'd been arranged in the same position.

"No pushing, no shouting, and no crying." John listed the rules. "If you piss me off, I'll shoot you and they'll take your price from my cut. I don't wanna do that, but if I have to, I will. We've got a journey ahead. I'd tell you to get comfortable, but I doubt possible. No talking and no crying."

Having said the latter twice, it must be the most important rule, or at least most important one to John. With a few clicks and mumbles, the van started to move.

In that position, she could probably get her hood off. But that might just piss John off and wouldn't really serve a purpose. She wouldn't have a window and wouldn't see where they were going to follow their progress.

Her thoughts returned to Rushe, still in that room, on the bed they'd made love on. He'd be driving himself crazy with the possibilities. That particular function in her own brain was in the off position. What lay up ahead didn't bear thinking about.

The thugs could make all the noise they wanted to. They ignored the sniffles initially. A couple of times John snapped at the women who cried. She tried to block it out, choosing to think about Rushe instead, about the things they'd done together. Despite everything, she felt lucky to have met him and been a part of his world, even if it was for too brief a time.

If it hadn't been for the dangerous predicament, he wouldn't have declared his feelings so spontaneously or voluntarily. But he had, and had vowed to come for her, to liberate her. Then what?

The only way through this was by thinking about her future with Rushe. He said there were things she needed to know, and she'd listen to every word. Once he explained his motivation and how he got involved in it in the first place, they could move forward.

Dreaming of a future with Rushe distracted her from the scuffles and whimpers. It helped block out what she was about to face. Not knowing the details drove her insane, but speculation only ended in worst-case scenario.

So she thought of Rushe. A man so powerful and enduring as Rushe struck her with awe. He'd picked little her to love, and he'd seen her at her lowest. Rushe would walk through fire for her and wouldn't give one thought to any pain he'd have to tolerate in the process.

One of the girls was crying again, John shouted back at her just as someone started scrambling around.

"Where you going?" John asked.

The scuffling paused. "I'm gonna have me some fun," Skeeve said.

She didn't like the proximity of his voice.

"You're gonna fuck her in the back of the van?"

"She deserves it."

"Whatever."

John's one word was her last line of defense. There, now, she had no way to defend herself and she knew, she just knew, he would come for her.

"Hear that, little girl?" Skeeve taunted.

Her hair was grabbed through the hood and yanked upward.

"Go to hell," she hissed.

"Where's your boyfriend now?"

Thrown from her seat, she landed on her face on the hard metal floor. With her hands still tied to the ankle bindings, her ass stuck up and out. Skeeve fumbled with her tee-shirt. Wedged in the aisle between rows of women, there were no routes of escape.

"Bet you're still wet," Skeeve said, pushing her tee-shirt up to her waist. "Nice of that superior sonofabitch to warm you up for me."

More women cried, but her horror zeroed in on one sound, the grate of his zip. Trying to go this way and that, she was trapped. Skeeve was going to rape her, and there wasn't a thing she could do to stop him. With the hood still over her face, she pressed her cheek to the floor.

"You're too chicken shit to tell him," she said. "You're so scared of him, you wouldn't dare challenge him. Remember in that shack, remember when you were crying and cowering from him? Begging him for your life like a pussy?"

"You fucking bitch!"

Skeeve's sticky hand landed on her backside as wheels squealed. On a thumping jolt, the van suddenly skidded, sending her and all the occupants bouncing off each other like silver bearings in a pinball machine. More crying, more shouting, the noise level grew to such a din, the screech of metal on concrete was almost drowned out. The van kept on going and with a thud, it rolled once, and then again.

It seemed to take forever, but they eventually came to a lurching halt. Hot, wet, panting filled the air. No one said anything, no one moved. What the hell just happened? The ticking of the engine, and rumbling of tires suspended in mid-air, bit into the atmosphere.

She tried to move, but something was on top of her. Shoving it aside took a lot of effort. Sitting up was no easier with her hands and feet still bound. Groaning and whimpering increased around her. Others were still alive… Burning, she could smell burning.

"Out," she said before thinking. "Everyone get out now!"

Much as she wanted to be liberated from the clutches of the gang, that wasn't actually her first thought. The smell of smoke meant fire. Rushe would never forgive her if she died less than an hour after leaving him.

Progress was slowed by the restraints, and the hood hid which direction to move in. With some shaking and flailing, she got the hood off and almost immediately wished to put it back on again.

She was on the roof, surrounded by bodies. In the darkness, the scent of blood drowned her reality. Pitching forward, she tried to move toward the back doors. Three women were moving, but at least two others were definitely dead. Skeeve lay at the edge of the space unmoving. She had no idea of his injuries and didn't care.

"What do we do?" Brianna asked, startling her

The bindings that once held Brianna's arms and legs together were loose. The gash on Brianna's leg, that must've granted her liberation, was nasty... and concerning.

"We get out of here," Flick said.

Brianna crawled over the unconscious bodies to untie Flick's bounds. "Good. Let's go."

She couldn't have put it better herself. When the women began to crawl to the back of the van, the doors flew open to reveal someone outside.

"Nobody move!"

The broad masked man aimed a gun into the van. Whoever he was, he wasn't screwing around.

"What's going on?" Brianna asked, raising her hands in surrender.

As she did the same, two other women sat up as well.

"How many of you are there?" the masked man asked.

"Seven women," Flick said. "Two dead, I think. I don't know about the men."

"Dead?"

"Yes," she said. "From the impact... did you see it?" That was a safer question than "*Why did you run us off the road?*"

"Hit harder than I meant to," he said.

"It happens," she muttered.

"You're Felicity."

Her posture righted fast. "How do you know that?"

"They got to you too... Rushe dead?"

"No, they locked him up," she said, unsure whether to be concerned or grateful that this person knew her identity. "Who are you?"

The masked man didn't answer. More groaning from around about didn't bode well. They were going to have more questions, and possibly more bodies, very quickly.

Lowering the gun slightly, he took the mask from under his chin, and pulled it off.

FORTY-SIX

IN THE SHADOW OF NIGHT, it took a moment to register his features. The second she did, a grin burst across her face as relief hit hard. To get to him, she climbed over everyone in her way, despite Brianna's exclamation against it.

Although she'd never met this guy before, when she clambered out, she flung her arms around him like they were old friends.

"Rushe told me you could be slow to warm up," he said.

She'd never been happier to see anyone in her life. More questions fired through her, but this was an ally. This was the man Rushe met in the diner while she watched from the safety of the car.

"He meant for me to see you," she said, releasing the stranger without leaving his side.

"Yes."

"I should've known."

"It's important to know who you can trust."

"You sonofabitch…" a male voice croaked.

The stranger automatically brought his arm out to push her behind his body, putting himself between her and danger, just as Rushe would.

She peeked around the protective arm. From that standpoint, the carnage inside was worse than first thought.

The voice had come from John, sitting on the van roof, that was now the floor, flanked by two dead men she didn't know.

"John," the stranger said in cool acknowledgement.

"Jansen."

Pieces began to slide into slots that had been vacant from the beginning. Rushe and Jansen were working together. Jansen had hit the van; he'd run them off the road. It was Jansen who worked with Victor until he intercepted the first shipment, and now he'd intercepted the second as well. Obviously, it was their mission to ensure these women never got to where they were going. Why hadn't he told her in their captivity that she would be freed enroute?

"We've been looking for you," John said.

"I know," Jansen said.

"Victor's gonna kill you for this."

"I'd guess he wants to kill me, but it won't be for this."

"Oh yeah, why—"

An abrupt shot startled her. A spot formed in the center of John's forehead and he fell to the side, landing on top of the body next to him.

"Because he's never gonna know I was here," Jansen said to John's corpse.

"What is going on?" she asked. "Who are you?"

"Jansen," he said to her, then dropped his gun arm to his side. "Women out."

"What are you going to do with them? Are you here to save us? Are you going to kill us or sell us? Or—"

"Rushe never told me you talked this much," Jansen said, helping the women out of the vehicle.

When Skeeve and the two dead women were the only ones left in the van, Jansen paused, seeming reluctant before he crouched to examine the deceased. Hesitation wasn't normal for men who could kill with abrupt determination, as he had done. The slowness of his deliberate movement to turn over the first woman was intriguing. With an audible exhale, he tensed and took his attention to the other woman to roll her over.

A second later, he was back on his feet, marching to the living women to cut their binds.

"What are you going to do with us?" Brianna asked.

Jansen produced a stack of banknotes and shoved them into Brianna's hands. "Get yourselves home."

"That's it?" Flick asked.

Jansen strode away. "That's it," he called back.

Brianna was taking care of the other women, so Flick ran after him. The road was dark and all but deserted. The bad guys were dead meaning the others should be okay. All they had to do was get to a house, or a car, they could call the police, get to a hospital, do whatever they needed to.

She struggled to keep up with Jansen as he disappeared into the night. If he got away from her, she'd never see him again, and she'd have no way to help Rushe.

"We have to go back," she said. "We have to go back for Rushe."

He snorted and kept on walking. "Good luck with that."

"No," she said. "You need to help me."

Jansen spun around. "They're gonna kill him. He's probably already dead."

"No," she said. "They think he's law enforcement or something."

Jansen smiled. "Rushe? I bet he loved that. He's been called a lot of things, but never anything quite that bad."

"If that's not it then, what?"

"He's an outside contractor," Jansen said. "Private enforcement."

"You work together?"

"Rushe works alone, he always has."

"You've known him a long time?" she asked.

"No… There's a reason he hasn't told you any of this," Jansen said. "Rushe doesn't open up to anyone. As far as he's concerned, there's only one thing women are good for. Sorry to let you down gently."

Either this guy didn't know how Rushe felt about her, or she was being played. "He told you to tell me that," she said. "If things worked out like this… if he was dead, or in trouble… You're supposed to make me think I'm embarrassing myself."

Jansen scrutinized her, gradually his chin came up. "You're good."

"I learned from the best," she said. "And there isn't a scenario he hasn't planned for."

"Except this one," Jansen said. "He's locked up in there for a reason. When Victor works out who Rushe is, one of two things happens, he uses him, or he kills him."

"Uses him for what?"

"You better be glad they let you go before they uncovered his identity. Victor's MO is to use women men care about. If he wants something from you, he'll find your pressure point and push. You're Rushe's pressure point, and the only one he's ever had, if the stories I've heard are true… You're his weakness."

"I know."

"But Victor's sold you on, or he thinks he has. With you out of the picture, he has no way to exploit Rushe, so Rushe will refuse, and eventually… Rushe will die."

She shook her head. "No, he's coming for me."

"Yeah," Jansen said. "All the trying in the world can't change the facts."

"You don't try, you don't succeed."

"The definition of insanity is doing the same thing over and over again and expecting different results. Rushe isn't getting out of there alive. Emotional torture is sort of Victor's forte."

"You can't expect me to walk away and leave him there."

"I'm doing you a favor," Jansen said.

The gun still hung loose in his hand. While his form was formidable, he didn't have the fight of Rushe. He didn't have the angry energy that made him capable of anything. The only time Rushe appeared this broken was when he knew there was nothing he could do to save her.

"We can get him out," she said. "If you help me."

"Give it up," Jansen said. "You'll only drive yourself insane. Take it from someone who knows."

He walked backward a couple of steps, then turned to continue his walk into the night.

"I need your help," she said. "You were working with him! You have to help him!"

Jansen kept walking. "No, I'm done. I'm not going back there."

If she let him go, she'd never be able to free Rushe on her own. "She's alive," she called out. More pieces slid into place when he came to a slow stop.

"That's why you intercept the shipments of women. You're looking for her."

"You don't know what you're talking about."

When he took another step, panic pumped in her chest. "Serendipity! You're here for Serendipity."

When he flipped around, she recognized that determination, that brick wall of anger she'd seen in Rushe.

"What did Rushe say to you?" he asked.

"Nothing."

"He told you about Serendipity?"

"No," she said, shaking her head.

He came back to her, the warm metal of the gun pressed into her arm when he grabbed hold of her. "Then how the fuck do you—"

"I saw her," she said. "Separate from the other women."

"I don't believe you."

"Are you willing to risk her life on that?" He hesitated. "She's alive. She's been there for six months."

"She's alive?"

"Yes."

"Why hasn't she been in the shipments?"

"Victor was going to kill her," she said, mindful of the flicker of hurt on his face. "He was going to kill her when you screwed him over."

"I screwed him over?" Jansen scoffed. "What version of history are you working from?"

"I can only tell you what they told me. Victor wants to find you. He kept Serendipity alive because he wants an audience. He wants to make it painful and slow, and he wants you to see it."

"How do you know?"

"Shiv told me," she said. "Are you going to leave her to that fate?" While he seemed to be processing her words, he didn't look at her, though he kept her in his grip. "Rushe wouldn't leave me to that… maybe he loves me more than you love her."

"Dead does her no good," Jansen snapped. "Damn thing Rushe kept repeating. Dead does her no good. Dead does her no good!"

Jansen released her with an eruption that hurled her backward so quick she almost lost her footing.

When he started walking again, she ran to catch up. "Where are you going?"

"Away from here."

"What?" she asked. "You're going to leave her in there?"

"No," he said. "No, I'm not. I've got a car parked around the next bend, and a motel room twelve miles from here."

"I don't understand."

"Flying in there guns blazing won't do anyone any good. Rushe and I thought we could play the long game on this, but this is… I can't sit on my ass anymore, and now he's locked up in there. And he has a woman, Rushe has a woman…? No one saw that coming. Victor's one fucking bastard."

He stopped long enough to grab hold of her.

"What are you doing?"

"You're coming with me."

"I am not," she said, trying to yank herself away.

"You're coming with me. We're gonna get you cleaned up, and fed, then you're going back in there."

"You're sending me back to Victor?"

"I said you were going back. I didn't say you were going alone."

She couldn't get out of Jansen's grip. Much as she wanted to go back to Rushe right that minute, she could only do what Jansen told her. Following his orders was her only option, she needed his help. Rushe was still in there. If word got back to him the shipment had been run off the road, and that there were casualties, he would think the worst.

Though Victor might not tell him. Letting Rushe think she'd been sold would get his blood boiling. Which was likely Victor's overriding intention. Men were intimidated, they were threatened by Rushe. They believed him to be superior, which he was. John had almost dared Rushe to fight, and he had known there were backup fighters in the passage ready to jump in when Rushe dispensed with the others.

So she did as told; Rushe would be so proud of her. But anything could happen at any time. She wanted to get back there, to get Rushe out without him being hurt, and before he did anything rash.

Jansen walked with determination in his gait. How had he got through six months without a woman he clearly cared about? When he'd intercepted the first shipment of women, he must've been certain Serendipity would be among them. To be wrong would've broken his heart.

After seeming to screw over Victor, Jansen couldn't go back to that house. Still, it didn't make sense. If Jansen was Victor's number two, why would the latter need to hold Serendipity at all?

Jansen said this was Victor's modus operandi, and she'd seen how Victor enjoyed tormenting Rushe with her. Playing games with people, mentally torturing men by using the object of their love against them was Victor's hobby.

They had to fight back.

In taking the object of someone's love all Victor achieved was the complete focus of the persecuted party. He would get no mercy. She had her own anger toward Victor, but that would be nothing compared to the anger of Jansen, and now the anger of Rushe.

It's all fun and games until someone gets hurt and Victor had done the hurting. Rushe and Jansen would ensure that after laughter came tears, and those tears would be Victor's, of that she was certain.

FORTY-SEVEN

JANSEN FED HER after she showered to clean out her wounds. He patched her up and demanded that she sleep. Of course, she objected. Rushe was in captivity. She wanted to liberate her love without delay. They came to an agreement she would try to sleep for half an hour, and if sleep didn't come, they would talk about a plan.

She opened her eyes. Half a second later, she sat up. Clutching the blanket to her chest, she tried to figure out where she was… a motel room, murky light, and the smell of… pizza.

"It's still hot," Jansen said.

She swung around to see him sitting on the bottom corner of the bed. "I fell asleep."

"Yeah, I won that bet."

"What time is it?"

"Five."

They hadn't got back to the motel until around that time in the morning, so it had to be in the evening. "You let me sleep all day?"

"Victor wouldn't have known the shipment didn't get to its destination until his crew returned, or in this case didn't return. Their orders would have kept them out until at least midday, maybe later. When they didn't get back on time, he'd have given them another couple of hours before asking questions, sometimes there are holdups. We've got time. It's only about now he's getting the news the girls never got there. He's probably on his way to talk to Rushe as we speak."

"Then we should get over there," she said, throwing back the covers only to remember she'd slept without clothes, because her tee-shirt had been torn and soiled.

Jansen took another bite of pizza and didn't seem to notice her quickly covering herself again. "Clothes in the bag on the floor beside you."

She grabbed up the white plastic bag with its top scrunched down and tipped out its contents. No underwear, just a pair of jeans, and a black cotton scoop neck about three sizes too small for her chest. They'd do. Something was better than nothing. Rushe would agree given she was alone with another man. As she put on the clothes under the covers, Jansen pushed the pizza box toward her.

She grabbed a slice. This Jansen was tough to get a read on, but he wasn't as blank as Rushe. Around six feet, his hair was longer and thinner than Rushe's, hooked back behind his ears. Still, a rather fierce looking tattoo sprouted from his tee-shirt, covering his neck from his shoulder. Maybe he wasn't as hard as Rushe, but he sure didn't look much softer.

"Is she your wife?" she asked. Jansen stopped chewing. "If you don't want to talk about it—"

"Ex-wife," he said. "Sorta. We got married real young, I fucked around, and we split. But a couple of years ago…"

"You got back together," she said when he didn't.

"Yeah," he said, flinging his pizza slice into the box. "After this she'll never want to see me again."

"You don't know that."

"I do," he said. "This whole mess is my fault. I got her into it, Rushe too, and now you. If I hadn't fucked up in the first place…"

"What happened?"

"I needed money," Jansen said, wiping pizza grease from his hands onto the thighs of his jeans. "Got it from Victor."

"You didn't pay him?"

"I paid him back, all of it," Jansen said. "That's the kicker. I could've walked away."

"But you didn't?"

"No," Jansen said.

"Serendipity found out you were working with him?"

"Nothing that simple, Victor wanted me to work with him. So I did. Then the jobs got… serious."

"You said no?"

"Tried to," Jansen said. "But he picked up Serendipity, just ripped her off the street. It wasn't about money anymore. When he got Serendipity, he had me. He knew I'd do anything to keep her safe. First couple of months were bad enough, but Victor was acting… invincible, then he got an idea. A contact wanted something, a big shot client, I don't know. But he got this idea about the trafficking in his head, and a guy knew a guy, which is always the way it is…"

"You were in over your head."

"I'm not a bad guy. I don't know how it came to this, I make bad decisions… which Serendipity will tell you is an excuse, but I make the decisions, I know it's my fault."

"So you called in Rushe?"

"Victor made a few comments that made me think Serendipity would be in the first shipment. That it was the best, the easiest, and the quickest way to get her out of his hair. I think he wanted to see what I'd do; he likes to have rats in his maze. If I let Serendipity go in the shipment, then my loyalty to Victor would be proven. If I could turn my back on the woman I loved for him…"

"But you couldn't?"

"I tried to make him think I'd go along with it, but I knew a guy who knew a guy…"

"Which is always the way it is," she said with a smile, and he exhaled a laugh.

She tossed what was left of her pizza into the box and moved it to the entertainment unit.

"Rushe just appeared one day, he doesn't really exist," Jansen said as she sat beside him. "I mean he does but… he's sorta known for being a shadow. Surveillance is part of his gig. The guy's got infinite patience."

Not always. His patience receded when she took too long getting her clothes off. "Yeah."

"He can watch a guy for months without ever making a move. Just watch him, constantly, all the time. I'm not talking about interesting people with interesting lives, we're talking Joe Normal."

"Why would he—"

"People want information for a whole bunch of reasons, and if you want information under the radar there's only one guy to go to. Rushe is the master of information extraction. He checks out every story. He does his own background check on anyone who wants to use his services, every person who hires him, and their stories. He takes nothing on faith. He doesn't trust a soul. He checks out every avenue before he makes a move."

"A move?" she asked.

"Surveillance is his bread and butter I think, but… he can find out anything, about anyone, he can watch and watch… and if he can't see it, he asks."

"Nicely?" she asked, suspecting she knew the answer to her own question.

"Rushe is a ghost. He can do what he wants because he doesn't exist. He's also been known to…"

"What?"

"He's been known to disappear people, if you know what I mean."

The watching thing didn't surprise her. Her man could sit for hours saying nothing. And the way Rushe had spoken to Skeeve, the things he'd said to her in the car about Robert proved, as she'd once told him, he was capable of anything.

Rushe found out things, extracted information, disappeared people. He was, as Jansen had put it, private enforcement.

"You didn't know," Jansen said. "He kind of has a specialty… which is how I ended up getting his attention."

"A specialty?"

"Cases involving female victims," Jansen said. "He takes cases in defense of women."

"Why?"

"I don't know. Like I said, I knew a guy who knew a guy. Since I hired Rushe I've heard stories, seen him in action. But nobody knows him personally, he doesn't have friends. I didn't even know what he looked like until this. He spends his life predicting everybody's next move."

Another thing she knew. "So you've been working together all this time?"

"Kind of, Rushe got involved through a friend of mine. I could never afford Rushe on my own. I know he turns down more jobs than he takes. This was supposed to be a quick one. Easy in, easy out… it hasn't worked out that way."

"You wanted Rushe to find Serendipity?"

"I thought she was going to be in the first shipment, but Victor didn't trust me. Rushe came in on his own, nothing to do with me, or so Victor thinks. But now Rushe is in it, and you're in it too."

"We'll figure it out. Is there anyone we could ask to help us?"

"No," Jansen said. "I don't know Rushe's contacts, though I guess he has them. If I thought… I mean if I'd known Serendipity was never going to be in a shipment then I'd… I wasn't even sure she was alive. Going in gung-ho seemed reckless when I didn't know her location. You've seen her?"

"Yes."

"How is she? I mean, how did she look? Did she say anything?"

That lifeless woman whose only action was to blink? "It's been tough on her," she said. "She'll need time. But the sooner you get her out of there, the sooner you can start making it better."

"Where is she?"

"The basement," she said. "Not far from Rushe… Maybe if we go back to the scene of the crash last night…"

Jansen was shaking his head. "The cops will be all over it. That's why I said I was done, and why I know time is short. They're closing in. When Serendipity wasn't in the first shipment, I let the women go, but they went to the police. They didn't give details about me so far as I know, they didn't know who I was, but the cops are sniffing around. I told Rushe I was done. I wasn't going anywhere near the shipment last night. I told him it was over. But I… at the last minute I… Anyway, last night…

those women will have told law enforcement, the net will be shrinking."

"Maybe we could call the cops, ask for help—"

"They'll raid the place. If they believe us, they'll raid the place," Jansen said, correcting himself. "If Victor hasn't already, he'll make sure no one makes it out of that basement alive."

"What do you think we should do?"

"There's two options, either we go in the front, we go in fast and loud… but with there only being two of us, and you… you don't look like the gun, or hand-to-hand combat, type."

"I've shot a gun," she asserted.

"Yeah?" he said, with a flash of surprise. "Do you have training?"

"No," she said, somewhat deflated. "It was just once."

"Right, so the bad guys will shoot us."

"I don't like that idea."

"No," Jansen said. "They're not gonna bring Serendipity out voluntarily. Now you say she's alive, I'll go in for her. I'd rather die trying than give up and leave her there… If you come—"

"I'm coming."

"You've got to be ready to die for him, Felicity. Are you willing to die for him?"

"Yes," she said, without hesitation. "And everyone calls me Flick."

"Okay, Flick, if we go in, we'll have to do it quietly. If we can get Rushe out of wherever he is, then we can get out of that house. We won't bring the bastards down, but we can get the people we love out."

"That's our main priority," she said.

"You're a woman, and they've sent you out in one shipment. If they know now how Rushe feels about you… it could be bad for you, Flick, very bad."

"You don't have to warn me," she said, placing a hand on his knee to comfort him. "I've seen what these people are capable of. I don't want to be back in their hands. But I won't see Rushe imprisoned there, just as you won't abandon Serendipity."

"Okay," he said. "I've got some supplies in the car. We'll wait until it's dark then we drive to a couple of streets over and walk to the house. It's an old house and Victor doesn't want to draw attention to the fact it's there, or that he's living in it. So there's as little traffic as there can be, and he doesn't patrol the perimeter. They lost a few guys last night, so their numbers are down slightly. We sneak in, get our people out, and go home."

Jansen made it sound so easy, in, get people, out again. It would not be easy. If it had been, Rushe probably would have brought Serendipity out that way in the first place.

Rushe was the key. If they got her love out of his cell, they would get out of that house. But that meant if they didn't have him, they were stranded. If Rushe had somehow freed himself, it would take him too long to realize she had gone back to that place for him. This would have to work, or it would be the last thing she'd ever do. But like she'd told Jansen, she would die for the man she loved, fighting for him was worth it.

FORTY-EIGHT

NERVES WERE ALREADY PLAYING a part out there in the cold. She would've been more confident taking orders from Rushe. When Jansen put a gun in her hand, her anxiety hit the stratosphere. This was real. They were going into Victor's place to get their people out, but it was no game, they'd have to shoot to kill or risk being killed themselves.

"The safety's off just point and shoot," he said. "Don't point it at me."

He closed the trunk and put on his backpack. When he started into the night, she followed. Getting lost before they started wouldn't do anyone any good. She wasn't supposed to be the one needing saved. With the camouflage paint on her skin, and the Lara Croft up-do, she looked the part more than felt it.

Jitters could only get them hurt. Except the thing was, throughout this experience, Rushe had been the one guiding her, giving instructions to keep her alive. Things only went wrong when she ignored those instructions.

She didn't like acting without his word. Her love would get her through this, his advice and instruction, but she didn't have it. She didn't have the option of it, much less the luxury. Now she relied on a man she'd known less than twenty-four hours. He'd screwed over Victor, that was pretty much the foundation of her trust.

Serendipity had been locked up for half a year and Jansen hadn't managed to retrieve her. He'd tried and failed. She couldn't imagine the depth of his frustration. As Rushe told him, dead does her no good. Still, somehow, she couldn't imagine Rushe being aware of her location for that long without taking action. He was a man with infinite patience… or so she'd been told.

"Come here," Jansen said, steering her back against a brick wall. "When we get around this wall, no more talking." She nodded. "I'll get you into the basement, but we'll have to go through the front."

"The front of the house?"

"The broken windows at the front are the quickest way. There is only one door in and out of the basement. If they come in with any women while we're—"

"Okay," she said. "Let's do it."

Jansen didn't hesitate. With purpose, he led her forward, around to a section of wall with some loose bricks. He took half a dozen out of place, adding that space to the existing one, giving them enough room to squeeze through. He went first, taking the time to scan the area before bringing her through.

All around them were trees. Where was the house? Just as she began to panic they might lose their way, Jansen pushed her past a group of small bushes, and there it was, the house.

Victor was such a fraud. A man who squatted in a dilapidated house had ideas of grandeur, but like she'd said to his face, he couldn't back them up. Now crouched behind these bushes with Jansen switching his weapon, and retrieving something from his pack, she had time to look at the structure properly for the first time.

On the side view, it still appeared grand. The blacked-out windows reflected back the night giving it an intimidating, sinister air. The red brick and white eaves were classic, but the only sign of life was the smoke billowing from the tall chimney. Bad people were in that building. There in its shadow she felt feeble. She and Jansen were nothing but insects in a bird's nest. How could they come out on top?

All the confidence in the world couldn't alter the laws of nature. Victor and his gang were bigger, stronger, and much better prepared. In that place, she'd found the strength to stand up to Skeeve. Asking Rushe to kill her hadn't been easy, but she'd done it with him at her side. Was she capable without him? What if he wasn't in there at all? Maybe Victor had already killed him or moved him; the possibilities drove her insane.

"What?" Jansen hissed.

She hadn't seen her guide go, and he'd said no more talking. That went out the window when he moved and she'd stayed put. At the edge of the lawn, a few feet ahead, Jansen was exposed. She couldn't do it. She couldn't. Fear would win, she'd let it. Rushe would be ashamed of her.

Rushe. As quickly as she faltered, she shifted to a crouch, and ran in behind Jansen. If Rushe was in there, she was going to get him back. He'd promised to come for her. Why shouldn't she offer the same dedication? She had to try. Failure would be better than never giving hope a chance.

Jansen led her to the narrowest stretch of gravel. They had to cross it; the house was an island in a sea of stones. They had no choice. Damnit. Every footstep rang in her ears like the bass at a heavy metal concert.

Following Jansen's example, the trick was to own it. He just went, straight out there, straight across. He set his goal in mind and kept moving. She blocked out her uncertainty and did the same.

Thankfully quicker than she would've thought, they reached the house, and ascended the side stairs to traverse the long stone porch. The whole way, her heart pounded louder than the noise of the gravel.

An impulse to heave a sigh of relief when they stopped almost won out, but she kept it in. When she and Rushe were joined later that night, she'd make up for this silence by making all the noise she wanted to.

Jansen pointed and crouched to boost her up to one of the broken windows. Grateful for the lift, she did her best to check the darkened room beyond. No movement, no sound, no light. She crawled inside. Mostly stripped out, the floor was spongy signaling this wasn't Victor's refurbished wing.

Her cohort came in behind her and grabbed her hand on his way to the door on the perpendicular wall. He wasted no time in getting to where he was going. His goal was set, and there was no time to look around. Out of that room, he swept the foyer, piloted her through another door and down a set of stairs.

Her head spun. Was she going to remember her way around the basement? Would she move with the same purpose and urgency? Jansen opened a door. Where were they going? How long was it going to— thrust into another room, her questions stopped. Empty… No one was inside, but… there was a door opposite them.

Rushing to the center of the room, optimism won out. "This is the room. The one I was in when they sent him away with Simone."

Despite not knowing the story, he didn't ask. "Okay, you know where you are, that's good," he said, swinging his bag around to retrieve a small lock-pick.

Turned out he didn't need it. They were equally surprised to find the door unlocked. Anything that saved them time was positive, she sure wasn't complaining. They progressed into the corridor together.

"There," she said, dashing to the door further down on the left.

Pressing her body to it, she listened for movement inside. Rushe should be in there… if they hadn't moved him. The deathly silence of the hallway sent her uneasy. The women had been held in this place; their screams echoed in her mind as if ghosts of vengeance hung in the air.

The clunk of the gun on the wood startled her, until she realized it was the gun in her own hand. She hadn't even thought about the thing and was grateful she hadn't been surprised anywhere along the way, or goodness only knew what she'd have shot.

Jansen tucked his own gun away, then took the pick and opened the locks on the door. Both paused and looked at each other, this was the make or break moment. Rushe was here, or he wasn't, and if he wasn't…

Jansen reached up for the high bolt, and she crouched to the lower one. With a finger count, they pulled their locks, and gave the door a shove. As quickly as it opened, Jansen was gone, yanked over the top of her into the room. Rushe held his throat, pinning him to the wall three feet off the floor.

"Let him go!" Her hand leaped to her mouth to suppress her volume, but Rushe dropped Jansen in an instant.

There may not have been time for him to register whom he had pinned to the wall, but at the sound of her voice, he whipped around. She hadn't given any thought to their reunion, about what she would do when she saw him again. Her body acted on instinct. Running straight to him, she leaped into his arms, seeking his mouth.

Kissing him once, and again, dipping her tongue into his mouth, then licking his lips, and diving in for more, her arm wrapped all the way around his head.

"Rushe," she exhaled. "Oh, Rushe."

All she wanted to do was mate with him, right there, immediately. Her animal drive to bond had her legs trying to climb higher on him, until her lower limbs locked around his diaphragm.

"Kitten," he said. "Okay, Kitten."

Like a limpet on a rock, she didn't want to let go. "You're here. Oh, you're still here."

His hands sought her ankles, and he tried to pry them apart. "When we get out," he said, still trying to free himself, but she kissed him again. "Kitten."

At his stern tone, she relaxed and slithered down his body. Her feet might have touched the floor, but her body remained against his.

"I think she likes you," Jansen said, tossing a tee-shirt to Rushe.

The amusement in his voice was a surprise. It hardly seemed like the time, but… yeah, maybe she wasn't in a position to judge.

"You gave her a gun?" Rushe asked, yanking on the tee-shirt, and snatching the weapon from her hand, while she rubbed her face in his chest.

Whether she was trying to scent him, or get his scent on her, it could go either way. Both were achieved. Thank God Rushe was where she'd left him. Now he was with them, they couldn't lose.

"I thought she should have the means to protect herself," Jansen said.

"I'm surprised you made it here alive," Rushe said. "The safety's off."

"She doesn't know how to use a gun."

"I know. Why did you bring her?"

"She saw Serendipity."

Rushe took her shoulders to force her body an arm's length from his. "You saw Serendipity? Alive?"

"That's the only reason we're here," Jansen said. "I was leaving you to rot."

"Figured," Rushe said. "I heard the shipment didn't make it, there were fatalities."

"During and after the crash," Jansen said. "Yeah."

This was all lovely, everyone catching up, but being away from Rushe's body reminded her of where they stood… of this room and this place.

She backed toward the door. "I want to leave."

"Where's Serendipity?"

"End of the corridor," she said. "The very last door on the right."

FORTY-NINE

JANSEN DIDN'T WAIT, he went out and she was about to follow when Rushe caught her wrist.

"Do you think now was the best time to start following my instructions?" he asked.

"What?"

"You're not wearing underwear."

"How do you know that?" she asked, looking at her chest.

"The girls like me, but not that much. No bra means no panties."

It defied credulity. "We're breaking you out of the evil lair and your main concern is my breasts?"

"No," he said, appearing offended by her question. "Don't complain about chaffing later is all. I'm fucking you senseless when we get out of here. It's gonna be hard and dirty and constant, I don't want you bitching at me."

Was he serious? His humor could be dry…

On her own smile, she wanted to leap back up into his arms. "Do I have a choice?"

"No."

"Okay," she said.

Keeping hold of her, Rushe led the way out to Jansen who was already picking the lock of Serendipity's room.

"When were you in here?" Rushe asked.

"This is the room with the…" she started and trailed off. "John and Shiv brought me here."

She didn't want to elaborate for Jansen's sake. If he heard what happened to her, it would follow that Serendipity may have endured the same experience.

When the final lock was opened, Jansen stood and looked over her head to Rushe. A lump pounced to her throat. These men had worked together on freeing this woman for months, and until now they hadn't been successful.

She'd been so grateful to see Rushe, and be back in his arms, after less than a day apart. Imagine half a year apart… she was amazed either of them made it.

Jansen had expected to see Serendipity after the first shipment, and he hadn't. He'd commandeered their shipment last night in a final ditch attempt to free the woman he loved.

Part of him had to be torn. Opening that door could reveal the relief he'd been anticipating, or there could be more disappointment waiting for him.

With a deep breath, Jansen opened the door and pushed it away. Standing there on the side-lines with Rushe, she couldn't read Jansen's expression at first. Then there was a gasping scream, a wail of torture and delight. Jansen's own throat bobbed, and he rushed into the room.

Rushe made no move to enter, she didn't either. Witnessing the naked love of those rediscovering each other would be moving, but it was also private. So many things had happened to each of them. Both must have thought all hope lost, yet there they were.

She swiped at the tears on her face, and cleared her throat, reminding herself she was supposed to be a hardened warrior now. Except she wasn't. When Rushe's hand slid up her back to the nape of her neck, she curled into his embrace to bury her face against his chest.

"I thought you were dead," he murmured.

"Can't get rid of me that easily," she said, consoled by his heat.

"You shouldn't have come back here."

"You can punish me later."

"I plan to," he said. "Will you ever do what you're told?"

"I might surprise you one day," she said. "But I doubt it."

Rushe guided her around out of the way, and she lifted her head to see Jansen carrying Serendipity in his arms. Even in this blackness, she could see the glisten in Jansen's eyes, but there wasn't time to soothe or comfort.

"We have to get out of here," Rushe said.

Jansen nodded. The four made their way down the corridor to the room they'd entered by. She could taste freedom; she could smell it. They ascended the stairs, and Jansen carried Serendipity into the foyer. They were home free.

Then, from nowhere, she was grabbed from behind, and in the suddenness lost Rushe's hand. Immediately, he turned, Jansen too.

Unfortunately, she recognized the owner of that stench. "Little girl, you came back for me."

"You're a worm," she growled. "You should've died like a dog at the side of that road."

"We were in the middle of something," Skeeve said. "We weren't through."

The barrel of a gun touched her temple. When the letch's hand cupped her breast, Rushe bared his teeth and bounded forward, but she held up her hands to stall him.

"No," Skeeve said. "No. No. I got her now. You don't want me to hurt her, do you?"

"You're gonna die," Rushe snarled.

"Your girlfriend here was giving me a ride, did she tell you? Oh yeah, in the back of that van, she was primed and ready for me, you left her all juiced up."

Skeeve backed her away from the other three. Jansen tucked Serendipity into the room with their entry window.

"She's a screamer," Skeeve said. "Maybe we should do it right here. Right in front of your boyfriend, let me show him how you really like it."

"Okay," she said, much to the surprise of everyone. "Let's do it."

"Yeah?" Skeeve asked.

"You're right, we never got to finish. Let's do it. Right here. Let him watch, yeah, it'll turn him on. Maybe you can take turns."

Each word she spoke increased Rushe's blood pressure, until she thought he might actually burst. "Kitten."

"Just exploring my curiosity," she said to Rushe. "Skeeve, get your dick out."

"You think about it—"

"Ignore him," she said, cutting off Rushe's words. "We'll do it right here. Bend me over and fuck me stupid."

"You want it?" Skeeve said, with all the glee she expected.

"Damn right, all these guns, the cold, hard metal, and the testosterone. It turns a girl on." She unbuttoned her own jeans and pulled down the zipper, one tantalizing tooth at a time. "You gonna do it or not?"

"I'll take you upstairs," Skeeve said.

"Oh," she said, zipping her jeans back up. "I know you're scared Rushe does it better, but you said to me that… if you're limp, I can help you. I've heard a lot of guys have that issue, it's never happened to Rushe, but—"

"No problems here, little girl," Skeeve snapped, and released her to go for his fly.

She ran out the way, turning to witness the flash of horror in his eyes at the moment everyone realized the game had changed. Skeeve was now the prey.

Before any of them could make another play, noise and movement from the top of the stairs drew their attention. Shiv, Glen, and the Kid appeared in front, with Simone close behind, and Victor in their wake. All the players were on the stage for a showdown.

Without realizing it, she'd got to Rushe who shoved her behind his back.

"I've got all the guys out looking for you. Here you are, right under my nose," Victor said. "Surprised to see you, Jansen. Thought you'd have killed yourself by now."

"Wouldn't give you the satisfaction," Jansen said.

"Heard you put a bullet in John last night. How you gonna explain that one to your superiors?"

His superiors? Victor's men were surprised too.

"I'm not gonna lose any sleep over it," Jansen said. "I know what he did for you."

"Every man here has a purpose, or had one, men like John are difficult to find. He was competent, unlike most of the bastards around here."

Victor shoved Skeeve out of the way when he reached the bottom of the stairs.

Shiv, Glen, and the Kid stayed on the stairs. Shiv was the only one of the three with a weapon trained on her, Rushe, and Jansen. Luckily, Serendipity was hidden but if the shooting started, she doubted it would stop. If they were slain, Serendipity wouldn't be saved either.

Victor had a weapon with a silencer attached hanging loose in his hand at his side.

"And little Felicity Hughes," Victor said. She poked her head around Rushe. "You turned out to be quite a distraction, didn't you? You just wouldn't give up. But we had you, I really thought we had you when we sent you out with that shipment. Who knew the pig was going to pop up again?"

"Pig?" Glen asked.

"That's right, boys. Don't know Jansen as well as we thought. He was part of the gang, of the crew, one of us, but all the time he was a cop. A cop here to bring us all in."

A cop? During the day they'd spent together, he might have slipped that into conversation. Maybe it was habit to cover his true identity. So how much truth was there in anything he'd said?

The murky air around them was ominous. Only the gleam of moonlight slithering its way through the cracks in sharp wedges illuminated them. The room was cold and with its two-story domed ceiling, the cavern echoed the voice of the villain holding court.

"Let the women go," Jansen said. "This has nothing to do with them."

"It has everything to do with them," Victor said. "They're here because of you. Both of them. We found out your friend Rushe isn't a cop; you brought him in to save your woman. We brought his girl in to keep him quiet, just like we did to you, Jansen. Your Serendipity did what she was told. Felicity on the other hand…"

Though Victor sounded pissed off, she took the statement as a compliment. She rested her head on Rushe's back, not in the slightest bit apologetic for her actions or mouthing off.

"Are you regretting it now?" Victor asked. "I offered you a deal, Felicity. If you'd agreed to my terms, you'd be on this side of the standoff now. Instead, you stand with the losers."

On opening her mouth wide, she inhaled intending to skirt Rushe, but his arm came around to enfold her against his back, holding her in place. Presumably foreseeing her retort, Rushe apparently thought she wouldn't make things any better. She probably wouldn't, but Victor would win the war of words if no one else got a chance to play.

"What are you gonna do?" Jansen asked.

"Maybe we sell your women," Victor said. "With both of you here, there's no one to stop the shipment going out."

"This was your last deal, and you didn't deliver," Jansen said. "Your benefactor is gonna be out looking for you now. They fronted you a lot of dough."

"Let me worry about that, you worry about your woman being tied to some bed in Asia and raped by every businessman with a credit card. You think she'd like that?"

"You're full of shit," Jansen said.

"We might just let them have her for free."

"Why you fucking—" Rushe grabbed the back of Jansen's pack to prevent him crossing to Victor.

"Always cool, Rushe," Victor said. "I can understand now. I think we'd have to pay them to take Felicity off our hands. But she's got a body, oh she has... maybe we just cut out her voice box, make more room for the thousands of dicks she'll have to swallow to pay her way in the whorehouse she's shackled to."

"Yeah." Skeeve laughed. "Send her out to swallow for a living, see what shuts her up then."

"Why don't you shut up," Victor snapped over his shoulder. "Sniveling piece of shit."

"That's all you are," Rushe said to Victor. "You're no better than Skeeve, scum who thinks he's something, but you'll never measure up. You'll never be the best. You can't even get being the worst right."

"What the fuck would you know?" Victor barked.

"I know a lot," Rushe said without intonation. "I know about the cash you've got overseas. I know about the money that's missing, the eighty grand… and I know about the two million fronted to you, money you promised you'd pay back."

"I did. I did pay it back," Victor said. "I sent you with the ransom and…"

"That's right," Rushe said. "You sent me."

"John," Victor said. "I sent John too, you both…"

"He drove," Rushe said, pausing to let Victor comprehend the truth. "I know about your high school sweetheart who fucked you over for your best friend. They've got six kids now, did you know that? All inferiority issues, it's why you're threatened by Skeeve."

"Threatened by shit like that?"

"Skeeve, you ain't never getting respect," Rushe said. "I don't respect you. Victor sure doesn't. None of the men do, and the women think you're lower than scum. You want to know how to get a woman like Flick? How guys like us, bottom feeders with nothing to offer, get women like Felicity Hughes, who could have any man in the world she wants? When you've got respect like that you don't need to rape women, Flick begs me to fuck her every minute of the goddamn day. Just now, downstairs, she's desperate for it, I have to pry the bitch off my cock, and we could get shot in the head by any of you fuckers any second. She doesn't care, she wants it so bad—"

"Shut up!" Victor said. "No more!"

"You've got to take control," Rushe said, still talking to Skeeve. Why was her love appealing to the weakest man in the room? "You follow around like a fucking sheep, and they'll lead you to the slaughter."

"I'm sick of this shit," Shiv said, starting down the stairs.

Skeeve brought his gun up, aiming it at his colleagues, and everybody stopped.

FIFTY

"DON'T BE A FUCKER, SKEEVE," Victor grumbled. "He's playing you. You want to shoot somebody? Shoot Rushe."

"No, man, no, I don't need to work for you," Skeeve said, holding his gun in both hands, backing in the direction of the door, widening his target angle. "You're no better, no better than me. This ain't your house. I could get me one of these, bring in bitches, get my own crew."

She wasn't ready to move, but when Rushe started walking backward, guiding her in the direction of the room Serendipity was in, she let him lead. But if he thought she was going in there without him, or leaving him behind, she would have her own speech to deliver.

"Yeah right, and where are you getting the money?"

"Shiv's been skimming off, where you think the eighty grand went?" Skeeve cackled.

Victor spun in a rage to observe the wide-eyed Shiv, then he looked to Rushe who nodded once. When

Victor raised his gun, Shiv began to babble and fumbled for his own weapon. It fell from his fingers, but it wouldn't have mattered. Victor pulled his trigger, and the look of shock froze on Shiv's face. A dark circle of blood on his head oozed as his body fell back onto the stairs and tumbled down landing at the bottom with a thud.

"Anyone else got authority problems?" Victor asked.

Glen said nothing, while the Kid stood as still as a statue.

"This is very tiresome," Simone said, examining her fingernails.

"You know you're the only guy in the building she hasn't fucked," Rushe said to Skeeve.

"You shut it," Victor said, aiming his gun at Rushe.

The red mist in Victor's focus scared her, although she tried to move, Rushe held her in place. "You kill me," her love said, "and you'll never know where the money is."

"Then I'll shoot your puta. Felicity, come on round, don't be shy."

"She's not going anywhere," Rushe said, using his strength against her.

"Why's she special?" Victor asked. "One bitch is as good as the next, what's different about her?"

"She can suck a golf ball through a garden hose."

"With a mouth like that, I'll bet she can," Victor said, with a flicker of a smile, like he knew better.

"You won't find out," Skeeve stuttered. "You won't find out! She don't want you, you're no better than me."

"Be quiet!" Victor called.

"No," Skeeve said, walking with his shaking gun closer to Victor. "No, you're gonna give me respect. You respect that dumb bitch, and you don't respect me!"

"That dumb bitch stands up for herself," Victor said over his shoulder.

The bang almost burst her eardrums. Glen jumped from his skin when dust from the wall by his head exploded. She peeked around Rushe again, looking for clues as to what had happened, and that's when she saw Victor's body on the floor, as motionless as Shiv's.

"You killed him!" Glen exclaimed. "You killed our money!"

"Rushe is money, he knows where the money is," Skeeve said, practically giddy, his gun fell from his hand to the floor. "Rushe, can tell us."

"He can, but he won't," Glen said, having seen what Skeeve hadn't, Rushe with his gun aimed at the murderous weasel.

"I told you no second chances," her love said.

She held her breath. Everyone seemed to hold their breath, waiting for what he would do next.

"Wait…" Skeeve said.

"Kick the gun over here," Rushe said.

"Boss, now—"

"Do it!"

Now he and Jansen were the only two armed people left in the room. She stepped back from Rushe but stayed behind him. Glen and the Kid were still on the stairs, Simone stood at the bottom. Skeeve remained in place, only a couple of feet from Victor's corpse. Skeeve did as he was told, and the weapon skittered across the floor to Rushe's feet.

"What are you going to do to him?" Simone asked, apparently aroused by this turn of events.

"We're gonna have a little fun," Rushe said.

His focus remained on the transparent Skeeve. "But… bu—bu… you're the boss."

"That's right," Rushe said.

"Are you going to shoot him?" Simone gushed.

"A gunshot's the least of his worries now," Rushe said.

The room hung suspended in silence. What should she do? What was going to happen? Skeeve was terrified. Glen and the Kid couldn't feel any better.

Rushe didn't move. He stood, infinitely patient, as Jansen had said, letting imaginations make what they would of the situation without giving a thing away.

Being in Rushe's presence could be intimidating enough at the best of times. But there he stood letting everyone get used to the fact there was a new sheriff in town.

Skeeve didn't blink, but on his jeans a dark stain filtered down one leg. He'd wet himself.

Simone snorted in disgust, and Jansen laughed. Rushe didn't move. She wanted to check his facial expression but wouldn't interrupt him at work.

"Get the women out of here," Rushe said.

That bassy tone came from his chest, from deep, low inside him, that cloudy place she'd witnessed herself.

Despite hearing his words, it was only when Jansen stepped backwards that she realized Rushe meant her.

"I'm not leaving," she declared, maybe the only entirely unintimidated party left in the building. Rushe might have remained static, but she heard the hiss of breath he drew through his teeth. "I'm not leaving without you."

"Isn't she precious," Simone mocked, and tittered at her seeming naivety.

Rushe was in charge now. With him at the helm, she had nothing to fear, so why would she leave?

"I have work to do," Rushe growled.

"I'm not leaving either."

All except Rushe turned to the unexpected voice. Serendipity was on her feet, in the lobby with them. On first seeing the woman, she'd looked frail in her catatonic state. Now she stood tall, though perhaps not vibrant, there was a determination in the set of her jaw, and the width of her shoulders that she respected, and could identify with.

"Serendipity, baby," Jansen said, lowering his weapon to approach her.

"No," Serendipity said. "They've been in control of me for months. Let's see how they like it."

"You heard the woman," Rushe said, and used the gun to gesture at the stairs. "Everyone up."

Glen and the Kid complied, and with an eye roll Simone did too. Skeeve was visibly reluctant to turn his back on Rushe. That said a lot about the little weasel because Rushe wouldn't shoot a man in the back.

Serendipity strode on, Jansen stuck to her side, determined in her certainty. Jansen kept his gun on those in front but whispered to Serendipity on the ascent.

"What are you going to do with them?" Flick asked.

"You stay down here," Rushe said, watching the group on its journey while he remained at her side.

He stroked her hair without even looking at her, then went for the stairs with his gun aimed ahead.

"Like hell I will," she said, hurrying to join him.

Rushe stopped on the stairs, and the others went out of view, which clearly pissed him off. "You don't want to see this."

"What are you going to do?"

"No one touches you," he said, letting his gaze meet hers. "I love you, Kitten. God damn you, woman, I love you."

She took his empty hand. "I know."

"I'll hurt anyone who hurts you," Rushe said. "There will be consequences for anyone who tries to wrong you."

"Rushe," she said, moving in closer. "You can't ask me to walk away from you. I won't do it."

With another grumble, he hooked an arm around her neck, over her shoulders, and kept her at his side when they went up the stairs. They followed the corridor, passing the room she'd been kept captive in, and went straight through the double doors at the end, into Victor's office.

Jansen was herding the four hostages into the side room she'd been introduced to by John. Serendipity sat on the couch, staring into the dying fire. Rushe made a move to follow Jansen when he disappeared through the black velvet curtain, but she caught his arm.

"Please don't get hurt," she murmured, knowing Rushe wouldn't be happy at the implication he might be fallible.

As she would've expected, he muttered to himself. Though the strength of his angry brow remained in place, and the space behind his eyes appeared void, Rushe ducked to press his mouth to hers. Briefly enough to reassure her, without taking him from the task at hand. She stayed rooted to the spot and watched him vanish through the drape.

She crossed to sit on the couch with Serendipity. The woman didn't say anything, but Flick got a good look at her gaunt appearance. Color smudged her dirty skin, bruises in various stages of their cycle: some new, some not. Closing herself in her own embrace, Serendipity kept staring. It wasn't the same vacant stare she'd first seen in Serendipity's eyes. This was a woman with vengeance in mind.

"I know where there are clothes," Flick said, hoping there would still be things in her old room. "There's a shower too if—"

"I want to make them pay."

"I know," Flick said. "I can understand that. You must have been through quite an ordeal."

"They had no right…"

Serendipity remained intent on the hearth. Gently, she touched her wrist and let her hand slide into Serendipity's. Very slowly, the woman turned to look her in the eye.

"Our men won't let them go anywhere. Let's get you cleaned up."

FIFTY-ONE

SERENDIPITY ALLOWED HER to lead them from the study, down the corridor, and into the room Flick had been held captive in. Because her own paranoia came into play, she left the door wide open. Just in case.

Trying to find a subtle way to ask if Serendipity had been sexually violated was impossible, so she asked out right. Washing away evidence of the crime would hurt in the long run. Thankfully, as it turned out, Victor gave the order Serendipity shouldn't be touched like that. He'd given that same order about her once. The arbitrary line was infuriating. Glad as she was that she and Serendipity had been spared that horrific ordeal, why had Brianna, and at least one of the others, had to endure it?

They stood together beside the drawers looking through the clothes. There were new things in there, thank goodness, because Serendipity was much taller than her. The new variety meant a better chance of finding something that would fit. Though it did leave her wondering who Victor was expecting to receive next.

"I don't know how she does it," Serendipity said, going to seat herself on the bed, letting the clothes fall from her fingers.

"Who?" Flick asked, stopping her own search.

"Simone, she works for the guy bankrolling the trafficking. I think she's biologically related somehow, I don't know. She was here to keep an eye on Victor, make sure things went smoothly."

"Things went anything but smoothly," Flick said, going to sit next to Serendipity.

"It didn't matter, she was drunk on the power. Victor said more than once that it was Simone's job to look after the women, make sure they were suitable to be sold on. She starved us so we'd lose weight."

"So you'd be weaker or more marketable?"

Serendipity shrugged. "Initially, I was terrified, waking up in that cellar…"

"I know," Flick said. "I was too."

"They kept me with the others until… they came and took them all away, treated them like cattle."

"But you were left behind?"

Serendipity nodded. "They separated me. Took me into that room, chained me to the wall… At first, Simone was the only one to visit. She taunted me with stories about what the men were doing, about what happened to the other women… about what they planned to do with me."

"You must have been scared."

"By then… talking did nothing, I'd tried to escape, but… when I did, Simone was vicious. She enjoys watching others in pain."

"Like Victor, Shiv, and the others."

"She was supposed to look after us. Keep us alive. Keep us in shape, healthy… Her job was to tell the money what to expect, what they were getting, so they could arrange buyers further down the line… It's horrible, isn't it? How could anyone sell a person?   A human being?"

"I struggled with that myself," Flick said. "But you're free now. Rushe and Jansen made sure none of those women got to where they were going. They're all safe… Simone will have a lot of explaining to do. I don't imagine her boss will be happy."

"No."

Serendipity had withdrawn again and stared blindly into the distance. She moved the clothes aside and took Serendipity's hands to pull her up from the bed.

"Get in the shower, I'll find clothes and put them in the bathroom for you. Wash away the memories… it will get easier. You've got to give it time."

Both did as she said. Clean clothes wouldn't magically erase the horror. Maybe getting out of the rag she'd been imprisoned in would be in some way freeing, symbolic of Serendipity's liberation.

The water went off, and she listened to the noises of Serendipity going through the motions. When she came out of the bathroom, Serendipity had tears in her eyes and rushed over to hug her. It was good her new friend still had access to her emotions. Was the anger still there too?

Serendipity had just tied back her damp hair when thunder joined them.

"What the fuck do you think you're doing?"

The women turned to see Rushe just inside the room. Serendipity took one look at him, then one at Flick, and filtered out, presumably going back to Jansen in the study.

"Me?" Flick asked.

"Don't wander around. Don't go looking for things," Rushe said. "Stay where I leave you."

"How has that worked out for you in the past?"

"If I have to tie you to something—"

"Why did Jansen come to you?" she asked, ignoring his fuming bull imitation. "If he was a cop, couldn't he go to his superiors?"

"Jansen came to me because when Victor found out he was an undercover cop. Victor kidnapped Serendipity and wanted Jansen to feed his superiors misinformation. Not just about his own shit, but others too. Jansen did it. It put Victor in a position of authority with other guys, showed he could get things done."

"What has that got to do with—"

"Jansen's not the only cop lowlifes have on the books. But he was the only one whose job it was to spy."

"Except he became a double agent," Flick said.

"Right. When he tried to talk to a superior about it, Victor found out."

"How?"

"Jansen didn't know, still doesn't."

"So he couldn't trust anyone."

"Right, and Jansen had done a bunch of illegal things by then. Victor had him over a barrel; both of them knew it," Rushe said, and stepped back to gesture at the door.

She didn't move. "Why do you take cases in defense of women?"

The question surprised him. "What? Who told you that?"

"You have a reputation for it."

He came deeper into the room toward her. "What do you know about my reputation? Jansen was supposed to tell you to scram."

"He did," she said, sitting on the edge of the bed.

"But you ignored him, sure."

"You paid my ransom." Again, she surprised him. "You personally ensured my freedom, but you paid the ransom anyway, didn't you?"

"Yes," he said, without moving his lips.

"I can't believe you would do that. No one's ever cared for me like that."

"No one's ever cared for me at all," Rushe stated. "I can't get rid of you. You're like a yappy mutt at my ankles, all the fucking time."

"You wanted me to see Jansen in that diner," she said. "You deliberately provoked me in the motel. You woke me up, and threatened me with cuffs, to goad me into it. You wanted me to think coming with you was my idea."

"It was."

"Yeah, but you had it first, didn't you?"

"Yes."

"Why couldn't you be honest with me?" she asked, pushing back up to her feet. "Was it just about deniability?"

"I told you at the shack not to trust these guys. I didn't know how it was gonna play out. If something happened to me, there was nothing to stop them coming for you. If I couldn't be there, you wouldn't have a chance. Damn right I paid the ransom, I wasn't gonna let Vic think he'd lost money or face. I paid it. I told them it was from your father, and he believed me."

"And Jansen?"

"I didn't trust Victor," Rushe said. "I knew he'd figure out my connection to Jansen eventually. Jansen was the only person, other than you, who knew I was here, and why."

"I didn't know why."

"Victor didn't know that," Rushe said. "He sent Shiv and John to torture you in the basement because he thought you knew everything, everything he didn't."

"I could've told them. How did you know I wouldn't?"

"You didn't know his name, or who he was," Rushe said, then hesitated.

"What?"

"If it had meant guaranteeing your freedom, I'd have wanted you to tell them."

Though his stature was subdued, she could read the fortitude in his eyes.

Was she hearing him right? "You wanted me to give up you and your friend, to save myself?"

That determination inside him, that glowed down onto her, didn't waver. "I'd give up anything to save you, Flick, anything."

"Why were you at the shack?" she asked. "In the first place, I don't understand what—"

"Jansen wasn't supposed to know me and the other guys from the shack were on Victor's crew. The meeting you walked in on was Victor making plans with the guys bankrolling the trafficking operation. Guys like that want the profit at the end but aren't interested in how the sausage gets made."

"Deniability."

"Some guys are squeamish," Rushe said. "The guys at the bar and shooting pool, everyone hanging around were from various gangs. Everyone there had people with them, everyone blended to one."

"So Jansen wasn't supposed to know you, Skeeve, and Shiv, Glen and the Kid were working for Victor? You were a backup crew?"

"Victor started me working for him independently. I had to make it clear I wanted more. I had to be hungry for it. Victor was impressed with me. My goal was finding Serendipity, Victor just couldn't know that. I wasn't going to find her collecting cash on the streets. Victor put us in the shack, out of the way, ready to move in if he needed us. He was worried Jansen might get Serendipity out on his own, or get the cops involved. He didn't tell us that. As far as we were told, we were enforcing, collecting Victor's debts, proving to him we had what it took to move to the next step."

"Trafficking."

"That and I think he wanted rid of Skeeve. No one will have to worry about that again after tonight."

"You killed him?

"Broke a few fingers," he said. "I don't work quickly. If you work slowly, make it clear there's no hurry, people are usually tipped over by the wait. You let them torture themselves."

"In their head, like Skeeve downstairs."

Rushe tucked his gun into his jeans and came to her, resting his hands on her shoulders. He opened his mouth, then paused and took a breath, before taking another shot.

"When I was twelve or thirteen… there about, I was a kid. I never stuck around in the same area, and tried to keep my nose clean as best I could but… I've always been in trouble, Kitten, I'm never gonna lie to you about that. I'd been arrested for fighting, and stealing, joyricing, vandalism, kids' stuff. But I'd been on my own, part of the system, all my life. I ran away from more than a couple of group homes. I'd been on my own on the streets for a while. I'd always looked out for myself, I always had to."

Flick didn't know where he was going with the story, but she'd give him all the time he needed to get it out. Opening up to her, to anyone, was unnatural to him, and she could sense his unease. But he'd never surrender to fear, even the psychological kind.

"One night, sorta by mistake, I… I saw a woman come out of her apartment, she put this pizza box in the dumpster and… I went in after it. I was too busy scarfing down the food to notice she'd come out again. She tried to talk to me but I…" He shook his head and his eyes fell from hers. "She started putting food out for me a lot; she was good to me, I... I don't know why..."

"What happened?" she asked, sliding her hand up to his jaw.

"She tried to talk to me..."

"You didn't talk to her?"

"No," he said. "She didn't make me eat out of the trash, she cooked for me, but I wouldn't go inside. I didn't want to be inside. I knew by then you couldn't rely on people, that you couldn't trust them... One night I was eating in the alley, and she brought me a beer. I was always tall and broad; I never told her how old I was. She was drinking one too, and I... I couldn't believe that someone, anyone, would want to share a beer with me. I didn't know that such casual situations existed."

"That's a good thing," she said. "She was trying to reach out to you."

"Yeah," he said. "This group... this gang, I didn't know their colors, but they were... there were a dozen of them, maybe more, they started hassling us. She was cool but..."

"But...?"

"I heard her scream... I knew what they would do to her, but... there were so many of them, I couldn't take them all."

FIFTY-TWO

"YOU RAN AWAY?"

"That would've been the smart thing to do," he said. "No, me, like an idiot, I fought. I didn't stand a chance. I should've left. I should've got help, not that I trusted the cops but… a few of them were beating me and I saw… I watched them carry her out the end of the alley."

She didn't want to push him, didn't want to see him in the torture he'd clearly endured all these years. "You did your best. You did what you thought was right. You were a kid."

"I passed out; I was unconscious for… I don't know how long. I got myself patched up at a free clinic. I didn't tell them anything. It wasn't so bad… for me."

"If you were unconscious for that amount of time it would've been terrible, so many of them, and only one of you."

"I went back there a couple of days later, as soon as I saw the yellow police tape…"

"They killed her?" she said in a rush of breath, without considering her words.

"Eventually," he said in such a distant voice it was as if he wasn't there with her at all. "It was in the newspaper, the things they did to her… it was horrific… and I'd been right there. I let it happen."

"They raped her? And beat her," she said. Rushe wouldn't look her in the eye, he just lifted his head in the slightest of nods. "You've blamed yourself all these years. That was why you couldn't let them… with me, in Dell's… why you need consent, why you despise these men… Oh, Rushe."

With a long exhale, she threw her arms around him, and held him as tightly as she could. He'd never sought her affection. In fact, he'd spurned it frequently. He didn't know how to deal with it because he didn't think he deserved it.

"You're a good man," she said into his chest. "You're an incredible man. I love you."

His hand rested on her head. "You should be ashamed of me."

"Never," she said, lifting her head to find his eyes. "I could never be ashamed of you, Rushe. And I'm going to spend the rest of my life proving it to you."

His features relaxed though his turmoil remained. Before either could say more, a sharp bang startled them both.

"That was a gunshot, stay here."

"No," she said, following directly behind him when he left the room to race down the corridor.

Rushe paused at the double doors with his gun already drawn, and flattened his hand to her abdomen, pressing her back against the wall.

"Please, Kitten, stay here."

She shook her head. "You don't work alone anymore."

The half a beat of eye contact they shared was broken by another gunshot. Rushe turned away and opened the office door without going inside. Serendipity was crouched, hiding at the side of the desk.

As Rushe crept inside, he held her at his back.

Jansen came out of the side room backward, his gun pointing behind the drape for a second before he turned to bolt deeper into the office. "Dipity?"

"Oh my God," Serendipity said, poking her head over the desk.

"What happened?" Rushe asked, not more than three feet inside the room.

"I released Skeeve," Serendipity said. "I wanted to—"

"You shot him?" Rushe asked Jansen.

The question was answered when Skeeve came into the room brandishing a weapon of his own. Though the weasel stood proud, one of his hands hung limp and useless, at his side.

"He got it from under the bed," Serendipity said. "He shot the Kid and Glen too."

"Now who's in charge!" Skeeve crowed.

The next bang startled her, she jumped closer, her hands landing on Rushe's back. Past his outstretched arm, she watched the splurge of red grow on Skeeve's chest. The dismay froze on his face as he fell to the floor, his gun dropping from his fingers. Everyone seemed to take a minute to establish what had happened.

Jansen spoke first. "You shot him."

"Because I said no second chances," Rushe said.

She thought of all the women who would be saved from Skeeve. He could terrorize no more.

"You hate shooting people," Jansen said.

"Not when they're asking for it," Rushe replied.

"I'll remember that."

"Any more issues?" Rushe asked.

Jansen headed back to the side room, stepping over Skeeve in the process. As soon as he pulled aside the drape, his attention snapped back around. "Simone is gone."

"Made a run for it," Rushe said. "Down through the basement."

"Yeah," Jansen said, crossing to his backpack on the desk to retrieve a phone. "You two better clear out if you want to miss the cavalry."

Rushe joined him at the desk while cleaning the weapon he'd shot Skeeve with. Jansen dialed and put the phone to his ear. After the handover of the gun, he smacked Rushe's arm, then they shook hands. Rushe nodded at Serendipity on the way past and grabbed her, his own woman, to rush them from the room, down the stairs and out the front door.

"Where are we going?" she asked Rushe when they started to run down the gravel drive. "Shouldn't we wait for the police?"

"Jansen's a cop."

"But we're witnesses."

Rushe didn't answer. He took her out the gate, slinging an arm around her to keep her pressed into his side.

"Won't he get in trouble? He was lying to them. How is he going to explain it?"

"That's not our problem, Kitten."

"Won't we get into trouble for leaving the scene?"

"They'll never know," Rushe said. "You want to be my girl, you've got to get used to some things."

"Like what?"

"Like that I'll never appear on a database of any kind. You'll be dating an apparition."

"As long as your dick isn't imaginary, that's fine by me."

"Serendipity was Victor's insurance policy. Jansen knew that Victor had him by the balls. I got involved because I'm not official, I can go under the radar and do pretty much what I want. I'm the guy people come to when every other avenue has been exhausted. I'm the last resort when everything else fails."

"Okay."

"Jansen's been tap-dancing both sides of the fence for a while. I'm here because of him, because of Serendipity. Damn sure he doesn't want his bosses talking to me. I don't exist and getting you or me into it only makes things worse for Jansen."

"And Victor took me as an insurance policy against you?"

"Right."

"I can't believe… this is so… it's…"

"You have to understand. Sometimes I'm on the side of the good guys, and sometimes it's the bad. So long as I believe in the case, I can be on either side. I take the cases I want to because I dedicate time to the mission. I give it my focus. Distractions or bad intelligence in this game can get you killed."

She considered his revelation while following his lead through the streets. Rushe was so determined, he had to have a plan. She was still absorbing the fact she'd been right all along, Rushe wasn't a bad guy. He helped people.

"Got any money?" he asked her.

"Uh…"

She dug for the bills Jansen had given her. Scooping them from her back pocket, she handed them over. Rushe counted them quickly in one hand, then stuck them in his own pocket.

"We'll stay local tonight. I'll make a few calls; get us out of here first thing in the morning."

"Out of here to where?" she asked.

"Home."

"I meant to… the ransom… you paid it. But the money, I don't…"

"Job pays well, Kitten… And I know people."

"Okay," she said, knowing it didn't make an ounce of difference to her. "What's next?"

"Sex."

His face was blank, his brow angry, and she had to take three steps for each one of his. They'd almost lost their lives. Either of them could've been killed at any second, and he was thinking about sex.

"It has been a while," she said.

"Yeah," Rushe answered, ignoring her sarcasm. "Did he touch you?"

"Who?"

"Shit sucking Skeeve. I didn't have time to get details."

"He's dead," she said. "I told him you would kill him. I didn't know I was right."

Rushe stopped them abruptly and shoved her into an alley. Pushing her past the dumpster, he thrust her back against the exposed brick of the wall and planted his hands above her head.

"Tell me," he growled, baring his teeth. "Tell me what he did."

"No," she said. "He didn't have sex with me."

"But he tried. I wanna know how far he got."

She recognized this side of him, this caged animal look, teetering on the edge of reason. This Rushe was capable of anything. "Does it matter?"

"Yes."

"Why? He's dead."

"If he hurt you, I'm gonna track down anyone he ever cared about and—"

"Rushe," she said, hooking her hands into his jeans pockets. "Let's forget he existed. I don't want him to take up another second of our time. He's not worth it."

"I'm gonna protect you," Rushe said. "You're my woman now… right?"

And if she didn't know him better, she'd say that last word was uncertain.

Her smile spread. "Right."

"You have to know… you have to know what I am, what I've done."

"I trust you, Rushe."

"I told you not to do that."

"And how am I at following instructions?" she said.

Though he didn't smile, his eyes traveled south. "Take off your clothes," he grumbled.

"No!" she squealed. "I'm not getting naked in a dirty alley. Find a car and then we'll talk."

"Motel," Rushe said, grabbing her hand and yanking her along behind.

The journey from snatching her arm to snatching her hand had been a long one. Somehow, they'd made it. In his strong grip, she ran along behind him. The distant wail of sirens would be heading to the place they'd just escaped from. Would they ever find out what happened at that house after they left?

FIFTY-THREE

QUICKER THAN SHE'D EXPECTED, Rushe had them at a motel. The girl at the front desk looked at them like she expected they'd want an hour rather than a night.

"He likes to take his time, and he can afford it," Flick said. "He pays extra for the bruises… and if there's blood, I get a new pair of Manolo's."

Flick raised her crossed fingers and the girl's jaw sank. Rushe said nothing, just dragged her out of the reception and threw her into the motel room.

"Take off your clothes," he snapped.

This wasn't a man preoccupied with sex. "What? I was just having some fun."

"That girl's gonna remember you," he said. "She's gonna remember me, and there could be cops poking around."

She hadn't thought about that. "We don't want to be remembered."

"No, we don't. Get. Naked."

Getting naked wasn't very difficult. She whipped off her top and kicked off her jeans. That was it. Naked.

"Get on the bed."

She crawled onto it. "I have a lot to learn about being a criminal."

"You're not a criminal," he said. "You've done nothing wrong."

"I shot a guy."

"In the leg," Rushe said. "That doesn't count."

She dropped from all fours onto her back. "What does count? Are their degrees of criminality?"

"There are degrees of everything. Stop talking."

The light still wasn't on and the glow of the neon red motel sign outside their window gave the place the air of a brothel. But there was only one man, and only one woman. She lay there completely naked, while he stood at the end of the bed just looking at her. In the previous motel they'd shared he'd done this, looked at her, examined her. Being observed by him churned her insides.

Except now it was different. Now they had a future. Now there was a part of her in him. A part that lived in his heart. A part he'd give his life to protect.

"No one touches you," Rushe growled. "You will never be touched by another man. Do you understand me?"

She nodded and breathed through his lingering scrutiny. "He's dead," she murmured, provoking his curiosity. "The guy I lost my virginity to when I was twenty, he died in a car crash three years later."

"Were you close?"

She shook her head. "I hadn't seen him for years, I read about it in the newspaper… Looking at you now, I think he took the easy way out."

Her hands slid from the bed, across her hips, and her waist, until they covered her breasts. The sharp point of her nipples prodded her palms. The contact shimmered through her torso to the nerves all around her center, that he was about to dominate.

They'd been joined in that cell, but it felt like a lifetime since they'd had their own rules. Sharing that room in the shack may have been under siege, but she had no idea the depth of this plot until they were more than halfway through the adventure.

Rushe had protected her when she didn't know she needed to be protected. She'd cost him. By his own admission, she'd fucked up the job. But his feral eyes feasting on her body held no regret. She had none either. Walking into that bar had given her the most important gift, one that would prove to be the core the rest of her world rotated on.

"What do you want to do to me?"

"I'm gonna fuck you," he said. "I'm gonna pound that little pussy 'til it knows just who it belongs to. I'm gonna fuck you so deep that your throat's gonna taste me. I'm gonna fuck you all night, then you're gonna climb on top and fuck yourself on my cock. All day and night just how I tell you. Open your legs." She did. "Wider. Lift your knees."

She did as told. When he sat onto the bed, she waited for him to undress, to do just as he said.

He didn't.

Holding his weight on the arm he braced over her, he slipped one finger inside her. "You like that?"

She purred, moving in time with his advance, her juices gushing over him. "Mm."

"You like it when I finger fuck you," he said, and jabbed another finger into her.

When his digits retreated, she tried to wriggle down toward them, to keep them inside her.

He stabbed into her again, curling his fingers inside. "You don't move," he rumbled. "You get what I give you. I'm running the show."

"Rushe," she gasped and squeezed her breasts.

"Hands off your tits, your body's mine. You don't get to play unless I tell you."

While he pumped his fingers in and out of her, she struggled to stay put. Squeezing her eyes closed, her focus narrowed to that space, the space inside her that craved him, that was being teased for his pleasure and her torment.

His tongue flicked her clit, and she sobbed out his name. He was there, right there, concentrating on delivering pleasure. She hadn't seen him move, hadn't expected his mouth. But it was only just getting started. His fingers withdrew, his tongue took their place, he lapped her juices then closed his mouth over her opening, sucking the taste of her from her passage.

The heat of climax burned in her. Her pelvis bucked up, so his hands clamped her hips in place on the bed.

"Not until I tell you," he said, grazing his teeth over her clit.

His mouth traveled upward to kiss each nipple before he took them between his fingers, tormenting the points with his thumbs.

"You like that?" he asked, ascending on top of her, his mouth almost on hers.

"Mm hmm," she said, unable to form words.

His mouth touched hers, then his tongue plunged inside to sweep across hers. "Do you taste that? Taste yourself? You've got one sweet little cunt. I told those guys, I told them you were desperate for my cock. You want it, don't you?"

"Yes," she exhaled. "Yes, Rushe, please."

"You begging, Kitten?" he growled. One hand left her breast to stroke her clit. "You want me to fuck you?"

"Yes," she said, trying to push up, but he pushed her back down.

She heard him open his jeans when he kissed her again.

"I love you, Flick," he said, without the tone of his sex talk.

Her eyes popped open, was he…? It was a wonder to her that such an incredible man could love her, want her. Yet, losing herself in the vulnerability of his gaze, it seemed he felt the same about her.

"I love you too," she whispered. "I love you so much."

"I don't know how it happened."

"Does it matter?" she asked.

"I didn't think that I would ever be able to…"

"To what?"

"To love anyone…"

"We'll learn together," she said, lifting her mouth to his. After a long kiss, both of them were looser, warmer, enraptured by each other. "What are we going to do next?"

"I gather information by watching, listening, and talking. You gather it by research and reading, I think we'll take it from there."

"Okay," she said, proud that their futures could merge as she'd always wanted them to.

"You don't give a fuck that I called you a horny whore who's hungry for my cock in front of those guys?"

"I'll never be angry at you for telling the truth," she said, smiling.

"Good."

"I've never heard you talk so much, like you did in there, to Victor," she said. "Outside of the bedroom I mean… or wherever we happen to be having sex."

"Kitten, I just followed your instruction."

"My instruction?"

"Yeah, I learned from your doing."

"They do say that actions speak louder than words," she said.

"Why have one when you can have both?"

"But how did you know that Skeeve would shoot Victor?"

"Because you told me."

"I did?"

"You were never gonna let Skeeve fuck you, but you knew how to get him where you wanted him."

"Yes," she said. "I did."

"You knew how to rile him, how to appeal to his immature ego. I followed your lead, Kitten. Now, leave the rest of the words and actions up to me."

"Aren't you forward?"

"You gonna let me fuck you?"

Her smile spread when he revealed his own elusive one. "Yes, sir."

FIFTY-FOUR

SHE YAWNED AND STRETCHED out from the tips of her fingers high above her head to the ends of her wiggling toes. On her relax, she opened one eye, her mattress was... a mattress.

Thrusting her hands under herself, she shoved up to look around. The bed was empty, the room was empty. Scrambling off the bed, she ran to the bathroom without thought for her nakedness.

"Rushe!" she hollered.

On throwing open the bathroom door, she saw it was empty too. That didn't stop her from dragging aside the shower curtain. Empty.

How could she get in touch with him? She couldn't. By his own admission, he wasn't on any database. Jansen called him a shadow. If Rushe ran out on her, that would be it, she'd have no way to track him down.

She heard the front door and dashed out to find... Rushe. Relief loosened her muscles.

He closed the door and began to raise the small paper bag in his hand but paused. "What?" he asked.

Her stance must have conveyed her panic. "Nothing."

"You thought I'd run out on you."

"No, I didn't," she said, knowing the truth was written all over her face.

"I got breakfast," he said, tossing the bag to the bed. "Eat."

She sat on the corner of their mussed bed to retrieve the bag. "Thanks."

Opening it, she tore a corner from the bagel, and munched quietly. Rushe brought a chair from the corner and sat down, resting his elbows on his knees, just looking at her.

"What?" she asked, swallowing down the lump and putting the bag with the bagel in it aside.

"I never bargained on you," he said.

"I was one thing you never foresaw."

"Right."

"Now you don't know what to do with me," she said, leaning back on her hands, glad now that her body was still bare.

She traced her toe up his jeans.

He caught her foot when it grazed the inside of his knee. "If I tell you everything… it could put you at risk. But there are people who will assume you know everything, even if you don't."

"Like Victor did?"

"Yeah," he said. "I don't know what to do about you."

"Keep me chained to your bed," she teased.

"I considered that. But I like screwing you in the shower."

"Look…" she said, leaning forward to take his hands. "I didn't bargain on you either. I have skeletons in my closet I should tell you about."

The concern on his face gave way to that angry brow. "Tell me."

"Rushe—"

"Is someone trying to hurt you? Tell me, Kitten, and I—"

"I love you," she said, sliding to the floor to seat herself between his feet. "I have to account for your trigger finger when I talk, don't I?"

"What do you mean?"

He stroked her hair, threading his fingers through it in wonder. Softness was foreign to him. Until her anyway. It was nice he was going through his awakening with her and was comfortable enough to let himself explore.

"If I tell you the guy at the coffeeshop shortchanged me, or the guy at the bus stop hit on me…"

"I can find out who he is, and who he cares, about within twenty-four hours, and I'll break whatever he hurt you with."

"Are we going home today?" she asked. "Have you heard from Jansen?"

"They've got Simone in custody, but she's not talking. I'm waiting for Jansen to return a call."

Sliding her hands up his thighs, she shifted to her knees. His hands caressed her upper arms, to her shoulders, and he pushed her hair away to cup her neck.

"Rushe," she whispered, seeking out his mouth.

With this gentle kiss, she pressed closer, dipping her tongue into his mouth, then retreating as his chased after. Tilting her head, she urged closer, and pushed him back to open his jeans.

Taking his member in her hand, she squeezed his shaft and began to pull causing him to hiss. She smiled into his growling eyes and dipped her mouth to swallow him. While she tasted, he slid his hips to the edge of the seat. On a deep breath, the head on his shoulders fell backward.

Sucking him deep, she kept bobbing up and down, working her fist in unison with her tongue. She cradled his testicles and with a gentle shake he groaned out. His hands landed in her hair and curled into her locks to increase her pace. Doing her best, she pushed him deep into her. Surging upward, his grip on her hair grew, and liquid spurted in her throat. Swallowing him down, she purred as she let him fall from her mouth.

"Feel better?" she asked, putting him back and refastening his jeans.

"You're getting damn good at that, Kitten."

"I hope you plan to stay over a lot, a girl shouldn't make a habit of missing breakfast."

A knock on the door startled her.

Rushe was out of the chair, between her and the noise. Stark naked and on her knees, she froze.

Rushe snapped his fingers. "Bathroom."

Yes, good plan. She retreated into the room where she'd sought him out earlier. Through the wall, she listened to the mumble of voices until they stopped.

Suddenly, the bathroom door opened. She pounced away from her listening post.

"Get dressed," Rushe said, giving her breast a squeeze. "I got a call at the front desk. When I'm back, we're leaving."

He ducked to suck her nipple into his mouth.

She laughed and shoved his shoulder. "Most men kiss your mouth goodbye."

"I'm not most men, Kitten," he said.

She welcomed his lips when they grazed hers, at the same time his finger dipped into her pussy. She hit him again, but he backed away sucking his finger into his mouth.

Though as stoic as ever, his dry playfulness made her grin. A man in love should glow. It might be invisible to others, but to her he was neon.

FIFTY-FIVE

WHEN SHE GOT OUT OF THE SHOWER, Rushe was waiting in the open doorway that stayed open while she got dressed. He bundled her into a car she didn't know they had and drove for hours.

By the time she directed Rushe into her street it was dark outside. He parked the car and she once again had to ask her super for a key. It was on the guy's lips to complain… until Rushe came into his eyeline and all complaints evaporated.

Upstairs, she got them inside. Every time she'd come back to her apartment after each apparent end to the trauma, she'd been emotionally drained.

That time, when Rushe's arm came around her body to snake his hand under her top to clasp her breast, drained was the last thing she felt.

Rushe buried his face in her hair in an attempt to kiss her neck. His other hand had already loosened her jeans to give him access, and his finger dipped into her.

"You're wet enough," he grumbled, and bent her over the kitchen counter to yank down her jeans.

She opened her mouth to speak, but he drove into her and began to pump fast. They'd barely managed to get into the room and he was already fucking her like he'd been celibate for months.

"Rushe," she gasped, pushing back.

He rammed her forward, locking her between him and the countertop. Shoving her top up, he clasped her breasts, and groaned. All it took was a quick swipe of her clit, and one more push sent her tumbling into pleasure.

She called out his name, screamed for him as he threw her into orgasm. Although her body tensed around his cock, he pounded on through her second, then her third climax before his grip bit deeper on her hips. With this pressure, and with a roar, he pulled out and the stream of his seed covered her ass.

She took time to steady her breathing. His huffs punctuated hers. "You've been holding that in," she said, they hadn't had any sex on their journey, which was unusual for them.

"You consider the pill."

"Was that a question or a statement?" she asked.

"Both."

"I thought you didn't want to come inside me. There are condoms in the nightstand."

Rushe slapped her clean butt cheek. "Why?"

"Just in case. There might have only ever been two dicks in my pussy, but I've rolled around with a few guys."

He spanked her again. "I want a list of names."

"Are you going to tell me about every woman you've made love to?"

"If you want me to," he said, withdrawing and wandering around the kitchen counter to explore her cube.

Except as soon as you were in it, all exploring was done. She'd used two sets of shelves to divide her bed from the rest of the room. An open plan kitchen living room, small bathroom, only big enough for a shower cubicle, was the extent of her space. Observing it now, her whole apartment was about the same size as the upstairs room she'd been held captive in at Victor's.

"It's not much, but it's home," she said. "Do you live in a mansion?"

She wriggled out of her jeans and took off her top at the same time.

"No," he said, dropping onto her couch and laying his arms along the back. "I have an apartment."

"I'm going to shower. I should go by the coffeeshop, find out if I still have a job."

"Okay," he said. "I'll meet you there in a couple of hours."

"Meet me?"

"I've got a few things to do," Rushe said.

"You will..." she said, tiptoeing closer then pausing.

"What?"

"You will come back, won't you?"

"You don't trust me?"

"I do," she said. "But... I have no way to get in touch with you, or..."

"Come here," he said. She complied and he pulled her onto the floor to sit between his feet. "You're my girl. I've been alone... Always thought nothing could change that. Getting used to you is gonna take time but I don't... I'm private."

"I know that but—"

"You're not a separate entity." His finger touched her chin. "You're an extension of me. I wasn't prepared for this, but I'll adjust."

"You don't want to be in love with me," she said. "Do you?"

"Would be a lot easier if I wasn't."

When he scissored her hair in two fingers, he tucked it away behind her shoulder. "Can I make it easier?"

"Starting tomorrow you're going on the pill. I'm gonna shoot my load in you, every day you're walking out the house with a pussy full of come, you hear me?" She nodded. "I'm gonna take care of you, Kitten… I'm just not sure how yet."

"You don't have to look after me," she said. "I know we'll take our time. You won't want to rush. I mean, I know you're an independent guy. I don't want to—"

"I have to take care of some things."

"Okay."

"Get clean, take a nap, or whatever," he said. "I'll come and get you from the coffeeshop. You can tell them you don't need your job."

"I have bills to pay, Rushe—"

"I'll transfer money to your account. You don't have to worry about money anymore."

"I can't live off you," she said. "That's not fair."

"On who?"

"I have to do something."

"You will," he said, stroking her hair.

"I give up my job to become a hooker?"

"What?"

"That's what you're suggesting, isn't it?" she asked. "I live off your money, and service you when required."

"You do that already, and I haven't paid you a dime. You don't want a career in coffee."

She couldn't argue that point. "I have to find a job."

"You're gonna work with me."

"If we're wholly dependent on each other, we'll be in a forced position. I don't want us to be together because we have to be. I want us to want to be together. If we split up—"

"You better hope we never split up," he said, holding her breasts and grazing his thumbs over her nipples. "No man touches this; no one touches what is mine. You'll never be touched by another man, not for the rest of your life. You are mine, Felicity. You are my woman, and I belong to you now. Once I have committed to something, I don't turn my back on it. We won't split; I won't allow it. If something makes you unhappy, we'll change it."

"And if something makes you unhappy?"

"You know me well enough by now, Kitten. I take what I want."

Lowering his mouth to hers, she hummed against the delight of his kiss. "Shower with me," she whispered.

"There are things to take care of."

"Sex has to be a priority in our relationship," she said on a smile. "That will make me happy."

She took her hands from his shoulders and lay out on the floor at his feet.

"You make a helluva sight, Kitten."

"Somehow I always end up naked while you're fully clothed."

"Just the way I want it."

"I want you in me," she said. "Please, Rushe, fuck me."

He considered her. After a long silence he got on the floor, holding his weight on his arms when he lay over her. "No."

"No?"

"One," he said, admiring her naked figure, then he kissed her one way and the other.

"What?"

"You asked me about every woman I've made love to. There's only been one. You."

For a charmless man, she was definitely charmed. "I want you to be happy too. Tell me if I'm doing something wrong, won't you?"

"You're beautiful," he said. "I wish I could…"

"What?" she asked, sliding her hands from his chest to his neck.

"You're a princess. I mean you're a goddess, and I'm not… it's like beauty and the beast."

"Rushe, I love that you take what you want from me. I love that there are things that go unsaid between us. Flowers and diamonds, those kinds of things, are nonsense. Superficial and meaningless. I love you. I love how you're aware of me at all times. I love that you care for me and anticipate my needs before I have them. I love you, and I don't want you to change a thing."

"I'm not what you'll be used to. All the romance, and they—"

"I left my family to get away from that frivolity. You say what you think. I've been on scores of dates in my life. I must have dated a hundred men."

"Point, Kitten?"

"There's a reason I didn't let them into my bed. But I slept with you from night one." They might not have had sex, but they'd slept. "I want to be your woman and only your woman."

"Damn right."

"What about you?" she asked. "Will I have to share you?"

With another kiss, he smiled down at her. She liked that it came easier to him, at least when they were alone.

"I couldn't sleep with Simone," he said. "I could've fucked her. Maybe things would've been better, easier if I had. She was all laid out buck naked, that skinny little ass, and her tits—"

"I don't want to hear this," she said, trying to push him away.

Rushe gave her more of his weight, pinning her in place. "She was naked, a hot naked woman lying there primed and ready. I've had hundreds of women. Any time a woman was on offer, I took it. On the job, or not, I took sex. I convinced plenty of gangs I was on their side by screwing the right woman at the right time."

"This isn't turning me on," she said, trying again to push him up. "Please move."

"No."

"I think I'm going to hurl."

"I was limp," he said. She relaxed and drew her eyes to him. "It wasn't just that I didn't want to fuck her, I couldn't. In my life that has never happened. I can always get it up, but… I looked at her spread out on the bed, and it was nothing. I didn't give a fuck. Her body was nothing to me."

Her smile spread slowly. "Lover."

"What?"

Rushe really was as clueless as he sounded. Once again, he'd romanced her without knowing it.

Simultaneously, she wrapped her arms and legs around him. "He really likes me."

"Who?"

"Your dick, he doesn't want to be in anyone else. He likes his home in me."

"He does," he said. "But I'm gonna be honest with you, Kitten. I'm never gonna fuck around on you, but in the course of what I do—"

"I know," she said, holding his face in her hands. "On top of the clothes I'll let you get away with, in the line of duty, but…"

"But? Kitten? Speak."

"Come home to me alive. I don't care if you have to fuck your way through twenty women, picture me if you have to, but come home to me. I won't be there the next time to pull you out."

"I'll always come home to you, Kitten."

"You better. I'll keep a list of every man who looks at my breasts."

"I'm not sure there are enough bullets," he said. "You'll always be able to contact me. I'll make sure of it… by proxy if nothing else."

"By proxy? I thought you worked alone. I don't want to endanger you. You come home to me, I promise I'll be waiting."

"You're gonna learn that being my woman is more complicated than that."

"Does being your woman involve sex of any kind? Your cock's been trying to get out of your jeans. If you loosen up a little, I can help him. You can keep talking if you want, I'll fuck myself if you sit up."

"Mm," he hummed, taking a bite of her neck. "My dick's got great taste in pussy."

They had other things to talk about, but her trust in him filled her with contentment. Whatever the future brought, they had each other. Rushe would look after her, even when she didn't need him to. She'd have to be sly about it, but she was determined to look after him too. Rushe would deny needing help, but that wouldn't stop her from giving it to him in any way she could.

FIFTY-SIX

AFTER THEIR LONG SHOWER, Rushe left her alone in the apartment. Being separated from him prickled. Her discomfort had a lot to do with what they'd been through over recent weeks. So many times, they'd been apart, sure they'd lost each other for good. It was difficult not to feel that way again.

Over time, she would get used to it, used to being with him, and being away from him. Right then, she craved his embrace, but once she got over the recent trauma, they would find a rhythm.

After Rushe was gone, she procrastinated at home until she couldn't put it off anymore. The idea of going back to the coffee place to explain herself wasn't a fun one. How could she explain?

So when the manager was unmoved by her tale and confirmed she was out of a job, she wasn't sorry or surprised.

On turning to leave the shop, she came face to face with Hayden.

"Good God, what happened?" Hayden asked, guiding her to sit at a nearby table.

What was he…? Oozing concern, he touched her face.

"Oh, the bruises?" she asked, taking a second to catch up.

"Yes! What happened?"

"It's a long story," she said.

"You look terrible, someone hurt you. Have you been to the police? The hospital?"

Hayden continued to paw at her face, she guided his hand away and held it on the table. "I'm fine."

"You should've called me," Hayden said.

"What for? I apologize that I missed our dinner… again."

"No, don't think about that. I'll take you out another time. Are you busy tonight?"

"No."

"You really have to tell—"

"No," she said. "The story isn't important, and I can't have dinner with you."

"If you're busy—"

"It's not that—"

She was yanked up out of her seat by someone… no points for guessing who. Hayden blanched, then sat back. The grip on her arm only loosened when her back fell against his broad chest. She didn't need to see Rushe to identify who'd handled her with such ownership. Rushe's arm fell across her shoulder, his hand draped over her breast. While he didn't grasp it, the thought was there.

"Problem?" Rushe grumbled.

From the vibration of his chest against her back, she could tell his lips hadn't moved and his angry brow was secure in its place.

"What is this?" Hayden demanded, standing up. "Who do you think you are?"

"You really don't want to be confrontational," she murmured.

"What?" Hayden asked her.

"I met someone," Flick said to him.

"You met someone?"

"This is Hayden," she said to Rushe.

Her love would recognize the name. She must be getting used to this shadow thing because she deliberately didn't introduce Rushe.

Hayden was clearly disturbed and putting the pieces together all wrong. "Should I call the cops?"

"No." She grinned and took Rushe's hand from her chest to kiss his knuckles. He hooked both hands on her opposite shoulders, embracing her from behind. "This is my boyfriend. My man. He protected me."

The description felt somehow inadequate.

"Problem?" Rushe asked again.

"It was good to see you again, Hayden," she said. "I wish you all the best for the future."

"That's it?"

"Yeah," she said, backing away in time with Rushe. "Have a nice life."

ON THE WALK BACK to her apartment, Rushe didn't say anything. Brooding was part of the package, she got that and practiced her own restraint. They passed the spot where she'd been snatched off the street by John. Despite reliving it in her mind, the memory didn't consume her. With Rushe's hand in hers, she was safe, he'd always make sure of that.

They hadn't discussed plans, but they were going back to her apartment, so she guessed they'd sleep there that night. Beyond that, she didn't know.

She unlocked and opened her apartment door, ready to cozy up to her man, when she noticed someone was already there.

"Jansen."

Rushe closed the door and passed her to join Jansen in her living room. The men shook hands.

"Everything done?" Rushe asked.

"Yeah," Jansen said.

Apparently Rushe was expecting the cop or had known he was already there.

"How is Serendipity?" she asked, getting over her surprise to join them.

"They checked her out in the hospital," Jansen said. "She's as good as can be expected. Her injuries weren't... it'll take time."

"You're moving in the right direction."

"She was taken because of me," Jansen said. "Because I cared about her. That was the only reason Victor... It's difficult to explain to her why it happened. Why she went through what she did. It's tough to know if having me around is hurting more than it's helping."

"It'll take time," she said. "Don't abandon her just because things are hard. She'll let you know what she needs from you. Right now, she won't know herself what she needs. Hold her hand, that's all you can do."

"Did you get it?" Rushe asked.

What was he talking about?

Jansen pulled a letter-sized brown envelope, folded lengthways, from his inside pocket.

Rushe took it and tucked it into his own back pocket.

"Simone's still not saying much. Most of Victor's guys are in custody," Jansen said. "Your names have come up, but you know they'll never find you."

Jansen's pointed look at Rushe was curious.

She frowned. "What?"

"You're not so tough to find," Jansen said to her.

"I'm already on it," Rushe said. "We'll be out of here within the hour."

"We will?" she asked.

She hadn't considered that the police, or the bad guys, might come looking for her. Naively she'd assumed the drama was over. From how these guys spoke, a whole new chapter could be starting.

"I can give a statement," she said.

"Eventually maybe," Jansen said. "Victor didn't work alone, and he owed a shitload of money to men who won't be happy to walk away without it. Bet your boots Simone's already been in touch with them. Do your family know where you are?"

"No," she said. "Not specifically. They wouldn't be able to get in touch with me. Should I—"

"No," Jansen said. "The cops will establish that for themselves. They'll look for you but…"

His attention switched back to Rushe at her side.

"Pack your things," Rushe said without looking at her.

"I don't understand, why can't I just tell the police—"

"I'm not the only cop in the world who's ever been blackmailed," Jansen said. "And that's not counting the guys who are downright corrupt. Why do you think I ended up with this guy? The cops won't protect you. They might try but… these criminals are pretty high up in the food chain. Take the risk if you want but… don't say you weren't warned."

And, damn, she'd seduced Rushe into sex that day when clearly there were other more important concerns.

Better understanding the urgency, she went to her bedroom to grab her suitcase without asking more questions. While she packed her belongings, the men continued to talk. Their serious expressions hinted at the mood of their words.

Putting the last of her jewelry into her case, she went to retrieve her things from the bathroom. When she came out again, Jansen was gone.

"Where did he go?"

"Back to Serendipity," Rushe said.

After dumping the last of her things in the suitcase, she zipped it up and got her jacket from its hanger in the closet.

"I can protect you," Rushe said, filling the space in the shelves that acted as an entryway for the bedroom.

She put on her jacket. "I know that."

"No," he said. "I mean… I work alone, but there are people I trust. If you want to stay here… I can get you security guys."

"Why would you need security surrounding us every time we go on a date?" His fixed expression didn't change, but clarity found her. "You mean me. You mean if you leave me here."

"It's your last chance, Flick. If we walk out that door… if you come into my world… it's not gonna be a nine to five, Kitten. If normality's what you're looking for—"

"Your world is an adventure. Normality has never worked for me."

"I want you to know, there's a choice. If you're not sure about this, I'll walk away now."

"You would walk away from me?" she asked. "You love me."

"Yeah, I do," he said. "But…"

"You're scared," she said, and he did falter then. "Every time you've known what's best for me, or thought you knew what was best, you acted to make sure that was the path I was on. You pushed me away after the shack. You threw me onto my parents' doorstep, but… if I stay here alone, I could get hurt."

"If you walk out that door with me, I can't guarantee you won't."

"I know," she said, hauling her suitcase from the bed to the floor to lug it over to him. "Being with you thrills me, Rushe." Propping the case against the shelf, she took his hand. "I have to know how this story ends. I can't be away from you, Rushe. Even when you've forced us apart, we always end up back together. I need you, Lover, and you need me too. Even if you resent me for it."

"I don't resent you," he said. "I love you."

"You've never given me a choice about together or apart. You trust me. You respect me. We're equals now. You're giving me the choice, because you can't guarantee what's best, for either of us. I won't abandon you, just as you won't abandon me. You said it yourself; we're an extension of each other."

"You ignored my instruction that first night. You've ignored me since," Rushe said. "I'm not giving you any instructions now. You've seen what I can face. What my world can involve. I'll always love you, and I'll always protect you to the best of my ability. But this is it, Kitten, your choice."

"Are you being a good Samaritan?" she asked, letting herself smile.

"No, just an honest one… Our future won't always be pretty, so I still say you want to keep walking… far away from me."

"Actually," she said, skirting around him, pulling the handle of her suitcase up. "I don't."

"Kitten," he warned.

She went to the door, and after unlocking it, deliberately left the key on the kitchen counter. "We have a new life to get to… Heel!"

On her order, his eyebrow sloped up. "You're gonna pay for that one," he said, but complied. Reaching around her to open the apartment door, he took the suitcase from her grip.

"You tell me to 'stay' like I'm a dog."

"You're my bitch. I thought we were clear on that."

"Punish me later?"

"Count on it," he said, smacking her ass, sending her out of the apartment, and into whatever lay ahead.

TO BE CONTINUED...

Thank you for reading this tale!
If you can, please take the time to review.

~

Ask your local library for more Scarlett Finn novels!

~

For all things Scarlett Finn
check out:

www.scarlettfinn.com

BOOK TWO

OUT NOW!